BOLTGUNS AND DUCT TAPE

SPACESHIP MECHANIC
BOOK ONE

JAMIE MCFARLANE

FICKLE DRAGON
PUBLISHING

To Diane, I'll see you in the stars.

PREFACE

FREE DOWNLOAD

Sign up for my newsletter and receive a free Jamie McFarlane starter library.

To get started, please visit:

http://www.fickledragon.com

1

NOT LOCAL

"Anyone home?" a voice called into the mechanic's bay.

"Strange," Rix Banner said aloud. He hadn't heard the bing bing of tires rolling across the air hose sensor letting him know someone needed gas. He set his wrench aside, grabbed the Oldsmobile 88's frame and rolled out from beneath. "Hold on!" he called.

Sitting up, Rix brushed his hands on his coveralls and then stood. It was late in the evening and the only reason he'd left the filling station open was because he was catching up on work. Having returned from WWII where he'd served as an airplane mechanic in the Army Air Corps, the urgency of transmission repairs, oil changes and filling gas for the folks of Cranberry Cove, Wisconsin, was perfectly his speed.

"Well darn," he said, scanning the driveway where the pumps stood. "Guess I missed 'em."

"Not hardly," the same voice answered.

Stepping from the gloom, a figure wearing a pair of tight blue coveralls, stepped into the dim glow of the mercury vapor light over the second bay. The tight fit of the coveralls caught his attention and he quickly schooled his eyes.

"Oh, didn't see you," Rix said, stumbling with the words, working through the fact that the narrow woman wore coveralls with a red polka dotted scarf tying up her hair. The dissonance with her garb to his 1950s sensibilities drew a grin on his face. "How can I help you, ma'am?"

"I understand from your advertisement that you can fix anything," the woman said. As he inspected her face, the only safe place to look, given her tight coveralls, he wondered where she was from. He'd travelled quite a lot in the war and felt like he was good at placing people. Not so much for this woman.

"Didn't catch your name. I'm Rix Banner. I own this place and the diner next door," he said, extending his hand for a shake. "I'm sorry, but they closed up about thirty minutes ago, so if you're looking for supper, you're out of luck in Cranberry Cove."

"Oh, right, I read about this," she said, eyeing his hand and extending her own in response. "Kel Warp."

Limp as a noodle. Rix figured the handshake had been too forward, so he released her hand and wiped his palm on his cotton coveralls, having picked up some sweat in the exchange.

"How can I help you, Ms. Warp?"

"I understand you're a mechanic," Kel said.

"Yeah, folks around here come to me to fix just about anything, from diesel tractors to crop dusters to automobiles. I guess motors are my thing. How can I help you?" Rix asked.

"Well, the advertisement I saw said you could fix *anything*. You even had a picture of a spaceship," Kel said.

"Why, you got a spaceship to fix?" Rix asked, chuckling.

"If I did, could you fix it?" Kel asked.

"I suppose it depends on how it's made," Rix said. "And I'd need manuals for it. Not that that sort of thing exists. Have you been drinking? Chief Andy doesn't take to public intoxication; you might be careful."

"You think I'm drunk?"

"Not judging," Rix said. "I've been known to take a snort once in a while. I saw things in the war a guy has a hard time forgetting."

"Which war?" Kel asked.

"Right," Rix said, shaking his head at what felt like a rhetorical question. The sound of brakes squealing alerted them they were no longer alone. "Oh shoot, there's Chief Andy now. You'd better come in the shop. He sees you in that giddyap and talkin' drunk like and you'll be waking up in the tank, for sure."

"Be serious," Kel said. "I'm not in any danger from any law enforcement here."

"I agree," Rix said, grabbing Kel's arm and leading her over to the Oldsmobile of which he was finishing up a transmission replacement. Opening the door, Rix pushed Kel in and closed the door.

"Hey Rix, come over here a minute," a new voice called out.

"Comin', Andy," Rix answered, jogging over to where the chief of police sat in his patrol car. "Nice night, don't you think?" he asked as a form of greeting.

"Not a social visit, Rix," Chief Andy said. "But you're right, I sure do like it when we switch from winter to warmer weather."

"You look a little flustered, Andy. Can I help you with something?"

"Did you see that light in the sky just east of town?"

"Sorry, I was under Old Man Baker's Oldsmobile, finishing up a transmission swap," Rix said. "What kind of light?"

"Falling star, maybe," Andy said.

"How low in the sky?"

"Real low, had to have hit ground. Bob Davis said he saw the whole thing. Big fiery crash on his cornfield. Saw a strange guy on the road after that," Andy said. "I told him I'd take a look, but I didn't see anything."

"Is that so? What's Bob's concern? Seems to me, his cornfield is just dirt this time of year. If an asteroid struck, there should be scorch marks, but those'd be hard to find at night. Probably better to look in the morning. And Bob's an old snoop, you know that. Nothing against the law to be walking down Highway 6. Probably someone just enjoying the warm weather, like we are," Rix said.

"You don't get too riled up about anything, do you? Some folks came home from the war messed up. Seems like you did just fine," Andy said.

"Like I've said before, I never had to fight much, Andy," Rix said. "I just turned wrenches and kept our airplanes in the air."

"I think you're being modest," Andy said. "Word is you saw action. What was it like, Rix?"

Rix gave Andy a polite smile but shook his head. "Nah, it wasn't anything to write home about, Andy. Just fixin' airplanes. Why don't you run by and grab me in the morning. I'll go out to Davis's field with you, and we can look around."

"Would seven o'clock work?" Andy asked.

"Sure will, but let's meet at the diner. I'll have Jenny pack some of her sweet rolls and coffee."

"That'd be swell, Rix. Hope you finish up soon. It's getting late. It might not be the sort of night a fella wants to be caught unawares," Andy said.

"Well, I'm sure it's not as bad as all that," Rix said. "But I'm about ten bolts into finishing up and you know how Old Man Baker can be."

"Jessie's all bark and no bite, Rix," Andy said. "Say, I'll let you get back to it. Wife's got a pot roast in."

"Have a good night, Andy," Rix said, patting the chief's door.

"See you in the morning."

Rix turned back to the shop and focused on the windows of Baker's Oldsmobile, trying to catch a glance of Kel.

"Kel, you can come out now, Andy's headed home," Rix said as he entered the garage.

Rix startled when Kel stepped down from the doorway which led into the garage's waiting room instead of exiting from the car. "Sorry about that," Kel said, dipping her head. "I figured it'd be easier to explain my presence if I wasn't hiding out in your old vessel."

Rix stared at Kel for a moment as if assessing the situation. "Automobile, that's what we call them," Rix said. "Say, you're not from around here, are you? Where'd you say you were from?"

"Well, Rix, we didn't much have time for that conversation," Kel said. "And I was looking around for a terminal, but you don't seem to have anything more sophisticated than neon lights in this place. What's that about?"

"A terminal? The train doesn't even stop in Cranberry Cove," Rix said. "And I quite like our neon lights; they do a great job of attracting customers. They weren't cheap, I can tell you that for sure."

"I didn't say anything about a train," Kel said, pulling a tiny device from her ear and tapping it against the palm of her hand. "I guess my language processor must need some sort of update."

"You asked about a terminal."

"Computer, I think is the right colloquial term," Kel said.

"A computer. Like a UNIVAC? I'm just a simple mechanic. What could I possibly need with all that techno-jazz? And who could afford such a thing?" Rix asked.

"Hells, I missed all the signs. Your planet isn't part of Galactic Empire, is it?" Kel asked. "And you've never seen a spaceship, have you? You have no idea what I'm talking about."

"I know what a spaceship is, I'm reading *The Martian Chronicles* right now," Rix said. "And I think it's time we get you back home so you can sleep off whatever you've been drinking."

"That's the problem now, isn't it," Kel said. "I'm not from around here and my space ... automobile, as you call it, is broken down. I need a competent space ... automobile mechanic to get me going so I can go home."

"Which is where?"

"Let's leave that a mystery for now."

"Okay, so where is your vehicle, then?"

"I'm gonna guess it's out in Bob Davis's field, from what Chief Andy said," Kel said.

"Are you putting me on?"

"Not even a little bit."

"I'm headed out there in the morning with Chief Andy," Rix said. "We'll take the wrecker and bring it back if that's where it's at. Was it on fire? Andy said it put on quite a display."

"What would it take to have you go out there tonight, Rix?" Kel asked ignoring his question. "I don't need law enforcement getting involved in this. When you see it, you'll understand why. I'm asking, one traveler to another."

"Traveler, huh?" Rix asked. "How about this. Give me twenty minutes to get this transmission buttoned up. If you're not passed out by then, we'll take a run out to Davis's farm and see about your spaceship."

"I called it an automobile," Kel said weakly. "And you do advertise you can fix anything."

"There's a difference between anything and any time," Rix said.

"I'll make it worth your while," Kel said.

"Twenty minutes," Rix said, sitting on the creeper that sat next to the Oldsmobile. With practiced ease, he leaned back and slipped under the vehicle with wrench in hand.

As promised, twenty minutes later, Rix slid out from beneath the car and started putting away the array of tools he'd used that evening after carefully wiping each one down, which took an additional twenty minutes.

"Are we good now?" Kel asked impatiently.

"Treat your tools well and they'll always be ready for the next job," Rix said, pulling on a chain which caused the tall, overhead garage door to close. "Talk to me about what's broken on your auto."

"That's why I'm here," Kel said. "Something to do with the motivator something-or-other. I couldn't completely understand what Philo was saying. When he gets excited, it's not always clear."

Next to the standing tool chest Rix had just loaded was a much smaller, portable toolbox that he brought with him on recovery jobs. "You left Philo with your car?" Rix asked. "And we'll go through here," he said, gesturing toward the man-sized door that sat between the two tall garage doors. "Is he shy or something?"

"Something like that," Kel said. "And say, would you like a nip?"

"Get in on the other side," Rix said, noticing that Kel had followed him around to the driver's side. "And nip of what? If I'm working, drinks are off the table."

"Suit yourself," Kel said. The flash of a silvered flask drew Rix's attention, and he rolled his eyes. It was turning out to be a long night.

"If you feel sick, tell me, I don't need you leaving behind your dinner in my truck," Rix said.

By the time Kel was loaded into the wrecker, she'd stashed her flask and was grinning. "This is seriously old-school stuff. I mean, what kind of fuel does this even use. It smells so badly. And wheels! It's adorable!" Kel said.

"This one runs on gas. I'd rather a diesel, but this is the frame I found, and the engine wasn't in that bad of shape," Rix said.

"Wait, you built this?" Kel asked.

"If by built, you mean that I found parts in a local junkyard and put those pieces together in a new way, then yes," Rix said. "I didn't come up with the design on my own. I just merged a few different ideas, and this is what I came up with."

"Is it always this bumpy?" Kel asked as they drove from the parking lot and onto the main road.

"Bumpy? Well, I suppose so," Rix said. "This isn't bad. Wait till we get into Davis's field. You haven't seen bumpy yet. We'll stop by Bob's house before we head into the field. I don't need him coming out with a shotgun to run us off."

"Are you sure that's wise?" Kel asked.

"Not sure what you're getting after. Bob's a farmer, he won't take kindly to us being on his land without his permission," Rix said.

They'd ridden in silence for fifteen minutes when the asphalt road turned to gravel. "This is crazy. Look at all that dust and it feels like you're going to fall off the road any minute now."

"We'll be fine, we've plenty of traction," Rix said.

Ten minutes later, Rix pulled onto a long lane that led up to a house where there were only a few lights left on.

"This is where Bob Davis lives?" she asked.

"Yeah, and you stay in the truck. Bob can be ornery. We don't need him making trouble," Rix said. Hopping out of the tow truck, Rix made his way up to the door and knocked. A few minutes later, an older, heavyset man wearing a white t-shirt and matching underwear answered the door, holding a shotgun. Words were exchanged and Bob made a show of shielding his eyes to look out toward the tow truck. After that, Rix returned to the truck.

"What was that all about?" Kel asked.

"Like I said, he can be ornery. We're good to go. I had to promise to show him where you crashed. He'll want some money if you broke fences or anything like that. I'll let you work that out, though."

"There was a fence next to the road, I didn't break anything," Kel said, which earned her a cautious glance from Rix. Checking her wristwatch often, Kel finally pointed, even though there was no outward evidence of a car having run into the field. "Two hundred meters in."

"Meters, eh? We measure things in yards around here, but it's about the same," Rix said passing the location she'd pointed at.

"What are you doing?"

"There are cows back in there and so there's a gate up a little further," Rix said, turning onto a built-up section, his powerful lights shining on three strands of barbed wire.

"That stuff is sharp. Why in the world do your wires have pokey things in them?" Kel asked.

"Keeps the cows in," Rix said, jumping out. As he walked over to the gate, he shook his head in disbelief. Who in the world didn't know what barbed wire was?

"Just over that hill to the right," Kel said, once again consulting her wristwatch when Rix rejoined her in the truck.

"What in blazes?" Rix asked, awe filling his voice, as he crested the hill and his lights fell on a sleek, twenty-meter-long spacecraft that sat in the middle of the empty field.

"Oh my fraks, it's being attacked by those massive beasts! Philo is inside. Are they trying to eat him?"

"The cows?" Rix asked with some confusion as he approached the craft. "How'd you even get that in here? I don't see any wheels."

"Which part of *spaceship* did you misunderstand?" Kel asked.

Rix stared with disbelief for a moment and then sighed. "How are we going to tow it? There's nothing to hook up to."

"Cows, you say that like they're not attacking my baby," Kel said with distress.

"If Philo is inside, he's completely safe," Rix said. "Cows eat grain and grass, not spaceships and people. Now, if there's a young bull in the mix, that could get interesting, but we should be fine."

"Should be?" Kel asked.

"Holy cow," Rix said, not listening as he stepped out of the tow truck to get a better look. "This really is an honest-to-God spaceship. Does it actually fly? Or did you build it in your garage? Is it a balloon? How'd you get it over here? Did you drift off course?"

"Uh, Rix, help?" Kel said as a particularly nosey angus ambled up to her.

"Shoo, now," Rix said, waving his hands and stomping the ground in the cow's direction. It took the hint and rumbled off.

"And no, it's not a balloon, Rix," Kel said. "I told you what it is, you just didn't want to believe me. Now can you fix it, or not?"

Rix was working his way around the spaceship, shining a flashlight above and around so he could get a full view of the entire, long vessel. "I don't understand. It's not sitting on anything."

"Right?" Kel agreed, not understanding the question.

"How?"

"Oh, gravity repulsion I think it's called," Kel said. "We landed hard, but the repulsors are heavy duty."

"You have some carbon burn marks aft. Like maybe someone was shooting at you," Rix observed.

"Space travel can be dangerous," Kel said noncommittally.

Just then the ship made a loud clanking sound, its nose shivered, and then dropped to the ground, coming to rest after a loud whump.

"Is that usual?" Rix asked.

"Well frak, no, that's new," Kel said, sighing. "Add that to the list of things that need fixing."

"And you're not a German?"

"I don't know what a German is."

"We just won a war against them. This looks like something they might try to put together," Rix said.

"No, I said we're not from around here, and by here, I mean this solar system," Kel said. "I need you to get shiny with the idea that you're looking at a gal-jabbed spaceship, because when I introduce you to Philo, we're going to start this all over again and I don't think we have that kind of time. I need to get *Calypso* off the ground within a couple of days or some unpleasant people are going to show up and make trouble in a way Chief Andy can't do much about."

"Are you making threats?"

"Not at all. Bad people are chasing me. I bet they've figured out I landed on Earth and even with the Galactic Empire quarantine, they'll be coming, either way," Kel said. "The only reason I'm here is because my ship broke down and you advertised that you can fix spaceships."

"That might have been an exaggeration," Rix said, scratching the back of his head. "I've never actually seen one of these before."

"But you're good at fixing things."

"Well, sure I am," Rix said. "But I don't have the first blessed idea about any piece of your technology."

"Will you at least look?"

"I could do that. You said you had the manuals on all this? It might take a bit of reading, but I'll give it a go."

"That's the spirit," Kel said. "Now, I need to warn you about Philo. He's not exactly human and by Galactic Empire standards, he's semi-sentient, kind of like humans."

"What do you mean like humans? You're human," Rix said.

"I look human, but there are some differences," Kel said. "It's not important. Now, Philo is Korrali. He looks mostly human but shorter and can get excited. He's my buddy, so I don't need trouble. He knows things even though he might sound like he doesn't."

"Okay, sure," Rix said. "As long as I don't get bit, I'm fine with whatever."

"Good for you," Kel said, tapping on the side of the craft, which was now angled down, with its nose lying in the dirt.

"Kels!" a high-pitched voice said excitedly when a hatch opened in the side of the spacecraft and bright light spilled out onto the field. A slender ramp extended from a previously hidden compartment and settled on the dirt. And just like Kel had promised, a short manlike being appeared, with even shorter legs and a gray and black biker beard that had recently been trimmed. "Oh, you found Mechanic Man! Bad repulsors. Needs fix. Mechanic Man come fix?"

"For the love of God, what have I gotten myself into?" Rix asked, stepping onto the ramp and following Kel into the spaceship.

2

SIMPLE FIXES

"This is incredible," Rix said, startling when a small hand grasped his own.

"It okay, Mechanic Man," Philo said. "What fix first?"

"I don't even know where to start," Rix said honestly. "Everything is so foreign."

"Fix push push," Philo said. "Good information. Mechanic Man fix fix."

"He's talking about the gravity repulsor," Kel said. "Here, take this tablet. You can ask it questions, and it will give instructions. Philo, go get the toolbox for Rix. And yes, Rix is the Mechanic Man." Without another word, Philo ambled off aft, presumably in search of the toolbox Kel asked for.

"I don't know what to do with this," Rix said, holding the electronic tablet in his hand but away from his face.

"That's a computer, Rix," Kel said. "Where I come from, they're smaller and connected to just about anything. In truth, that tablet isn't anything, it can just connect with the intelligent devices around it. That's helpful because when it gets near the repulsors, it'll read all of the diagnostic data and be able to help you figure out what's wrong."

"If it's so easy, why didn't you do it?"

"I have a stellar record of breaking things," Kel said. "And I don't tell anyone I know how to fix spaceships."

"You need to stop with that," Rix said. "It was an advertisement and everyone else who read it knows I'm joking about spaceships, because we all know they're not real."

"Does this feel like it's not real?" Kel asked, gesturing to the spaceship's interior.

"Kind of," Rix said. "I mean, it's dirty, but there are lights and weird little doodads everywhere."

Kel grabbed the electronic tablet and pushed it in front of Rix's face. As soon as he did, an interface showed up.

Scanning for identity. Identity not found.

"It says it's searching for my identity," Rix said and then raised his voice to almost shouting. "I'm Rix Banner, from Cranberry Cove, Wisconsin."

Rix Banner, Cranberry Cove, Wisconsin, United States, Earth, Sol. Human, thirty-one years old. Mechanic. Owner of Cranberry Cove Diner and Filling Station.

"It hears you fine," Kel said, peering over Rix's shoulder as the device displayed. "You're an unknown entity so it's creating a Galactic Empire record to keep data about you squared away. Don't worry, all systems have excellent privacy."

"It's not like I'm taking this to the bathroom," Rix said.

Kel blinked her eyes and thought for a moment and then laughed. "It won't take pictures of you in the bathroom."

"Good."

"Tools tools tools," Philo said, holding a heavy, deep toolbox easily in his right hand. "Come come!"

"You better follow him," Kel said.

"To where?"

"Push push."

Rix had heard enough of the conversation to figure that push push was the gravity repulsor and fell in behind Philo, who stopped after a few meters and pulled a tile up from the deck, exposing an entire network of complicated wires, pipes and devices that were all far beyond Rix's comprehension.

"Oh boy," Rix said as Philo set the toolbox next to a narrow ladder and started climbing down into the 'tween deck as Rix would soon discover it was called. Following behind, Rix descended the ladder only to find that he was forced to stoop as he followed Philo forward.

"Broke," Philo said simply, dropping the tools on the rounded hull they'd been walking on. "Mechanic Man Rix, fix now."

And with that, Philo grabbed an overhead truss and arm-over-arm swung himself back to the open hatch and disappeared up into the ship.

"What have you gotten yourself into this time, Rixy old boy?" Rix asked, sitting down on the hull still holding onto the electronic pad. "Just exactly which of these things is the gravity repulsor? Why am I doing this again?"

"Hold tablet in front of face and scan the compartment." The voice emitted from the tablet and instead of following instructions, Rix jumped, dropping the device on the deck. When he recovered, he managed to gather his wits and looked at the instructions that were also written on the display.

"How are you doing this?" Rix asked nobody in particular.

"If you are asking about the display of text on the simple electronics device you are holding, the answer is related to interconnectivity of computational devices that is likely beyond your current capacity for technological comprehension."

"I'm not sure, but I think you just called me dumb," Rix said. "I'm not dumb."

"Assessment accepted. You have existed in an environment without complex, interactive systems and lack the requisite knowledge to proceed without elaborate descriptions. Alternatively, simple instructions can be provided and details filled in when you wish to learn more."

"That sounds like a winner. Once again with how I locate this repulsor?" Rix said.

"Treat this electronic notepad as a window and look *through* it. This will allow the repulsor systems to be highlighted so you may recognize them without the notepad."

"Now that makes perfect sense. The window thing was helpful," Rix said, holding the pad up and noticing the components two yards ahead of him that were highlighted. "Also, that's really neat the way you gave them color. I'd like to understand that more when there's a chance."

"Yes, again, a lengthy description is required. In short, however, consider the coursework in your secondary education called geometry. What if there was a device that was capable of calculating millions of geometric equations every second and that same device could make measurements as long as the camera was unobscured. Could you then imagine how easy it would be to then add color over the top of located items?"

"Shoot, we're going to get along just fine. I assume you are just such a device and have those capabilities," Rix said.

"It's always a little more complicated than that, but you have grasped the essence of the conversation quite nicely. If you place this tablet next to the device highlighted with a green halo, you will interface with the diagnostics system. Once that is complete, those diagnostics will be combined with known operating parameters and a remedy will be formulated."

"I love your confidence," Rix said, holding the tablet next to the green halo.

"Diagnostics uploaded. There is an important part that has become dislodged due to the failure of a clamp. In that *Calypso* does not have a manufactory, we will need to locate a resource on this planet capable of manufacturing the correct part."

"Show me what's broken. I want to see it with my own eyes," Rix said.

"Yes, of course. Withdraw the wrench that looks like what is currently displayed. You will remove the fasteners that are highlighted in orange."

"Are you a person?" Rix asked.

"Not in the way you are thinking," the pad replied. "Technology of Galactic Empire is sophisticated and replicating human conversation is not difficult."

"You think I'm dumb, huh?" Rix asked, locating the wrench after a bit of trial and error which was immediately corrected by the fact that the highlighted item wasn't his first choice. "You didn't exactly answer my question."

"A survey calculating human intelligence has been completed. On the well-accepted galactic sentience scale, humanity scores as low as forty-nine and as high as ninety-two. Anything below one hundred is considered semi-sentient. You are provably *dumb* as you say."

"Don't you go sugarcoating anything," Rix said, pulling off a cover plate and setting it aside, leaving the retaining bolts resting within. "What now? Where's the problem?"

"There is no reason for you to be opening this device," the tablet responded. "A repair is well beyond your capacity and this instrument is delicate."

"This is where the *I can fix anything* part comes in," Rix said. "Delicate or not, I can't fix what I can't touch. Besides, according to you, you're looking for a replacement part. How about you show me what that part looks like and what the actual problem is."

"If you insist."

The pause that followed begged a response and Rix obliged. "I insist."

"The repulsor lattice core has a gravity coil array that has two states. Hold the tablet up for a demonstration."

On the screen, Rix saw a stripped-down version of the lattice core that lay at the bottom of the device's compartment. Segregated into sixteen cells were individual gravity coil arrays. The disconnect between what he could see and what the tablet displayed were additional parts between him and the broken part.

"Looks like that might take a minute to disassemble," Rix said. "I'm going to need a place to lay all this out, so I don't forget how it is assembled."

"That is unnecessary, I am able to record where each part is located for your easy retrieval."

"Thanks, but this is my first job, I need to make sure I'm doing things in a way I can support," Rix said. From the toolbox, he pulled a small tarp and spread it out on the hull. He moved the repulsor's lid to the top left corner. "Now what's next to come off?"

"You are wasting time," the notepad said.

"Just so we're clear, I haven't ruled you out for being a person. You arguing isn't exactly working toward your cover."

"Is this a sentience test of sorts?" the notepad asked. "Perhaps the test young Alan Turing of Manchester has just proposed?"

"I'm not familiar with anyone named Turing, I was just putting you on notice that I hadn't ruled anything out," Rix said.

"Why is this important?"

"You're trying to stop me from fixing this vessel. I'd like to know why."

"I am not, but if I were a person, I might have ulterior motives," the tablet answered. "Remove the anti-mass regulator next."

"You're as good at answering questions as you are at avoiding them," Rix said, grabbing a new tool highlighted through the tablet's glass panel.

Twenty minutes later, Rix found himself looking at the repulsor lattice core. "Is there power to that lattice right now?" he asked.

"Negative. You would have already been injured had it not been turned off."

"In the future, warn me and show me how to turn it off," Rix said. "I like to learn the whole thing instead of just the pieces you think are important."

"The power is off."

"Which of the gravity coil array thingamabobs is busted?" Rix asked. In the aft row, second in from starboard, a gravity coil array highlighted. "I'm going to guess that just slides in there. Is it attached to anything beneath?"

"There is no additional coupling."

Without further questions, Rix reached into the lattice and nimbly plucked the broken gravity coil array from its location. Turning it slowly in his hand, he found that there was indeed a small cylinder about the length of a bobby pin that was loosely connected and moved when he gently pushed with his thumb. Upon further inspection he discovered that something akin to a soldered joint had detached and there was separation when the cylinder was pulled downward by gravity.

"This probably worked fine in space, although I'm not sure why that would matter if it's only used on planets," Rix said. "What are these soldering joints made with?"

"A melted alloy that requires considerable heat."

"How much heat?"

"Six hundred twenty-three degrees using your Celsius scale."

Rix pondered for a moment. "That's hot. Maybe three times as hot as my soldering equipment."

"And how would you repair it if you had a machine that would get this hot? Do you have more material?"

"Hang on," Rix said, setting the part on the sheet he'd laid down. Setting the notepad next to the part, Rix turned and scurried up through the hole in the deck and ran out to his truck.

"Where are you going?" Kel called after him, following him out as far as the ramp.

"I just need something," he answered, rummaging in a tool chest bolted to the wrecker. "Ah, there it is." Proudly, he held a roll of duct tape up to show Kel. "Doesn't look like much, but it'll likely do the job."

"There's no part on my ship that looks like what you're holding."

"Oh, sweetheart, this stuff is magic. They made it back in the war for fixing wounds quick, but it does way more than that. It's a darn miracle is what it is."

"You're crazy," Kel answered, laughing as she followed Rix back through the ship and even down into the 'tween deck. "Oh, for frak sake, you've ruined my ship. What are all those parts doing out like that?"

"You asked me to fix it. This is me fixing it. Now, do you want me to get back to work?" Rix asked.

"You better not break it worse," Kel said, plucking a part from the sheet.

"Put that back just like you found it. If you move it or rotate it, I won't remember where it goes."

"You better be right."

Rix pulled a two-inch length of the duct tape off and cut it with his pocketknife. Placing the tape on the broken part, he created tension which would hold the piece together temporarily. Reseating the part into the lattice, he started reassembling the larger component.

"How do you know what you are doing?" the notebook asked.

"Am I doing it wrong?" Rix asked.

"No, but even a galactic sentience rating of ninety-two, humanity's max, would not allow for this level of recall."

"I've always had a good memory," Rix said. "Just need the field containment shroud and we'll be ready to seal this old girl right up."

"Girl?"

"Planes, boats, cars are all considered feminine. It reminds us to be gentle when we work on them."

"You have unusual mannerisms."

"I haven't heard you say you think my fix won't work."

"I do not know if it will. There is some heat generated. I do not know if your duct tape will hold. I estimate it will last only a matter of a few hours."

"Nifty," Rix said. "How do I turn the power on so we can test it out?"

"It requires a command through *Calypso's* main system. Power in five, four, three …"

A line of circuits connecting the three gravity repulsors that sat next to each other glowed with a dim yellow light which pulsed several times and then faded. The repaired repulsor then glowed initially red then switched to yellow while at the same moment the front end of *Calypso* lifted from the field and levelled out.

"You did it!" Kel said excitedly. "You're a genius! How did you do that?"

"Not every repair requires a new part. It's like you guys are so sophisticated that you don't see the simplicity of the devices that comprise your system. We need to get your ship back to my shop so I can fix it for real, though. My patch probably won't last that long."

"*Calypso* won't move right now," Kel said. "What do you propose?"

"It doesn't look too hard," Rix said. "I'll just rig up a harness and we'll pull you behind my wrecker. Do you have any sort of steering controls?"

"You're really going to use that truck as a tug for my beautiful girl?"

"Unless you see another way," Rix said. "Back at my shop, I have a lot more supplies for fixing things."

"This is so humiliating," Kel said, following Rix from the 'tween deck back outside of *Calypso*.

At the truck, Rix picked up a bucket that held a heavy-duty towing chain and hefted a length for Kel to see. "Do you have anywhere we can connect this?"

"Philo, turn on the forward magnetic clamps," Kel said and then looked at Rix's grip on the chain. "Better let that go, clamps might pull it out of your hand."

"Hold on a second, then," Rix said.

"Wait one, Philo," Kel said.

Rix looped the chain around the back end of his wrecker and laid the chain out in a straight line. "Let's see how that works."

"Now, Kel?" Philo's voice sounded from Kel's wrist where there was just a flat black band.

Rix nodded and Kel answered, "Go."

A hum preceded the chain jumping up from the ground and pulling toward *Calypso*. The sound of groaning metal warned of metal fatigue and then Rix's wrecker truck started slowly sliding toward *Calypso*, dirt piling up behind the locked rear dual wheels.

"Holy buckets!" Rix called, racing over to the truck and jumping in to release the brakes. With freedom of movement, the wrecker was pulled the final meter until the chain was held solidly in place by the clamp. "Well, that's nifty. Never seen anything like that before."

"I'm a little leery of how this is going to work. You want me to steer while you pull with that little truck? You do know that my girl here out masses that truck by fifty times, right? If I start sliding around, you're coming with me."

"I guess you know what that means, then," Rix said.

"I do?"

"Yeah, don't slide around."

"It's probably not the dumbest thing I've ever done," Kel said. "Although, it's probably going to be in my top five."

"You pull me into a ditch and roll me over and it won't even dent my top twenty," Rix said.

Kel laughed. "You got a good nature about you, Rix Banner. And apparently, you can fix spaceships, too."

"Let's not get ahead of ourselves. Duct tape isn't likely going to be a permanent solution," Rix said.

"And I just need another couple dozen lightyears of wear and tear to reach civilization," Kel said. "Hey, Philo wants to know if it's okay if he rides in the truck with you. I told him about it and he's curious."

"Sure," Rix said.

"Rixy!" Philo said in his high-pitched, excited voice as he peeked out from the side of *Calypso*. "I'm coming, Rixy!"

Rix grinned at the small alien's antics and watched as he wobbled down the ramp as if either his knees were damaged or, more likely, his lower legs were inflexible. Either way, Philo made decent time.

"Just sit over there, Philo," Rix said, gesturing to the passenger seat instead of being behind the wheel. "These trucks are double clutched and she's a bit finnicky so, with a load, I'll probably do the driving."

"Philo good with running trucks," Philo said.

"I have no doubt, friend," Rix said, "but this old girl is my responsibility, so go ahead and slide over. I have some M&M candies in the console here." Rix pulled open a box of colorful candies and showed it to Philo.

"Eat eat," Philo said excitedly taking the box and tipping into his open mouth. "Candy good."

"Can you hear me, Rix?" Kel's voice sounded over a black band that was on Philo's wrist.

"Sure can," Rix answered. "Are you set? I'm going to start pulling. Release brakes if you have them on."

"I'll try, but remember, if I start sliding to the side, I'll pull you right along with me."

"I understand."

More groaning metal from the stresses of taking on the burden of *Calypso* sounded and the wheels on the wrecker spun, digging in the dirt.

"I'm giving you everything," Kel said. "Be careful."

As Kel fully released what amounted to brakes on *Calypso*, Rix's tires bit into the hardpacked soil and they started forward with the large spaceship in tow.

"There's a bit of a hill, I'm going to match your acceleration going down," Rix said. "It might get a little bumpy and we'll turn left at the bottom."

"I don't know left," Kel said.

"Can you see my truck?"

"Of course."

Rix turned on the left blinker. "That's left."

"Ah, we're good. Fast down the hill and then left. You're really going to test my abilities with these side thrusters. I almost never do this work myself," Kel said.

"You're talking alien gobbledy gook," Rix said. "Just let me know if you're hitting the brakes."

Together, they moved up the slight hill and then, as *Calypso* crested and started sliding down the opposite side, things started to get a bit more chaotic.

"Brake!" Kel said just a little too late. The front end of Rix's wrecker was lifted from the ground after a strong enough jolt that Philo and his M&Ms were thrown into the dash.

"Are you okay, Philo?" Rix asked.

"Candy candy," Philo said, plucking M&Ms from the floorboards.

"Sorry Rix, go again," Kel said.

Through the gate, Rix pulled *Calypso* over the fence and onto the road. Every tenth of a mile they travelled, they got better at their task, although there were fits and starts as Kel had to hit brakes without warning a few times. After the second time, Rix had Philo put the candy away, promising he'd return it to the affable alien once they were settled back in Cranberry Cove.

"This isn't that bad," Kel said. "These roads are really good. We don't have much like this on the planets I go to."

"Well, if you all have repulsors, I don't see the value," Rix agreed. Just then, headlights coming from the opposite direction crested a small hill. Rix turned on his emergency lights to warn them of their approach. "Hey, we'll need to slow down. I don't know how we're getting around this guy."

"There's not enough room," Kel said. "He'll have to get out of the way."

"That should be interesting," Rix agreed.

It became obvious when the driver of the other vehicle finally caught what Rix was towing as the car slammed to a stop and there was no movement for a time.

"We'll go right over him, don't worry," Kel said.

"It's going to be tough to explain all this," Rix said.

"One problem at a time, Rix," Kel said. "That's the only way to make it through some nights, if you know what I mean."

"You're not wrong," Rix agreed.

A family of four sat inside their new station wagon, their faces pressed against the windows as Rix tugged *Calypso* down the road and right over the top of the stalled vehicle. Rix waved, but it seemed they only had eyes for the spaceship, which he felt was reasonable.

Taking the long way around, Rix oriented the long spaceship with the side of his shop. It was longer than the shop was deep, but there was plenty of land and they fit just perfectly.

"I'm setting brakes," Kel said.

"Go ahead and grab the M&Ms, Philo," Rix said. "We're stopping for the night."

"Okay, Rixy, this good. Like ride," Philo said. "And candy."

Rix climbed out and walked back to where Kel was already exiting the spaceship. Over the top of the shop, a bright streak of light showed the path of something entering the atmosphere.

"Did you see that?" Rix asked.

"Frak. They found me," Kel said.

3

COVERING UP

"Who's they?" Rix asked.

"Nobody important," Kel said. "Pay you double if you can fix this tonight?"

"That might be interesting, but we haven't even talked about payment," Rix said. "I don't even know what's wrong. Plus, that light in the sky was up in the atmosphere. There's no way they could possibly find you. Cranberry Cove is about as tucked away as a little town can get. There are millions of other little towns all over the globe, I don't get it."

"They tracked *Calypso's* energy signature or something," Kel said. "I don't know how they did it. I do know that they're here and we're all in danger."

"Just turn it off," Rix said.

"Turn what off?"

"*Calypso*," Rix said. "I have some heavy-duty wood six-by-sixes. We could slide them in under the bottom of her and then you just shut her down."

"You can't just shut a spaceship off, Rix," Kel said.

"His solution, while overtly simple, would work," said a voice from Kel's wrist.

"Notepad is talking again, only she's doing it from your wrist," Rix said. "I see you, Notepad."

"This isn't the time, Rix," Kel said. "Talk to me about this wood. What are you saying?"

"I have pallets of beams sitting out back. I'll just run them over with the forklift. It'll take a bit of effort, but give us a couple of hours, we'll be set. Maybe you could ask Notepad the best place to put stuff while I'm fetching them. And I know someone who's got a few big old tarps from when the circus was in town. We'll pull those over top."

"How are you so levelheaded about this?" Kel asked suspiciously. "Two hours ago, you didn't think there was such a thing as spaceships. Now, you're some sort of expert at hiding them?"

"What do you think an airplane mechanic in the war did?" Rix asked.

"What war?"

"Oh for the love of God, Kel," Rix said with frustration. "We haven't been out of the war for more than two years here. Just about every nation on Earth was involved. We won, but not without heavy losses."

"And you fixed airplanes."

"Yes, that dropped bombs and some that were used by fighter pilots who tried to keep the enemy from bombing our airplanes," Rix said.

"Hiding airplanes was a survival mechanism," Kel said.

"Same as fixing them, Kel. The more planes I kept in the air, the more likely it was that me and all my friends got to come home," Rix said. "Do you want to talk more or do you want to stay alive? You choose, because I've got nothing in this besides a wasted evening."

"It's not wasted. You fixed my repulsor," Kel said. "And I appreciate that a whole lot."

"You haven't seen my bill yet."

Kel chuckled. "Crash landed on a quarantined planet, I doubt there's an actual bill that's too high for fixing my old girl, here," she said.

"I'll keep that in mind," Rix said. "Now, are you going to help?"

"Tell me what to do."

"I'm going to need help moving lumber. It's going to be heavy," Rix said. "Are you up for that?"

"No, but Philo is," Kel said. "He's a lot stronger than he looks."

"That works," Rix said. "Explain it to him. I'll be back with some beams."

Rix set off at a jog and disappeared behind the back of the shop. The cool air of the evening, and the fact that he could no longer see the spaceship, helped regulate his nerves. He knew better than to give in to the nerves and steeled himself as he jumped into his old forklift.

Spinning around, he lowered the forks and slid them beneath the pallet which held a heavy stack of six-by-six beams he'd been storing for no other reason than he didn't want to see them lost, having accepted them in trade in lieu of money from a recent card game.

Kel and Philo stood beneath *Calypso* talking as Rix ambled toward them, his forklift bouncing along the gravel, feeling a little tipsy due to the weight. Kel pointed at a location for him to stop but he pulled up next to them and lowered the engine RPMs to idle so they could talk.

"Do we know where the structural points are so we don't bend your frame?" Rix asked.

"What do you know about *Calypso's* frame?" Kel asked.

"I was inside and saw a super structure," Rix said. "I'd bet she's heavy enough to poke through the hull if we don't line the beams up right. Best not to make new problems, right?"

"I don't know about that," Kel said, glancing at her wristwatch. She sighed and pulled the notepad out from a pocket and handed it over to Rix.

Instead of asking further questions, Rix looked *through* the notepad until a piece of ground was highlighted and a proposed lattice structure was superimposed with glowing artificial beams.

"Apparently someone does," Rix said, moving the load next to where they were to be unloaded.

"Philo strong. Help mans," Philo said, grasping the side of the fork-lift as Rix lowered the pallet of wood.

"Did you see this?" Rix asked, showing the drawing to Philo.

"Good good," Philo agreed, jumping off eagerly and making his way over to the stack of beams.

As promised, Philo was plenty strong and knew exactly where to set each beam. They worked together quickly and built two bunks in less than thirty minutes.

"We'll need another pallet or two to get this done," Rix said.

"Philo make machine go," Philo said. "Philo good."

Unlike the wrecker, Rix wasn't quite as worried about the forklift as it topped out at a couple of miles per hour. "Are you sure you can drive this?"

"Philo good," Philo said, looking expectantly at Rix.

"Be my guest," Rix said. "I'll hang on the side until you get the hang of it."

"Fun fun," Philo said, grasping the controls. At first Philo's driving was erratic and Rix had to swing in and tap the brakes, but after reassurances from Philo in his stilted speaking pattern, the odd little alien seemed to get it and drove right back to where the other pallets were sitting.

"Go slow with the load, it'll get real tippy where the ground is uneven," Rix warned.

"Slow," Philo responded.

Not one to overthink things, Rix hopped off the forklift and walked back to beneath *Calypso,* holding the notepad up for inspection. "You sure do a lot of thinking, Notepad," Rix said as he located four more bunk locations, which included two drop points for pallets. He was about to show Philo where to unload the current pallet when the smaller alien did just that and then turned around, presumably for a third load. "What, nothing clever to say?"

"Was that a compliment?" Notepad answered. "Are you pleased that I am capable of computation?"

"Yes, a compliment," Rix said. "Assuming your locations are taking into consideration the superstructure, you're likely saving *Calypso* from further damage. I don't suppose you'd like to share your name with me, would you? I think we're beyond thinking you're actually part of this device I'm holding. I heard you talking through Kel's watch."

"My designation is 49231125-0-B," Notepad answered. "Would it be more comfortable for you to interface with me using this designation?"

"That's a mouthful. I'll probably stick with Notepad unless you have something easier to remember."

"Beverly as it is a colloquial reference you will not struggle with."

"That's fine, but maybe you could lay off on the judgy thing you're doing about my intelligence. I'm perfectly happy not to have that pushed in my face every time you're feeling insecure," Rix said. "Can you tell Kel I'm headed off to grab that big tarp?"

"Yes. And I am not insecure," Beverly said.

"If you have to say that, it's less effective," Rix said.

"I am not sure I like you, Rix Banner," Beverly said.

"Why? I feel like we're off to a banging start," Rix said. "You finally admitted you're not just some electronic computer machine thingam-abob. I feel we're getting along swimmingly."

"There is plenty of artificial intelligence that could have responded just as I have," Beverly answered. "You have no proof positive."

"Aside from your choice of wording for most of this conversation," Rix said. "It's okay, I don't need you to expose yourself in a way that's uncomfortable. It'll be our little secret."

"You are impossible, Rix Banner."

"This ... this I've heard," Rix said, slowing the truck he'd taken over to a warehouse owned by one of his friends. Hopping out and letting himself inside, he struggled to move a trio of massive canvas tarps into his truck, but managed, all the same. "I've noticed that Kel has a wristwatch you like to talk through, but Philo does not. Does this mean you're part of Philo in some way?"

"You've intuited this through observation?" Beverly asked.

"I'm not sure there's another way," Rix said. "Do you need me to stretch these tarps out so you can give us the best coverage plan for Calypso?"

"It is unexpected that you so easily turn over these tasks. I believe

29

it is within your capacity to utilize these tarps at some level of efficiency," Beverly said.

"And yet, I can't do millions of calculations in seconds," Rix said. "And geometry was fun, but I don't think I remember all that much of it."

"Yes, if you stretch the tarps, I will design an efficient plan for deploying them. I presume you have rope available."

"I do and I'll grab it once you're ready."

Arriving back at the filling station, he saw that Philo had made significant progress with the remaining bunks and had started using the forklift to position the beams so that limited effort was required on his part. Instead of doubling up on the work, Rix started unfurling the tarps and once that was done, he ducked into the shop after retrieving a large spool of twine. Returning to where Philo was working, Rix then helped the small alien complete the task.

"Kel, can you hear me?" Rix asked, holding the notepad in front of his mouth.

"Yes, is the wood all positioned?" she asked.

"Lower Calypso slowly. I'm concerned about puncturing your hull. I imagine that's important once you get out of the atmosphere," Rix said.

"I've got this," Kel answered. Almost immediately, Calypso started dropping at a rate of one centimeter per second.

Thirty seconds later, the first part of the hull settled onto the heavy wooden beams. "Nice and slow now," Rix said. "You've made contact."

"I can see," Kel answered. "We're holding just fine." She slowed the descent by a factor of ten but continued. Wood shifted and popped under the extraordinary weight of the spaceship, but the bunks held and finally the ship stopped moving. "I think we're good," Kel said. "I can't come down any further."

"Slowly reduce your braking," Rix said. "I want to make sure you don't slide."

"Have a little trust. Beverly is good with this," Kel said. Just then Calypso seemed to jump to the side a few centimeters as the wood bunks accepted the final stresses placed upon them. "Frak! What's going on, Rix?"

"You're good. It's just settling in," Rix answered. "Damn fine work, Beverly. Can you start shutting it down? We'll get those tarps in place. It's getting late and I have an early morning meeting with Chief Andy."

"What are you going to tell him?"

"Like, am I going to tell him spaceships and little green men are real?"

"Yes, very much like that," Kel answered.

"He'll notice this ship on the side of the building. Lots of people will. Now, if we keep it covered, they might not jump right to spaceship, but some will. No, Chief Andy is in this one way or another," Rix said. "He's a good guy and I bet he'll prefer to keep the peace over making trouble about this."

"What kind of trouble could he make?"

"I imagine he could call the FBI. Those fellas are real smart and probably want to know about spaceships landing on Earth. Heck, maybe they've already covered up a few like this. Either way, if we can keep it quiet, I imagine that's what Chief Andy will lean toward."

"You sound very certain."

"Certain enough," Rix said. "Why don't you and Philo grab some clothes. We'll finish up here and you can take the guest room at my house. It's not fancy, but it keeps the rain off my head and there's food and beer in the refrigerator."

"I could drink a beer," Kel said. "And Philo will want a couple, too. He's been working hard."

"Suit yourself," Rix said, pulling on a tarp.

The trio worked for another forty minutes at the end of which, the tarps had been pulled into place. As promised, the three of them piled into Rix's truck and he drove them to a small, but well-maintained house a few blocks away.

"No lights?" Kel asked.

"It was light when I left this morning," Rix said. "How would they get turned on?"

31

"That's amazing," Kel said. "Your house has no idea you're here."

"I'm not sure how it would," Rix said, leading the pair. A flash of light from across the street drew Rix's attention. His neighbor, Ella Gourding, was peeking out the window, curious about Rix's late arrival. That he was in the company of two others would likely make the rounds before he'd even gotten to bed.

"Just so you know, neighbors watch everything. Try not to act alien," Rix said.

"You are taking all of this quite well," Kel said. "Care to explain?"

"I'm not sure what an explanation would look like," Rix said. "You weren't shooting at me, so I don't see a reason to get worked up. I got over all of that in the war."

"World War II," Kel added.

"Assume that's what I'm referring to when I say anything about a war."

"I understand."

Entering through the back and into the kitchen, Rix hung the truck keys on a hook and pushed the light switch in, turning on a yellow, overhead bulb. "She's not much, but I call her home," Rix said, walking straight across to the cabinets. "Say, you all up for trying something different? I have this cocktail I make. It's not for everyone."

"You should understand that everything will be different for us," Kel said.

"I try something new," Philo said.

"It's an adaptation of a drink called Fisherman's Folly. I call it Rix's Folly. It just takes a minute," Rix said, pulling a jar of dill pickles from the refrigerator, setting it beside a bottle of Gin, a smaller bottle of Sake, and a smelly spritzer that was already preloaded with fish sauce. "I just need to juice a couple of grapefruits."

"You have a lot of smells going on there," Kel said, wrinkling her nose.

"That's its appeal," Rix said, continuing to work on the drink. Several minutes later, he handed the deep green colored drink first to Philo and then to Kel, keeping one for himself. "Bottoms up!"

Taking only an easy drink from the top of the glass, Rix savored the experience.

"Oh, Lords of Gavenar, this tastes like the hind end of a mud-dwelling reptilian corpse-sucker," Kel said, spitting back into her glass.

"Like I said, not for everyone," Rix said, turning to Philo. "What do you think, little fella?"

"Good good," Philo said, finishing his glass of Rix's Folly.

"There's a beer in the refrigerator, Kel. It might be more to your liking," Rix said. When she made no move to open the refrigerator, Rix pulled a bottle out, opened the top and gave it to her. This time, when she tested the drink, she had a smile on her face.

"What a treat," Kel said, grinning as she held the bottle up to the light. "This looks hand-brewed and bottled."

"I imagine it was a big enough batch," Rix said. "I think they do the brewing in Madison. I suppose everything where you come from is done by machines and computers."

"More than you can likely imagine," Kel said, taking a long drink. "Fruits of Xandarj, this is amazing."

Philo didn't set the bottle down until it was fully drained. A quiet grin spread across the odd little biker-monkey-alien man's face.

"Philo sure got quiet," Rix observed.

"He needs another beer," Kel said, which earned her a grateful look from Philo. "The alcohol hits his nervous system fast and helps him relax. We should figure out where we're sleeping, he isn't going to make it much past another fifteen minutes."

Rix handed the small alien another bottle and set one out on the table for Kel, who had just about finished her own. She nodded with satisfaction, finishing off the bottle and flashed a smile at Rix when she picked up the next.

"How about I show you where you can sleep," Rix said after Philo finished the second beer and then walked from the kitchen.

They'd no more made it to the living room when Philo climbed onto the narrow couch and seemed to fall immediately to sleep.

"I'm not sure we're getting him away from here," Kel said. "Is that a problem?"

"Not really," Rix said, pulling a nearby blanket over the sleepy alien. "Are you hungry?"

"Why are you being so nice to us? You don't know me at all," Kel said.

"Feels like the right thing to do," Rix said. "And, I'll admit, I'm curious. You don't meet people flying spaceships, or aliens for that matter."

"You could turn us in."

"Sure. Maybe tomorrow," Rix said, returning to the kitchen with Kel in tow.

"That's not funny."

"Right, so what are the chances the guys chasing you will find you in Cranberry Cove?" Rix asked.

"They will find us. It's a matter of time," Kel said.

"I don't understand. How is that possible? There's no power. It's under a tarp," Rix said, turning the oven's temperature control to 350.

"Right, but we're being chased by bounty hunters who have technology designed to locate people," Kel said. "It's a disadvantage that Earth has such little technology. Their locator drones will find *Calypso* based on her smell. The only advantage is that Earth has a large population that covers the globe."

"How long do you think?"

"Three days, maybe a week."

"We're good for tonight, then, right?"

"Definitely. Another beer?"

Rix gave her a surprised look. "Any food?"

"I figured I'd drink my dinner."

Rix pulled another beer from the refrigerator and opened the bottle, handing it to her. He didn't figure it was for him to judge another's proclivities, and he wondered if he could draw her in for the meatloaf his neighbor had made for him. Placing the meatloaf's pan in the oven, he joined her at the kitchen table, where he'd left his own beer.

"Talk to me about bounty hunters," Rix said, kicking back so he balanced on the back legs of his chair.

"What do you want to know? Are you asking why we're being chased?"

"It's not a bad place to start," Rix said. "You don't have to tell me anything you don't want."

"Sure. You'll probably think less of me, but I can share since you've been so hospitable," she said. "Maybe a little context would be helpful, though. I'm from the planet Caelanth, our species name is Velari. This is in the Forantic Quadrant of the Janesk sector of Galactic Empire space. I know that's not a lot of context, but it should help you understand the scale of the Galactic Empire. So, there are a lot of regional governments that are part of Galactic Empire and there's a lot of trouble between Forantic and Minga quadrants."

"What kind of trouble?"

"Well, there are old wars, but Galactic Empire demands a limit to the conflicts. There is a lot of tension and it's hard to make ends meet," she said. "I mean, I'm lucky to have *Calypso*. I don't know what I'd do without her."

"You're defensive, Kel," Rix said. "I'm not making judgments. But just so we're clear. You haven't answered my actual question. I feel like you're doing things you're not proud of. Maybe you don't need to tell me. I'll get you going and you don't have to feel badly."

"No, no, it's not that," Kel said. "I'll own up to my life. I thought it was a simple courier job. Pick up a case of electronics from point A, deliver to point B, get paid."

"Good pay?"

"Sort of. We took fire right after pickup and that caused the trouble that eventually caused us to land here," she said. "Now, if we survive, we'll be lucky to break even after repairs."

"Which is where I come in."

"I had hoped," she said. "And you've been a real sport here, Rix, but I don't have any real expectations that you'll be able to bail us out of this mess."

"What happens if those bounty hunters catch up with you?"

"Best case, they take the cargo and just leave."

"Worst?"

"Blow up my *Calypso* and take me and Philo prisoner."

"Let's hope that doesn't happen."

"What is that smell?" she asked.

Rix smiled. "That's the meatloaf. Are you sure you don't want some?"

"I kind of do."

4
DRAWING ATTENTION

"What is wrong with you?" Kel asked, looking at Rix through barely open eyes.

"It's early, but we've a meeting with Chief Andy," Rix said. "You need to get up. We'll grab breakfast at the diner."

Kel had slept in her jumpsuit and hadn't even bothered to take the red polka dot scarf off from around her head. Shaking her head, she pulled the cover with her as she rolled back over.

"Is that how it's going to be?" Rix said, moving over to the window next to the guest room's bed. Pulling it open, he let the near-freezing air fill the room, sending Kel further under the covers. He grinned as he grabbed the covers and yanked them away from her, dragging them from the room to her great disappointment.

"You are a horrible beastly human rat-man with extra-large sphincters," she yelled after him.

Contemplating her words, Rix shook his head, smiling at her creativeness if not eloquence. At the bottom of the stairs, he dumped the covers in the laundry room and then walked out to the living room where he expected to need to wake Philo.

"Mechanic Mans! Philo happy."

"Good morning, Philo. Did you sleep okay last night?"

"Beers good. Bed soft."

Moving into the kitchen, Rix eyed the notepad that he'd left on the counter and picked it up. "Do you sleep, Beverly?" he asked.

"In a manner of speaking, although perhaps meditation is more accurate," Beverly responded.

"Am I right that your presence is linked to Philo's?"

"You ask a question that has security implications for me," Beverly said. "Would you accept that I am a sentient being like yourself, but my form is so different you would struggle to perceive me in a meaningful way?"

"Boy howdy but can you pack a thousand words into a tiny sentence," Rix said. "And if you're so good at drawing things with your notepad display, why not just make up something that we can relate to."

"I don't understand—make up something?"

"Like a puppet, but you know, it's got some Beverly attributes or things you think represent you in a human way," Rix said. "It's not different than what you're doing with talking. There's no way you all speak English, so, you're adapting to me, because I can't adapt to you."

"Adapt visually," Beverly said.

"Yes."

"Are all humans as perceptive as you?"

"Hold on there, did you just compliment a semi-sentient, knuckle dragger?" Rix asked.

"I don't understand 'knuckle dragger,' but you are certainly well beyond the upper range of intelligence attributed to humans by Galactic Empire," she said. On the notepad screen, a woman wearing a featureless gray robe appeared. So unremarkable was the clothing that, to Rix, it looked as if her head were floating in space.

"That's better," Rix said. "And I'm sure you'll get the hang of all this."

"You sound disappointed. Have I not done what you asked?"

"I guess I thought with all your intelligence and galactic travel, you'd come up with something a bit more fanciful than choir robes."

"Why would that be important?"

"I just don't know too many women who would be interested in that look."

"I've never considered such a thing. You're talking about fashion."

"Right. You don't have fashion where you come from?"

"No. Clothing does not make sense for my people. In fact, the idea of visual information is not part of our biology."

"Wow, now see, that's alien. I know Philo is an alien, but he's not all that hard to figure out. He's kind of a mix of an ape and a good-natured guy. Kel is just a regular woman but you, you've got a story."

"Hmm, interesting first impressions," Beverly said. "Could you give me examples of fashion?"

"Well, I don't have anything here, but down at the diner we have a stack of magazines you could look through."

"I cannot look through printed material without help," Beverly said. "Your civilization does not have electronic media. It is very quiet here."

"What about broadcast TV?"

"Do tell."

Rix walked back into the living room and turned on a small black and white TV. "This is broadcast. Maybe you could figure out how to intercept it."

"I did not know this, Rix. Thank you very much."

"Can someone explain to me why we are awake at such a rude hour?" Kel asked, stomping down the stairs and turning into the living room.

"Chief Andy is going to have questions," Rix said. "It's not like those tarps are going to hide anything from him."

"Earth is quarantine. We can't tell him anything. The risk is too high," Kel said.

"Risk of what?" Rix asked.

"Exposure of the bigger universe that's out there."

"I towed your spaceship through town. People saw it," Rix said. "It seems like the word is going to get out."

"Frak. Then you're right. We need to get back to *Calypso* and see what needs to be done to get her fixed," Kel said.

"None of that happens if we're sitting here," Rix said.

"True," Kel agreed. "So let's get going already."

"See Beverly, like every human woman ever. She changes her mind in an instant and we're all just supposed to keep up."

"Careful, Rix Banner," Kel said. "I still have some alien tricks up my sleeve. I don't need your sarcastic mouth making trouble."

"Truly just proving my point and doubling down on why I'm happily single," Rix said. "Also, if you're not looking to raise eyebrows, you'll want to keep Philo aboard *Calypso*. He'll likely draw quite a lot of attention. It'll be bad enough with the clothes you're wearing."

"What's wrong with what I'm wearing. It's comfortable and a whole lot smarter than what you're wearing," she said.

"I doubt anyone here would call that smart fashion," Rix said. "I'm just saying you won't fit in and will draw attention."

"A risk we'll have to take. I'm not changing from my jumpsuit."

"Fair enough," Rix said. "Shall we get going?"

"Fine."

The trio piled back into Rix's truck and he pulled out onto the quiet paved streets of Cranberry Cove. The drive was only eight blocks but as they got closer to their destination, the traffic significantly increased.

"This isn't good," Rix said.

"What concerns you?" Kel asked.

"This traffic. It's like everyone in Cranberry Cove is out this morning," he said. "I don't like it."

"Is it not normally like this?"

"No. At this time of the morning, I'd expect to see maybe ten vehicles," Rix said. "Something is up … like someone saw a spaceship and the word is out."

"How? You don't have wireless transmission capacity. Aside from that television, which I believe is one way. Is it not?"

"Dang it," Rix said swearing beneath his breath. "We have telephones and busy bodies. Put those together and you'd be surprised how quickly word can travel."

Rix continued the drive and eventually, it got to the point where cars were backing up on the street. Worried about what he'd find at the shop, Rix moved over and drove against opposing traffic for the last two blocks, only to find a mass of vehicles parked in the filling station's drive.

"Someone has removed one of the tarps," Kel said.

"Or it blew off, either way, that's not good."

A large tarp was laying on the ground in front of *Calypso* while a dozen brave individuals tentatively peeked around the ship, clearly nervous to get too close. Irritation surged through Rix and he started honking to get people out of his way. At first, he was successful, but then, the cars were too tightly packed together and couldn't move.

"Stay in the truck," Rix growled, hopping out. "Move. You're blocking my shop." He waved his arms and managed to brow beat a few to move on. "Hey, get away from that!" he shouted as a few men, emboldened by his appearance, got closer to the shiny, chromed vessel. "Come on, guys. You're trespassing."

"You can't stop us," one man Rix didn't recognize said. The man went as far as to shove Rix, which didn't have quite the intent he'd expected. Instead of shoving back, Rix stalked off to his garage, where he opened the door, went inside and grabbed his Marlin over-under twelve-gauge loaded with salt pellets. At close range, the pellets could be fatal, but he wasn't expecting to point the shotgun at anyone.

"He's got a gun," one of the men who was tapping a hand against the hull said nervously.

"Yes, he does," Rix said, breaking the twelve-gauge open and sliding a couple of shells into the barrels. With practiced ease, he snapped the gun closed. Previously emboldened, many of those near the garage lost their nerve at the sight of a gun and jogged back to their cars. Even so, a couple remained defiant. "You're on private property. You best get moving or you'll be picking salt from your behinds for the next week."

"What is this, Rix?" Rob Blaken, a man Rix often played cards with and generally got along with, asked.

"It's a new circus ride for that outfit in Minneapolis. They got a motor burned out," Rix said, lying easily. "And whoever took that tarp down is gonna lose me my money so you best all get now, you hear me?"

The grinding whine of a police siren started up, which was probably the only reason Rix didn't end up firing into the air to run the recalcitrant curious off.

"People, you will move along and clear the street. If you don't have business at the filling station or diner, I'm going to start handing out tickets," Chief Andy called.

"I didn't see who took the tarp off," Rob said. "Sorry, Rix, it's just something you don't see all the time. Beth told me that there was a spaceship down here. I just wanted to come take a look. We weren't causing any harm."

"No, I know," Rix said. "But it will be trouble for me."

"Look, I can help you get the tarp back on. Say, Jeff, help us get this covered up, would you?" Rob called to one of his friends.

"Sorry, Rix," Jeff said sheepishly as he joined the men wrangling the tarp. "Circus ride you say? Doesn't look too easy to get in."

"Not much in there. All the work is on the exterior paint, trying to make it look real," Rix said.

"Well, I can see that. It's a good job. It feels realistic," Jeff added.

"You boys better get going. Chief Andy has his ticket book out," Rix said.

"Martha will be all over me if I get another ticket," Jeff said. "And, Andy has had it out for me since I beat him out for captain on the basketball team."

"Well, there's enough chaos down here that if you get going now, there's no way he'll write you up, Jeff," Rix said.

"Good thought," Jeff said. "Let's get together for cards, soon?"

"Seven tomorrow night, my place?" Rix asked.

"Sounds good. I'll bring Martha's tuna casserole."

"Everyone, go home," Chief Andy called again over his loudspeaker.

The crowd that was starting to break up did so more quickly now that the front end of *Calypso* was once again under the tarp and no longer visible. Rix looked around for the man who'd knocked into him but couldn't locate him.

"Get along now," Rix said, leaving his shotgun leaning against a wooden bunk as he shooed the final onlookers away. It took another twenty minutes to clear the road, but people got the idea that Chief Andy wasn't going to put up with poor behavior and they either walked over to the diner or drove away.

"What in tarnation are you doing, Rix?" Andy asked, walking across the drive.

"Hang on, let me bring the truck in off the road," Rix said, jogging out to where Kel and Philo were patiently awaiting his return.

"That was quite a crowd," Kel said. "I think that could be trouble if word travels too far."

"I wouldn't be surprised if a news team from Tannerville comes up," Rix said. "We'll just keep the tarp on, though. It's not much to look at and I don't think I saw anyone with a camera in the crowd. Besides, it was dark, without flashes a camera wouldn't do much. Now, you need to let me do the talking with Chief Andy."

"Sure."

Rix jumped out of the truck and rejoined Andy who looked skeptically at Kel and Philo. "Who are they?" Andy asked.

"I have to be honest, I don't know them very well," Rix said. "Far as I know, their vehicle had a break down and I was going to see if I could help out. But then all these folks were crawling all over my shop because of this other project."

"What is it?" Andy asked, looking at the tarped spaceship. "I got a glance. It looks like some sort of airplane or other."

"Well, I'm just getting into that now," Rix said. "Best I can tell, it's some kind of prop made to look like a spaceship. They're trying to keep it hush hush, but someone got nosey, apparently."

"Were you pulling that down main late last night?"

"That was me," Rix said.

"You need a permit for something that size. Did you get into any power poles?"

"No. I figured if I dragged it in late, nobody would much care," Rix said. "Say, are you on for cards tomorrow night?"

"Gambling, drinking and smokes?" Chief Andy asked.

"Not if Linda asks. We'll buy in at five bucks if that's not too rich for everyone," Rix said. "Apparently, Martha is making tuna casserole."

"We're not done with the conversation about that permit, Rix," Andy said, "But, we should probably get back out to Bob's house and see what he's all worked up about."

"I took a run out there last night," Rix said. "I didn't see much. Maybe we'll see something in the daylight."

"Trouble sleeping or something?"

"Nothing like that. I just started worrying that maybe someone had run off the road and wanted to make sure we weren't running up on a dead body," Rix said.

"Well, I appreciate that, Rix. Have you had breakfast? I hope all those lookie-loos haven't taken all the sweet rolls," Andy said with dismay. "Grab you one?"

"Absolutely," Rix said. "Let me get these folks squared away and we'll get going."

It was midday when Rix returned to the shop. Having run across Davis's field, looking for a wrecked car or asteroid and finding nothing, Andy was satisfied there was no further mystery to resolve. But as things went, the owner of the Oldsmobile was ready to pick it up and several customers were waiting for Rix to return for a variety of smaller issues, like flat tires and the like. It wasn't until three in the afternoon when Rix closed the mechanics shop and left an employee in charge of the full-service pumps so he could talk with Kel.

"You were gone forever," Kel said after Rix found the small open hatch that allowed him to climb into *Calypso* without utilizing the blocked main hatch.

"Believe it or not, the universe continues on, even when your ship is grounded on Earth," Rix said. "Why is it you don't ask Beverly to help you fix whatever it is that's wrong with your ship?"

"I can replace some parts," Kel said. "And so can Philo, but we've tried and, far as we know, we need a custom manufactured part in order to get going again. And then we picked this forsaken planet with no appreciable tech on it. We're screwed."

"Maybe spend less time worrying about what we can't do and a bit more time on what we can," Rix said. "What's the problem?"

"Flux coupling manifold is cracked. It's been needing an overhaul forever, but who has money for that?" Kel said.

"Now we're getting somewhere. Where's that notepad?" Rix asked.

"What, you're just going to go back in there and fix a flux coupling manifold?"

"I fixed your gravity repulsors."

"Right, that was cute, using that funny gray tape and all," she said. "A flux coupling manifold is extremely sensitive. If it's off by just a little bit, we all go boom." Kel mimed a small explosion in front of herself, which she seemed to watch with great satisfaction.

"You're telling me you know this has been broken for a time and now you're saying it's extremely sensitive. Pick one, it can't be both," Rix said.

"How are you standing there telling me about my own spaceship?" Kel asked.

"Spaceman bad," Philo said. "Listen betters."

Rix grinned. He'd worked with a lot of people who wanted to tell him how to fix tractors, airplane engines and big truck diesels. Words amounted to just about nothing when compared to just getting your hands on things. "Nah, just a difference of opinion, Philo. Would you mind grabbing that toolbox again? You can show me where this broken manifold is."

"Work work," Philo said and trundled off.

"He's a good sort," Rix said, watching the short alien walk away.

"You don't get easily aggravated, do you?" Kel asked.

"That's not my thing," Rix agreed.

"Why is that and don't tell me 'The War,' because that's not a description," Kel said.

"Doesn't make it not true," Rix said. "Once you've had a bomb land a hundred feet from the plane you're working on and have it flip over, you'll reset your threshold for things that ruffle your feathers."

"I've never done that," Kel said. "I've had plenty of people shooting at me, though."

"That doesn't sound like a very good line of work," Rix said.

"We don't always get to choose our jobs, Rix Banner," Kel said. "I grew up dirt poor with a dad who drank too much. Most people would say he wasn't that good a man, but I liked him and he took mostly good care of me. Why, I remember sitting on his lap, flying his runabout while he was out of his mind drunk. Turns out, I'm a natural when it comes to flying things. Wouldn't be here talking if I weren't."

"I'll have to take your word for it," Rix said, accepting the notepad back from her again. "You liked your dad then?"

"Yeah, he was a good man with a good heart," Kel said. "Just a little misunderstood. You know, kids don't much care what a parent does as long as they love and protect them, right?"

"Got me there. Parents died when I was young. Grandparents took care of me, but they passed several years ago. The war successfully ended any kind of dating life for me, so I'm just a guy who likes working on things. So no, I don't know much about kids."

"You have a good life here," Kel said. "Manifold that's broken is aft. I'll show you."

Rix fell in behind Kel and they walked through a narrow corridor where she stopped and unlocked a hatch on the right side of the vessel. The locking mechanism required her to rotate a handle clockwise half a turn and when she pushed it inward, there was a hiss of gas when pressure equalized.

"Pressurized?" Rix asked.

"Sort of," Kel said. "Engines can have their own trouble, so, we like to keep them closed off from living spaces. Earth pressure is a little different than what we had in the compartment."

"Hmm, I suppose that makes sense," Rix said.

"Say Rix, I think I overheard you talking about a card game," Kel said. "If I'm around, I don't suppose you'd invite me along, would you? I love cards. Especially if there's drinking to be done."

"Kel, you gotta stop talking like that, at least if you're not around me," Rix said. "People around here will think there's something wrong with you. Women don't talk like that."

"Because I like cards and drinking?" she asked scandalized. "Who doesn't like that? What kind of place is this?"

"It's a small town with small town values," Rix said. "If you don't want to attract attention, it'd be best if you fit in while you're here. If we work hard, maybe we can get *Calypso* fixed and you can get outta here before your friends show up."

"That's the spirit," Kel said.

5

SMALL MISUNDERSTANDING

Rix set down his welder, flipped up his hood and inspected the gravity coil array's end. Having set his welder on the lowest setting applicable for aluminum, he'd, with painstaking slowness, melted the conductive points of the coil and added a slight dab of aluminum from a stick.

"I don't love it," he said, holding the notepad between the part and himself so the camera would allow Beverly to see his work.

"I agree," Beverly said. "Very rudimentary work if compared to an automated manufactory. But that's not the right lens, is it?"

"I don't understand," Rix said. "Honestly, I'm not sure what your manufactory is capable of or even what it really is. Where is this lens?"

"No, what I mean is that a comparison to the highly sophisticated machinery, which is the manufactory, to a sapient's use of hand tools is not reasonable. The work you've done is extraordinary. I thought you were completely mental when you said you'd be using that red welding box which barely controls the voltages passing through the wires. It never occurred to me that you, or really any human, could handle such delicate work."

"Did you hear that, Philo? I think she just gave me a compliment," Rix said.

"Candy? Philo bored," Philo answered.

"Sure, why not," Rix said, setting his helmet aside and turning off the welding machine. "We're celebrating."

"Philo like Rix. Rix good with machines. Make go," Philo said.

"Well, we haven't looked at that manifold just yet," Rix said. "But, between you and me, I think that's probably an easier fix, as long as we can match the metals well enough. What say we get your candy, and you help me remove that broken manifold. It looks like that might take the two of us."

"Candy first. Grav cart help move," Philo said.

Rix walked back into the shop's reception area and grabbed a box of M&Ms from the shelf. So far, he'd learned that not only did Philo have a sweet tooth, but he also preferred plain M&Ms over the other candies. Also, he'd learned, that Philo was considerably more helpful with candy in his pocket than without.

"There you go. Now, show me this cart you're so proud of," Rix said.

Philo nodded his head and bounced forward happily as he pulled one small colorful sugar-coated candy out after the next, savoring each for several moments before moving on to the next.

"What are you two up to?" Kel asked, catching Rix as he entered *Calypso*.

"I believe I have a more permanent fix for that repulsor completed," he said. "We were just getting started on the flux coupling manifold."

"Do you really think you've fixed the lattice?" Kel asked. "Those parts are expensive. I'd have to pay eight hundred credits at a major port, twice that on a backwater world like Earth. And that's if they even had access."

"The broken piece was the gravity coil array," Rix corrected. "And assuming I didn't disrupt the circuit too much with the added aluminum, I think it should hold for the foreseeable future."

"Are all humans this good fixing things?" Kel asked with genuine interest. "Be honest. I don't need all that humble crap you're always doing."

"Humble is a good place to start from," Rix said, grinning. "Some folks like to talk themselves up. I'd prefer to let my work do the talking. And no, fixin' stuff has always been something I'm good at."

"Good at. From what I can tell, you're some kind of genius," Kel said. "Have you ever thought about getting out of this place? Go adventuring?"

"You forget. I've done plenty of adventuring," Rix said.

"I know; in the war and all that," Kel said. "But that's not adventuring. That's relocating into hostile territory and working your ass off to try to stop people from shooting at you."

"I've thought about traveling," Rix said. "It's hard enough to make the rent on this place working sixty hours a week. Just putting food on the table keeps me plenty busy. I don't know when I'd have the time or money."

"I can see that," Kel said. "Say, about your payment. We're going to have to talk about how we take care of that. I don't exactly have human money. I might have some things that could be interesting, though."

"No," a voice from Rix's pocket said.

"What was that?" Rix asked, after he pulled out the notepad and held it between himself and Kel.

Beverly's face appeared on the notepad. "Humanity is quarantined. You cannot leave Galactic Empire technology with a human. As it is, we're breaking over a dozen laws just being here."

"We didn't have a choice. My engine wasn't working," Kel said defensively.

"Where there's quarantine, that doesn't matter. This planet is under an 'avoid at all costs, including injury to self' advisory," Beverly said.

Rix held up his hand. "We've had this argument," Rix said. "Don't sweat it. We'll get you fixed and on your way. There'll be a rumor of a spaceship. That's hardly news anymore for as often as it happens. As long as you've moved on, there's nothing your Galactic Empire can do to prove you were even here."

"Don't be so sure of that," Beverly said.

Rix shrugged and allowed Philo to pull him away from the conversation and back toward the engine compartment.

"Thank you, Philo. That was a boring conversation, anyway."

Philo approached the bulkhead at the end of the short hallway and deftly unlatched a board that was otherwise pinned to the wall. As the board fell over due to Philo having let go, Philo deftly stepped aside and allow it to fall to the deck. Surprising for Rix, however, the board stopped falling when it was six inches off the deck.

Philo gave Rix an amused smile and popped another candy into his mouth. "Carry manifold," Philo said.

"Gravity cart," Rix filled in.

"Rix good," Philo finished. "Philo bring tools."

Rix opened the hatch that led to the starboard engine bay and pulled out Beverly's tablet. Holding the notepad up, he felt silly waving it across the highlighted area that was on display but when the manifold's cradle highlighted in green, accompanied by a satisfying beep, he knew he'd done the right thing.

"How do we get the manifold out of the cradle?" he asked.

No longer interested in questioning Rix's potential success, Beverly showed a list of actions required and then highlighted the first parts that needed removing. Getting right to it, Rix laid out the same tarp he'd used for the gravity repulsor repair and started removing parts.

"Philo, buddy, grab the other end of this," Rix said, as he pulled back the top side of the cradle and realized it was well over eighty pounds and awkwardly placed.

"Rix Rix, big heavies float," Philo said, recognizing what Rix was attempting.

"I'm not following, Buddy."

"The gravity controls within *Calypso* operate in multiple ways," Beverly said from the ledge where Rix had set the notepad.

"Talk to me about that," Rix said.

"Perhaps a demonstration."

All hands warning. Artificial gravity changed to zero point two gravities.

Rix felt the lessening of weight on his feet almost to the point where he thought he might float away. It was like he had suddenly lost the solid grip on the floor that he'd taken for granted his entire life.

"Whoa there," Rix said.

"Move part now," Philo instructed, grabbing a nearby handhold and pulling himself up with a single arm until he sat high overhead, still stuffing small candies in his mouth.

Rix nodded and gently pulled on the heavy cradle part. At first, trying to move anything in an environment where his feet weren't seated firmly on the ground felt awkward, but he soon got it, and leveraged the part's movement in a way that forced his feet downward. Different than he'd expected, the part was hard to move at first, but as soon as it started moving, it wasn't difficult to keep moving.

"Well, that's darn handy," Rix said, slowly moving the part off the top of the engine and then pulling it toward his body. His first mistake was in misunderstanding that once a heavy part started moving, it was nearly as difficult to stop as it had been to start. As a result, the cradle part pushed him into the hallway where his feet dragged along the deck, plowing through his neat lines of parts. "And that's not handy at all," he complained.

"Rix figure it," Philo said encouragingly from his high perch.

"Yeah, thanks buddy. Beverly, maybe just a little more gravity. I love this is so light, but maybe a little more gravity would be helpful."

All hands warning. Artificial gravity changed to zero point four gravities.

Rix's feet settled more firmly onto the floor and the part weighed more heavily in his hands, but it wasn't anything he couldn't handle. Moving forward, he found the next open spot on his rumpled tarp and set the piece down. With the heavy piece out of the way, Rix rearranged the tarp and placed the pieces back in line.

It turned out the broken manifold was fairly deep into the engine and minutes turned into hours as Rix patiently removed part after part, manually unbolting and drilling out semi-permanent fasteners that held the engine together.

"How's it going?" Kel finally asked. "It's getting late, you know and you've made quite a mess of things."

"I have questions," Rix said. "Without Beverly, I'd never have taken this thing apart right. What's with all the rivets?"

"I don't know what a rivet is," Kel said.

"Beverly calls them permanent bolts," Rix said.

"Oh, those," Kel said. "They're exactly what you think. Bolts that are permanently installed so they aren't removed during high stress maneuvers."

"And how do you install them? Some sort of rivet gun?"

"Stop saying rivet. We use boltguns. It's not extraordinary technology. I'd have thought of all the things, this would be something humanity had."

"We do. We call them rivets," Rix said. "But we'd never use them in this kind of environment. Our normal bolts hold things well. Let me guess, you have a better way to remove them than drilling them out like I've been doing."

"The boltgun has a setting for removal," Kel said, turning to look up at Philo. "You could have told him about that."

"Rix fast. Rix no need Philo," Philo said, pursing his lips.

"Oh, someone ran out of candy, didn't they?" Kel said.

"You're a scamp!" Rix said, grinning but also jumping up toward Philo.

Philo let out a squawk and started scrabbling away, but on his high perch, he had only a few options, which Rix cut off, tackling the little alien and bringing him down to the engine compartment floor.

"Rixy! Rixy!" Philo called out with equal parts joy and terror.

"You're getting it now!" Rix said, poking the wriggling alien with his fingers, which caused Philo to continue shouting. It took a few minutes for the ruckus to end as Philo turned on Rix and the two lightly wrestled around but both soon tired.

"That was unexpected," Kel said laughing. "It's getting late. Are you still expecting to play cards and drink tonight or will you continue working?"

"Oh, crap, what time is it?"

"In your local time, I believe it is four o'clock in the afternoon," Kel said.

"Oh, shoot," Rix said. "I only have a couple hours left before I need to get going. Are you still interested in playing tonight?"

"Philo, will want to sleep. Do you have sufficient beer?"

"That's an odd question. For Philo?"

"Yes, carbonated drinks help his stomach when he sleeps."

"And the alcohol?" Rix asked.

Kel shrugged. In that moment, Rix wondered if Kel was for sure a woman, or at least a female alien. She talked more like the men he'd gone to war with and wasn't curvy like the women of Cranberry Cove. With short cut hair, her moderately low voice would certainly pass for a man.

"You're looking at me funny," Kel said.

"I have an idea," Rix said. "You're probably not going to like it."

"Nothing good ever starts with words like this," Kel said.

"I'm aware," Rix said. "People around here don't expect women to be drinking and playing cards with a bunch of guys."

"That sounds like an undeveloped culture, which tracks with Cranberry Cove," Kel said.

"No need to be pokey about it," Rix said. "We're about the same size and if you wore a pair of my pants and one of my shirts, you'd pass for a man all day long."

"And then you would feel comfortable with my drinking and playing cards?" Kel asked.

"Well, I suppose yes," Rix said. "You agree that we want to keep things on the down low, right?"

"I'm not even sure what that means, but if you mean to not make a public spectacle, you are right," Kel agreed.

"Well, then good. It's settled. We'll get you fixed up with some man clothes, then," Rix said.

"Tell me, how much more work do you have on *Calypso* before you know if you'll be able to fix her?" Kel asked.

"Gee, honestly, I think I just need to take that manifold I just removed out to the shop and do a little shaping with my grinder and then do a little metal filling. Maybe an hour, two at max," he said. "After that, I probably have another three hours of reassembly, presuming the boltgun works the way I think it should. I'd like to at least get it welded tonight. Maybe Philo could help me move it out to the shop."

"Philo help Rixy," Philo said with a dumb grin on his impish face.

"I did not know I was going to need to look out for your antics, my friend," Rix said, poking Philo companionably.

"Rixy not ask. Philo not dumb."

"Lesson learned," Rix said.

Moving the manifold out of *Calypso* turned out to be less of a hassle than Rix had anticipated. Between low gravity conditions and the gravity cart, it was simply a matter of strapping the manifold to the cart and moving it between the ship and the shop.

Setting up to weld was more difficult, given the weight of the manifold, but within his shop, Rix had lots of options for moving heavy equipment, including engine hoists and an overhead gantry complete with chain lift.

"Are you sure this is going to work?" Kel asked when Rix finally finished up cleaning, deburring, welding and grinding.

"I'm surprised you don't know how to do this," Rix said. "It's just a little labor and a little skill with a buzz box. Look for yourself. What do you think?"

Kel looked at the manifold which was cooling down from the welder's heat. "If I hadn't seen the crack, I'd never have known it was there. How do you know it will hold?"

"I don't," Rix said. "But Beverly gave me specifications and we talked about what they meant, so I'd say we're at least sixty-forty odds on this being a good fix."

"What happens if it fails?"

"Depends on how deep in space you are," Rix said.

"Oh, you think you're so funny," Kel said, poking Rix in the chest like he'd done to Philo.

Rix grabbed a rag and wiped at his hands. "You can send me a postcard when you get where you're going," he said. "Assuming the patch doesn't blow a hole through your ship and you lose all your precious oxygen while your engine dies."

"You are a stink hole!"

"Funny translation. Are you ready for cards? I think we're out of time for tonight. First, Philo, help me put the manifold on the grav cart. That way if you're still asleep in the morning I can get it into the ship."

"Fine but then let's go play cards!" Kel said.

"I thought you'd never ask," Rix said.

With the overhead gantry chain hoist, moving the flux coupling manifold from the workbench down to the grav cart was a matter of positioning the cart and holding it steady. To secure, Rix lashed the manifold in place with a length of rope and clever knots.

"You're just a man of many talents," Kel said as Rix closed the mechanic's bay and left instructions for his employee who was working the full-service pumps.

"Let me tell you about the card game we're playing tonight," Rix said, not sure how to handle Kel's compliment. "Are you familiar with poker?"

"Not specifically," Kel said. "But I've played a lot of card games, give me the ten-thousand-meter view."

"Our decks have fifty-two cards with four suits," Rix said. "Every player gets two cards to start with, but you're building a best hand for a total of five cards."

"How do I get more cards?" Kel asked.

"Good question, you get more cards by the common cards that every player can use or not, depending on how helpful they are," Rix said. "The common cards are shared, not picked up. There are betting rounds with limits on how betting takes place. Everybody buys in at five dollars, I'll spot you, and in place of that five dollars, you get chips of differing values. End of the night, the person with the most chips takes home the entire bank."

"I imagine there are details I'm missing."

"For certain you are," Rix said as he started up the truck after Kel and Philo were loaded in. As they drove the short distance to his house, he continued to describe the cards, their values and what winning hands looked like.

"I've played a few, similar games," Kel said. "Can you buy in when you're out of chips?"

"Before nine o'clock, yes, after that, you're an observer," Rix said. "Otherwise, the game would go all night. Mostly, we just play cards, drink and talk about dumb stuff. We should probably talk about your cover story."

"I don't know what that is."

"Why you're in Cranberry Cove. How we know each other. Where you're from. What you do for a living. All of that."

Kel held her watch to her mouth as she spoke. "Beverly, is that something you could manage?"

"It is already accomplished, Kellan Goddard," Beverly answered. "You are Rix Banner's second cousin from Saint Louis, Missouri and are passing through on a multi-state sales tour where you're selling industrial brushes. It's both specific enough to be realistic and boring enough to minimize questions."

"That was fast," Rix said. "I suppose you do that with geometry too, then?"

"Rix Banner, you have already intuited that my calculations are significantly more complex than fast, simple math," Beverly said.

"It's nice to hear it out loud," Rix said, pulling into the parking lot of a liquor store. "You two stay here, I'll be right back."

"This looks like exactly my type of store," Kel said. "I'm coming. Philo, you stay in the truck and we'll bring back something for you, okay?"

"Philo, stay."

With Kel along, Rix's purchases quadrupled as the alien woman continued to pick out item after item with almost child-like interest. He finally had to end the browsing by paying the clerk and walking from the store.

"Hey, are you upset?" Kel asked, catching up with him.

"No, we're just on a schedule."

"Oh, okay."

Arriving home, Rix quickly brought Kel up to his room and

handed her some clothing. "It should fit over your coveralls if you like."

"I need to run these through a suit cleaner," Kel said, running a finger down the center of her chest, which caused a slit to appear in her relatively tight-fitting space suit.

"Oh, hold on, let me give you privacy," Rix said when she shrugged her hands into the sleeves preparing to remove the suit.

"Okay," Kel said, nonplussed.

Suddenly, a loud, high-pitched warble sounded from the notepad that Rix still held in his pocket. The same sound emitted from Kel's wristband as well as Philo's.

"What in blazes!?" Rix asked anxiously pulling the notepad from his pocket.

Beverly's face appeared on the notepad and on her face was a look of grave concern. Kel, *Calypso's* scanners have discovered a Dravari Police cruiser running a standard Dravari search pattern. I estimate discovery of *Calypso* within the hour."

"Ah frak, frak, frak," Kel said. "How long did you say it would take to put that manifold back in place?"

"Police force? I thought you said you were being chased by pirates," Rix said.

"Did I say that? That's so weird," Kel said with a far off look in her face. "But really, Dravari Police are like pirates, so that makes sense. We really need to reschedule this card game. Those Dravari are going to have questions. It's not safe."

"Kel, what have you dragged me into?" Rix asked.

"It's just a misunderstanding," Kel said. "And, trust me, Dravari are not the good guys here."

"And you are?" Rix said, putting hands on his hips. "Kel, I'm not going anywhere with you until I get the actual truth."

6

NIGHTMARE

"Can we walk and talk?" Kel asked. "Seriously, those Dravari aren't to be messed with. They'll track me right to your house and they won't play nice, trust me."

"Oh, hell, what have you gotten me into?" Rix asked.

"It's not good," Kel admitted. "I was hoping to be gone before Dravari showed up. Heck, I didn't even know those guys were onto me. Dravari Police really aren't all that interested in a little concern like *Calypso*. At least, that's what I thought."

"You've got to be kidding me with all this," Rix said.

"Not at all, Rix," Kel said. "Look, you have no reason to believe anything I tell you, but it's not what it must look like. Dravari are on the wrong side of this."

"Make it simple for me, why are they chasing you?" Rix asked, crossing his arms stubbornly. "I saw the soot marks on the side of *Calypso*, someone was shooting at you."

"They were just trying to disable the ship," Kel said.

"Not an explanation," Rix said.

"Fine, we took something important, and I thought we were away clean. Somehow Dravari knew what we were up to way before it could have been reported. They came for us almost immediately after we snagged what we were after."

"Define snagged."

"Stole, pilfered, absconded," Kel said.

"You're thieves," Rix said simply. "Get out and take Philo with you. I didn't ask to get involved in larceny."

"You don't understand," Kel said. "We took some equipment that we need back home. Without the equipment, people will die. You must believe me."

"It must have been extremely valuable equipment if you have both pirates and police chasing you."

"Very valuable," Kel said and watched as Rix's expression turned hard.

"And this is the point where you try to get my participation by offering me a cut."

"Well, I hadn't ruled it out," Kel said pragmatically.

"I thought you were grabbing a piece of life-saving technology. How do you make money from that?" Rix asked.

"We didn't *just* grab the one thing. It was too tempting," Kel said and turned her conversation to hopeful tones. "But it goes to a good cause."

"Right, you? You're the good cause?"

"No, the kids back home," she said. "Look, are you helping us or not? Because, someone needs to be putting that manifold back in place or we're going to get turned into dust. Trust me, Dravari are coming to Cranberry Cove. Best thing we can do for your friends is to get *Calypso* out of here."

"You're some piece of work, Kel," Rix said.

"I know," Kel said. "What was I supposed to do? My engines were broken. And it's not exactly my fault, you know. Some of the blame is yours."

"How's that, exactly?"

"You advertised you could fix spaceships."

"Oh for heaven's sake," Rix said. "You can't be serious."

"If you were qualified to fix my ship, I'd have been gone thirty hours ago," she said.

"That's the dumbest thing I've ever heard," Rix said, walking into the kitchen and then out the back door, which he slammed behind him.

Kel followed, having to reopen the door which he'd just slammed. "What are you doing?"

"I'm going down to the shop to fix your damn ship," he said. "And then you're going to leave and good luck to you."

"What about getting paid. You care about that, right? I have a small amount of precious metal. I'll give some of it to you."

"Just stop," Rix said, firing up the truck.

No sooner had Philo and Kel loaded into the truck's front bench seat than did Rix spin wheels in reverse on the gravel drive next to his house. Slamming the truck into first, he let the clutch go a little quickly, which jerked them all forward, but sent them speeding along.

"Kel, there is an update," Beverly's voice sounded quiet from the watch around Kel's wrist.

"Talk to us Beverly," Kel said.

"You have a maximum of fifteen minutes before that Dravari Police cruiser starts scanning the search grid that encompasses Cranberry Cove," Beverly said. "They've picked up some sort of trail."

"Do you know where they're at now?"

"Not yet. I'll keep you apprised of the situation as it develops," Beverly said.

Rix frowned in concentration as he careened through the small town's quiet streets.

"You're being quiet," Kel said.

"I'm thinking," Rix answered in clipped tones.

"Look, I'm sorry, Rix," Kel said. "I really did think we'd just drop in and get a couple of parts installed and be on our way. I didn't think you or really anyone would get dragged into all this."

"You didn't think. That sounds like the problem right there. We're just a bunch of semi-sentient hicks. Who cares what kind of trouble you bring," Rix said. "Not like we got any choice in it, did we?"

"You've every right to be mad," Kel said. "I'm sorry for involving you and your town. You have a nice thing going here and I've made a mess of things."

Rix clamped his jaw tightly. He wasn't even sure how much of what he'd seen and heard was real, but the last day and a half had been almost like a dream or what was quickly becoming a nightmare. That Kel was scared was obvious and even as much as he hated her in that moment, he couldn't discount the very real possibility of danger.

"I'll get you going. Once I do, you leave and don't come back," Rix said. "Deal?"

"More than fair, Rix," Kel said.

"Fine."

Rix came up to *Calypso* fast and jammed on the truck's brakes, skidding in the soft dirt next to his shop until they came to rest a few meters from the ship. Opening the truck, he ran over to a side door they'd been using to move between his shop and *Calypso*.

"Philo, get that ship opened up, I'm coming in with the manifold," Rix ordered, running through the shop and pulling hard on the chain which opened the tall overhead door of the shop. With strength borne of need, he pushed the grav cart quickly, his feet skidding as the mass of the heavy part gave him a quick lesson in inertia. By the time he made it around the ship, the loading ramp was extended. Philo grabbed hold of one end of the cart and between them, they scooted up the ramp.

"Rix grumpy. No good fix," Philo said simply.

"Focused," Rix corrected. "Bring the boltgun, Philo. Beverly, I need low gravity so I can get this manifold into place."

"Very well, Rix Banner," Beverly answered as Philo trundled off in search of tools.

Rix pulled out a pocketknife and cut the ropes that held the manifold to the grav cart. Normally, he'd have preferred to unwind the knots by hand, but that work required time, a commodity he was convinced was in short supply.

Grunting under the strain of the manifold's mass, Rix worked to push the heavy piece through the short hallway and into the engine bay.

"Oh, hells!" he said through gritted teeth when his speed got the better part of him and the manifold mashed his left hand against the doorframe leading into the engine compartment. Snapping sounds alerted Rix to the fact that he'd fractured bones and he grimaced, even as he redirected the path of the manifold.

"What happened, Rix?" Kel called from behind him.

"I think I broke my hand," Rix said, struggling to keep the pain out of his voice.

"We can fix that, it'll take a minute," Kel said. "I'm grabbing the medical kit."

Rix exhaled the breath he'd been holding as he looked at his battered hand, which throbbed painfully. Not one to sit around in an emergency, he continued pushing the manifold toward its final desti- nation, but with only one good hand, his moves lacked the elegance required to get it properly seated.

"What are you doing?" Rix asked when Kel pulled at his arm.

"Trust me."

"Funny," Rix said, his tone anything but joking. Something in Kel's expression softened his anger and he allowed her to have his hand.

"First one will help with pain and swelling," Kel said, pressing the tip of a screwdriver sized instrument that had a cushioned head at the end against his hand. At first, the pressure of the device caused a spike in the pain, but then small pricks against his skin were followed by immediate relief.

"What in the heck is that?" Rix asked.

"If you're going to be on the run, good medical kits are a must," Kel said. "Hold on a second, I can give you some use of your left hand, it'll probably hurt some and you should go more slowly, but this should do it."

A second application of the small device made his left hand feel like it was full of lead. Woodenly, he moved his fingers, but she wasn't wrong, she'd restored some function to his hand and he wouldn't look the gift-horse in the mouth, even though he wasn't completely convinced angry aliens were coming for them.

"Are you good?" Kel asked.

"Not sure that's what we're going for," Rix said. "I can work though."

"Good, I'm going up front to get ready to try your new engine," Kel said. "Once I power up, that Dravari cruiser is going to lock right onto us. We'll only get one shot at this."

Rix took the notepad from his pocket and placed it facing his work on the ledge he'd used before. The orientation was one that Beverly had suggested gave her the best vantage point for observing his work.

"Go," Rix said, struggling to move the manifold into place. With less control, the manifold immediately slammed into the engine making way more noise than felt comfortable. Kel's sudden intake of breath told of her anxiety, but to her credit she said nothing and exited the engine compartment.

"We should avoid that kind of contact," Beverly said. "Also, while it is dangerous to do so, *Calypso's* engine can operate without the entirety of the assembly being replaced."

An explosion rocked the ship and with the low gravity, Rix was tossed through the doorway, where his shoulder caught on the jamb and spun him into the opposite wall. "Aww, crap!" he said mentally inspecting himself for new damage.

"Is everyone good back there?" Kel called, her voice full of worry.

"Barely," Rix called back. "What was that?"

"Looks like Dravari found us, they just dropped a rock on your shop. I'm really sorry, Rix," she said.

"Rocks don't explode," Rix said angrily.

"Well, in my world they do," Kel said. "And if you don't get that manifold bolted down, they're going to drop one of those rocks right on us."

"For Pete's sake," Rix growled, struggling to get back into the engine compartment. Once in, he pulled the manifold back to where he'd been trying to set it and seated it in place. "Philo, I need that boltgun now!"

"Boltgun boltgun," Philo's voice carried through the hallway, preceding the nimble alien's swinging trek. Cradled between his knees, he held a chromed tool about the size of a large pneumatic impact hammer.

"Impact in three seconds!" Kel's voice called over the ship's public address. "Brace!"

Rix grasped the manifold and held tight to the engine housing as *Calypso* was rocked once again by a heavy explosion.

"What is going on out there?" Rix asked, flailing for the boltgun Philo still held.

"Nothing good, Rix," Kel called. "Where are we at? I'm powering up systems."

"Not freaking yet," Rix answered. "Give me a blessed second already."

Rix twisted the manifold again, reseating it. "Beverly, where are you?"

"On the deck under the engine."

"Hells," Rix said. He wanted the virtual alien's review of his positioning on the manifold but was certain that he didn't have time. Inspecting from all sides he could manage, he made a quick decision, settled the boltgun in place and activated it. Or so he thought, but there was no outward indication of the tools operation, beyond a clicking sound, which in his experience suggested some sort of failure. "This thing is broken!"

"What thing?" Beverly asked.

"The boltgun," Rix answered.

"Double check," Beverly said.

Rix trapped the boltgun under his arm and tried to move the manifold. It was, in fact, secured in place. And while the plan called for twelve bolts to hold the manifold in place, it felt more than secure to him.

"Kel, I've got a bolt in," Rix called out grabbing the bolt gun from under his arm and moving around the manifold as he one-by-one permanently secured the part.

A whirring sound preceded a deep thrumming as *Calypso's* engine struggled to start but then sputtered and became quiet, the whirring no longer increasing in frequency but slowing.

"What's wrong, Rix? Something's not happening," Kel called.

Rix looked at the engine and quickly realized he had no idea what the problem might be. "No idea, try again."

Again the whirring started and was followed by a deep thrumming that started to gain intensity, but once again, both stopped. "It's not working," Kel said excitedly.

"Hang on a second," Rix said mostly to himself as he lowered himself to the floor in search of Beverly's notepad that had fallen from its perch. "You've got to be kidding me." Beneath the engine was a narrow space which had allowed the notepad to slide beneath. The space was barely wide enough for Rix's hand and forearm and certainly wouldn't accommodate the rest of his arm. Even so, he tried, only to be foiled. An idea popped into his mind. "Philo! I need you here. Please help!"

Within seconds Philo appeared in the doorway and looked at Rix with interest. "Philo help?"

"Beverly's under here. I can't reach it," he said.

"No, she not under," Philo said, shaking his head.

"Buddy, please, I need the electronic thingamabob that slid under here."

"Under?" Philo asked, kneeling next to him.

"Yeah!"

The biggest explosion yet rocked the ship and Rix careened off the engine and once again fell halfway into the hall. His focus, however, was locked on the notepad that slipped out from beneath the engine and had slidden across the deck. He pushed against the wall and scrambled, jumping back into the room, pouncing on the device.

"Beverly!" he said. "What'd I do wrong?" He faced the device at the manifold and did his best to give her a complete view of the work he'd done.

"There is nothing wrong, Rix, but you need to lock down the cradle before that engine can keep going. It's moving too much and puts the engine out of phase which is why it's shutting down," Beverly said.

Rix gained his feet and raced into the hallway, looking for the cradle, which of course, had been thrown around, but was fortunately heavy enough that it hadn't gone far. Forgetting the pain in his hand, he grabbed the cradle and struggled to bring it back to the engine, this time not forgetting the lesson about inertia and lower g-forces that had caused so much damage to his hand.

"Philo, boltgun, I need it!"

"Point," Philo said, showing up a moment later wielding the boltgun.

Ordinarily, Rix would have questioned the sanity of letting Philo use the boltgun under the stressful situation. Something just seemed right about the short alien's understanding of the boltgun and Rix simply pointed at the attachment point for the cradle. *Ki-tack, ki-tack, ki-tack,* Philo snapped three permanent bolts into place in as many seconds, following Rix's directions.

"Nicely done, Philo," Rix said. "Kel, try it again!"

The same whirring sounded and was followed by the deep thrumming, which this time continued to gain intensity, which Rix figured was probably a good sign. Not wanting to be caught off guard again, Rix grabbed the tablet and spoke directly to Beverly. "Show me the next part."

Having just disassembled the manifold the day before, Rix was familiar with the part in question and had *Calypso* not been beaten about by explosions, he'd have easily located it. As it was, he had to use the tablet as a window to scan the hallway and was grateful when Beverly highlighted the tumbled part.

"Point," Philo directed again when Rix set the part in place.

Rix's gut dropped out from beneath him and he nearly fell to the floor. "What in the heck was that?" he asked, struggling to keep the part in place. Recovering, he pointed at the attachment point to which Philo responded by tacking it into place.

"*Calypso* has lifted from the wooden bunks," Beverly said, highlighting the next part.

"Hold on to something," Kel called back.

Rix had no sooner grabbed onto the doorframe when he felt the sudden rush of acceleration and then nothing. Shrugging it off, Rix grabbed the next part. His original estimate of a couple of hours turned out to be wildly inaccurate as the result of the extraordinary efficacy of the boltgun.

"The remaining parts are not required for immediate operation, Rix," Beverly said. "I recommend advancing to the cockpit. Kel is preparing to launch from the surface."

"No, hold on!" Rix said, racing forward. *Calypso's* bridge wasn't difficult to locate as it was the forwardmost room on the ship. "What are you doing?" Rix asked, bursting through the cockpit door.

"Saving our asses," Kel said.

Rix looked through the glass of the cockpit and out over Cranberry Cove. Beneath him, the town spread out and when he oriented himself and located his shop, he found that both the shop and diner were burning, a large black cloud rising above them.

"My shop!" Rix said, his hands going to the sides of his head. "Everything I have is in there."

"I'm sorry, Rix. Dravari had an idea we were near and was trying to shake us out by blowing up the building," Kel said.

"You've got to be kidding me! What about your precious Galactic Empire, surely they have to do something about that," Rix said. "What am I going to do? I can't possibly afford to start over again."

"How about we just stay alive. Sit down and strap in, this is going to get real dicey for a few minutes," Kel said.

"I want off," Rix said.

"Not right now," Kel shot back. "We're not slowing down enough for you to get out. And for your information, Galactic Empire won't do anything against the Dravari unless they're outside of their jurisdiction. The only reason they're chasing me is because I swiped a device they were barely using right out from under their noses. They can't afford to let me escape because people would get wise to their crappy security."

Rix stumbled into the wall as Kel turned sharply and then nearly fell as she repeated the maneuver. He grabbed for the side of the chair she'd indicated and pulled himself into place, just barely managing to get the harness over his shoulders where he held on. One more violent turn and Rix managed to snap the harness into place.

"What can I do?"

"Do you know how to limber a needler?" Kel asked.

"I barely know what you just said."

"Probably not, then," Kel said. "Just sit back. I've been in worse spots. I sure hope your fixes hold. This isn't a good time to lose power. If we lose that engine now, they'll turn us into scrap parts within a couple of minutes."

"Beverly, show me how to do the needle thing," Rix said, talking to the tablet.

"Good plan, Rix," Kel said.

7

IN DEEP

"The needler turret is starboard, amidship," Beverly instructed, showing an image of the narrow hallway that ran from just behind the bridge all the way back to the engine compartment, which was about ten meters in length. As promised, halfway back, there was a high-lighted hatch where the words Needler Access were a dead giveaway.

Rix struggled against the restraints he'd barely managed to clip into only moments before, his task made more difficult by *Calypso's* sharp turns and heavy impacts against the hull. "What's happening?" he asked, anxiously, finally managing to free himself. His question was quickly answered by the sudden appearance of a hole in the ceiling above his head.

"Are you okay?" Kel asked, grunting as she slammed the ship's flight controls hard to starboard and *Calypso* answered her actions by rolling in a lazy arc in the same direction.

"My leg, crap on a bucket but that hurts," Rix said, checking out his leg, only to discover holes through the cuff of his pants and then a hole in the decking where he stood. A fine rivulet of blood ran down his leg. Suddenly concerned, he grabbed at the hole in his pants and ripped it open, exposing a finger sized furrow that ran a few inches along his calf. "I'm hit." His voice carried importance but not panic as it was not the first time he'd been hit in combat, and he'd seen plenty more grievous wounds.

"Philo, med-kit, quick," Kel said. "Frak, these guys are good."

"Yup yup," Philo answered from somewhere aft.

Rix grabbed the narrow railing that ran overhead down the length of the hallway and started limping aft. "What are you doing, Rix?" Kel asked, jerking again at the flight controls, which had the effect of knocking Rix's legs out from under him. Fortunately, he had a solid grasp of the overhead bar and managed not to fall.

"Needler." It was all he could manage between the pain in his leg and the *Calypso's* pitching deck.

"Seriously attractive right now," Kel said under her breath, not loud enough for Rix to hear, or at least so she thought.

Beverly's face appeared on a panel which just moments before had the picture of a handprint on it. "Put your hand on this panel. It's a security feature. I need to register your palm print to *Calypso* so it'll work for you."

While Rix could barely imagine the technology required for recognizing his handprint, or even more perplexing, Beverly's ability to tell *Calypso* what his handprint looked like, he wasn't currently in the business of questioning things. Whatever this needler was, he was singularly focused on it, as Kel had suggested he'd be able to contribute to their current predicament. Placing his right hand against the panel, the hatch didn't immediately open, although the panel heated almost to an uncomfortable state. And then, the hatch opened.

Rix wasn't sure what he'd been expecting, but his understanding of the volume of *Calypso* had him thinking that he'd be looking at a room that extended to the ship's exterior. Instead, he was looking at a metal ladder that led directly up.

"Rixy, Rixy, wait!" Philo called, arm-over-arm swinging toward him from even further aft. Looped over Philo's shoulder was a bag, from which, when he dropped to the deck, the small alien pulled a bottle.

"Make it fast, Philo," Rix urged.

Philo wasted no time, first ripping off the lower pant leg with ease that suggested significantly more strength than Rix had expected and then spraying foam from the bottle he'd pulled from the medical kit bag. Instantly, relief flooded Rix's leg as the pain was numbed.

"Go, Rixy," Philo urged.

Rix grabbed a ladder rung and was just about tossed out of the hatch when a triplet of impacts shoved *Calypso* to the side and new sunlight shown through, aft of their position.

"They're targeting the engine, that was close," Kel called over the public address. "There's something wrong with the engine, I can't get all the power I need. Can you do something?"

"Which is it; needler or mechanic?" Rix called back.

"We're gonna die without that engine working," Kel answered.

"Ah, hells," Rix cursed under his breath, releasing the ladder rung and racing aft. He hadn't entirely finished putting the manifold back together, although, per Beverly's analysis, none of the remaining parts were critical for immediate operation. His only thought was to continue replacing parts, at least until he arrived in the engine room and discovered a new hole that punched through an adjacent part. "Beverly, what is that?"

While he didn't have the notepad with him, he had noticed that when Philo was in the room, Beverly didn't seem to require the notepad to see things. When she answered, she confirmed this suspicion. "Rix, that is a vacuum collector. It's not a standard part for this engine but it was a cheap fix. That hole prevents the collector from operating correctly."

"I just need to close it off, then?" Rix asked. "So it can develop vacuum?"

"We don't have any spare parts," Beverly said.

"Boltguns and duct tape, Beverly," Rix said. "That's all we need for field repairs." And before she could answer, Rix had a thin sheet of steel in one hand and a boltgun in the other. Deftly, he placed one edge of the steel sheet on the device and bolted it into place.

"What are you doing? You can't just bolt things to a sensitive part like that," Beverly said with great concern. "And more importantly, that sheet can't hold vacuum."

Rix ignored her complaints and bent the sheet over. It wasn't a perfect fit, so he left one edge hanging as he bolted that side in place, covering the combat incurred hole. Setting the boltgun aside, he pulled a flattened roll of duct tape and peeled off a length, slapping it along the edge of the sheet on all four sides.

"What did you do!?" Kel called back as *Calypso* jolted forward and then rolled to port, throwing Rix into a bulkhead and tossing free parts and the boltgun around dangerously.

"Philo, help me get this crap outta here," Rix said, landing on the deck and pushing the parts out the door as quickly as he could manage. Philo joined in and soon the engine was free of loose parts. As soon as that worked, the two exited the engine compartment and closed the door behind them.

"Rix, talk to me, what happened?" Kel called.

"I applied a temporary fix to the vacuum collector," Rix said. "It's a bit of a Frankenstein but it should hold for the time being."

"Seriously, you fixed my engine, again?" Kel asked. "How is that even possible? Earth has no technology to speak of. I just don't get it. I still need you on that needler. If we don't show these guys we can bite back, they're gonna just stay on us. Eventually, they'll finish the job."

Rix glanced over at Philo who was bending over with a spray can in his hand, spritzing foam into one of the many holes that had punched through *Calypso's* hull. Filing the action away in his memory to consider later, he kept moving to the needler hatch and this time pulled himself up into a small bubble that sat dead centered at the top of *Calypso* and provided a 360-degree field of view. Also, with *Calypso's* rounded shape, he noticed that he had visibility over both sides of the ship.

Within the bubble sat a narrow chair that would barely accommodate his frame. A light shape crossed overhead and for the first time, he caught a glimpse of the vessel that was attacking them as it fired a stream of bullets in their direction. Just before the stream of fire started, however, *Calypso* ducked downward and turned away from their enemy's direction of travel, quickly separating the two vessels. "Good job," he muttered as he struggled to pull restraints over his shoulders and wiggled his backside to get seated correctly.

"What's the drill here, Beverly?" Rix asked, quickly scanning the weapon turret's cockpit.

Ideally located just above his beltline, a pair of hand controls flanked a pair of displays. The displays didn't have information that made much sense to him at first but after asking for Beverly, she appeared on the rightmost display. "The needler weapon is a simple device that expels thin, extraordinarily hard projectiles made of iridium-tungsten alloy needles at high velocities. Advantages are hull penetration, due to size and speed of weapon. This weapon is only useful within medium range and is compromised within the atmosphere if range exceeds fifteen hundred meters. Also, this weapon has a significant rate of fire that could deplete *Calypso's* already meager supply."

"Talk to me about meager," Rix said.

"At the highest rate, perhaps thirty seconds of sustained fire," Beverly said. "Give or take three seconds."

"Set rate of fire to medium low, whatever that looks like," Rix said.

"You will have to make that adjustment, I do not have access to weapon's systems," Beverly said. "Look at the display on the left. There is a slider control with which you can adjust the rate of fire."

Rix had no idea what a slider control might be but looked at the display all the same. "How?" he asked, seeing a representational bar that was solid red.

"Poke the red bar with your finger and drag down while maintaining contact with the screen," Beverly explained.

Rix shook his head. Her words were clear enough but between getting shot at and being asked to use technology he'd never conceived of before, his brain was on full overload. Fortunately, when he touched the screen, the red bar diminished in size even before he moved his finger, and when he slid his finger across the glass in a downward motion, the slider followed suit and text displayed – *two hundred rounds per minute.*

Rix whistled at the idea, over three needles per second would be discharged at one third of the weapon's capacity. Just as extreme was that presumably it would all be done with magnetics. He struggled to put the ideas aside, knowing that his focus was needed on operating the weapon.

"Okay, I'm in, Kel," Rix said. "I can't see the bogey."

"He's ahead fifteen kilometers and working on making another pass at us," Kel said. "You should be able to see him on your tactical display."

"Sure, like I even know what you're talking about," Rix said.

"Display on your right," Kel said. "*Calypso* is always dead center on that display; you'll see the little ship coming your way. The lines are meaningful but maybe just turn that off for now."

"Fine, here goes nothing," Rix said, grabbing the controls of the turret. Without warning, the turret spun, responding to Rix's hand motions, even though he had no idea what he was doing.

"Try using left hand only, first," Beverly said, blanking out the tactical display for a moment with her face.

"Man, we don't have time for me to learn this," Rix fretted.

"It doesn't matter what time we have," Beverly said. "Just do what you can. We have no other choice."

Rix sighed and removed his right hand. As he moved his left, he became aware of the cockpit's movement responding to his small motions. The larger the motion, the faster the cockpit moved. He had no expertise, but it wasn't overly difficult.

"If you lose track of the primary combatant, you can press the follow button and the ship will aim you as much as possible at your enemy," Beverly instructed. "The button is the little lug beneath your left thumb. "Depress it now."

Rix did just that and the turret spun several degrees forward and up even more degrees. Referring to the tactical display, Rix tried to make sense of what he was looking at. The purpose of two lines on the display immediately began to make sense. One line showed the direction of *Calypso's* travel and another showed how his turret was aimed. "Well, that's helpful as heck."

"They're closing, Rix," Kel called back.

"Eighteen hundred meters," Rix answered. "I see it."

"Rix, on your right control, press and hold the button with your thumb. Rock it up and down for a zoomed view on the targeting display," Beverly said.

Rix did as instructed and suddenly, a wicked looking spaceship, oriented directly at them, appeared. The ship was bright white with boxy features and stubby little wings. Superimposed over top of that spaceship was a targeting reticle that enough resembled anti-aircraft iron sights that Rix had no trouble understanding their implication. The reticle was jumping around so much that he struggled to keep it aimed suggesting it wasn't a good time to return fire.

"What are you doing, Rix? You need to fire, they're closing on us," Kel urged.

"Hold on," Rix said. "Need to see the whites of their eyes first."

"Crazy human gonna get us killed," Kel grumbled under her breath.

"You know I can hear you, right?"

"And I need you to shoot at that ship, already!"

"Calm. They don't know we have an active turret," Rix said. "They've been attacking with impunity. Let them think this is nothing different."

"Man, you do know they could knock us out of the sky, right?" Kel continued. "Do you really think you'll hit them? I just need them to be concerned, maybe give me a little wiggle room for maneuvers."

"Good talk," Rix said. The enemy craft was closing fast and he couldn't continue to maintain the conversation and also focus on learning how to utilize the swiveling turret. "Beverly, tell me if I'm getting off!"

"Make sure to use the auto-targeting if you feel like you've lost your target. You'll have to make the final adjustments, but it should get you close."

"Good call," Rix answered, tabbing the auto-target, which jerked the turret a few centimeters on both axes. When the range indicator counted down to six hundred meters, he pulled and held the trigger in place. At first, the indicator for hits showed no joy, but with a combination of re-centering with the auto-targeting and slight adjustments, he started getting a hang of using the weapon. "This is just like an anti-aircraft turret, except a hundred times easier to move."

"What are you on about?" Kel asked. "Whoo hoo, you tagged him good on the nose! Way to go, Rix! Frakking Dravari!"

"I lost him," Rix said, tapping the auto-target which refused to respond, given the position of the enemy ship being on the opposite side of *Calypso*.

"Oh no, you didn't, he's licking his wounds," she said. "He sure wasn't expecting that."

"Good, what now?"

"Oh, don't get your spacesuit in a bunch," Kel said. "We're not out of this yet. That was just their fastest ship."

"You need to take me home," Rix said.

"Oh, bad news, Rix," Kel said. "Your shop is messed up. Those Dravari were targeting hotspots and your shop was venting heat and drew all those missiles."

"What do you mean, messed up? I haven't even paid off the mortgage on that thing," Rix said, his voice rising with concern.

"Well, heck, I'll show you. We're plenty close," Kel said, swinging *Calypso* around and diving toward the ground. "Darn good idea, too, they'll never expect to find us back where we started. That'd be dumb."

"Hey, I'm catching a new ship out there," Rix said. "Are you seeing that?"

"Ah, frak, yes," Kel said with obvious disappointment. "That looks like another Dravari cruiser, we'll have to make quick time of visiting Cranberry Cove."

"What in the heck are you talking about? I need to go home and get my shop fixed," Rix said. "You need to drop me off. I got your ship working for you. Pay me and let me go already."

"Oh, buddy, you have no idea. Life just changed for you and you don't even know it. Dravari Police will do an investigation, and they'll come find you," Kel said. "I'm afraid that your time as an earthling is over."

"Knock it off," Rix said. "I demand to go home!"

"You need to trust me on this," Kel said. "You don't want to be there when Dravari show up."

"What about everyone else in Cranberry Cove?" Rix asked as stomach acid coated the back of his throat.

"They'll be fine," Kel said. "Dravari can't expose Galactic Empire any more than I can. The problem is, you're part of the system now so you're fair game."

"What do you mean, 'part of the system'?"

"You were registered into the Galactic Empire database," Kel said. "Like it or not, you're one of us."

"*You* did this to me! Dammit, Kel! You've messed up my life. I was barely making ends meet as it was!" Rix said. "I finally had my business started and I was paying my bills! Now you're telling me that I can't go home? Baloney! Take me home!"

"If that's what you really want, Rix," Kel said. "But you can stay on *Calypso*. We need a mechanic, clearly. We'll take you home where you can get registered as an immigrant to Galactic Empire. It's a whole new life. Don't you want to try new things? Think of how exciting it would be to explore a whole new world, actually new worlds. There are thousands of them."

Rix climbed down from the needler and joined Kel in the cockpit. "You're a real piece of work, Kel."

"Yeah, if it's any consolation, I didn't mean to mess up your life," Kel said. "I was just trying to get my ship fixed. I didn't think Dravari would find me so quickly. I don't think all the publicity we got from moving the ship to your shop helped us any. I'll drop you at home if that's what you want. Maybe you have insurance?"

"Insurance for a spaceship attacking with missiles?" Rix asked.

"Do you really think an insurance adjustor would put that as the cause?"

"What do you know about insurance and adjustors?"

"Look, while my language translator is good at mapping ideas, it's not that big of a concept," Kel said. "I just figured you'd have something like that, and you guys call it insurance, which sounds straightforward. So do you have it?"

Rix sighed. "Sort of. The building is probably covered. I have some insurance for my tools. But it'll take forever to rebuild the building and who even knows if my landlord will even take on the project?"

"So come along with me and Philo. We'll take good care of you. Besides, a good mechanic can find work anywhere. That's especially true where I come from, even more so when word gets around about how you fixed *Calypso* with your bare hands and your crazy foil tape."

"It's like you've lost all common sense about what you're flying around in," Rix said. "You have no common sense about you."

"Hey now, let's not get personal already," Kel said. "And here comes Cranberry Cove out the starboard side."

"Is that over here?" Rix asked, pointing to the right. He'd heard starboard and port at some point in his life, but it wasn't the sort of thing that was often referenced in his world.

"Yes."

Rix looked out the window as Kel dropped *Calypso* along the outskirts of Cranberry Cove. Where his mechanic's shop and diner had once stood was nothing more than a pile of cinderblocks and neon signage laying in a smoldering heap. Two fire trucks were on the scene pumping water into the wreckage, but even from their high vantage point, Rix could see the buildings were completely destroyed.

"Let me out," Rix said. "I'm gonna be sick."

8

HOME ADVANTAGE

"Take this," Kel said, handing Rix the electronic notepad he'd been using to communicate with Beverly. With all the excitement at his shop, Kel had landed at a cemetery on the opposite side of town where it was quiet.

"You can't leave alien technology here," Rix said, looking skeptically at the device.

"No, I can't, but I'm going to," Kel said. "I've put you in danger and that device is the only way for you to have a chance of contacting friendly support if Dravari come for you."

"Bye Rixy," Philo said, his voice heavy with disappointment.

"Goodbye, big man," Rix said, bumping the smaller alien on his shoulder as Philo had done to him before.

Rix stood in the cemetery and watched as *Calypso* lifted without so much as stirring the freshly cut grass from the graves. Quietly, the ship zipped away, its only noise being the whoosh of air across its less-than-aerodynamic surfaces. Turning for town, he walked along a gravel road which soon turned to pavement, each step putting distance between his recent experiences and his otherwise firmly grounded reality. Thirty minutes later, he arrived at his shop where the fire was no longer raging, and it looked like the firemen were starting the wind down process.

"Rix Banner, just the man I was looking for," Mike Renn, the fire chief for Cranberry Cove's volunteer firefighters said. Chief Renn was the only paid position and he took his job seriously.

"Chief," Rix said, extending his hand.

"We were worried you'd gotten caught up in the fire. Word was you cancelled your card game and then disappeared," Renn said.

"What happened?" Rix asked. Fortunately, it was just past midnight and darkness masked what Rix thought was likely a poor poker face on his part.

"Neighbors reported several large explosions," Renn said. "Did you keep propane bottles indoors?"

"Sometimes," Rix said. "I don't recall any, though. But I definitely keep welding gasses for the cutting torch. Did you recover any bottles?"

"That will have to wait until things cool down in there," Renn said. "I imagine Andy is going to want to talk to you about where you were tonight."

"Are you thinking this was arson?" Rix asked.

"Why would you ask that?" Renn's response was pointed, like he felt Rix was hiding something, which, of course, he was.

"You said Andy wants to know where I was. I can't think of two reasons for why that's a question."

"A big fire like this calls for an arson investigation. Do you own the building?" Renn asked.

"No, Norm Saunders does. I'm leasing. We were just talking about putting together some sort of permanent financing, but, well, … now this," Rix said, leaning into the loss he felt. "I had insurance on my tools, but it's not gonna get close to covering what I lost."

"I feel you, Rix. Fires like this are devastating and people never have enough insurance to put things right," Renn said and then turned to look over Rix's shoulder. "What? Who in the heck is that?"

Rix followed Renn's gaze. A black Cadillac Series 60 had just pulled up and a pair of men in dark suits, black ties and bowler hats stepped out. Their eyes turned directly to Rix, and they started walking purposefully toward him.

"Do you know these guys?" Renn asked. "Look like spooks to me. What are you into, Rix?"

"Well, heck, I don't know," Rix said. The men walked with a predatory grace that was unexpected for the suited men. Rix considered running but stubbornly stayed put. If he was to play the innocent, he couldn't turn tail and run every time he felt uncomfortable.

"Rix Banner?" One of the men asked. Wearing sunglasses, even though it was after midnight, the man barely moved.

"That's me," Rix said. "Who am I talking to?"

"National Security Task Force," the same man answered, flashing a leather wallet that opened to expose a shiny golden badge and a photo ID. "Chief Renn, we're taking custody of Mr. Banner."

"I'm afraid your timing is off," Renn said bravely. Rix couldn't be sure but thought it possible that Mike was trying to use whatever small authority he had to keep Rix from being taken away. "I have Mr. Banner in custody of the Cranberry Grove Fire Department on suspicion of arson."

"National security interests supersede local matters. I'll note your interest and once we're done with him, he'll be returned so you can complete your investigation," the man said.

"I'm going to need to see that badge again," Renn said, growing bolder. "I didn't catch your name, nor did I get your badge number."

"Take up your issue with Washington," the unusual man said in his monotone. "Fornak, apprehend Rix Banner."

"Well, hold on there," Renn said, stepping between Rix and Fornak who hadn't yet spoken but had growled as he approached. "We have laws here in Cranberry Cove."

Fornak stiff armed Renn, pushing him backwards and to the ground. Rix felt he'd seen enough and turned and ran. Instead of running directly away, he instead ran at the Cadillac Series 60, which still had doors open and the motor running. As he ran, he silently prayed that there wasn't a third agent waiting for him. Reaching the car, he jumped through the passenger door and slid across the new seat, grabbing the steering wheel.

"Well, hello there, Hydramatic," Rix said, pushing the car's automatic transmission into gear. The pair of suited men were just about on him when the back wheels started throwing gravel and the car lurched forward. A pair of heavy thumps against the side of the vehicle warned of their arrival and he was grateful that the passenger door had closed automatically as he'd taken off.

A loud crash sounded as one of the agents punched a fist right through the window of the back door. With the power required to break a window, Rix quickly understood that the agents weren't normal people. The Cadillac wasn't exactly a sportscar but with the pedal pressed to the floor mats, it had gained significant speed, even though Rix was struggling to control it, due to split attention. Bumping up over a curb, Rix jerked the steering wheel to the left, trying to correct. This only made things worse as he rammed into another vehicle which lifted the Cadillac's front end.

"Oh, craaap!" Rix complained as the Cadillac rolled over, sending him tumbling inside the vehicle at a low speed. For a moment, the world simply turned upside down as the vehicle spun around and skidded on its top, finally coming to rest against a third vehicle. An otherworldly cry sounded as one of the agents got caught between the two vehicles.

Stunned, Rix struggled to figure out what had happened. Fortunately, he hadn't hit too hard and started to gain his faculties when the back window blew out, and a dark figure struggled to enter the vehicle. Rix tried the driver's side door and to his amazement, it swung open. He wasted no time and took off on foot, ducking into the neighborhood at full speed.

Muffled footsteps behind warned of a pursuer and Rix, who'd been a sprinter in high school called on long-lost muscles to kick in. And for a few moments they did, until they didn't. Breathing heavily, he looked over his shoulder only to find that one of the agents was chasing him. Only the so-called agent had lost its hat and glasses and there was no question in Rix's mind that the agent was not from Earth. Without hair and sporting a bony skull with pointed ears, Rix had no reference for what was following him. That it had survived a car crash while riding on the outside, Rix had no doubt he was no match, physically for it.

"Stop, human," the agent called in a commanding, gravelly voice. "Do not make this worse for yourself."

The smallest essence of a plan formed in Rix's lizard brain that wanted nothing more than to run away as fast as he could. He turned toward the middle school football practice field. He recalled a Saint Bernard that was chained up in the ditch that ran along the side of the field. Not exactly legal and certainly not safe for the kids who practiced, the dog had a reputation for aggression and as such had been teased unmercifully by the middle school kids as they'd run just out of reach through that ditch, antagonizing the poor animal.

"Josie, wake up!" he called still twenty meters from the doghouse. His legs felt like lead, and he could hear the alien's incessant approach. He feared his ability to make it up the other side of the ditch, given his waning strength, but he also knew this might be his only chance. If only Josie would wake up and participate.

With only the stars overhead to illuminate the doghouse, Rix ran down the slope of the ditch and lost his footing, rolling head over heels as he slipped on something unpleasant that Josie had left behind.

"Stay down," came the command from his alien pursuer.

Rix got to hands and knees and crawled over to the side of the dilapidated doghouse and banged on it as hard as he could manage. A startled bark was his reward, and he turned to find the alien agent holding some kind of weapon and descending into the ditch.

Like a mortar from an artillery launcher, Josie launched herself from within the doghouse, her heavy chain clanking against the doghouse door frame as it passed. A flash of light and a fizzling crack from the alien's weapon sounded as an energy round slammed into the wet earth next to where Rix was still on all fours.

"Holy crap!" Rix said as Josie met the alien and unleashed years of pent-up anxiety and anger over her poor treatment. Rix struggled to get to his feet and was about to run off when he noticed the alien's weapon, which had a lighted dial on its side, had been thrown clear of what was devolving into something quite grim.

With renewed energy, Rix scooped up the weapon and dashed across the practice field. On the opposite side was a band of trees on the side of a hill. Without hesitation, he scrabbled onto the hillside and struggled to climb, his legs once again feeling like they were made of cement. Halfway up the hundred-foot climb, he leaned against a tree, listening for what had come of the fight between Josie and the alien. Josie's barking suggested that the agent was clear, which was enough to convince Rix to continue up the hill.

With only twenty feet to the top of the hill, however, he was completely out of gas and turned, sitting hard on the spongy ground. It was then that the notepad he'd been carrying in his pocket pushed against his side.

"Come on, Kel, don't abandon me yet," he said, pulling out the tablet and looking at it, which had previously been enough to call Beverly's attention. This time, however, it didn't work. He was just about to throw the notepad into the trees when his finger discovered a small button along one edge. He pressed the button and the screen lit up.

"Rix Banner, did you miss me already?" Kel asked, her face appearing on the screen. "We're just about to get moving here. What's shakin'?"

"You gotta come get me. I'm being chased by a … well I don't know what it is. Dravari maybe, definitely not human, though," he said. "Said they were from National Security Task Force."

"Describe them," Kel said.

"Human looking, funny heads?" Rix said. "Dropped his gun, though. He was just about to shoot me."

"Well, you definitely grabbed a good break there," Kel said. "Sounds like Dravari and they're not known for being sloppy. Can't imagine it'd be that hard to shoot an unarmed human. They're extraordinarily strong and their skin is tough. Make sure to hit them in the gut if you get a chance to shoot one. They're not as strong there."

"Are you coming to get me?"

"You need a ride, now?" Kel asked. "I thought you wanted to stay on Earth, figure out how to make a comeback and all."

"Hey, you got me into this trouble," Rix said. "You could at least have the decency to come get me."

"And then what?"

"Quiet," Rix said in a harsh whisper. "I hear something coming up the hill."

"Better get moving," Kel said.

"I got nothing left in the tank. I'm gonna make a stand," Rix said, pulling the gun around after setting the notepad on the ground.

"Terrible idea," Kel said. "You can't take on a Dravari by yourself. Even if you have its gun. Their weapons have a friend/foe recognizer and won't actually shoot friends."

"Piss!" Rix exclaimed and tossed the weapon into the trees. Turning on the hill, he struggled to climb, effectively crawling the final distance to where the wildness gave way to a suburban back yard.

Just as he made it a few meters into the backyard, a light shone on him, illuminating him. Like a deer in headlights, Rix stopped moving and raised his hands. For a moment, nothing happened but then a thin metal cable fell on the grass and suddenly Philo dropped in with a vest connected to the line.

"Philo hold, Rix hold," Philo said, stepping in close to Rix and wrapping his arms around him. Before Rix had a chance to respond, Philo's backpack started ascending the line bringing Philo and Rix along with it. Instinctively, Rix grabbed Philo, not wanting to fall off.

"Hold on, kids, we have friends," Kel's voice sounded over Philo's wristband.

And then, without any more warning, *Calypso* flitted off with Philo and Rix hanging on for dear life, swinging in the wind. Just as Rix thought they were clear of the Dravari, the agent that'd been chasing him leapt up and grabbed onto the thin line that played out beneath Philo and Rix's feet. Impossibly, the Dravari started climbing.

"You've got to be kidding me!" Rix said with disgust.

"Dravari bad," Philo said.

"Yeah, got it," Rix said. "Can you cut the cable?"

"No, cable strong," Philo answered.

"Take us down," Rix said.

"Dravari bad," Philo repeated.

"Down."

Fortunately, that was the extent of the argument and Philo started lowering the pair even as they swung out over the roof tops of *Cranberry Cove*.

"What are you doing, Rix? Get in the ship," Kel called.

"We picked up a stowaway," Rix said, kicking at the Dravari's hands which gripped the thin cable. The Dravari was strong, but it was also heavy, and the cable had been biting into its hands. At first, Rix dislodged one hand, which caused the Dravari to release, which destabilized everyone on the line and sent them swinging around. It managed to replace its hand a few moments later, but Rix was waiting and kicked, sending the Dravari falling.

"Up now?" Philo asked.

"Yeah, little buddy, up now."

Entering *Calypso's* hold through a round hatch roughly a meter and a half in diameter, the pair bumped against the threshold but were pulled through without too much pain. With a deft maneuver Rix hadn't thought Philo capable of, the pair were unclipped and landed on the deck, falling over each other in a tangle.

"Welcome aboard, Rix," Kel called over comms. "Philo, get that hatch closed. There's a Dravari patrol ship warming up twenty kilometers south of Cranberry Cove. We need to hit it fast because I'd bet anything we have Dravari sitting out behind that moon waiting for us to launch."

Philo rolled away from Rix and fished the remaining cable out of the open hatch before closing it tight. "Kel, go go," he called, offering a hand to Rix, who was lying on his back on the deck, trying to catch his breath. "Rix hurt?"

"No, my little friend," Rix said. "Rix is tired from running from a Dravari agent."

"Rix is smart. Dravari hard chase."

"Don't know about the smart thing," Rix said, taking the offered hand. "Oh, crap, hold on." Rix's stomach roiled as he stood, the exertion in combination with the danger that had mostly passed was too much. He leaned over and retched the contents of his stomach onto the deck.

"Rix popped," Philo said simply.

Rix was about to respond as he attempted to straighten but leaned over and finished up what had remained in his stomach and then proceeded to dry heave for a few moments.

"How's it going back there?" Kel asked over comms, sounding sincerely concerned.

"I'm struggling," Rix said. "Thanks for coming back for me."

"We owed you that much," Kel said. "For whatever it's worth, I didn't think our landing here would bring you so much trouble. I figured we'd get *Calypso* fixed up and be on our way before anyone knew what we were doing."

Rix sighed. He still felt bad about having been involved in the whole affair. Had Kel never shown up, he'd still have his shop and wouldn't even know that aliens existed. In that moment, he'd have gladly reset the clock and gone back a couple of days, but he was also enough of a pragmatist to know that wasn't how the universe worked.

"How do I get this cleaned up?" Rix asked, his legs wobbling as he stood. "Do you have a mop or something?"

"Easy, Rixy," Philo said cheerfully. "Rix go sit. Philo clean."

Rix nodded. The idea of sitting for a minute sounded just about right. Making his way forward, he moved through a pair of doors that separated the hold from *Calypso's* interior cabin. That two doors were so close together got him thinking and he suspected it had something to do with the changes of pressure a space born vessel might incur, but wasn't certain.

"Oh, man, you should probably get in the shower," Kel said as Rix entered the cockpit. "There are a handful of extra vacsuits in the cupboards next to the head. Have Beverly help you with sizing. I'd guess you're a forty-nine narrow."

Rix looked at his front and realized his race for freedom and the subsequent barfing hadn't been at all kind to his clothing, which was now in deep need of cleaning. "I think I lost the notepad. I had it until Philo grabbed me, but ..."

Kel lifted an identical notepad out of a pocket on the side of her chair. "Use this one. We'll get you an earwig once we're somewhere there's a manufactory."

"I don't know what that is ... hold on, are we in space now!?" Rix asked, looking out into the inky blackness. The stars, which he'd so often looked at in the night sky, were brighter than he ever thought possible, and the distances seemed so extraordinarily vast. The experience made him feel small and insignificant.

"Is this your first time?"

"For humanity, best I know," Rix said.

"Well, that's for sure not true," Kel said. "Welcome to the club, though. Check this out."

Kel rotated *Calypso* so that Earth came into view. Tears welled in Rix's eyes as he took in the beauty he'd only imagined. "That's remarkable," he said quietly.

"Earth is a real gem," Kel said. "One of the prettiest planets I've seen in a while. That is, if you like a water-land mix, which I don't mind admitting I do."

Rix's wobbly legs started to give out and he moved quickly so he could sit. "What have you gotten me into, Kel?"

"Yeah, really am sorry about that," she said. "It's not like I had much of a choice. The engine was shot and we're being chased by Dravari. I just didn't have many options. I'm sorry I screwed up your life."

"Tell me you're more than a petty thief," Rix said.

"Would that make you feel better?" Kel asked.

"Never mind."

9

SPACEMAN RIX

Hot water pulsated against Rix's back as he leaned against the small shower's wall, his head resting against his arms. He was experiencing the inevitable crash that followed stressful situations. It wasn't an altogether unfamiliar pattern as his experiences in the war as a forward operating mechanic had put him in harm's way more than a few times. Deliberately calm focus in the midst of crisis had served him well, but it came with a price to be paid.

"Rixy, Rixy, Rixy, what have you gotten yourself into this time?" he muttered. Even as he spoke, his mind worked to process his surroundings. He'd been standing in the shower for twenty minutes, waiting for the tank to run cold, which was typically his prompt for exiting. Aboard *Calypso*, that just wasn't happening. He added a mental reminder to understand the seemingly infinite, hot, clean water aboard a sealed vessel. His imagination offered solutions, but he wanted to understand the actual reasons such was possible. "And tell me you're not starting to dig this gig. You should be wiggin' out. What's wrong with you?"

A knock on the door to the head broke Rix from his stupored musing. "Hey, are you okay in there?" Kel called through the door. "I don't have access to your bios. Just tell me you're still alive, eh?"

Rix sighed. Kel's voice brought him back to Earth. He shook his head as he considered the phrase. He wasn't back to Earth, exactly, but he knew better than to focus on the rabbit trails of random thoughts. "Yeah, I'm cool," he said.

"You can turn the heat higher," Kel responded. "Philo is making pasta. He's a great chef. Why don't you finish up and join us. A little food will help you get settled."

"I don't have any clothing," Rix said. "I didn't find anything."

"Oh, no problem, Beverly gave me your size, and you're in luck. Philo had an old earwig he's going to give you. You'll be a modern man in no time at this rate."

"I *am* ...," Rix started but then realized he was hungry and his responses weren't likely going to be helpful. "Fine. Just leave the clothing by the door. I'll need a towel, too."

"Okay, it's there," Kel answered cheerfully.

"Yup, good," Rix answered, not interested in conversation.

Rix turned off the water and allowed it to drip for a few moments. He was intentionally dragging his feet. Processing the fact that he'd effectively been Shanghaied by an alien burglar and her pet monkey and dragged off to space in a spaceship he'd fixed was just a lot to process. How would he ever pay off his loans for the shop? If he was unable to pay the rent on his house, what would happen to his stuff? Would they take his truck? How would he ever get home? He had so many questions and he was certain Kel wouldn't have answers for any of it.

Opening the door, Rix found a towel which might as well have been a tea towel in his grandmother's kitchen for as large as it was. Shaking his head and picking it up, he figured it wasn't the biggest of his problems. To his surprise, the towel had no trouble absorbing the residual water from his shower. He looked around for a hamper to toss the towel into but found nothing, so he set the towel on the deck and found that instead of a single spacesuit, there were two. The topmost, sleeveless suit was made of a thin, almost transparent material that was soft to the touch. Pulling it on first, Rix found that the legs ended just above his knees.

"Doesn't exactly give a guy much privacy," he said, looking down his front. A noise in the short hallway alerted him to someone's presence so he got right to pulling on the spacesuit which sat atop a pair of thin boots. Fitting more loosely than the under garment, the spacesuit slid over top of the thin material. The last to be equipped were the boots, which adjusted slightly and self-sealed once he'd pulled them on.

"Now you look like a right and proper spacer," Kel said appearing in the hallway from around the corner. "What do you think? I bet it feels strange, given your old clothing."

"Its soft," Rix said. "I'm afraid I'm going to rip it."

Kel nodded. "Philo is ready to serve, trust me, you don't want to miss this."

"Where are we going?" Rix asked.

"Aft. Galley is furthest aft before the airlocks. Technically, there's storage, but it's a different kind of hatch. You'll catch on, *Calypso* isn't very big by spaceship standards," she said. "Although, she does a great job of atmospheric entry and escape, well, as long as the engines and gravity repulsors work, that is."

Rix nodded and followed Kel aft. "How exactly did we get away from everyone chasing us?" Rix asked. "And who's driving or flying, whatever you call it."

"Sailing," Kel answered. "And we don't need someone always watching the controls. *Calypso* knows the navigation plan and if nothing changes too drastically, she'll handle things. Did you put the earwig in?"

"I have no idea what you're talking about."

Kel stopped and turned around. "It's a little thingy about this big," she said holding her finger and thumb half a centimeter apart. When she saw Rix's blank expression she nodded understanding. "Beverly, did you see what happened to it?"

"Yes, it rolled off the towel and is lodged against the port bulkhead just beneath the hatch to the head," Beverly's disembodied voice explained.

Kel made to step around Rix but he held his hand up and turned with her. "I heard her fine. I've got it," he said.

"Are you still mad, Rix?" Kel asked. "You sound mad."

Rix shook his head, choosing not to answer the question as he stalked back to the head where he found, right where Beverly had described, a small chrome-colored bead, which he picked up.

"Put it in either ear, Rix," Beverly said, not waiting for the question.

"Is it going to hurt?"

"Not excessively."

Rix had grown to trust Beverly, if not Kel, enough that he did as she'd suggested. "What's this going to do for me? Ouch, dang it!" Blinking back tears from an intense but short-lived stab in his ears, Rix suddenly became aware of a ten-centimeter-tall woman floating in *Calypso's* hallway just in front of him. She wore a spacesuit, complete with glass helmet and rocket pack identical to what had recently been on the cover of a magazine not more than two months prior.

"That's real?" he asked and then seemed to catch himself. "Of course, it's not. You saw that on my issue of *Popular Mechanics*. But, how?"

Beverly's smile was ear to ear as she nodded. "You remember! That's so much fun!"

"I don't understand. How am I seeing this? I thought you weren't real."

"I'm very much real," she said. "I'm not big enough for you to see, is more accurate. And you're seeing this because I can transmit information to your earwig, which is directly tied into your optic nerve as well as your vestibulocochlear nerve."

"Ooh, that's super cool," Rix said with genuine appreciation. "How do I know if what I'm seeing is real anymore then?"

"You are indeed very smart, Rix," Beverly said. "The device you're wearing can be removed by tapping your left ear five times with your index finger. Tap twice and you'll get a menu which allows you to configure security settings. Currently, I am the only entity that may present anything beyond extended controls and reading surfaces. If you wish, you may eliminate that access as well."

"I see," Rix said.

"Funny," Beverly said, laughing as she pulled off the glass bubbled helmet and held it in her arm.

"What?" Rix asked and then smiled as he put together his use of the phrase *I see* with the fact that Beverly was presenting visual hallucinations.

"All good here?" Kel asked.

Rix swiped a drop of blood from his ear and looked at it. "Aside from the violence of getting attuned to Galactic Empire technology, I am."

"Oh right, I'd forgotten about how the earwigs get installed," Kel said. "There isn't that much that causes pain. Mostly, people don't like things that hurt. And, it's not Galactic Empire technology, not all of it. Galactic Empire are just the guys on top right now. They've only been in charge for maybe three hundred years and their reach really isn't that wide for most stuff."

"You're talking like someone who works in the gray spaces of the law," Rix said.

"Are you a black-and-white kind of guy?" Kel asked.

"Hold on, why has your voice changed?" Rix asked. Kel's voice had previously held a tinny quality and now it was fuller, almost otherworldly. "Is that the earwig?"

"Yes and no. I'm not speaking English, like you think. Before you had an earwig, I had a translator that was cancelling the soundwaves of my speech and translating from Galactic Common to English. It tries to match voices, but it's always a little off. Now, you're hearing my real voice, or as close as you'll get until you can speak Galactic Common."

"So much to learn," Rix said, following Kel through the hatch into a smaller room that smelled heavily of garlic. There was a table just big enough for four people if those people weren't overly large.

"Rixy!" Philo exclaimed. "Pasta and sauce! Earth food. Yum!"

Rix couldn't help but smile at Philo's enthusiasm as dishes were loaded with spaghetti and red sauce. If he wasn't on a spaceship with a pair of aliens, he wouldn't have questioned what he was looking at. As it was, the smell was right enough and he was hungry enough that he was more than ready to give it a try.

"Lay it on me, Philo," Rix said.

Philo looked questioningly at Kel who quickly made a guess at the translation. "I think he just wants a plate, Philo."

"That's what I said," Rix said.

"Translator didn't understand that," Kel said, eliciting a shrug from Rix.

With three steaming plates on the small stainless-steel table, the unconventional crew found seats. As soon as Philo was seated, he dug with metallic chopsticks, something Rix hadn't even tried to use in his life.

"Hold them like this," Beverly said, holding her hand out with chopsticks laying between fingers and over her thumb. "Pinch them so the tips meet. You'll figure it out quickly, but you should pick up your plate like Philo is doing. You'll make less of a mess."

It took some work, but Rix was determined and figured it out enough. "This is really good, Philo," he admitted after several bites. "Did you get this recipe from my kitchen somehow?"

Instead of Philo answering, Beverly answered for him. "I had Philo scan all the books and magazines in your house as well as at your shop. The encyclopedia set took a long time but was very useful."

"When, while I was sleeping?"

"Yes. Philo sleeps a couple of hours at a time."

Rix looked around the galley and found that he recognized very little of what he was seeing. Apparently reading his glances, Beverly caused projections of labels to appear above points of interest. The longer Rix looked at something, the more detailed the description became.

"That's neat," Rix said. "Not the sleep thing, but what Beverly's doing."

"She is smart," Kel agreed. "And you call this spaghetti? It's wonderful. How close is it to what you're used to, Rix?"

"Close. It's very fresh-tasting. More like what my grandmother made than the canned stuff we get nowadays. How'd you manage this? Did you go shopping while we were there, too? How did you have all this time?" Rix asked.

"No, our galley has the ability to mimic flavors and textures," Kel said. "Philo is really good at reading recipes from odd sources. Is this a keeper? I mean, from my perspective, yes, but as an Earth dish, what do you think?"

"Definitely keep it," Rix said.

"Your mood is improving with food," Kel said. "I feel like I need to keep apologizing. I never meant to get you caught up in all of this. I'm afraid you'll never get to go home and that's fully my fault. I am so sorry. I feel so guilty."

"I kind of need to let people know where I've gone so they can do things. I hate leaving debt behind and putting my trouble on others," Rix said.

"Like I did to you," Kel said.

"I'm not getting into all that. Is there any way for me to send letters? I could tell my friend who is a lawyer. They could deal with things until I get back," Rix said.

"You can't go back, Rix," Kel said. "You've seen too much. The quarantine works both ways. You've seen enough that you could change the development of Earth. It could destabilize the planet's governments. You could end up being responsible for the end of humanity."

"How do you figure?"

"Nuclear bombs sound familiar? One government has the potential to blow up the entire rest of the globe. Imagine if you've seen things that are even more powerful than that while aboard?" she asked. "Galactic Empire won't allow you to go home. Dravari shouldn't have landed and come after you. I guarantee they've marked you as an enlightened human. They couldn't have been shooting at you otherwise."

"They can just do that?"

"Dravari aren't good actors on the galactic stage, but they are allowed to operate by the Galactic Empire because they police large swaths of space. Trust me, they'd have liked to kill you, but not until they'd questioned you in a way that was very painful."

"You're talking about torture," Rix said. "That's illegal, even on Earth."

"Is it? What if they use a different name for it?" Kel asked. "Bad people do what they want and justify it later. There are plenty of folk like that in the Galactic Empire."

"Is that how you justify stealing?"

"That's a simple way to think about it, but I suppose you're not wrong," Kel said.

"How is it that they haven't chased us down yet?" Rix asked. "Surely, *Calypso* isn't faster than the best Dravari have access to, right?"

"We're burning hard right now and we're about to your moon," Kel said. "That ship that blew up half of Cranberry Cove couldn't exit Earth's gravity well easy like *Calypso* can, so they either stashed a second ship on the opposite side of your home world or behind this moon. I'm betting on this moon."

"So why are we here!?" Rix asked, setting down his chopsticks as all interest in food had disappeared.

"They think I think we're clear, which I don't," Kel said. "We're going to pull an old smuggler's trick that I think will do the job."

"Which is what?"

"We're going to let that moon's gravity pull us in and slingshot us on an arc about four hundred twenty degrees around," she said. "We'll do that fully powered down, wearing our spacesuits so we don't get too cold. You see, all their sensors are designed to pick up electromagnetic signals emitted by equipment and ship systems. We'll look just like any other free-floating piece of space junk, too small to pick up with passive optical equipment, assuming they're even using stuff like that. We'd have to be unlucky for them to find us."

"Define unlucky."

"If we end up passing within a thousand kilometers or so, that'd be unlucky," Kel said. "They'd have a hard time not seeing us if we did that, if you know what I mean. But space is big, the odds of that happening are infinitesimal."

"And what happens then?"

"Oh, who knows?" Kel said. "Depends on how soon we figure it out and how quickly they respond. I mean, basically, it becomes a footrace to the transit point. Once we get there, we engage the transverse engines and skedaddle off to Xandarj and then scoot around to Argon and then finally we take a long, old ride out to the final leg of our trip to the Narlux-4 system."

"What happened to Narlux one through three?" Rix asked.

"Four is a designation that means the system was part of the original expansion of the Janesk Sector. That history is over a thousand years old, so I'm not completely certain. Ask Beverly if you have time to kill for a history lesson," Kel said.

"How many people are in Narlux-4?"

"Beverly?" Kel asked.

"Twelve billion spread out across three planets and one moon, providing you don't count Tarnis, which only accounts for a few thousand brave, hardy souls," Beverly answered.

"Feels only fair to include them," Rix said.

Beverly smiled. "You're funny."

"Doesn't seem right to exclude them if they're both brave *and* hardy," Rix said.

"Fine, twelve billion two thousand forty-five, including Tarnis."

"Why brave and hardy?" Rix asked.

"Tarnis is close to the Narlux-4 star and supports no life on the sunward exposure," Beverly said. "Fortunately, the planet has no spin of its own and is locked to always face the system's single star."

"Like our moon, then."

"Very good," Beverly said. "Just like that, Rix."

"You know things," Kel said. "That's impressive, given your prior lack of technology."

"I like to read. How soon until we make this big maneuver around the moon?" Rix asked.

"Thirty minutes, give or take."

"Cutting it close, don't you think? If I hadn't asked about things, would you have even told me? What if I'd stayed in the shower when you cut power?"

"You didn't. So that's not a real question."

"Where do I get a helmet?"

"Like Beverly, you don't need one. It's already in your spacesuit," Kel explained. "Let's go."

Rix stayed behind for a moment and helped Philo place dishes in the cleaner. Taking only a few moments, the dishes came out spotless and to boot, the Galley Pro 1000 next showed a slight increase to the ship's stores.

"Tell me, it didn't just scrape our plates and it's going to feed that back to us," Rix said.

"Why? It's very efficient. You don't have to worry about germs, it's perfectly sanitary and every meal is nutritionally balanced," Beverly explained. "Many long-term travelers prefer to bring their own foodstuffs along, but for a ship as small as *Calypso*, that's not practical, given how much time it's designed to be away from home."

"I noticed my towel was missing when I went back looking for the earwig. Where did that go?"

"Garonze Textile Cleaner 15," Beverly said, smiling. "Its name is a misnomer. It is only the third revision of the original Garonze invention and it also can manufacture undersuits and even repair Garonze brand spacesuits if the damage isn't too great."

"I'm wearing a Garonze spacesuit then?"

"That's right. The Garonze Textile Genie 1200, which is considerably more expensive, also manufactures the suits on demand. Genius marketing if you ask me," Beverly said.

"Genius," Rix agreed without as much conviction.

"You'll want to strap in for this next maneuver," Kel said. "I'll be removing most of the atmosphere and the gravity generators won't work while we're playing possum."

"How do you know about possums?" Rix asked.

"Playing dead isn't unique to Earth possums," Kel said. "And for the record, I didn't say possum or play, the translator put that together for you to hear as it was the best translation."

"That's incredible," Rix said.

"You've said that a lot lately," Kel said. "I think you're going to like being a spaceman."

"But not the first Earthling you've met," Rix said.

"Not even close. It turns out that the Galactic Empire isn't great at enforcing the quarantine on your planet," Kel said.

"But they're good at keeping people from coming home," Rix said.

"See, you *are* catching on."

10

DARK SIDE OF THE MOON

"Just lean forward," Kel said.

The two were seated in *Calypso's* bridge quickly approaching Earth's moon. Tension was rising as the result of a countdown timer projected on the forward glass and was showing thirty seconds to full system shutdown.

Fabric pushed uncomfortably at the back of Rix's neck and at Kel's instruction, he did as she suggested. A transparent fabric quickly enveloped his face and for a moment, Rix's heartrate spiked as his fingers slid off the slippery material. "Kel! What is happening?" he asked. Claustrophobia had been one of Rix's biggest struggles as a mechanic, which often required him to squeeze into tight spaces. Having a bag over his head was not something he could easily deal with. And before Kel could answer, the transparent panel in front of his face disappeared. "Oh, crap, that was bad."

"What's going on, Rix?"

"There was a bag over my head."

"Still is, it's called a spacesuit," she said. "And that bag is your helmet. It's still there."

Beverly appeared on the forward bulkhead just above the navigation and flight displays. "I've mitigated it, Rix," Beverly said soothingly. "Just breathe naturally. Your suit is drawing atmosphere from the chair. You are not in any danger. Close your eyes for a minute and relax. You're perfectly safe."

Rix closed his eyes and imagined he was anywhere but on a spaceship on a collision course with the moon, behind which likely lurked a powerful enemy waiting to shoot them down. The details floated through his head, and he struggled to manage the feelings of helplessness. Kel's hand rested on his own and she gave a gentle squeeze.

"I forget, this is all new to you. It must be overwhelming," she said.

Rix forced his eyes open. "There's a lot going on."

"You're feeling out of control, Rix," Kel said. "Trust me, I've got this, Rix."

"What choice do I have?" Rix said, gripping the arm rests flanking him.

"That's the spirit! Now, I need to hit this just right so we grab an unstable orbit at just the right heading so this big, beautiful, gray girl sends us packing in the right direction!" Kel said, talking to no one in particular. "Oh, no, not there! Come on you squirrely little sweetheart! Listen to me, just slip over a tad. That's right, like the gorgeous little spoon you are. Kill power!"

"This is the worst idea ever," Rix said, watching the events unfold through the forward screen as the display panels held virtually no information that made any sense to him. That they were sailing only a hundred kilometers from the moon's surface resembled falling from orbit much more than it did the fancy maneuver Kel had described. "Without power, we're going to crash!"

Kel watched with amusement as Rix's mouth moved. Tapping the side of her helmet she shook her head. Rix's look of confusion further spread the grin on her face. Finally, she took pity on him and leaned over so that their helmets touched.

"We can't … with … touching," her voice echoed in his helmet as he adjusted away from her. For a moment, the words didn't make much sense, but when she pushed her head toward him more insistently, he allowed the helmets to maintain contact.

"Let me guess, radios are shut down," Rix said.

"Good guess. I dumped ship atmosphere, too. If we weren't making an orbital maneuver, I'd tell you to unclip your harness and try zero-g. I'm afraid you might barf, though, and we don't really have time for that," Kel said. "No air means we can't communicate unless our helmets are touching. And even at that, it's not that great."

"How long are we without power?"

"We'll see once we pass over to the dark side of your gray lady-in-waiting," Kel said.

Rix nodded and then sat back in his chair. Connecting with Kel was uncomfortable, and his stomach was threatening consequences for new adventures. Once his head came to rest on the headrest, however, he immediately felt more grounded. And as the moonscape flew by beneath, he was finally able to start enjoying the extraordinary events of the moment.

They sailed for what seemed an impossible length of time, but likely only amounted to an hour before they approached the dark horizonal line cast by the sun. Rix was on alert and watched with considerable interest as they entered a space never seen by any human before him, or at least, not one still living on Earth.

They continued in dark for another period when blinking lights in the distance caught his attention. "Kel! There!" He pointed at the source.

Still unable to communicate without touching helmets, Kel nevertheless looked out the window and then back to Rix.

"Beverly! Shoot!" He said, and then an idea struck him. He searched the pocket on the side of the chair he sat on and his gloved hand caught on a tablet. Pressing the tablet to his face, it stopped in midair on the suit material that he couldn't easily see. "Beverly, do you see through the window thing? I think I see Dravari!"

Without waiting, Rix held the tablet between him and the blinking light. For a moment, nothing happened, but then, a dashed green rectangle formed around the lights and zoomed in. Excited for the discovery, Rix handed the tablet to Kel, who then handed it back to him. Leaning over, she touched her helmet to his own.

"Good find and that ship is way too close for comfort," she said.

"We're going to pass it with maybe five hundred kilometers between us. Hang on, this could get dicey."

Rix nodded. Once again, there was nothing he could do about it, which he hated. Placing the tablet between him and the lights updated the view. "You can just hold the tablet, Rix," Beverly said, her voice much clearer than had been Kel's. "If we're in contact, I can send visual and auditory data through touch sensors and avoid the radiation that would give away our location. And you have very good eyesight to have picked that out."

"Are they going to see us?"

"Probably," Beverly said.

"You could have lied."

"I could have."

With much anticipation, Rix watched as the Dravari patrol ship seemed to accelerate toward them, even while not being directly oriented in their direction. He realized his sense of who was accelerating and who wasn't was skewed. There was something about the extreme quiet of their travel that was messing with his understanding of things. At least in cars and airplanes, motor noise and vibration were a large part of the experience and provided clues as to how fast the vehicle was moving. Not so in a spaceship at least when in a powerless vacuum. There were a lot of physics involved in the idea and it comforted his mind to posit those ideas even as they sped toward potential doom.

Kel grabbed Rix's hand as they zipped past the Dravari ship. "We made it! They're not moving! They didn't see us!"

"How are you talking to me?"

"Beverly reminded me that our touch sensors could be configured to pass along messages," Kel said. "It didn't occur to me before."

"So this isn't a regular thing for you?"

"It's sometimes a regular thing," Kel said, grinning. "Feels good to get around him."

"We may have a problem, Kel," Beverly said. "That Dravari patrol vessel has changed orientation and is lining up on our current arc."

"Oh boy," Kel said, blowing out a hot breath and releasing Rix's hand. In response, Rix reached over and placed his hand on Kel's leg, earning him a questioning look. "Whatcha doing, there, sailor?" she asked suggestively.

"Touch sensor."

"It looks like we're going to have to do this the hard way," Kel said, leaning forward and flipping switches on the forward bulkhead. Immediately, lights turned on in the cockpit and Rix's ears popped as atmospheric pressure pressed in on his suit.

"Do I need to get in the needler turret?" Rix asked.

"Oh, do I love your can-do attitude," Kel said, grinning. "That won't be necessary. Do you have any idea how many g's humans can take? I don't have much data regarding your species, and I'd hate to stop your hearts or something like that."

"Heart, singular," Rix said. "I think our best pilots can take seven g's with special equipment. I'm certain mere mortals can deal with five without blacking out."

"You just know this?" Kel asked. "How do you know this?"

"I read it in *Popular Mechanics*," Rix said. "They had an article about test pilots which I found interesting."

"Hmm, that is impressive. Personally, I just rely on the computative devices that are part of being a citizen of the Galactic Empire," she said and then glanced at him appraisingly. "Right. Not a citizen. I get it. Hold on. Here comes the hammer!"

"What?" Rix asked but it was too late for answers as *Calypso's* engines kicked in and flattened him against the back of the seat. "What in the heeeeeelllllll!" His question was cut off as he struggled just to breathe.

For almost an hour, Rix struggled against changes to the g-forces with *Calypso* approaching the darkened horizon of the moon under constant acceleration. Just when he thought he couldn't take any more they sailed through to the opposite side, and out into the full light of the sun.

"Keep it up, Rix. Dravari were caught with their spacesuits down and they're behind the acceleration curve. I sure wish our inertial dampers were working to full spec. This would be a whole lot easier. Frak, I think they're catching up," she said.

"I can't very well be fixing your ship while we're running like this," Rix said.

"Ooh, that's right, you're good at that sort of thing," she said. "Let's try something crazy."

"Crazier," Rix corrected.

"Touché."

Instead of exiting the moon's orbit and slingshotting off to the transition point for the Xandarj system, Kel killed the engines and allowed the moon's gravity to keep ahold of *Calypso.*

"What are you doing?"

"Going dark. Beverly, give old Rixy a quick rundown of the inertial systems. Maybe he's got a fix in him."

"I barely have any tools," Rix complained. "I'm not a magician."

"Could have fooled me," Kel shot back. "Besides, we're not escaping without a new plan, so, hang on to your panties already."

For the next hour they coasted quietly in orbit, surprisingly without the Dravari patrol finding them. "How are they missing us?" Rix finally asked, touching Kel's suit.

"They thought we were going for escape orbit and so they're searching local space. This was a brilliant maneuver if I do say so myself," she said.

"So why didn't you just make it your plan?"

"There's a second ship, probably. If there are two ships, this gets a lot harder."

"Why are they so crazy about finding us? This is a lot of effort," Rix said. "What did you take?"

"It's technical," Kel said. "You wouldn't understand."

"Try me."

"Fine," Kel said. "It has something to do with generating atmosphere on space stations. My client needs whatever this thingamajig is, so I grabbed one."

"From a locker," Rix filled in. "Could it be that expensive that they'd send two ships?"

"Expensive, yes, and I wasn't entirely truthful about the locker thing."

"That's hard to believe," Rix said.

"Don't be petty. I'm telling you now," Kel said.

"Where'd you get this doodad?"

"From a Dravari outpost," Kel said. "Intelligence said it was unmanned. And mostly it was. Just a few dozen people. The devices have rare parts and are hard to get. My client's problem is those parts are hard to come by. It was totally unguarded, too. We just dropped in, disconnected the system and borrowed a couple of parts. It's not like they were really using it. The atmospheric regenerator doohickey thingamabob is good for a station serving thousands and like I said, maybe two dozen were on the outpost that was *supposed* to be unmanned. So, it's not exactly my fault."

"It's entirely your fault. You have a ship, you could be making money with legal loads, instead of stealing, couldn't you?" Rix asked.

"Now you're an expert on intergalactic transport and delivery? No, Mr. Genius Earth Boy, I can't make money with legal loads. I can't afford a freighter license for Empire travel lanes. Without that license, nobody legit will work with me so I have to take the jobs I can find."

Rix pursed his lips. Her explanation wasn't entirely outrageous, even though her actions seemed to be.

"It's still stealing and that's not okay, even in your Galactic Empire."

"You're gonna take those words back, I swear it, Rix Banner," Kel said and for the first time, she looked angry. "You have no idea what you're talking about."

Surprised by her defensiveness, Rix decided it would be best to leave the conversation alone. "What now?"

"Glad you asked," Kel said, flipping *Calypso* end for end as they crossed over to the dark side of the moon once again. "Time for the hammer again."

Rix was once again pressed back in his chair and this time, the darkness came for him as his vision grayed out and he drifted into unconsciousness.

"Time to wake up, Rix," Kel's voice said plainly.

As Rix opened his eyes, he discovered he was still aboard *Calypso* and it was dark throughout the ship with only starlight providing illumination. "You knocked me out on purpose," he said accusingly.

"Still learning your limitations," she answered flatly.

"Sure, let's go with that," Rix said. "Where are we? I assume dark side of the moon and all."

"I set down in an impact crater. There's no way they'll see us down here, even if we power up essential systems," she said. "Time to get to work."

Rix wanted to argue with her and even more he wanted to tell her off for the way she'd handled things. That they were still alive, however, wasn't lost on him. "Philo, can you grab tools please?"

"Yup yup, Rixy," came Philo's disembodied voice.

"Down the hatch, Beverly?" Rix asked.

"That's right, Rix," Beverly answered. "I don't think much has been done with this system for a time. It hasn't operated correctly for twenty months, using Earth measurements."

Rix nodded, not exactly sure why she was clarifying her use of measurements as he believed the translator was doing that sort of work constantly. He decided it wasn't a mystery that needed immediate resolution, given the circumstances.

"Can it run one of those self-diagnostics?" he asked, opening the 'tween deck hatch and lowering himself in. He felt considerably lighter than he had on Earth and wondered if he was feeling the moon's gravity, which he knew to be roughly twenty percent that of Earth.

"There is no power to the device," Beverly said.

"Did we check to see if it's plugged in?" Rix asked.

"I don't believe it has been looked at after initial failure. Kel is a talented pilot and able to operate *Calypso* without inertial compensation," Beverly said.

"You sound defensive," Rix said.

"Perhaps your questions suggest a distrust in the application of common sense," Beverly said. "Common sense suggests that only trained and qualified engineers should attempt repairs on spaceship systems. The danger is unexpected, catastrophic failure leading to a slow death in an unpowered spaceship."

"Let's hold that thought for moment," Rix said. "Please show me where the inertial system components are."

Not expecting the system to be quite so comprehensive, Rix gasped when Beverly highlighted a network of thin bars of an unknown material, all strapped to the underside of the main deck. And when he looked down at the lattice of incomplete decking which made up the 'tween deck's floor, he saw even more of the highlighted bars.

"What's the deal?" Rix asked. "Kind of looks like big locust tree leaves. I take it we're passing some sort of field through that alloy to simulate gravity and adjust for inertial differences?"

"I don't understand how you even formulated that sentence given even exceptional human comprehension," Beverly said.

"I'll take that as—*yes, Rix, that's how this works,*" Rix said. "I've experienced the artificial gravity. It feels like that part is working. Let's eliminate that from my view."

"You're correct, Rix," Beverly said.

"Thanks," Rix said, inspecting the components that remained, which turned out to be located directly next to the gravity repulsor components. "That makes sense. These guys need to communicate, right?"

"Guys?" Beverly asked.

"Repulsor, artificial gravity, and inertial systems all do fairly similar work," Rix said. "Right?"

"You have uncanny instincts. You have never worked on advanced technology before, correct?" Beverly asked.

"I worked on the most advanced technology the good old U.S. of A. had back in the war. Didn't compare much to this, though, I'll admit that. Show me where this box gets power. It really feels like it's just not getting any."

Beverly highlighted a vast network of wiring that ran along the outer hull. "Discovering a power break will be quite difficult," Beverly said. "There is power throughout this area."

"Trust me, if I can troubleshoot a new Caddy's wiring harness, I've got this," Rix said with confidence he didn't entirely feel. "And I see the problem already."

"That is unlikely, Rix," Beverly said. "Where are you looking?"

Rix looked over to Philo who'd been standing quietly by, holding Rix's travel toolbox and a pouch of tools that had been on *Calypso* already. "Hand me the inch-and-a-quarter open-end wrench there on the left side, would you, Philo?"

Philo set both tool carriers on the deck and opened Rix's. After a few moments, he handed over a simple eight-inch-long tool to Rix. "Rix fix?" Philo asked.

"I see a couple of options. I could break it, too," Rix said. "Beverly, from which side does power flow? Does it come from here?" Rix pointed at a thick line.

"Yes. What are you doing, Rix?"

"Earth tools are made of varying grades of steel. What we care about is that it's conductive," Rix said, carefully tugging at a piece of foam that lay across the thick cable. The foam didn't move and he discovered he was unable to pick at it to pull it off. "Is there some sort of solvent to break this foam down?"

Philo reached into the bag that was part of *Calypso's* inventory and held out a tube. "Careful, Rixy. No air after foam."

"Good call, Philo," Rix said. "Hand me the putty knife from my toolbox."

It took only a couple of moments for Philo to locate the tool and hand it to Rix. Dabbing a small amount of the solvent along the edge of the putty knife, Rix experimented with sliding it beneath the cable, trying to slice through the foam. The solvent worked, freeing the cable from being trapped against the hull. With a quick squirt, leaving the putty knife in place to guard against overspray and opening up the hull patch, he removed the foam from the cable, exposing a break in the wire.

"Impossible," Beverly said.

"What do you mean?" Rix asked.

"That you intuited that issue without seeing it."

"Oh, sister, trust me. I've earned that Boy Scout badge a long time ago. You have no idea how many airplanes, shot up by enemy anti-aircraft, had busted wires and hydraulics. This was an easy call. Now comes the tricky part."

"Be careful, Rix, there is a lot of power in that line."

"Turn it off a minute?" Rix asked.

"It is off."

"Philo, I need the seven-eighths open-ended," Rix said, holding out the larger wrench to pass back. Philo swapped tools in Rix's hand. "And a length of duct tape if you don't mind. Two inches should do it."

Placing the head of the wrench in the break of the wire, Rix taped it in place. "Stand back when we power this up. If we're lucky, it'll weld itself in place."

"What if unlucky?" Philo asked.

"Big bang and maybe some shrapnel," Rix said. "I'm pulling for the welding thing. Beverly, give us power?"

A loud pop sent Philo and Rix jumping away, but after the initial noise, the deck returned to quiet. "Who are you, Rix Banner?" Beverly said, her voice full of wonder.

"I take it we now have power," Rix said.

"We do, in fact, have power to the inertial system," Beverly said. "Most remarkable."

11

JUMPSPACE

"Diagnostics are complete," Kel said after Rix returned to the bridge. "Would you bet your life on your fix staying in place?" She hadn't been overly excited about Rix's description of using a wrench as a bridge for the power conduit.

"I'm not in the habit of betting my life on anything," Rix answered. "But it should hold for now."

"What was the problem?"

"Do you recall anything about when it stopped working? Like maybe you were in some sort of fight where you were being shot at?" Rix asked.

"Yes, and I already knew that. That doesn't explain how you figured out how to fix it."

"Apparently, spaceships aren't really that different from cars. I just started tracing to where the system failed and found a spot where there was that foam Philo uses to plug holes in the hull," Rix said. "Power on one side of a line, nothing after a big hunk of foam. Doesn't take a genius to put that together."

"Copy that, try to keep it down, Dravari are right overhead, hunting for us," Kel said.

Rix stopped in the galley on the way by and poured a cup of coffee into a weighted stainless-steel cup. Joining Kel in the bridge, he slid into a seat next to her. "Are we just hanging out here in this crater, then? By the way, those are words I never thought I'd say."

Kel laughed and kicked her feet up to rest on the forward bulkhead. "They just *think* we're around here," she said. "If they *knew*, they'd drop down and get a closer look. Dravari ships all use the same search software."

"A nap, then?" Rix asked, reclining the bridge chair, his eyes wandering across the permanent night sky. "Man, the stars and the view of the galaxy are clear. Kind of makes me feel small."

"We are small," Kel said. "But don't get tripped up by that. Everyone is important in their own way. Your actions define your value to the universe."

Rix wrinkled his eyebrows but didn't respond to Kel's statement.

"What, you don't think a *petty thief* can have deep thoughts?"

Kel had thrown Rix's words right back at him and he knew better than to respond. He'd offended her with the truth, and he wasn't about to apologize. Instead, he took a long sip of his coffee.

"What am I going to do, Kel?" Rix asked. "Who's going to need a Luddite mechanic in a highly advanced scientific community?"

"Do?"

"Yeah, for work? I imagine a person needs to make money where you come from, right?"

"I'd bring you on as crew, but I can't really pay much," she said. "I hardly make anything as it is."

"You see my quandary, then," he said.

"Galactic Empire is a big place, full of opportunity," she said. "By putting you into the registry, you'll get an immigrant ID. I'm not sure if they'll let you own property right away, or not. The whole 'humans are semi-sentient' thing might be a problem."

"What kind of problem?"

"Philo can't own things or enter into long-term contracts without a co-signer," she said. "If that's your classification, that rules out living on any of the major core worlds."

"This just keeps getting better and better," Rix said.

"If your skills as a mechanic keep translating as they have for me, people will need you on the outer rim planets and settlements. Not everyone can fix spaceships with a boltgun and a roll of duct tape," she said. "Now that I think about it, I bet Garba Klex would rent out the old small ship dry dock back home. It's not like anyone's going to be using it anytime soon."

"Who's Garba Klex? And you're talking about Narlux-4?" Rix asked.

"Man, you've got that good memory. Narlux-4 is the system," Kel said. "We're headed to Patience Station in Surnak Belt which is an asteroid belt in Narlux-4. Garba Klex is the mayor of Patience Station and owns a bunch of it."

"You live in an asteroid belt."

"Mostly, I live aboard *Calypso*," she said. "But when I'm catching downtime, it's mostly on Patience Station. I have people there."

This caught Rix's attention. "Family?"

"Some. Older sister and a nephew, but most of the people of Patience Station are family," she said. "What about you, what kind of family do you have?"

"Parents died a few years back," he said. "Grandparents died while I was in The War, and I have no siblings. I'm what most people consider a loner."

"Is that how you see yourself?"

"Not really," Rix said. "Right woman comes along ... well, I suppose that's not likely anymore."

"Keep an open mind, Rix," Kel said. "Most folks you consider alien really aren't that different from you or me."

"I guess I don't know what you are," Rix said. "You look human enough, at least mostly."

"Are you sure I'm not human?" she asked.

"You could be," Rix said. "But you talked about how you didn't have the money for a freighter pilot license, which has to be a contract. Therefore, you're not human."

"Asking about a person's species can be considered impolite," Kel said. "In some cases, like Fimil, it's obvious."

"Fimil?"

A ten-centimeter-tall quadrupedal alien hologram appeared in front of where Rix sat. Humanoid for the most part, the alien had gray skin and a nose that was more accurately described as a wrinkly elephant's trunk and hung to its chin.

"Thank you, Beverly," Kel said. "Yeah, or Vred."

The elephant headed alien that was floating in front of Rix shifted to that of a reptile skinned alien, complete with dark green pebbled skin along the back of its neck and pale green, smooth skin on its face and down its front. The alien's hands were thick and ended in clawed points, although there was a keen intelligence evident in its face.

"Kind of a crocodile type of thing, huh?" Rix said. "Are there a lot of those around?"

"Fimil and Vred are prolific species, so yeah, lots of those around," Kel answered.

"But you don't want to say what you are," Rix said.

"It's dangerous for others to know my species," she said. "You'll probably figure it out because I'll end up giving it away before we get home."

"What do you mean, give it away?"

"You might as well see it now," she said.

"See what?"

"Give it a minute," she said.

At first, Rix didn't see anything different, but as he watched, Kel's face slowly started shifting. High, flat cheeks, thin lips and dead black eyes slowly morphed to a rounder, softer look, her eyes turned blue gray and her hair shifted from a medium gray, short cut to thick auburn as her once pallid skin shifted to a fair, freckled complexion. The spacesuit material made the sound of rubber sliding against skin and Rix noticed that Kel's chest seemed to expand, although not excessively even as her waist drew in slightly.

"Holy cow, you're a shapeshifter?" he asked. "Is this how people expect to see you?"

"This is my true form," she said. "I'm Tjelari and my species has the ability to change the way we look."

"Spy agencies on Earth would kill for that," Rix said.

"There aren't a lot of us around anymore," Kel said. "If the right people knew what I am, my life would be harder. They'd come for me."

"Because you're able to shift?"

"Yes. The shifts are more than cosmetic, the shapes I take are modeled after real people, down to their vascular patterns, DNA signatures, and most of the things that are recognizable by all but the most advanced security systems," she said.

"That must be handy for your line of work," Rix said.

"Get over it, Rix," Kel said. "You are in no position to judge Philo and me or the life choices we've made. Life out in the deep dark is a lot harder than you could ever imagine. Cranberry Cove is a lie. That kind of safety isn't the way most of the universe lives."

"Don't preach to me about injustice. I just got done fighting Nazis. I know how bad it can be," he said hotly.

"Fine," Kel said.

"Fine," Rix agreed.

They sat quietly for several minutes and finally, Rix lay his head back and allowed his eyes to close even as he replayed the conversation in his head. He wanted to argue with Kel more, but neither of them knew enough about the other's past to get overly deep. Instead, he allowed sleep to find him.

"Are you still grumpy?"

Kel's voice floated into Rix's waking consciousness. He'd been dreaming about working in his shop back in Cranberry Cove and had anxiety about not being able to pay rent, which wasn't a new dream.

"I wasn't that grumpy," he said, opening his eyes.

"Sleep good?" she asked, not pushing it further.

"How long was I down?"

"Three hours," she said. "Dravari moved out of sensor range almost two hours ago. And, in fifteen hours, we'll be at the peak for making a line to the Xandarj transition point. After that it's a footrace."

"Do you think Dravari know we're headed there? If they do, why wouldn't they just set up shop along that route and wait for us?"

"They might," she said. "But there are several transition points we could use. I doubt they know I prefer Xandarj."

"Clear it up for me," Rix said. "Why do you prefer Xandarj?"

"It's not a core planet," she said. "Xandarj people are great as a whole. They believe in independence so much that some consider them anarchists. If you get in trouble with someone on Xandarj, it's your problem to resolve. Their security people keep the peace more than enforce the few laws they have."

"How do they not fall into complete chaos?" Rix asked.

"It can get a little tribal," Kel said. "I have good relationships with Dralli Station, so if I have an important load, I'll hire a Dralli escort."

"How soon will you know if we're being chased by Dravari?"

"We'll know soon enough," she said. "Thirty minutes max."

"How long of a trip are we taking?"

"Three days to Xandarj transition, five days to get to the next jump, etc. Three weeks, give or take," she said.

"What in the world am I supposed to do for three weeks in this little ship?"

"First few days are always sleeping," Kel said. "Unless we're still being chased by Dravari, because that can get exciting. After that, there's ship maintenance, some of which I'm not very good at. And you could put the engine back together. There's always replacing the hull patches."

"You might be interested in getting qualified for ship maintenance," Beverly said, appearing on the forward bulkhead. "There's also basic ship handling and navigational classes that are publicly available."

"What about exercise?"

"Lots of options," Kel said. "If you like to run or hike, you can use the hallway like a track. The program projects a trail onto your retina and it's just like being in different places. There's a section of the deck that will adjust to the program's terrain."

"That seems like it'd be a short trip."

"Nah, it keeps you all in one place, but you hardly know you're being moved back after the first time or two you use it. Bigger ships with longer tracks do a better job. We can't play too many sports, though, because our track doesn't adjust quickly enough for side-to-side running."

"What are you replacing hull patches with?" Rix asked, changing subjects back.

"Like a welder from your world but a bit more sophisticated. It takes a little setup if you're working against vacuum. It's a whole process. A lot of times, it's easier just to wait until you're back home so you have access to the exterior. If you're impatient, though, it can be done using a hull patch system. It turns out the alloy used in the patch system is stronger than the rest of the hull, so it's worthwhile."

"How much of that do you have?" Rix asked.

"More than you could use. Why?"

"I've seen at least thirty holes in *Calypso*. If one of those gives away at the wrong time, that could be a big deal, right?"

"It's not pleasant," she said. "Especially if you're not in a spacesuit at the time, like you're in the shower. If that happens, the head seals up tight, so it's not too big of a problem. If you want to work on patches, though, I'm not going to stop you. It's probably worth seeing if Dravari are chasing us or not, first, though."

"Beverly, could you direct me to something that would show me the general classifications of spaceship systems?" Rix said.

"How many minutes of instruction would you like?" Beverly asked. "And do you want me to add any sort of testing at the end of the module?"

"It sounds like you're going to manufacture this course," Rix said.

"I am," Beverly agreed.

"That is next level," Rix said.

"Philo, get strapped in, we're going to launch in thirty minutes," Kel called over the ship's public address.

"Where does he get to sit while we're up here?"

"Philo's species requires more sleep than either of ours," she said. "He has a bunk that's just large enough for him to curl up within, but I need him to use his harness when we're making course corrections, which he doesn't love."

"Beverly, cue up the first navigation course, would you? I might as well get an understanding of what's happening around here," Rix said. "Kel, let me know when you're going to start doing things."

"Will do." Rix had barely started the coursework when Kel tapped on his arm. "If you look at the navigational display—the one to starboard, that is—you'll see *Calypso's* arc as she leaves your moon's surface and escapes its gravity well. After that, we'll constantly accelerate toward the Xandarj system's transition point. At the midpoint of our trek, we'll circumvolve and decelerate with the same force so we end up at a dead stop in relationship to our destination. Due to your fixes of the inertial system, we'll make good time and save fuel to boot."

"Circumvolve is the term for what we do at the middle?" Rix asked.

"It is," Kel agreed. "You can take the controls if you like. *Calypso* will provide feedback through the flight controls; if you're outside of the navigation plot, she'll try to push your controls back into place, but not so hard that you can't override her. If Dravari show up, I'll take over."

"I only saw a little bit about doing this," Rix said nervously. "I'm probably going to make a mess."

"You might. Just remember, smaller adjustments are better than large ones."

And with Kel giving him pointers along the way, Rix directed *Calypso* to lift from the moon's surface and guided the small ship around the lip of the crater and out into space. Suddenly, Rix's control sticks both stopped providing feedback, becoming limp in his hands.

"Strap in, Rix! Philo, hunker down buddy!" Kel called over comms as she slammed the acceleration stick forward and abruptly veered hard to starboard. Unlike the last hard maneuver where he'd been slammed into the back of the chair, Rix felt an increase of pressure that ramped up to a certain point but failed to reach the painful limits that had rendered him unconscious. "Look at the tactical display. You'll see the Dravari position."

Rix found it difficult to turn his head but not impossible. On the flat panel that sat inset in the forward bulkhead, a single Dravari ship arced toward *Calypso*. In addition to miniature versions of the Dravari ship and *Calypso*, there were faint lines drawn on the display. A single arcing line joined the two vessels; along that line was a triangle in the center displaying a positive number, which in that moment read four-hundred-twenty-one. That number was ticking down several points per second. Other lines extended from the aft of each vessel.

"Beverly, what am I looking at?" Rix asked quietly, not wanting to distract Kel.

"Are you referring to the navigational display?"

"Yes."

"The lines behind each vessel show acceleration and an average directional arc over the last several seconds," Beverly said. "The line between *Calypso* shows an estimated number of seconds before intercept."

"Three hundred forty seconds or six minutes before intercept?" Rix asked.

"Yes," Beverly said. "But look at the acceleration vectors for each vessel and also at the rate of change of the seconds on that TTI indicator."

"TTI—time to intercept?" Rix asked.

"Got it in one," Beverly said.

"Well, *Calypso* has a longer acceleration vector, maybe by thirty percent than the Dravari," Rix said. "What you're saying is they're coming in much faster in relationship to where we're headed, but *Calypso* is speeding up more quickly than they are."

"Again, you're right. Tap that triangle. Don't worry about changing things for Kel, the lines are projected by the earwig's electronics," Beverly instructed. Rix didn't question her instructions and did as she said. The data within the triangle showed a positive number in the hundreds. "That's the difference in acceleration in meters per second per second. Tap again and you'll get MDI or minimum distance interval, which I'm showing as thirty-four kilometers. That's close, but Dravari patrol vessels don't have armaments that are accurate at thirty-four kilometers."

"What in the world would be accurate at thirty-four kilometers on a moving target?" Rix asked.

"Intelligent guided missiles," Beverly said. "Our crimes aren't enough to warrant the use of missiles that cost one hundred fifty thousand credits, give or take. Or so we hope."

"You're taking this rather well," Kel said, glancing at Rix. "I assume Beverly is giving you the lay of the land for what's going on, then?"

"This is stressful. I'm not sure knowing the numbers is making things better. What if they use missiles?"

"We evade," Kel said, leaning forward and patting the forward bulkhead. "This old girl has more than a few tricks left. And now that we have operational inertial systems, they don't stand a chance. That was good work, Rix. I don't know how you knew what to do to get this old girl patched up, but I'm not about to question it."

"How soon will we know if we're going to make it?"

"I predict that, in a few hours, Dravari will peel off and head back home. Xandarj won't recognize their authority, so they won't get any help there."

"Space combat is a chess game much more than it's a dog fight, isn't it?" Rix said.

"'Dog fight' isn't a familiar term, but I think I get it," Kel said. "It can be both, depending on the pilots. I have no desire to stand toe-to-toe with Dravari, especially with my inertial systems working. We're small and fast and we give up too much armor to Dravari."

"How is it they don't just wait for you back where you came from instead of chasing you?"

"They have no idea where we came from. No, the data they can get from us is a much heavier vessel with different physical dimensions," Kel said.

"How's that possible?"

"Does it come as that much of a surprise that *Calypso* can change her shape?"

"I suppose not," Rix said, trying not to sound disappointed. He was starting to like the woman but struggled with her career choices.

"Want to take over the flight controls? We just bottomed out our

MDI. It'd be good for you to start logging some hours. You'll need them for your ship-handling courses. Most captains won't let anyone without at least a few thousand hours touch their flight controls, so it's good to get hours when you can."

"Sounds good."

Minutes turned into hours and hours into days. Rix shifted between the various tasks they'd discussed, including completing the repair of *Calypso's* engine. Each hour that passed, the mood aboard the ship elevated as it became clear that Dravari were less and less likely to give pursuit.

"We're coming up on the Xandarj transition, Rix," Kel said. "You'll want to get things put away since we'll be entering a whole new solar system. Xandarj transition can be busy on the other side."

"Talk to me about busy," Rix said.

"Lots of ship traffic," she said. "We'll be able to step up the acceleration in Xandarj space, though. If Dravari aren't on us now, they can't possibly track us through Xandarj, given all the traffic, so we can be more aggressive."

"I wondered if *Calypso* had more in her," Rix said. "I'd been reading about different ships and their capacities."

"You haven't seen what *Calypso* has," Kel said. "If that manifold was in tip-top shape, I'd have dared Dravari to chase us."

"I think you made the right call. My fixes aren't of a permanent nature and I'd hate to stress them unnecessarily."

"I'll be up in ten minutes. Does that work?" Rix asked.

"Take your time," Kel said. "I'll hang out on the transition point until you're ready."

With help from Philo, Rix cleaned up the tools and the debris from where he'd been replacing temporary hull patches. The device used to allow the titanium alloy to meld with the remainder of the hull was a technological wonder that worked so efficiently that Rix derived satisfaction from its use. His estimation of the number of holes in *Calypso's* hull had been grossly off as he'd fixed thirty spots already and found he was only halfway through the ship. That the replacement patches were stronger than the original hull material just added to his enjoyment of the process.

"Halfway done, Cap," Rix said, sliding into his chair.

"You've been at those repairs for days. I'd have thought you'd be done by now," Kel said.

"I think you've been in more fights than you'd like to admit," Rix said. "Philo and I have filled thirty and we're only halfway done. There's also damage to at least a third of your systems. You do know that getting shot is hard on those systems, right?"

"Thirty percent is an exaggeration," Kel said.

Rix pinched the list of repairs he'd been tracking since he'd started working through the ship and flicked it at Kel. His use of the gesture caught her off guard, but she accepted the small data packet all the same.

"All of these?" she asked, despair evident in her voice.

"Varying degrees of trouble," Rix said. "You're lucky the septic has a redundant solids collector."

"We'll put that on the top of the list," she said, handing him a small bag. "Now, transition can be disturbing for some species. If you need to vomit, use the bag. Also, it's likely your vision will play tricks on you. First time through, it might be a good idea to close your eyes."

"Great," Rix said, closing his eyes. A moment later, his stomach flopped, and bile rose in his throat. He pushed at the feelings and just as quickly as they'd onset, they dissipated.

"Welcome to jumpspace," Kel said. "Given our mass and other factors, we'll spend three days in jumpspace before we drop into Xandarj, so you might as well get comfortable with it all. Good job on not vomiting."

Rix opened his eyes and was met with an unexpected view out the forward window of the bridge. Where there had once been relatively static stars was now more a blur as stars seemed to be sliding past *Calypso* much like rows of corn slipped past on the highways back home.

"That's crazy," Rix managed.

"I don't love it," Kel admitted. "But the good news is, energy weapons don't work at all in jumpspace, and even kinetic weapons have limited use. Not only that, little ships like *Calypso*, move more quickly than those with higher mass. Point is, we're hard to catch now."

"Are you up for a game of hall ball?" Rix asked. "I wouldn't mind moving around a bit."

"Do you think you'll score this time?"

"Oh, I'm going to score," Rix said. "Mark my words."

12

MEMBER OF SOCIETY

"My gosh, this place is insane," Rix said shortly after *Calypso* transitioned into normal space within the Xandarj system. The trip through Sol had been one of sheer isolation as had been jumpspace. "There must be hundreds of ships out there. What are they all doing?"

"Xandarj is a major stop in one of the heaviest traveled trade routes in this sector," Kel explained. "The cool thing about Xandarj is that Dralli Station has a massive open trading floor that runs around the clock called The Trailer."

"I thought you weren't a licensed trader."

"I'm an unlicensed freighter captain," Kel clarified. "I can trade all I want, especially in a place like Dralli Station that's set up with an open market. What I can't do is make freighting contracts with Xandarj businesses and insure the loads. Without insurance, buyers can't get financing and it all just falls apart."

"Gotcha," Rix said. "Well, I won't be trading much of anything, given my current lack of citizenship and funds."

"We've been in space for eight days, how about we stop in and pick up fresh supplies. Xandarj is known for their fresh produce. I can't pay you right now, but I have enough to cover dinner," Kel said.

"Talk to me about manufactory machines," Rix said.

"Not much to know," Kel said. "There are a few different kinds, but mostly it's about how much mass they can output, how sophisticated their patterns can be and what kinds of materials they use. Difference between creating ship parts and clothing is a good way to look at it. That'll sound like industrial vs. personal."

"So could an industrial manufactory create a car, as an example?"

"Not in one go. First you need a pattern, also called IP, which stands for intellectual property. Each pattern has a cost of materials and a cost per run. If you're going to use the pattern a lot, you might consider purchasing the IP for infinite runs, but those prices are extremely high," she said.

"That's slick," Rix said. "Could we pay for a new flux coupling manifold?"

"Not with the money in my account," Kel said.

"My patch isn't going to last forever," Rix said.

"That manifold has been on its last leg since I found *Calypso*," Kel said, patting the forward bulkhead lovingly. "We'll get by just fine for the time being."

"How expensive could that part be?" Rix asked. "You're just paying for something someone thought up. Once they create this IP you're talking about, it's just a matter of having the right materials and that manufactory thing."

"You have access to their pricing," Kel said.

"How?"

"On your HUD, check out *local space,* then within that, *Dralli Station,* and then station services. That'll get you the publicly available manufactories. From there, search for the part using the model information you get from the engine."

As she talked, Rix opened the menus and started searching what turned out to be a vast library of items that could be manufactured. "Oh, I found it. The original manufacturer of the engine has the only available pattern. Is that usual? Back home we could get parts that weren't OEM and they were a bit cheaper."

"OEM?"

"Original Equipment Manufacturer," Rix said.

"They have the details so locked down that creating new parts is difficult. Now, if you had a pattern that was off brand you could run it for your own use, but that's like having an infinite use pattern and all that's expensive, or sometimes the parts don't even work. No, you're better off buying reputable patterns."

"Hmm, I see why it's so expensive," Rix said. "Their replacement package is half a dozen parts. If we could get a shim made from the right material, it would slip right over and I could lock it down with the boltgun. It wouldn't be pretty, but I'm sure it wouldn't affect engine performance."

"Now you're designing replacement parts for a spaceship engine," Kel said. "You do realize the best of the best create these engines, right?"

"And my hat's off to them," Rix said. "It's not like I'm creating a new engine design. I don't even have to know everything about the engine to see how to fix this one thing. How do I create my own part?"

"If it costs too much, I'm not doing it," Kel said.

"Fair enough."

"Ask Beverly to show you how to create a pattern. It's something you could do if you really want to try, but trust me, there are a lot of people out there thinking about this, I don't see how you could possibly create something new."

"Maybe I'm not looking for it in the right way," Rix said. "How long will it take us to get to Dralli Station?"

"Thirty-two hours if I push things a little harder," Kel said.

Rix made his way back to the engine room and removed the housing that he'd installed only a few days prior. He didn't need to take the engine completely apart, which wasn't possible under power, but he wanted a good look at the manifold.

"Beverly, how do I get measurements?" Rix asked. No more had he asked when a grid of green lines appeared on the parts of the engine which had Rix's attention.

"Nudge the lines with your finger to get it to lock onto whatever you're thinking about. I can help, but you'll have to tell me what you're trying to do," Beverly said.

Rix struggled for a time, trying to get the green lines into the right places. It was the sort of dexterity he hadn't much experience with and as he worked, he got better. "Can you stop that one from moving?" Rix asked, holding his finger in place to avoid bumping his perfectly placed line out of position.

"I've locked it, do you want me to mirror the same line on the other side of the crack? I think I see what you're doing," Beverly said. "I've run a simulation and checked specifications. I don't know how you did it, but the custom part you're proposing is within the engine's tolerance, which is something your welding has not achieved."

"Welding isn't nearly as precise as what we're drawing here," Rix said. "And yes, lock that side. I wish we could remove that weld so I could see the shape of the crack along the inside."

"Oh, I have that, Rix," Beverly said. "When you were welding back on Earth, I recorded the surfaces with considerable resolution."

"And we can use those recordings in this process?"

"You could do it without me. The computational assets you have access to through your HUD are considerable. Being who I am, my interpretation is more forgiving than your HUD's, but you would soon learn how to direct it correctly."

"Let's try this, pull the drawing out that we have so far and put only the inside surface of the crack into that drawing," Rix said. "Does that make sense?"

"Certainly," Beverly said, finishing the three-dimensional drawing and shading it in with the color of the manifold's alloy.

"That should fit like a glove. Any suggestions on how to get it to adhere? More welding or maybe tabs for the boltgun?"

"This is fun, Rix," Beverly said. "Who'd have thought to create an entirely custom piece to fix this? If we add a layer of flux, we can heat weld it in place just like you did your wrench."

"What's the run price, then?" Rix asked.

"One hundred forty-five credits per run."

"Let's look at a replacement section for that wiring harness. Can you show that to me?"

"Certainly."

The pair continued to work for a couple of hours as Rix proposed new ideas for previous repairs.

"You're saying we can't replicate the gravity coil array directly, but if we just make a replacement shroud that isn't broken, we're okay? What's the difference?" Rix asked after a heated exchange with Beverly about what the manufactory would accept as a pattern.

"That's exactly right. Your harness and manifold repairs can't be used by anyone else since they are specific to the damage *Calypso* received. The shroud for the array is what chipped. You're not creating a full replacement for that piece."

"That's a fine definition, Beverly. How certain are you that I'm in the clear on this shroud?" Rix asked.

"Completely. I submitted the pattern for review, and it came back clear," she said.

"Well, hold on a moment. What kind of clear?"

"I don't understand the question. We can have the part created and use it," Beverly said. "That's as clear as we need."

"But that part could be used by other people with the same problem," Rix said. "Could we put our pattern into the store somehow? We could do it for free, so other people don't have to buy an entire replacement part."

"Why free? You could charge a small amount and if it gets used a lot, you'd have income," Beverly said. "It would take a little work to create a vendor profile, but I could help. Is that something you're interested in?"

"How would they pay me?"

"I don't understand. The manufactories collect the money and signal the accounts for transfer."

"Like a check then?" Rix asked.

"Oh, I see your confusion," Beverly said. "All money is tracked through computers and transactions are stored publicly, but not in a way they can identify people. Point is, mostly there isn't physical money changing hands."

"That sounds like a good way to get ripped off."

"At one point that was a problem in our history, but not for hundreds of years," Beverly said. "You have immigrant status now, so you can establish a bank account with one of the major civilizations. Xandarj would work."

"Xandarj the solar system or Xandarj-3 the planet?" Rix asked.

"Neither. Xandarj the government, which is part of the Galactic Empire and therefore can move money throughout the empire," Beverly said.

"How long does that take?"

"Practically instant," Beverly said. "I can submit the request if you desire."

Rix whistled. "For every person in the Galactic Empire?"

"Only those who request, but our systems for tracking and recording wealth have few limits. A stable government is truly the most important choice and Xandarj is that."

"Why not, then? Is there a better choice?"

"I cannot anticipate your future with any accuracy, but Xandarj has a long history of treating immigrants to the same protections as its citizens," she explained. "Tell me you authorize my acting as agent for setting up your account and I'll see to the details."

"I authorize you to act as my agent," Rix said.

"You will owe me seventy-five credits, which is what I will deposit in your account to get it started," she said. "I do not need repayment until your finances are stable."

"I appreciate you, Beverly."

"What did she do now?" Kel asked. "And, if I understand your request, you want to spend four hundred thirty credits to fix the flux coupling manifold? Do you think it'll really work?"

"That's actually to repair the engine, gravity and inertial systems," Rix said. "I'm even creating a pattern for other people to use, assuming they know how to look for it. Is that too much money?"

"Not if you think those parts will work," Kel said.

"They'll work."

"I'll get them queued. Explain how you created a pattern?"

"I asked Beverly about it. It seems like the problem we're having could be somewhat common," Rix said. "Instead of buying a whole new subassembly, why not just buy the part that's broken? That's my thinking, at least."

"I've never heard of someone submitting a new pattern," Kel said. "Are you sure your part wasn't already available?"

"For sure it was not. Tell me, do we need to wear anything special when we get to Dralli Station?" Rix asked. "I'd feel weird wearing a spacesuit in front of other people."

"Spacesuits are common enough, although, if you want to find a pattern for some street clothing, I owe you that much," Kel said. "We need to talk about Xandarj. Some of the males can be very strong. Don't look them directly in the eyes, especially if they're drinking. Most Xandarj are friendly, but there are some who look for trouble with visitors. Dralli Station rules state that you have to take care of your own conflicts, so don't expect help out of a mess."

"Keep my head down and don't make the locals mad. That sounds familiar enough," Rix said.

"No eye contact."

"Like a junkyard dog."

"I don't understand the reference."

"Oh, holy cow, is that the space station?" Rix asked as a gleaming white object in the distance started to come into focus.

"Dralli Station," Kel said.

Three hours later, *Calypso* slowly approached and sailed through the open bay door where Kel neatly set down on a preassigned landing pad.

With excitement, Rix looked out the spacecraft's front window, catching his first real look at the colorful Xandarj aliens. Covered with brightly colored hair, Xandarj were shorter and stockier than humans. As a result of the hair covering their bodies, the clothing worn by the colorful aliens was considerably more revealing than what would be polite for humans.

"So many colors," Rix said.

"Let's go," Kel said. "Philo, are you ready?"

"Stairs are set, Kel," Philo said. "Pretty girl at bottom."

"What's that about?" Rix asked, tapping his suit so the helmet closed him in.

"The girl?" Kel asked and when Rix nodded, she continued. "Madis Bazer is the daughter of the man who manages this docking bay. She'll process the customs which will go fast because we have friends. Philo has a crush on her. She's a sweet little thing who seems to always greet us when we come in."

"Mutual crush you're thinking?" Rix asked.

Kel shrugged and as she did, Rix noticed that her facial features were hardening, and her body contours were shifting back to the more angular, less feminine version of her he'd first met.

"What's with the body morph?" Rix asked.

"I don't like to show my true form in public if I can avoid it," Kel said. "And you don't need your helmet up. There's atmosphere in the docking bay."

"How? The doors are open."

"In your free time, look up photonic barrier," Kel said.

Gathering at the exit hatch, the three followed Philo out of the ship and down the narrow stairs that were extended to the docking bay deck. Bounding across to where the young Xandarj stood, Philo excitedly wrapped her in a hug.

"Mads! Mads!" he said excitedly, spinning her around once.

"Set me down now, please, Philo," Madis said kindly. "I was so happy this morning when I saw that you planned to dock today."

"Meet friend Rix!" Philo said, dragging Madis along behind him. "Good with spaceships. Very smart."

"Hello Madis," Rix said, carefully avoiding her eyes as he got close. Madis tapped fingers to her chest and bowed slightly. It was a move easily replicated so Rix followed suit.

"Welcome to Dralli Station. I see here that you are a recent immigrant. Welcome to the Galactic Empire!" Madis said with excitement.

"Thank you, Madis!" Rix answered.

"Rixy made spaceship parts," Philo said. "Made own patterns."

"Is that right?" Madis said with a smile as she looked between Philo and Rix and then down at a tablet she held. "Oh, that's unexpected. You *did* create your own patterns and those will complete in two hours. And, just because I like you so much, Philo, I'll have those parts delivered right to your ship."

"Mads is best!" Philo said. "Have foods with Philo?"

"I told Dad you were arriving this afternoon, so I'm yours for the day!" Madis said, smiling widely. A low nap of bright green fur covered most of Madis's body aside from her face, neck and the visible part of her chest. She wore a short-legged jumper that sported a variety of similarly bright colors.

"Philo go now?" Philo asked, looking expectantly at Kel.

"Can you have him back by 0600 tomorrow?" Kel asked, looking at Madis directly.

"Oh, that's perfect!" Madis said. "I have a shift starting at 0800."

"You could make it 0800 if that's easier," Kel said.

"Yes yes!" Philo said enthusiastically and then he bounded off, pulling Madis along behind him.

"That was unexpected," Rix said as he and Kel watched the two bouncing through the docking bay, holding hands.

"Philo gets along well with Xandarj and Madis is his favorite," Kel said. "How about we get you some street clothing and then we'll head down to The Trailer. I have orders from some folks back home. We'll see if we can find what we're looking for."

"That works," Rix agreed. "Where's the clothing store?"

"Did you pick out a pattern you wanted?"

"Pants, a top and some boots," Rix said. "I couldn't find socks, though."

"I'm not familiar."

"They go between feet and boots. It's kind of gross if you don't wear them."

"I ... well, I'm not sure we have that. The shoes keep themselves clean, so I don't know about gross. And that's right over here," Kel said, leading him along a painted path on the docking bay deck to one of the soaring walls of the station. "Just palm your hand, it should recognize you since Beverly registered you."

"How does it get my clothing here? Do we wait?" Rix asked,

pressing his hand against the security panel. No sooner had he pressed his hand in place but did a door open with a pair of denim jeans, and a lightweight shirt folded beneath and a pair of boots behind it. "I don't get it."

"Beverly knew where we were docking so this was the obvious choice for your textile manufactory," Kel said, pointing at an alpha-numeric designation right above the window and security panel. "There are only four of these in the docking bay, so even if she missed, we wouldn't have had to walk far. You can change in the restroom, right over there."

Rix struggled not to feel completely out of place as he walked by himself into the facilities accompanied by various aliens of different shapes and sizes. Recognizing a Fimil, he struggled not to stare at the elephant nose as much as he'd struggled not to stare at Madis's green fur. His head felt a little swimmy as the events pressed on him and he was thrilled when he found a stall where he was able to close and lock the door.

"Are you okay in there?" he heard Kel call a few minutes later.

"I just need a minute," Rix answered.

"It's a lot, I get you," Kel said. "Take your time, I'll be outside."

It took Rix ten minutes before he'd gathered himself sufficiently to change out of his spacesuit and into the street clothes. That the clothing fit perfectly and the boots were comfortable was a welcome surprise. Finally, he mustered the courage to rejoin the menagerie that was Dralli Station.

"Your face lacks the coloring I have grown used to, is that signifi-cant for your species?" Kel asked.

Rix considered playing it cool but decided to be honest. "There's a lot going on. I'm adjusting. There are sometimes physical signs."

"You're probably as hungry as I am," Kel said. "I know this great place that's not far from here."

"Okay," Rix said weakly.

As they walked, Kel reached over and grabbed his hand without saying anything. Her hand was warmer than Rix expected, and he found that comforting. She didn't talk as she led him through the tall corridors until they reached the entrance to a shop called Cracked Cask.

A chime in Rix's ear caught his attention but he decided against reading whatever notification his HUD wanted to share with him. The pub's layout was surprisingly familiar as they passed booths and tables where patrons sat with tall towers of colorful fruits and chatted happily. He wasn't certain why Kel chose the booth she did, but he happily slid in and found that he could finally relax.

"You're doing well, Rix," Kel said, "In your position, I'd be completely freaked out."

"That's exactly how I feel," Rix said.

"Do you want me to order the food? I think I know what you'd like here, given what we've had on the ship," she said. "I've already checked. Nothing on the menu will poison humans."

"I suppose that's reassuring," Rix said.

"Hang on, I'll order." Kel's eyes got glassy, which Rix recognized as her tuning out so she could interact with her own HUD. Rix decided to check his notification.

"Hey, that's cool," Rix said, reacting to his notification.

"Cool? What's that?" Kel asked.

"I just sold a five-pack of the pattern I put out there for the matrix shroud," he said. "I think I just made twelve credits."

"Show me."

Rix pinched the data from his HUD and flicked it at Kel. For a moment, she concentrated and then dismissed the screen. "Look at you! You're a productive member of society!"

13

CROSSED

"This restaurant isn't that different than back home," Rix observed, setting down a utensil that was roughly the shape of a small fork. "The fruit is beyond good and maybe the drinks don't have the same punch. I don't know what I was thinking. And the people, these Xandarj, sure, lots of colorful fur but they're just not that different where things matter."

"What were you expecting?"

"Well, we're talking about aliens," Rix said. "Shouldn't it be more, you know, *alien?*"

"Oh, that," Kel said. "There's a theory that we all came from a common DNA seed and that's why we're so similar. Another theory is that evolution makes obvious choices and our shape is what survives the best. Truth is, we don't know why the species are so similar. You can trust this commonality isn't lost on the deep thinkers of the Galactic Empire. There are as many theories as there are species. Probably more."

"Is this a booty call stop for Philo?" Rix asked. "He seemed happy to see Madis. Or does he have a different girl at every stop?"

"He's quite friendly," Kel said.

"That makes me smile."

"Same."

"Where is this Trailer you're referring to?" Rix asked, noticing they'd come to the end of their meal.

"First level. Since you have twelve credits to your name, dinner is on me," Kel said. "Oh, and I know I owe you for the repairs. I just need to deliver our load so I can get paid before I can take care of you."

Rix nodded. As a businessman, he found Kel's words suspect. Taking off on a trip without money for incidentals like repairs seemed unlikely. Either she didn't have the money and was running on a shoestring, or she did and he was being strung along. Given the poor repair of *Calypso*, he was inclined to the former.

"I'm not sure we settled on a price for ruining my life and absconding with me off to space," Rix said flatly.

"You're right," Kel said. "Me showing up the way I did crapped up your life. For the record, Dravari shot up your shop, though. I was just looking for repairs you advertised. I feel badly that they did that to you, but don't be confused. That wasn't me."

"But you were running from the law. Doesn't that make you culpable for what happened next?"

"Dravari are the scourge of the Galactic Empire and they only have legal standing because of the treaties signed to bring our quadrant into the empire. They don't follow any of the *actual* Galactic Empire laws and they get away with it for the sake of peace. Meanwhile, people like me and the others back on Patience Station are being strangled to death by their taxes and regulations that are put in place to make sure we can barely hold on. It's completely fine if you want to blame me for ruining your perfect life, I get that, and you're right, but get your head out of your ass with Dravari. They ruined your life because you're meaningless to them. I'm going to The Trailer now. I'm done with this conversation."

Rix grimaced. He'd definitely poked the bear in a sensitive spot. The whole idea was confusing. He'd lost his business and his home because this alien woman had chosen to believe a stupid print advertisement that no one on Earth could have misconstrued.

In a huff, Kel stood up from the table and swiped a thumb across a terminal embedded into the table surface. Wordlessly, she turned and walked quickly from the pub, leaving Rix to figure if he wanted to follow along or choose his own adventure. Scanning the room, he saw only aliens and quickly decided to follow along.

"Hold up, Kel," he called, jogging to catch up with her.

"Fine," Kel said, slowing but only enough so he could walk half a stride behind her. Arriving at an elevator bank, Rix followed the narrow, angry woman into the car which dropped quickly and stopped just as fast.

The first thing Rix noticed about The Trailer was the vastness of the open space. Incorrectly, the word "trailer" had suggested a small enclosed object that could be towed. Like the open air bazaars he'd seen in northern Africa during the war, hundreds if not thousands of vendor stalls were set up, separated by colorful tents and temporary walls.

"Gold chain for your sweetheart?" a thin alien with brooding, sallow eyes asked, holding three lengths of chain over a hand covered in mottled purplish bruises.

"No, thank you," Rix answered. The alien's eyes grew wide and it advanced.

"Knock it off," Kel growled, grabbing Rix's arm roughly, pulling away from the vendor.

"What are you doing?" Rix asked.

"Until you get better at identifying alien species, you stick with me and avoid eye contact," she said.

"I thought that was with big Xandarj males," Rix said.

"Listen, Banner, this isn't your world. Not everything is safe and clean. You're my responsibility and as long as that's the case, you do as I say if you want to stay alive."

"That guy was going to kill me?"

"No, but there's nothing he's selling that's real. Graveborn are notorious thieves."

"You can't judge an entire species like that," Rix said, recoiling.

"Most of the time, I'd applaud your naïveté in this, but Graveborn are a special class of bad news," she said. "Dammit, Banner, just don't make new trouble for me, would you?"

Rix sighed. "Lead on. I'll try not to make trouble."

"We're going to see a Xandarj woman, Abistel, about some woven material. Her family works with fibers from the planet and makes material she uses."

"Abistel? Why wouldn't you just use the manufactory for fabric? I thought that was the point."

"Not everyone can afford to use a manufactory. Patience Station has two of them and they have very high fees because their queues are always full," she said. "Clothing is never a priority. Abistel's clothing is special."

"Lead on."

Winding through the throngs of shoppers, Kel expertly navigated, finding momentary gaps of open space and sometimes tailing others moving in the right direction. After twenty minutes, the crowds had significantly diminished and finally, Kel slowed as she approached a humble vendor booth where there were hundreds of rolls of brightly colored materials piled everywhere.

"Kel of Patience!" a friendly voice called out just before a short Xandarj female with bright cobalt blue hair came swinging out from behind a curtain, landing on a table so that she stood even with Kel. "Oh, my beautiful friend, I have awaited the gift of your arrival with much anticipation!" The odd pair embraced for long enough that Rix started to feel uncomfortable.

"Good to see you, too, Bopar! I brought three crates from Abistel, were you expecting them?"

"Oh yes. I have promises to buy several of the garments already. Let me send my children to recover these from your vessel this afternoon," Bopar said. "Is this one with you?" Bopar asked, looking at Rix.

"Rix Banner," Rix said, holding out his hand as if to shake.

Bopar looked quizzically at his hand and then tapped the top of it with her index finger. Once she'd done that, she looked at Rix for approval. "I am Bopar. I see you are an immigrant from Earth. I've never seen a human due to the quarantine, has that eased?"

"No. We don't have a lot of spaceships back home," Rix said. "Those with transition engines are even more rare, I suppose because we haven't discovered them yet."

"You're a funny one," Bopar said, smiling as she tapped Rix's nose in the same way she'd tapped his hand. "But, you look quite uncomfortable."

"My apologies," Rix said. "This is my first space station. Local customs aren't particularly obvious."

"You'll catch on soon. You seem like a bright one," Bopar said and turned back to Kel. "Did Abistel wish to purchase more of the fabric?"

"No," Kel said, a worried look crossing her face. "She's low on funds just now and hopes to purchase on my next trip."

"I am sorry to hear that," Bopar said. "Patience Station still suffers under Dravari's heavy hand. I wish things were different. I understand they were threatening an incursion. Is that still a possibility?"

"We've heard the same rumors," Kel said. "Dravari manage a blockade of the jumpspace lanes for commercial Galactic Empire trade, nothing beyond that at least right now. Patience Station would be too expensive for them to consider raiding us. Besides, what would they even gain? We're a poor station that's out of the way for commerce."

Rix listened carefully but didn't participate. Kel had promised him a home on Patience Station, if only a temporary one. Knowing what he was getting into was top of his priority list.

"Stay safe, Kel Warp," Bopar said solemnly. "You are a beacon of light in the darkness."

"You are too kind and even more generous, Bopar. We'll meet your kids in the Bazer docking bay in a couple of hours to help unload Abistel's wares," Kel said. "Let's go, Rix, we have a few more stops to make. It was good seeing you again, Bopar."

Kel didn't hesitate and started out once again, moving through the vendor stalls at a quick pace that Rix struggled to keep up with. It didn't take a local to recognize that they'd moved well out of the main selling space of The Trailer and that the clientele was significantly downgraded. Rix kept his eyes down but moved his head in such a way that he monitored those nearby with his peripheral vision.

"Stay here and don't get into any trouble," Kel instructed when she arrived at a booth where the tattered material of the walls was faded and pungent smoke hung heavy in the air. Scanning the area, Rix found they were alone, at least in visual range, but the sound of low voices murmuring and feet shuffling behind fabric panels indicated they were anything but alone. He nodded understanding and set his back to the booth's outside wall as Kel moved a flap and slid inside.

"Kel of Patience," a man's greeting floated through the door. "I did not expect to see you this soon."

"Or ever," Kel finished for the man. Rix had spent enough time learning Kel's various moods and he was certain she had no love for whom she was speaking with.

"Where is it?"

"Someplace safe."

"That's not how this works. You bring me the device, and you get paid."

"What's to prevent you from taking the device and neglecting to pay out?"

"My good nature."

"So you see the impasse, then," Kel said dryly.

"What's with the meat stick you brought along? Have you really brought protection? He doesn't look like much."

"Never mind him, do you have the money?"

"I have precious metal; you know the deal. I have no desire to have our collaborations tracked."

"Show me the precious and I'll tell you where your device can be picked up," Kel said.

"You should have brought it with you. I do not wish to be seen above the seventh level. There are those who would not treat me as I wish to be treated."

"Gorath, what are you doing!?" Kel asked, her voice suddenly tense with worry. "Rix, run!"

Rix grimaced, whatever was happening inside the tent was likely to soon become his problem. That he would run from trouble, however, wasn't something he was likely to do, though. Through the draped opening, a dark-robed figure appeared. Gray skin and pitch-black highlights on lips, eyelids and nose highlighted the alien's face. A grim grin of satisfaction lit on the alien's face as it saw Rix still in one place.

"Do not move or my weapon will see to your ending," the figure said. The voice wasn't the same as the one Kel had spoken to and true to the threat, it was holding some sort of alien looking pistol that Rix was convinced had the potential to do just as was promised. He raised his hands defensively.

"Hey, there's no need for any trouble," Rix said calmly.

"Come," the figure said, pushing Rix toward the opening.

"Dang it," Rix cursed softly as he entered a dimly lit room where Kel stood frozen in place with another of the gray-skinned aliens holding her head with a handful of her hair. With pockmarked light green skin and bloated with fat, the figure sat in a wide chair that hovered above the ground. He glared menacingly between Kel and Rix, a pistol in one of its chubby hands.

"Do I have your attention now?" the figure asked, staring at Kel.

Kel whimpered as the alien twisted her hair, pushing her forward, toward the repulsive alien. "Gondarg, I have your device. There's no reason for all this."

"You are more trouble than you are worth, Kel. Dravari have already put out a warning regarding the stolen equipment. What happened to a quiet operation? There are eyes watching you now. What am I to do?"

"Patience Station needed that unit," Kel said. "Dravari have more than they need."

"You disappoint me. You showed such promise," Gondarg said. "Send your Earth boy to get the device. I will trade your freedom for it. I assume he's smart enough to do something simple, like this."

"That's not our deal," Kel said and then whimpered as the goon behind her once again twisted her head.

14

OLD WEST LESSONS

"But it is now," Gondarg said, scooting his hovering chair forward as he leaned menacingly toward Kel. At the same time, the goon behind her increased the pressure, clearly trying to get her to cry out. That Gondarg had lowered his gun to make his threat more pressing wasn't lost on Rix.

Without thinking, Rix acted. In his world, women weren't treated like Kel was being treated. Taking a quick step forward, Rix felt a hand swipe at his back, trying to catch him. With balled fists, he punched at the side of Gondarg's flabby jaw. Shock registered on Gondarg's face as his pistol fired into the floor, the round ricocheting against several objects before embedding into the fabric wall. Rix didn't hesitate to follow up his first punch with a second and a third.

"Rix, no!" Kel cried out, but even as she did, she turned, throwing an elbow into the jaw of her captor.

Slowly, Gondarg's arm started to swing around. Rix grabbed the arm and realized that beneath the alien's considerable fat was also just as much muscle. "Oh, hell," Rix cursed. That Gondarg had been shocked by his first assault, Rix decided to change strategies and let go of his arm then slid behind Gondarg's chair while he flurried a combination of blows into the alien's head, each blow harder than the last, mostly due to a massive spike of adrenaline.

The weapon in Gondarg's hand clattered to the ground just as one of the gray skinned aliens reached him and grabbed his shoulders from behind, pulling hard. The grab was so unexpected, it sent Rix off-balance enough that the alien not only stopped him from punching Gondarg, but it also threw Rix to the ground. Thinking quickly, Rix barrel rolled beneath Gondarg's chair and lashed out, snagging the weapon that had fallen to the floor.

Heavy hands grabbed Rix's legs and pulled him out from beneath the chair. "It is your time to die," the alien's voice rasped with menace.

"Depends on how well this thing works," Rix said, swinging the pistol around and firing off a triplet of shots into the gray-skinned alien's chest. The alien's already oversized eyes widened even more as it dropped Rix's legs and reached for its chest, slumping to its knees.

"I'll kill her where she stands," growled the final alien. "Release the weapon."

Kel had not successfully separated from the gray-skinned alien that held her and was captured with an arm locked around her neck and a pistol pointed at her side. Rix shook his head, raising his pistol to point at the alien.

"Do what you want," Rix said. "She's just a job for me. Not worth me dying for. But you, you're a witness I don't need. Go ahead, shoot her, I'll finish you off. It'll make a nice clean story for the station."

"Rix, you bastard!" Kel cried out. As she did, however, she managed to move her head forward and to punctuate, she slammed her head back into the gray-skinned alien's face, crushing its nose. The gray-skinned alien's weapon discharged, striking Kel in the abdomen. Rix sidestepped and fired, killing the alien as Kel fell from his hands.

"Why'd you do that!?" Rix asked, catching Kel and bringing her to the floor. "Oh dang it, this is really bad. Beverly, can you hear me? Kel's been hurt, she needs help."

"Rix, yes, talk to me, what's going on?" Beverly's voice sounded in his ear. "Look at the wound. I can see what you see."

"What do I do?" Rix asked, with grave concern.

"It is bad, Rix. You need to get her to the nearest medical station. Where are you? I do not have access to your location data," she said.

"The Trailer? We're in the back corner, somewhere," Rix said. "How can I tell you where we're at?"

"Go out and look at the pillars above, they have location markers," Beverly said.

Rix hated laying Kel onto the floor but did as Beverly asked, even though Gondarg was starting to rustle around. With a quick peek out of the tent, he ducked back in after Beverly announced she understood his location.

"It's a distance. Perhaps it would be better to bring the emergency equipment to her," Beverly said.

"Not possible. Can't we get medics down here?"

"Station emergency response won't get involved due to your location."

"Okay, tell me where to go," Rix said, tearing a long strip of material from the wall. "This is going to hurt, Kel. I've got you, though." He wadded the cloth up and set Kel upright so he could tie a bandage around her waist and hold the wad of makeshift bandage in place. As he was just finishing, Gondarg groaned and took a deep breath.

"Shoot," Rix said. Jumping to his feet, Rix grabbed Gondarg's shoulders and pulled mightily, trying to unseat the fat alien. A strong hand slapped the side of Rix's head and had he not seen the blow coming and partially blocked it with his arm, he'd have taken quite a blow. As it was, Rix kept his feet and lashed out with another combination of blows, stunning Gondarg.

Not willing to waste time, Rix grabbed Gondarg's flailing arm and this time managed to pull him from his chair, sending the fat alien to the ground near Kel, who had lost consciousness. As the fat alien fell, the chair scooted back and slammed into the fabric wall which must have been backed to something unstable as there was a crash in the background.

Rix lifted Kel's arm and rolled his shoulders beneath, struggling to pull her into a fireman's carry. It took every bit of his strength to lift her and he stumbled over Gondarg's inert body as he dropped Kel into Gondarg's chair.

"That's handy," Beverly said with appreciation.

Rix turned and picked up Gondarg's pistol and stuffed it into the back of his pants. Pushing from behind, he struggled to navigate the chair through the bodies on the ground, but managed. The fabric door caught on the chair, but Rix wasn't paying attention to those sorts of details. With as much force as his panicked body could muster, he plowed through and in the process pulled a portion of the stall down atop Gondarg and his gray-skinned guards.

"What is this?" an alien with the body of an alligator asked as Rix pushed forward.

"Out of my way," Rix growled and was surprised when the larger alien stepped back, giving Rix the room he needed to push Kel's unconscious body through the narrow space.

"Turn left!" Beverly called as Rix ran forward. "Now right! Two hundred meters."

The urgency of Kel bleeding out wouldn't allow him to pace his response. His lack of conditioning, however, did just that and after a hundred meters, he was forced to slow his pace.

"How close?" Rix asked.

"Elevator, go to Level Twenty-Three, I'll set the car on private. It's going to use ten of your twelve credits, I apologize."

"Fine," Rix managed to answer.

Breathing heavily, Rix arrived at the elevator bank and pushed Kel into a car that already had someone aboard. A pair of female Xandarj took one look at Kel, the chair and Rix and decided they had no interest in being involved in the moment, so they disembarked.

"Level Twenty-Three," Rix demanded.

"Priority access granted," a calm voice answered.

"When we get there, you'll take a left. There will be a white room directly ahead with an autonomous medical android," Beverly said, just as the doors opened on Level Twenty-Three. "Go!"

Rix pushed Kel into the room.

"Unconscious patient identified. Move Kel Warp onto padded table. Do you need assistance with transfer?"

"No," Rix gasped, still out of breath. He then grabbed Kel and stood her up, kicking the chair out of the way and turning her around until she leaned against the table. And while it wasn't the most graceful maneuver, he slid her around until she was settled on the table.

"Please step aside for diagnostics."

Rix did as he was bade and then realized the door to the room remained open. Not knowing what kind of trouble he'd started, he closed the door for privacy.

"What now, Beverly?" Rix asked.

"You've saved her life, Rix," Beverly said. "The autonomous medical treatment is quite comprehensive and is subsidized by Dralli Station."

Rix looked on as arms came out from beneath the table and sensors were run along her body. When the time came, these same arms worked together to gently roll her onto her side. As the robotic doctor worked, Kel's body started to shift back to the softer, rounder form she'd shown him aboard *Calypso*. Cutting away much of her clothing, Rix found that he was uncomfortable watching the machine work and schooled his eyes to give her privacy.

"You're going to be all right, Kel," he said in a soothing voice as he stood next to her head. And for thirty minutes, the machine worked on her, although not as feverishly as it had in the first minutes.

"Where am I?" Kel asked groggily.

"Dralli Station, emergency medical room on Level Twenty-Three," Rix said. He'd had time to calm and was sitting in Gondarg's chair, searching its various nooks and crannies. In addition to unlabeled plastic bottles of both liquids and pills, he'd found an electronic notepad, another smaller pistol, a couple of knives, and several finger-length glass crystals. There was also food, dirt and grime in most of the nooks and crannies.

"What happened?" she asked. "Why are you here?"

"Do you know who I am?"

147

"Yes. Rix Banner from Earth. I don't remember us making it to Dralli, but apparently, we have. Was I shot?"

"You were shot," Rix confirmed. "Gondarg and a couple of his goons got a bit too frisky for my taste and the five of us struggled. You got shot in the side when you bashed your head into a gray-skinned alien."

"Is that why the back of my head hurts so much?" she asked, rubbing her head.

"I would imagine."

"Wait, we had a fight with Gondarg? That's universally bad. He is not a good person to be at odds with. Why don't I remember anything?"

"No idea," Rix said. "I saw it in the war, though. Guys got shot or blown up and they lost memories of the event. Maybe you'll get it back. Who knows?"

"Is that Gondarg's chair?" she asked, her eyes growing wide.

"I needed some way to get you to medical," Rix said.

"And you took his chair. Oh, Lords of Gavenar, this just keeps getting worse," she said. "Did I get paid?"

"No. We didn't deliver whatever it was," Rix said. "He was double-crossing you and that's when the conversation broke down. Apparently, he didn't like whatever it was you took for Patience Station, it drew too much attention. He wanted his thingamajig and was going to take it without paying whatever the two of you agreed on."

"Maybe it's not too late to make this right," she said, struggling as if to sit upright.

"Doesn't fit with what I heard in that tent," Rix said. "It was tense. He wasn't friendly."

"No, dang, that's probably right."

"How are you feeling?"

"Sore," she said.

"That makes sense."

"We need to give back his chair," she said.

"I bet he'd appreciate that," Rix said. "It's grimy and there's food debris all over it. If we wanted to keep it, it'd need a whole lot of cleaning."

"You looked through his chair?"

Rix held out a tray where he'd piled all the items he'd found in Gondarg's chair. "I'm not giving back guns. That's just bad business if you ask me. And I don't know what these are. They seem important," Rix said, pulling the finger-sized crystals out and setting them on the tray.

"Well, maybe this isn't as much a loss as I thought," Kel said, picking up one of the crystals. "Oh, hahaha, that's a big one. Gondarg is going to be out of his mind when he figures this out," Kel said.

"I don't understand."

"Credit crystals, sometimes called chits," Kel said. "Untrackable money. You can offload credits to a crystal like this and then exchange it. Galactic Empire hates it, but it's allowed under certain circumstances."

"How much?" Rix asked.

"Five hundred, four-sixty and twelve thousand," Kel said, holding up the crystals.

"How much does he owe you for whatever it is you took from that Dralli Outpost?" Rix asked.

"Twenty-eight hundred credits," Kel said.

"Can you take it from the big one?"

"Sure, we need to give the chair back, too," Kel said. "He's not going to be graceful about this, but I can't fix that."

"I know it's maybe not an alien thing that you worry about, but your clothing is cut and you're kind of showing private things," Rix said.

"See anything you like?" Kel asked, her tone anything but flirty.

"Best I could, I didn't look. Promise," Rix said.

"You didn't answer the question," Kel said, losing most of the hostility from her question.

"You're asking me if I find you attractive in a hospital bed after being shot," Rix said.

"Yes."

"Gah, you are too much, Kel," Rix said, shaking his head.

"Thank you, Rix."

"For what?"

"You didn't need to help me. I've dragged you into more and more trouble. You've been nothing but understanding and a gentleman. No one would know anything if you took this twelve-thousand credit chit and just disappeared. You could go somewhere remote. Gondarg would never find you," she said. "If you hang around me, there'll probably be trouble with all this."

"What if we put that part on his chair along with his stuff, including the credit chits?" Rix asked. "Tell him where it's at and let him know we took payment."

"I'm not sure if that would work, he'll think I'm weak and that I'm trying to get his favor by returning his money," Kel said.

"He already thinks you're weak, he wasn't going to pay you," Rix said. "You can live up to your end of the bargain, though. If he comes for you after that, your conscience is clear."

"My conscience would like thirteen thousand credits," Kel said.

"I'll let you work it out," Rix said.

"Help me to the chair?"

"Sure."

"And you really didn't look while I was unconscious?"

"At your bloody, half-naked body?"

"When you say it that way, it doesn't sound good."

"I saw a little," Rix said. "For the record, you're just as attractive as you think."

"Good, because I could come up with a different form if that was a problem."

"We're not dating, Kel. Why would it matter what I think?"

"No, you're right. That's my bad."

Rix helped Kel into Gondarg's chair but grabbed a blanket to throw over her lap, which covered up some of her nakedness and just as importantly, disguised much of Gondarg's chair.

"Back to the *Calypso*?" Rix asked.

"That's the best bet," Kel said. "And you're right. We'll deliver the chair, credit chits minus payment and the thing I stole for him from that Dralli outpost. I'm sorry to make you complicit in that job, but now I have you delivering things. I was trying to keep you out of all that, given your strong feelings on the matter."

"Well, like you've said, maybe I don't know everything that's happening around here. I don't know who Dralli are, or who those gray-skinned aliens are, or what kind of alien Gondarg is. I'm not much of a fan of being so ignorant, especially with the geo-political stuff."

"Work with Beverly, she should be able to give you a good understanding of geopolitical. The gray-skinned aliens are easy. Those are Graveborn. Gondarg's henchmen are trouble. How'd you take down three of them?"

"Just two plus Gondarg. You kept one busy while I mixed it up with Gondarg. In the chaos that followed, you got shot and I put down the other one," Rix said.

"I'm sure I have the video. I'll watch it later. Hopefully my memory comes back."

"Yeah, about that. I said some things that you might have questions about," Rix said. "I was posturing. Just keep that in mind."

"Oh, this should be good," Kel said. "What'd you say?"

"Nothing bad. I just pretended I didn't care if you got shot. It wasn't true. I did care. I do care," Rix said. "And then, you got shot. So, kind of my bad. But also, I think they were going to do worse things, so not as much my bad?"

"I will for certain watch this video and I may or may not have big feelings," Kel said as Rix pushed the chair from the emergency medical treatment room.

"That's fair," Rix agreed.

The trip down to the Bazer docking bay was uneventful, but at two hundred meters away, Rix saw a pair of Graveborn milling around near *Calypso*. "Hmm, that could be trouble," Kel said. "Most of the time, Mathad won't put up with those guys hanging around. I wonder if he sees them."

"What's our standing here?" Rix asked. "Can we just shoot them?"

"Sort of," Kel said. "If we damage any other vessels or structures with our fire, then we have to pay for that, especially if we're the initial aggressors. If those Graveborn start something, then, they're on the hook. Mathad, likes to provide a level of security and he's no friend of Gondarg's."

"Let's let it play out then," Rix said. "My guess is they'll want to intimidate. Hold this." Rix handed Gondarg's pistol to Kel, who placed it beneath the blanket with a lopsided grin.

"You're kind of a bad boy, aren't you?" Kel asked.

"How so?"

"Instead of calling Mathad, you're going to go face these guys down," she said.

"It's our trouble," Rix said. "Isn't that the Xandarj way? We're to take care of our own trouble?"

"For certain, you are right," she said. "And this is a nice pistol. Are you keeping it for certain?"

"Yup. I've got this thing about giving guns back."

"So I've heard."

Rix moved the smaller weapon he'd recovered from the chair to the front of his pants, which was still hidden since he was pushing Kel's chair. "You boys looking for us?" he called out when they were twenty meters away.

The ambient noise in the docking bay dropped significantly as the other freighter pilots, crew, and station stevedores stopped what they were doing and quieted. The tension was palpable, resembling that of an old west gunslinger showdown.

"You've got something of my boss's," one of the Graveborn snarled, his hand coming to rest on the gun at his hip.

"Sure do. Are you here to pick it up?" Rix asked, cheerfully. "And once we get Kel back on the ship, you can take his chair, too."

"That chair had important items aboard," the Graveborn who hadn't spoken first said.

"Credit chits, sure, we've got them," Rix said. "We'll give 'em back. Are you sure you want to be shouting out your boss's business across the docking bay here? I'm sure everyone here loves a bit of gossip."

"Be quiet, you fool," the first Graveborn snapped.

"Not exactly easy to figure who you're talking to," Rix said. "I'll assume that was meant for your buddy there, since I don't think you're looking to escalate things here in the open. Maybe take your hands off your weapons. Step away from *Calypso*, we'll put Kel up inside and I'll get you your things."

"What's to prevent you from getting in your ship and locking us out?"

"Definitely not your winning personality," Rix said and as he got closer, he lowered his voice. "If your boss had simply taken delivery as was the plan, this wouldn't have happened. We're not the ones running away from fulfilling the deal. That was you guys. Give me ten minutes and I'll return with whatever it was we're delivering, and you can take Jack Wagon's chair back."

"That's not going to work for us. We just needed this to be quiet," one said as both Graveborn pulled weapons.

15

NATURAL CONSEQUENCES

A flash of light filled the docking bay, and Rix was stunned to the point where he had to grab the back of Gondarg's chair to keep his feet.

"All hostilities will cease!" a loud, deep voice filled the docking bay.

"Madath, I'm guessing?" Rix asked, blinking rapidly to clear his vision. Slowly, his focus returned and when he turned, looking for the Graveborn who were no longer in front of Kel, he found them four meters away, lying on their stomachs.

"That's definitely Madath," Kel said and then raised her voice. "Sorry, Madath, didn't expect to bring trouble back with me!"

"You're in the clear, Kel Warp," Madath's disembodied voice announced. "Graveborn Jeefie and Krai, you are forbidden to enter Bazer Docking Bay for a period of three months. Leave peacefully within ten minutes or action will be taken."

"Let's get in the ship, Kel," Rix said, pulling on the handle that would extend the stairs leading up, into *Calypso*. "Can you stand well enough?"

"With your help," she said.

Together, they managed to get to the top of the stairs, Gondarg's chair left behind as an afterthought. After putting Kel into one of the soft sofas in the only crew room aboard, he returned to the open hatch. At the bottom of the stairs, the Graveborn Jeefie stared up at him as if he might attempt to come aboard.

"Hey, any chance you want to return with the device your boss was looking for? Behave yourself, and I'll go grab it. Do we have a deal?"

"There are credits and weapons, too," Jeefie said.

"Sure, I'll bring all that. If you're not both visible when I get back to this door, we're keeping everything, do you understand?"

"Yes. We will be here," Jeefie said.

"Perfect."

Rix returned to where Kel was sitting uncomfortably on the couch. "I need the thingy for Gondarg and you need to make a decision about the credit chits," Rix said.

"Under the captain's chair on the bridge, there is a wrapped package," she said. "Do not open it. I don't want you anymore involved in this transaction than you have to be. I'll have the chits ready when you get back."

"Okay," Rix said.

As promised, he found a package beneath Kel's seat and retrieved it. "Here you go, she held out her hand and offered a single chit."

"There were three of them, right?"

"One is yours, one is mine, the other goes back to Gondarg. You do know the likelihood of that chit making it to Gondarg with the same amount on it as now isn't that good."

"Those goons would cross him like that?"

"Impossible to prove the value we gave it to them with."

"Roll around with pigs, I suppose we can't complain when we get dirty."

"Earth wisdom again?" Kel asked.

"At least video the values when you hand them to me."

"If you hold them in your glove, your HUD will show the value," Kel said. "You do that as you hand them over. That isn't perfect proof, but I bet it's enough to keep those clowns from getting out of line. He's going to want his guns. I hate to belabor the point."

"Then don't," Rix said. "It's not happening. Do you have pawn shops here? I could sell it."

"They're worth a lot less without proof of ownership transfer."

"Of course."

Rix took the crystal and package and descended the stairs where the Graveborn were justifiably antsy, with Mathad's exile soon to be enforced. "Okay, one crystal with ten thousand four hundred sixty credits. The other twenty-five hundred was kept as payment, per the original deal. The chair is Gondarg's. The other nicknacks are here and the guns are staying with me." Rix emptied a small bag of the random items he'd recovered from the chair initially.

"You cannot keep the weapons," Jeefie said.

"They were used against me, I am for certain going to keep them," Rix said. "We can work this out at a future date if you're so inclined. Of course, if I have to look over my shoulder every time I'm here, I might decide that's too much stress and figure out how to deal with it. I propose we just all call this even. Don't you think Gondarg would like that?"

"He will not. You damaged his reputation."

"Well then, a couple of weapons probably won't tip the balance, then, will they?"

"No."

"Okay then, shoo already," Rix said. "Madath's wrath and all, right?"

Jeefie took the crystal and pocketed it, which Rix videoed and then the two Graveborn moved quickly until they'd exited the docking bay into the soaring hallway that led to the rest of Dralli space station.

"Well, that was exciting," Rix said, rejoining Kel, sitting across from her in an easy chair.

"I haven't been fair to you," Kel said. "I'm a disaster in your life and I'm sorry. Even with all that, you pulled my butt out of the line of fire. Why?"

"I can't decide if you're one of the good guys or one of the bad guys," Rix said. "I suppose you'll tell me it depends on the day."

"That and who you're asking," Kel said. "Hey, Bopar's kids will be here soon. Could you work on getting the big cargo bay door open? It's inset in the deck, I'm sure Beverly can show you."

"What's the work?" Rix asked.

"It gets stuck sometimes. We always manage to get it open, but last time we took off from that outpost, it kind of got snagged and we had to bring it in the hard way."

"Snagged on what?" Rix asked.

"I'm not exactly sure," she said. "Something that was attached to the station, though."

"And if we can't get it open?"

"We'll have to carry five hundred kilograms of cargo up through the center of the ship and down the stairs."

"We could get one of those gravity pallets," Rix said. "Five hundred kilograms wouldn't take more than ten or fifteen minutes if we could use something like that. I'm a little afraid to open up your hold if you hit it like you said. What if it takes me more than a day to fix it? I'm thinking we don't want to be here if Gondarg starts getting frisky."

"That's a good point. Are you sure you want to get involved in moving things by hand?"

"That depends on if you have something to carry it on which fits in the hallway."

"There's a narrow grav pallet in the hold. It should be strapped to the forward bulkhead on the starboard side."

"Care to help me identify the crates to unload?"

"Everything in that center stack. There's a blue strap over the top of them."

"Are we sure they're coming soon?"

"Bopar said they're on the way up."

Rix stood and walked aft to the hold, where he hadn't previously spent much time given its general, disorganized state and filthy conditions. As a shop owner, he'd always kept his garage bays and office areas immaculate. *Calypso* was dirty and many of the steel beams showed considerable corrosion, possibly to the point of rusting through in some locations. Like not fixing the cargo hold elevator, Rix had no intention of poking at the corrosion as it could open up a hole larger than he could repair.

"This should be fun," he said ironically as he located the grav pallet and dropped it to the deck, kicking it over to the pile of crates sitting atop a bent piece of decking, strapped firmly in place. Each crate weighed close to forty kilograms and while he was equal to the task of moving them, it was considerable work for him and the pallet would only hold a pair of them.

"Are you getting it okay?" Kel called as she heard him working up through the hallway. "I feel guilty not helping you."

"Do you have some sort of winch to keep this from flying down the stairs?"

"Winch? Can't you just walk it down and hold onto it? Strap the crates to the pallet."

Rix shook his head and walked aft, where he'd seen adjustable straps. In addition to the straps, he grabbed a length of twisted cable. After securing the crates, he looped the cable through a thick ring attached to the bulkhead opposite the open door and then to the end of the pallet. Pushing the pallet out the door he gently lowered it down the stairs by threading the cable through the ring.

"That's clever," Kel said, joining Rix in the hallway. "I always wondered what that was for."

"Well, I don't know if that was its job or not, but it worked for me. And, you're right, that elevator for your cargo hold is good and truly broken. It's fixable, but I'm going to need tools and material."

"And time," Kel said.

Rix went to the bottom of the stairs and brought the pallet back, repeating the process only to find a trio of energetic Xandarj who looked like children to him, although their small stature likely tilted his opinion in the matter. They drove an electric, multi-wheeled vehicle with a spacious bed behind an open cab.

"Kel!" the oldest of the group called out, running around Rix and clambering up, into *Calypso*. The other two chased along behind.

Unstrapping the crates, Rix returned for another load. At the top of the stairs, he paused for a moment and looked in on Kel, who, despite injuries, was wrestling with Bopar's kids and laughing with joy at the experience.

Getting back to work, Rix continued until he'd completed six and a half loads and by that time, the Xandarj kids were helping to load the crates onto their truck. "You're really from Earth? I'm Barnoie. I'm the oldest. Welcome to Dralli Station. My mother likes Kel a very lot and we love to play with Philo, but sometimes he's not here."

Rix grinned at the small Xandarj's energy. "It's nice to meet you, Barnoie. Thank you for the help loading the crates. They're heavy but you're plenty strong."

"Those aren't heavy. Sometimes we get crates that are twice that heavy. Have you moved heavy things when the gravity is off? It's much easier, but if you go too fast, sometimes it can't be stopped and that's real bad. Mom doesn't like it when we break things. She says we can't have nice things if we're just going to break them."

"My mother said the same thing to me when I was young," Rix said.

"Barnoie, we have to go! Mom is waiting," one of the siblings that had already loaded into the truck called.

"I'm coming!"

Suddenly and without warning, Barnoie lunged for and hugged Rix. The innocent gesture surprised Rix but he quickly recovered and returned the affection. "We'll see you, Barnoie."

"Okay." And with that, Barnoie bounded over to the truck and jumped into the back.

Rix climbed back into the ship and after retracting the stairs, plopped onto a chair opposite where Kel was starting to doze.

"Did you get it all taken care of?" Kel asked, not opening her eyes as she spoke.

"We did. That was heavy. Was that all clothing?"

"No, not only. Bopar specializes in exotic clothing, but she'll broker other goods, too. There are a handful of craftsmen and women on Patience Station. Anything they can pack in a crate is fair game."

"Do you have to worry about smuggling laws between planets?"

"Not so much with Xandarj. What must you think of me. Are all humans this narrow-minded?"

"You're just grumpy from being shot," Rix said. "I think it's reasonable, if I'm going to live here, to know what the laws are. I don't even know what someone would smuggle."

"I guess I am a little grumpy, but you've been judging me a lot, too."

"You're right. I'm sorry. I don't know anything about this universe and it's not fair."

"Thank you," Kel said. "Oh, and this is for you." She held out one of the credit crystals and handed it to him.

"What's this for?"

"Like it or not, you were part of the Gondarg deal and I pay my debts, well, what I can," she said. "There are two hundred credits on there. I think that's fair payment for your part in the deal."

Rix studied his HUD and found that the credit crystal was loaded just as she'd said. "So I just carry this around with me to make payments for things?"

"That's right. When you use it, you can transfer any amount you want as long as the person you're giving it to has a chit. And before you ask, chits are not expensive, when you get a chance, collect a few, that way you can transfer the right amount to an empty and give it as payment."

"Good advice, thank you."

"See, I like you when you're polite, which is most of the time," Kel said. "Want to play some cards? I don't think I'll want to go out to dinner tonight since I'm not sure what Gondarg's response will be to how things went down."

"Didn't he say he wouldn't go above Level Seven?"

"Sure, but clearly his goons will. We just don't need that kind of trouble. Nobody will try anything in a Bazer docking bay, which is why I like coming here."

"Do we have things to bring back to Patience Station? What about trade items to sell?"

"Sometimes I get crates of the popular fruit. I hadn't thought about that, but I think it's a stellar idea. Any more sales from the part pattern you put up for sale?"

Rix's eyes unfocused as he brought the HUD up. "Will you look at that," Rix said.

"You sold more?"

"Yeah, I'm getting about two and a half credits per run, one twenty over two point five is forty-eight. Forty-eight more runs. This is decent money. I'm surprised there's that much call for that part."

"You earned another one hundred twenty credits?"

"Oh, here's the detail. Yeah, total one hundred thirty-two credits, plus the Gondarg money. I don't even know what I'd spend money on. I suppose I'll need food. What would you think of me investing in fruit to bring to Patience? I could put in the two hundred from Gondarg. Will they deliver to the ship?"

"With a big enough order, they will. I'll put in four hundred and we'll split profits," she said. "I can also order a meal to be delivered since we're getting the fruit. Do you have any requests for food?"

It was early evening and besides taking a delivery for several crates of fruit and a meal, the night was uneventful. Early the next morning, Kel directed Bazer's crew to put on a load of fuel and water. It was 0730 when Philo returned home.

"Rixy! Philo happy to see you," Philo said with his usual energy.

"Did you have a nice time with Madis?" Rix asked.

"Yes yes, Madis is fun! Philo very tired. What work we need do?"

"I'm not sure," Rix said. "We've taken on fuel and water. I feel like most things are buttoned up."

"Oh, hi, Philo," Kel said, appearing in the hallway. "Glad you're back. I'd like to shove off as quickly as possible if you don't mind. I've already run the pre-sail checklist and diagnostics."

"Good, Philo sleep now."

"Good night, little friend," Kel said, ruffling the hair on Philo's head. "Rix, would you like to learn how to depart from a space station?"

"I sure would," Rix said, following Kel forward.

"First, you'll need to go outside and disconnect the umbilicus. You might ask Beverly to monitor your work so you're confident you have it stowed correctly."

"Umbilicus for what?"

"Station power, air, water and black water," she said. "Surely, you saw the big orange tube connected to the aft, underside."

"I did. I suspected power but should have guessed the rest."

"Wear gloves. Also, there's a well-known general rule when disconnecting that many first timers miss."

"What's that?"

"Keep your mouth closed when disconnecting gray and black water connections," she said. "You'll thank me some day for that one."

Rix laughed. "I suppose I will. Beverly, you'll give me instructions?"

"Yes, Rix," Beverly said, appearing in front of him wearing a head-to-foot blue protective suit with exaggerated filters in front of her face mask and elbow length gloves.

"Very funny."

Rix exited the ship and worked his way to the half a meter in diameter flexible tube that had been extended from the deck and connected to *Calypso*. Beverly manufactured a video of the disconnect process, which entailed sliding down the orange tube and then disconnecting the individual flexible pipe runs and slowly lowering them into the deck. With all of that, Rix had no trouble disconnecting *Calypso* and returned to the bridge a few minutes later.

"Good job," Kel said. "When exiting any normal docking bay or even an external pier, the communication protocol is the same. We'll contact the berth controller, this time Bazer Docking, and let them know of our plans to depart. After that, we'll contact Dralli Station to get permission to enter local space. They'll give us a departure window and an initial vector that will keep us free of local traffic and lead us out of controlled space. In some larger systems where there are more vessels, there could be a transfer from local space of a station to another traffic control, like Fimil-2 and Marska. Their controlled space extends all the way out to the jumpspace transition point."

"Because of population?" Rix asked.

"That's right. And you need to stay within your given vector or they'll pull you out of the traffic pattern where you could be forced to sit for hours waiting for an opening."

"Gotcha."

"Bazer Dock Control, this is *Calypso* requesting permission to disembark," Kel said and then muted her radio. "Also, you need to have all your bills paid. Vendors can report a ship as having debt and you won't get clearance until that's resolved."

"*Calypso*, you are cleared for departure." On the tactical display, Madis Bazer's face appeared with a big grin. "Safe travels, Kel. Bring my boy back when you can, okay?"

"Sure will, Madis," Kel said.

"Patching you over to Dralli Station with a pending departure request."

"Appreciate the hospitality."

"*Calypso*, your departure window is attached. Safe journey to you. Please return soon," said a disembodied voice.

"See the communication line on the tactical display?" Kel asked, pointing to the words they'd just heard from Dralli station. "This little icon tells you there's an attached navigation plan." Tapping the icon caused the navigation display to update with a timeline for departing and a heading upon exiting the docking bay.

"Slowly lift using gravity repulsors, we don't need much, just another meter so we clear the lip of the bay doors," she explained.

Having virtually no experience with the ship, Rix very slowly used the controls to lift *Calypso* as directed. Once he'd reached two meters, he started rotating the ship, so it pointed directly at the exit. Once he'd completed both, he looked at Kel for reassurance. "Good so far?"

"No complaints," Kel said. "Take us out at two meters per second."

"Turn right and up once we're out?"

Kel shook her head with slight disapproval. "Starboard fifteen degrees with twenty degrees of inclination once *Calypso* is five hundred meters clear of Dralli Station."

"Right, sorry." Rix's heart hammered in his chest as he struggled with *Calypso's* controls. "I'm slipping around all over the place. It's like I'm on a bed of hot butter here."

"Smaller adjustments, you're doing fine," Kel said.

"I just barely missed that blue spaceship."

"Seven meters clearance. I'm watching. Don't sweat it."

As *Calypso* lumbered toward the opening, Rix started to get a better sense for the controls and they passed through the light blue photonic barrier which held atmosphere within the station. Seeing what looked like a big drop-off, Rix felt almost panicked as they passed through. That *Calypso* didn't plunge over the edge felt wrong to him, but once he was fully clear of the station, the falling sensation settled.

"Accelerate to forty meters per second," Kel instructed.

"Okay."

"Generally, a good practice is to repeat what you've been told instead of saying okay. In that case, you could respond with—*Aye, aye, forty meters.*"

"Aye, aye, forty meters," Rix said.

"Perfect. We'll turn in fifteen seconds."

"Turning in fifteen."

"You're a natural."

"Funny."

16

PARTNERS IN CRIME

"How can this be worth your time? We've been sailing for weeks," Rix said as they approached yet another jumpspace transition point.

"There isn't a huge expense in these smaller ships," Kel said. "Fuel is nearly free, so I just have to cover the cost of food, which I'd need to do no matter where we're at. Maintenance is a thing, but mostly I've been lucky with that, at least until recently."

"You've made what? Forty-five hundred credits total? What are your expenses?"

"That's a personal question, don't you think?"

"I'm trying to make sense of the economy I'm entering. I saw the fuel prices and I agree, inexpensive, but even so, this trip burns two thousand credits in fuel. Food is maybe another six hundred credits, which should probably be more like twelve hundred, but you rely on powdered meals."

"Those are nutritionally complete," Kel said.

"Sure, okay, maybe that's how you all eat. It's just not what I'm used to," Rix said. "You had docking fees for another five hundred and then you bought fruit and I imagine you have to pay Philo something. When I look at this sheet, I think you're clearing maybe three hundred credits."

"You haven't factored in what I owe you," she said.

"What's your thought on that?"

"I imagine you have your own expectations."

"I've been running my garage for quite a while and there's a skill you develop when you fix people's rides. Want to take a guess as to what that is?" Rix asked.

"A person's ability to repay?"

"Got it in one," Rix said. "My guess is you run close to the line on expenses vs income. Further, I'd wager you have debt that's forcing you to take unsavory deals like with Gondarg. Risking your life for twenty-five hundred credits gives me an idea of the value you place on that amount. With three hundred, plus what we get from the fruit, you'll probably have to get creative with whoever holds your debt, which means, you'll be just slightly less broke, but broke, nonetheless. I'm not saying this to insult you, but so we're on the same page."

"You don't need to be so condescending. I know I don't have a lot of money."

"That breakdown wasn't meant to be condescending. I'm sorry it came across that way," Rix said. "I've looked up prices for repairs at several major cities and did the same for smaller hubs. If I were an accredited mechanic, which I am not, your bill would be close to fifteen thousand credits."

"That's robbery. I don't have that kind of money."

"Let's take some of the emotion out of the conversation. I'm trying to establish a baseline so we both can agree what a fair price is."

Kel sighed. "Fine, go ahead."

"Now, my repairs on the engine aren't permanent, so that affects the price, my repair to the inertial system is, and the gravity repulsor fix is somewhere between permanent and otherwise. Again, if I was an accredited mechanic for those components, a more realistic price is closer to twelve thousand credits. I can't put a value on you blowing up my life, so I think that's more of you owing me a lot of consideration with respect to helping me get settled, whatever that looks like, and yes, I understand, you don't have money for that."

"You're so emotionless in this conversation. Is this how you really think?"

"People put a lot of emotion behind money," Rix said. "I don't get it. It's just a tool that represents value."

"What do you mean consideration for helping you get settled?"

"You have connections, friendships and knowledge that I don't," Rix said. "The consideration I'm talking about is you leveraging those things to help me get established. You also have a spaceship, which I might need space on at some point in the future, and I'd expect the friends and family discount, as long as I'm not overly hindering your own business."

"You're a scoundrel," Kel said. "You've got your hooks in me and now you're going to bleed me to death."

"That wouldn't do me a lot of good now, would it?" Rix said. "In that you owe me, it's in my best interest to help you be successful, otherwise how will you pay me back? Like it or not, we've become partners, linked together by fate. If I remove the lens of business and think about this personally, I like our position in this. Despite my reservations about the kind of work you do, I find you to be both honorable and very likable. You're smart, otherwise you wouldn't have figured out how to procure a spaceship and sail it. I'm excited by the potential of our partnership. The two of us are stronger as a team than we are separated."

"You really mean that, don't you," she said. "I just can't figure you out. On one side of your mouth, you're telling me I'll be in debt to you for the rest of my life, living just slightly better than a slave. On the other side, we're a power couple, ready to take on the universe. Those are mixed messages."

"Why don't you think on things and you can tell me what you think after that," Rix said with a shrug. "Tell me where you think I'm off base or being punitive. Also, when will we get updated communications? I haven't seen an update on that part I was selling since we left Xandarj."

"The Korgul government is part of Dravari, so I've been sailing communication-free, otherwise Dravari would know we're in-system and we'd be at risk for them chasing us down. Argon is also under Dravari control, so, we're looking at another ten days, before we're in Narlux-4 system," she said.

"Narlux-4 is Dravari, too, right?" Rix asked.

"Yes, but Patience Station is in the Surnak asteroid belt. No Dravari patrol is about to follow us into the belt," she said.

"Why not?"

"Dravari are hated by everyone," she said. "Pirates, privateers and heck, just freedom-seeking refugees are hidden all over the belt. It takes about nothing to set up a turret with a fat energy pack and put it on auto so it targets Dravari patrols. And trust me, there are hundreds of those turrets that've been set up."

"I'd think Dravari would put together a big force and clean out the belt," Rix said. "Back home, the idea that a piece of a city or country is allowed to run itself isn't really a thing."

"Are you certain of that? Are there not places in your big cities which your law enforcement avoids? Or parts of your country where it's well known that it's unsafe to travel?"

"Well, I suppose you're not entirely wrong in that," Rix said. "And with the distances and times involved for transit, it'd be just that much more difficult. Dravari could target big installations like Patience Station, though, couldn't they?"

"Why don't you hold judgment about what's possible for when you actually get a chance to see where we're headed?" Kel said. "Patience Station is deep in the thickest part of the asteroid belt. Just getting there is dangerous for ships of any real size."

"I'll spend some time learning about Narlux-4. It sounds like I'm making assumptions that aren't working," Rix said.

"What have you been reading? I've watched. You haven't put down your reader since we started the trip."

"There's so much," Rix said. "Being interested in mechanical things, I started by getting high-level overviews of the ship's various systems. You won't be surprised to learn that there are hundreds of systems keeping *Calypso* in business. And, every last system is complex, something I'm not sure is a compliment."

"They're complex because we have synthetic intelligence to diagnose and fix problems. They're not made to be fixed by Earth mechanics," Kel said.

"As far as I can see, the current system of spaceship ownership and repair has an awful lot to do with keeping the original manufacturer well paid for repairs. I'm all about getting quality parts and not sacrificing, but you all have made an art out of keeping the expenses high. It's like that engine fix. Caraga Industries would have us purchase an eight-thousand-credit subassembly when my ten-credit part fully fixes the problem."

"Your piece isn't sanctioned by Caraga, though, so most people won't buy it."

"But, by including full instructions with my replacement part, I've made it just a little easier for people who have no other options and can't afford the eight-thousand credits."

"You want to open up a garage, just like you had back on Earth, don't you?"

"Well, like you said, I don't know what I'm getting into on Patience Station. Are there other mechanics?"

"Several."

"Are they good at what they do?"

"It's a small station and it takes forever for replacement parts to get shipped. They do what they can."

"You're saying they have a built-in excuse for sub-par work."

"I suppose."

"That sounds like a perfect opportunity for us."

"Us?"

"What does a legit captain's license cost for freighter work, so you can access the major trade lanes?"

"First level is twenty-five thousand credits. That lets me sail a deep space vessel capable of hauling twenty-five tons."

Rix whistled in response to the number. "That's a lot."

"I know."

"How many tons can you put on *Calypso*?"

"Fifteen if it's well packed. The engines and superstructure aren't rated for more, and really fifteen tons is pushing it."

"On Earth, our overland hauling has a lot of options. Local trucks are a lot smaller than long-haul. Is there any sort of license for an intersystem freighter? Narlux-4 has several cities and stations with spaceports that are set up for trade."

"*Calypso* is flagged for suspicious activity in Narlux-4. If we get boarded with illegal cargo, the cargo and the ship will both be impounded. It's a virtual guarantee that *Calypso* will be boarded every time it gets near any decent-sized port within the system."

"But no arrest?"

"I'm not sure. I don't know if Dravari have us for this last job for sure or not. They'll have their scans, which shouldn't match, but who knows what they have on us for sure."

"That is a pickle," Rix said.

"Let's get back to the partner conversation. How did we become partners, again?"

"We have a mutually beneficial relationship," Rix said. "What kind of debt do you have?"

"Again with the personal questions."

"I'm just trying to calculate things out. Is it really that important to you that I don't know your debt? I'm not trying to take advantage of you. What I'm trying to do is figure out how we can use the skills we both have to not just survive, but to also thrive."

"Why would you throw in with me? I'm not exactly winning at life."

"But you could be, with a little help and a partner that wants to see you succeed," Rix said.

"You're a strange man," Kel said. "I owe forty-seven thousand credits on *Calypso* and another fifty-two hundred that I've racked up trying to survive. I'm six months behind on the mortgage for *Calypso*."

"So about three thousand credits a month?"

"Fifty-two hundred."

"What?" Rix "That's like twelve percent interest."

"I have late fees that are tacked on."

"That's a terrible loan," Rix said.

"I didn't have any collateral."

"*Calypso* is collateral."

"I don't know. Those were the terms and it was the only way I could get a ship so I could pull myself out of the trouble I've buried myself in." Tears formed in Kel's eyes and she started to quietly cry. "I'm such a loser. I can't do anything right and when I try, I make it worse for everyone."

Rix reached across the distance between the two chairs and picked up her hand. "You've had a tough road, haven't you. I'm sorry, Kel, I really am."

"Why are you being nice to me?" she asked after a few minutes. "I owe you and now you know I can't possibly pay you back. I've messed up your life. You should hate me."

"I don't hate you, Kel," Rix said. "I think you're a good person who's been put into a ridiculously tough spot. I'm sorry I'm a jerk when I talk about things. I'm not trying to be mean, it's just the way I think about things."

"No, that's the problem, you're not mean at all," Kel said, her voice quavering as she tried to talk. "You should be mad at me and you're being nice. I don't deserve you, and I don't understand how you can be so upbeat. Thank you for being nice. I know I've been grumpy."

"How about I become a silent partner in *Calypso*?" Rix asked.

"What do you mean?"

"I'll buy half of *Calypso's* debt, you continue to operate her however you like, I share in the profits," Rix said.

"There aren't profits, every credit earned goes to paying debt. If Vigno calls the loan, we won't have *Calypso*, even."

"So that's our first order of business as partners," Rix said. "We need to get the loan current or get Vigno to give us some breathing room."

"That'd be a fun conversation," Kel said sarcastically.

"Not a good person?"

"Nailed it in one," Kel chuckled darkly.

"Partners?"

"This is a terrible decision on your part, Rix."

"Are you open to a conversation about *Calypso*?"

"What about her?" Kel asked suspiciously.

"You don't have to do that," Rix said. "I'm asking questions and trying ideas on for size. I'm not saying we need to do anything, but I'd like to understand where your head is at in things."

"I'm not sure I'm going to like this conversation but go ahead."

"What's your number one priority for repairs or refurbishment?"

"We can't afford anything like that."

"I fully agree. Today and for the foreseeable future, we can't afford non-critical repairs."

"We can't even afford critical repairs."

"Sure. Humor me."

"The hull needs resurfacing. We have a lot of damage where we haven't filled with alloy. And, where we've filled, we haven't polished the outside. There's a machine available on Grevlox that we could rent, but that's an intersystem trip that could put us in front of Dravari patrols."

"Okay, what I heard is we need to get you a short-haul freighter license for Narlux-4."

"And if I get arrested?"

"I'd be with you, so the question is, what if *we* get arrested? Wouldn't Dravari have to notify you if there's a warrant out for you?"

"I don't know."

"Okay, then step one, we need to figure out if you have an outstanding warrant, or anything related to *Calypso*."

"*Calypso* or the phantom image that we project for the Dravari sensors."

Rix typed as Kel was talking. "Good, got it. Any idea what the process is for that short-haul license?"

"Twenty-five hundred credits."

"Doggone, licensing is ridiculous. Okay, so twenty-five hundred to test short-haul deliveries. How are you at figuring who has product to deliver to or picked up from Grevlox?"

"Well, I guess I haven't really asked. It never mattered since I couldn't afford the license."

"Man, we need money and soon. Without it, we're just spitting into the wind, aren't we?"

"I've been trying to tell you this."

"You've been relatively patient, I agree. I believe our partnership's first objectives are to get us some room on the mortgage, then get you a short-haul freighter captain's license. So, fifty-two hundred and twenty-five hundred brings us to 7,700 being our goal, if you agree with the general idea."

"That's a lot to take in."

"Agreed, and I'm not pressuring you on any of this," Rix said. "Take as long as you'd like to think about it. I've got some of my own concerns to think about."

"Like what?"

"I'm a mechanic, not just by trade, but that's what I'm interested in doing. Being a spaceship mechanic feels a whole lot like being an airplane mechanic or even an automotive mechanic. I'd like to open a business on Patience Station to that end. Are there reasons I couldn't do that?"

"Rent and tools," she said. "You'll need equipment and maybe even a small manufactory. I'd guess all that's expensive. I can put in a good word to Garba, though."

"How many people live in Patience Station?"

"Eight thousand, but it was built for four times that."

"Since there are a few mechanics already, am I going to be stepping on toes if I find a way to negotiate shop space?"

"Well, I don't know about that," Kel said. "When people hear about how you fixed *Calypso*, you'll likely get inquiries. I suppose you could just go to clients and work on their vessel in situ, right?"

"That'd work for a while, but as I build up tools, it'll get harder and harder to do," Rix said.

"I wish I could be more helpful other than to tell you to talk to Garba."

"She's someone I should speak with, regardless," Rix said. "Hopefully, I can count on you for an introduction."

"Sure, we're not overly friendly, but we talk from time to time. I imagine she'll want to talk to you regardless," Kel said. "Also, we're about to transition. You might want to strap in, you seem to get a little queasy for a few minutes surrounding transition."

"Yeah, good idea. How long will we be in jumpspace?" Rix asked.

"Three days. Now, the good news is, that once we're in Argon, we'll turn off our hull projectors and turn on communications," she said.

"If Dravari was monitoring both sides of jumpspace, couldn't they do some sort of correlation and figure out the ship that went in came out smaller on the other side?"

"Maybe, but we'd know if Dravari had a ship sitting near the jump-space transition."

"Okay, I guess I'm back to reading," Rix said.

"You make me feel a little inadequate. I've never done as much reading on a trip as you're doing, aside from reading fiction," she said. "I can't imagine what you find interesting about technical manuals related to all that technology."

"It can be dry, but a lot of your tech solves problems I didn't even know existed, so I'm learning tons," Rix said.

"Well, that's cool, what's the most impressive piece of technology to you?"

"It has to be the earwig and speech translation," he said. "I don't see how the holograms are so perfect that I'd swear I'm looking at some-thing real. Also, I don't understand how my words get translated in real time without you hearing me speak, saying the wrong words. According to the description, the headsets are using some of the phonemes and noise-blocking others, so that it feels natural. I wouldn't even know what to think if I hear a real alien."

"You can turn off the translation if that's interesting to you," she said. "In some cases, like Vred, it's a huge difference. You should try that sometime. You and I have similar organs to generate speech, so you'd just hear a foreign language."

"That's great," Rix said.

"What else?"

"Manufactories. The idea is simple enough, but it's such a complex implementation. I can't imagine how they can put it all together in such a small space."

"So you're not impressed by jumpspace transition?"

"Right, or inertial dampers, gravity repulsors, artificial gravity on demand, anti-gravity with something as simple as a pallet. Where do you even start with some of this?" Rix said. "The computational requirements for the navigation systems alone are mind-boggling. Right now, computers on Earth take up entire rooms and they're doing little more than basic math after requiring some of our best and brightest to write programs by punching holes in cardstock."

"It's fun to see my world through your eyes," she said and then turned serious. "Are you going to cheat me, Rix Banner? I know I shouldn't be asking you this, but I've worked so hard to get where I'm at and I know I'm close to losing everything, but I don't think I can take one more disappointment. I want to believe in you, Rix. I want to believe that the three of us are more than we are individually."

"We're counting Beverly, right? Did you know she's only four hundred nanometers big? How is that even possible for someone so smart and capable?" Rix said. "I won't cheat you, Kel. I can't promise that we'll succeed, but I guarantee if we fail, it won't be because I've cheated."

"You know what? I believe you, Rix Banner. I'm in. I'll talk to Philo and make sure he agrees, but yes, I want to be your partner. Together, with Beverly, the *four* of us will be unstoppable."

"Dravari, look out!" Rix said enthusiastically.

17

NARROW PATH

"Welcome to Narlux-4!" Kel said. "Now the real fun starts."

Having shifted their relationship to that of partnership, Rix had taken a new look at *Calypso*. Rust and general decay marked most of the tired, old vessel. Taking stock, he'd spent a full three days inventorying and recording hull and structural damage using a three-point scale: critical, moderate, and cosmetic. As a perfectionist, each type of damage needed repair, but as a pragmatist, he knew that focusing on the critical was the right play.

"Pellian freighter projectors are off, transmitting auto-ship identification as Grevlox flagged, D-Class freighter *Calypso*," Rix said. Given the strength of the auto-navigation systems, a pilot's time was consumed by communication and planning tasks much more than course adjustments and fine maneuvers.

"I don't care where you've been, coming home always feels good," Kel said. "I've double-checked our projections and AIS. Well done, Mr. Banner. Now it's time for some basic Narlux-4 astronomy. Surnak Belt is roughly the distance of your planet, Mars from the Narlux-4 star, or one-point-five of humanity's astronomical units. The Argon jumpspace transition point, where we just arrived, is currently three-quarters of an astronomical unit. Are you with me?"

"Sure, depending on orbital position of the asteroid belt and the stationary position of the transition point, that distance changes. Is that what you're pointing out?"

"Yes, good," Kel said, pointing at the navigational display, which she'd zoomed out to show the entirety of the Narlux-4 solar system. "We're going there. That's Church Rock, where we'll enter one of the most volatile parts of the Surnak asteroid belt. And yes, that sounds contrary to a good location for a space station, but it's not, do you know why?"

"The Guardians?" Rix asked, having already researched the route. The Guardians were a set of six massive asteroids which slowly orbited the asteroid that had become Patience Station and screened the station from free-floating deadly asteroids that were otherwise common. "Aegis, Talos, Orcus, etc."

"You've done your research. Do you have a navigation plan for *Calypso*?"

Rix pinched at his HUD and pulled the navigation plan he'd created and flicked it at Kel.

"Good. Do you feel good about our plan?"

"I feel like that's a trick question. You have a surprise or something, don't you?"

Kel nodded her head. "You can't see them, but there are a pair of Dravari patrol ships that just went out of sensor range because they're behind Moxen, the big gas giant in position four. Assuming they're orbiting, we'll see them in an hour's time on the other side. The problem with your plan is that if we don't accelerate harder, they'll have a chance to overtake us."

"And you're sure they're coming? That's a lot of travel. Does *Calypso* have some sort of warrant out?"

"No, nothing like that, but our timing is suspicious for the events on Pertaf, even though it's so far away," Kel said. "We'll see what they do and adjust our burn accordingly."

"I guess that's the value of intuition," Rix said. "I didn't even see those Dravari ships on the list of the ships sailing through Narlux-4."

"They weren't there," Kel said. "I have access to data that shows the government patrol routes."

"You could have shared it."

"It's highly guarded, so I couldn't share it yet," she said. "You build a reputation as being someone who's on the right side, you'll get access to the list. For now, I've plugged those two Dravari into our sensor watch list."

"That's fair," Rix said.

"You should have data now, though. I've unblocked our antennae."

Rix glanced at the portion of his HUD which showed incoming messages. Instead of zero unread, he had nineteen new messages, most of which were from the daily reports from the manufactory market where he'd listed his part. "Oh, boy, this is adding up," Rix said.

"Talk to me, are we talking retire to Fergy Beach Moon, adding up, or are we talking fresh ingredients instead of meal paste adding up?" Kel asked.

"Well, food is expensive out here, so I think I'm looking at being able to afford my own meal paste, O2, and water consumption for the foreseeable future," Rix said. "I'm running a balance of eight hundred forty credits, so I earned about seven hundred while comms were blacked out. What kind of return do you think we'll see on the fruit? Speaking of food."

"We'll triple our investment," she said.

"We should have bought more."

"I've done that and lost money before. There's a limited group on Patience who will buy transported fresh food. With the crates we have, we'll sell out quickly and leave a little bit of demand on the table. If we flood our market, it works against us in the long run."

"Scarcity of supply props up the price, you're saying."

"Tried and tested economic theory," she said. "What are you working on today? I saw the work you've done in the engine room, repairing the oxidation and filling all those holes. It looks nice, but that's a ton of work. Are you planning on doing the whole ship?"

"I've divided the ship into four quadrants," Rix said. "My goal is to work through what I've deemed critical within a quadrant before moving on. That hole filling and fairing wasn't exactly critical, but I wanted to see how hard it was to work with the tools we have for more cosmetic issues. It's a lot more work than I was hoping for."

"Why are you doing it at all?"

"It's part of what I like about working on cars. I didn't run a body shop, but I had plans of building one after I got ahead on the garage," Rix said. "Back home, people pay good money to keep their vehicles in top shape and looking good. This work isn't that much different. By doing the work, I can get some idea of what I'd need to charge to do the work."

"Have you looked at better tools? I know there's some sort of dealio that you can attach to interior or exterior hull and bulkheads that'll do the grinding and sanding."

"Dealio? I'm rubbing off on you. And yes, it looks like for twelve hundred credits I could run a pattern for the Spaceship Fairing Device 12A."

"Are you going to do that?"

"Not yet," Rix said. "First, I don't have the money, but more importantly, I don't have a shop, or even the tools I'd need to do basic repairs. I don't mind spending free time working at something if it'll improve an asset. I really don't like sitting around, so this works for me."

"You're earning about a hundred credits a day on that part. Are you seeing any trends, are your sales growing at all?"

"After the first four days, it levelled off," Rix said. "A hundred credits a day isn't terrible, though. It's at least a start. Hopefully, that won't dry up. It's not like what I created is that hard to reproduce."

"You're already doing better than half the people living on Patience Station," Kel said. "It might be a good idea not to talk about it too much."

"Do you see that Dravari Patrol just popped out? I think it's going to be a footrace. They used Grevlox's gravity to put on some pace coming our way," Rix said. "I'm adjusting for a max burn profile. Any objections?"

"This is gonna suck," Kel lamented. "Go ahead."

Rix accepted the navigation system's prompt asking for verification of his burn schedule adjustment. The adjustment would mean that they'd spend the next two and a half days under a heavy acceleration load, which with the gravity system working with the inertial system would just make it seem like they were on a high-gravity planet, making walking and sleeping difficult.

"This projection line shows we're going to be close when we reach Church Rock," Rix said. "They really want us."

"Yeah, they've sent a heave-to order."

"We're not masked," Rix said. "Don't you have to comply? Otherwise, you won't be able to sail without projections in your home system."

"Their heave-to has no legal bearing this far out into uncontrolled space. That also means that if they want to shoot at us, filing a complaint with the Dravari government doesn't add up to much."

"So Dravari police get away with whatever they want, then?" Rix asked.

"It works out that way most of the time."

"What if they come on to Patience Station and make trouble? How do you deal with that?"

"They don't. Patience Station is too dangerous to get to for ships the size of Dravari patrol vessels. If they really want to make trouble, they could send a small scout out and unload half a dozen troopers. Patience Station has enough to resist a few, but the desire for peace is enough that Garba wouldn't make too big a deal over their visit. I just can't afford for them to board *Calypso* with stolen equipment in the hold. Once that's unloaded, they can come talk to me all day long."

"I don't love sailing like this," Rix said, settling his head back into the headrest.

"It gets better. It's never comfortable, and I'm not sure about human physiology, but after a few hours, you'll know. Just don't expect to get a lot done, aside from reading."

"Fair enough," Rix said. "Reading it is."

Long minutes turned into hours, and hours into days. What had been a thin, barely recognizable line of asteroids in the distance slowly grew, gaining shape and definition. Nervously, they watched the Dravari patrol vessels approach a point in the distance where there would be a confrontation.

"How is this even possible?" Kel complained. "They're going to catch us just before we're safe, we just need ten more minutes. I know this is an impossible ask, but is there anything you can think of that would give us just the least bit more acceleration?"

"I've been thinking about the problem," Rix said. "You're this hotshot pilot, right?"

"I don't think I like where this is going," she said.

"I'm right, though, aren't I?"

"Yes. I'm good. Better than good. What's your point?"

"Overshoot," Rix said. "Let off the acceleration for a moment, come in hot at Church Rock and deal with the consequences. I've been looking at the obstacles on the other side of Church Rock. We're decelerating right now, which of course is just backwards acceleration. If you stop for thirty minutes, we'll reach Church Rock a massive difference in relative speeds, right?"

"I'll make a spaceman out of you yet, Rix Banner," Kel said. "And, yes, thirty minutes would put us at Church Rock with likely deadly excessive relative speed differences. You do see what's on the other side, right?"

"I do, but look up here," Rix said, zooming in the local space near Church Rock. He'd already placed navigation lines that wove through the surrounding nearby asteroids with several key adjustments that required precise timing. "If you take this path, you can lose speed while in the asteroid belt. If Dravari don't already have this plot, there's no way they could follow us in."

"Do you have any idea what you're suggesting? Nobody can navigate with that kind of precision," Kel said.

"Nobody?" Rix asked, raising an eyebrow challengingly. "Is it really that impossible?"

"I hate you in this moment," she said, leaning over to focus on the navigational plots Rix had created. "Lords of Gavenar, how did you find this? You've even taken into consideration those screaming lunkers."

Rix grinned. The term "screaming lunker" referred to hunks of ice or rock that were neither stable nor orbiting another object. In the asteroid belts, these were often born in the moment of collision between two larger asteroids. "You like it then?"

"No, I don't like it! I repeat, there are a million things that could go wrong with this plan. If I'm off by twenty milliseconds making that first turn, we'll be just an icy, fine pink mist," she said.

"I ran it a couple of times, you have five hundred milliseconds of grace. That's half a second. The plan will update based on how closely you hit it, because, of course, if you're off, that changes our position. The good news is that we're constantly decelerating by that point and every maneuver gets easier because our relative speed to the main asteroid belt just gets closer and closer."

"Maybe I haven't been clear. The reason we don't get a lot of heat from Dravari at Patience Station is because navigating the asteroid belt past Church Rock is already too risky for their pilots. You want to add a whole bunch of excessive speed to the mix and have me decelerating through an already nearly impossible route. Am I getting this right?"

"I think that's about the sum of it," Rix said. "It was just an idea. If this is beyond your skill, let's come up with something else. I'd personally prefer not to die today if I could avoid it."

"That won't work with me."

"What? Admitting we're not skilled enough for an insane maneuver that people will likely talk about for decades to come?"

"Your mouth is going to get us both killed. You know that, right?"

"Seriously, Kel, if this is too much, don't do it," Rix said, his voice changing from the banter they'd been exchanging to an earnest tone.

"I know," Kel admitted. "The problem is, I'm certain I can do this. It looks nuts, but also, I really am that good. I guess the question is, do you trust me to do this?"

"I trust you to know your limits," Rix said. "If it's any consolation, I passed this by Beverly, and she said you have this in you."

"Kill the engines, we'll coast for thirty. I just wish I could see the looks on those Dravari navigators when they understand what we're up to.

"Maybe they'll break off pursuit," Rix said.

"No, they'll follow us in, if only to pick up the pieces. They've come this far; there's no reason for them to turn around now. Let's run those simulations a few more times, eh?"

"Aye, aye, Captain, rerunning simulations," Rix answered smartly.

And for the next several hours, the pair made minor adjustments to Rix's plan as real-time sensor data provided updates to the locations and vectors of each object within the proposed navigational path.

"One minute to first milestone," Rix announced somberly. "We're a solid eight thousand kilometers ahead of the Dravari Patrol and still adding. You've got this, Kel. Just execute by the numbers."

"I can do this," Kel said, taking a moment to blow on her hands. "Trust the plan. Clear my mind."

"Kel, there's a new spaceship that was sitting behind Church Rock, it's moved into our path," Rix said calmly, although the sound of his heart hammering in his chest could be heard in his voice. "You're going to have to move around it, they can't adjust in time."

"Dammit. Dravari must have spooked 'em. We're too late to abort I need a new plan!"

Rix tapped on the navigational display, forcing it to adjust. His first solution would send them careening into an asteroid two turns down the road. His second was only slightly better, giving the slimmest of clearances.

"Be your best, Kel, we have one that works. Trust the plot," Rix said.

"We're going to hit that ship," she exclaimed as the ship that had been hidden appeared directly in their path.

"No, it's going to feel that way. You've got this," Rix said.

"Please don't let this be the one that ends me," Kel seemed to pray. "I can do this."

"First adjustment in five, four, three …," Rix counted down.

At two, *Calypso* ripped over the back of the unexpected spaceship with scant meters between them. Rix noticed a blinking communication request on the navigation panel, but chose to ignore it. Just after that, Kel lit a bow thruster while simultaneously adjusting power to the main engine. Rix stared at the screens, willing the numbers to true up.

"Frak, that was close," Kel said.

"We're off by a smidge," Rix said. "I'm modifying to make up. Turn and adjust main again in five, four …"

Kel had no choice but to trust the display in front of her and with precision borne of necessity and skill, she shifted *Calypso's* travel, falling back into sync with the navigation plan Rix had created. A loud bang from aft reverberated through the entire ship. Neither had any question as to what had happened as *Calypso's* engines were supposed to clear the current asteroid by no more than twenty meters. Being off just slightly, had caused *Calypso* to kiss the object.

"Damage?" Kel asked.

Rix looked at the engine's reported capacity. It was down by ten percent, which was not fatal but would make future course corrections more challenging.

"We'll need a bit more thrust to get through this next adjustment. It's hairy. Oh crap, aft starboard thrustor is reporting total failure. You need that for our next adjustment," Rix announced. "Five seconds!" Stress filled Rix's voice as he recognized the trouble they were now in.

Without aid of *Calypso's* navigational system, Kel tapped the forward bow thrusters after tipping them hard to the same angle. The move caused *Calypso* to rotate on its horizontal axis and placed the aft port thruster in the same place where the starboard thruster had been only moments before. She then executed the turn as planned. *Calypso's* path bent around a massive cluster of small asteroids, which, given their current speed, striking any of which would have ended their day.

"That's some ridiculous sailing, Kel," Rix said after holding his breath for several seconds as she continued to rotate the vessel and make miniscule adjustments on the fly.

"Not really a choice now, is it?" Kel asked, sliding *Calypso* into a secret, if not well-known to her, path through the Surnak Belt. "I believe you owe me a drink, Mr. Banner."

"Don't get cocky. We still have to make it through all of this!" Rix said.

"This, I could do in my sleep," Kel said, flipping *Calypso* over again and lazily looping around Aegis Asteroid, the first of the six Guardians of Patience Station. "See how calm it is behind Aegis? That's his job, keep out the riffraff. Also, without our ship ident, we'd have been tagged by the sentry cannons."

"I don't see any cannons."

"That's ideal. If you can't see them, then they're a whole lot harder to remove," Kel said. "Garba has them moved about once a year, just because of that."

"Would they shoot at Dravari?"

"Some say yes, some say no," Kel said. "Garba doesn't share that kind of information. It's need to know."

"How does anyone come out here if it's well-known you'll shoot at them?"

"It's troublesome, for sure," Kel said. "I've tied into Patience Station's sensor net. See if those Dravari are still hanging around."

Rix tapped on the navigation display and found the resolution of local space objects had increased at least tenfold. Zooming out, he panned over to where the pair of Dravari vessels had slowed to a relative speed of zero with Church Rock.

"I think they're thinking about coming in," Rix said.

"I bet they're talking with Garba, asking for permission to dock at Patience."

"Will she allow it?"

Kel shrugged. "Doesn't much matter. If they don't have the path through the asteroids, it's probably too risky for them to follow us in. We have thirty minutes on them, regardless, so it doesn't much matter. Just in case, though, once we dock, I need you to knock off our communication masts. Philo and I will take care of unloading cargo."

"He really doesn't like deep space, does he?"

"Makes Philo tired," Philo announced, joining the pair on the bridge. "Now, time for play!"

18

WUNDERKIND

Rix stared in wonder as they approached Patience Station. Instead of a free-standing space station like he had in mind, Patience Station was seventy-percent rock faced with the other thirty percent a mixture of tall clear windows, metal expanses and machinery. The asteroid, easily twice the size of Aegis, was composed of iron and silicate with a deep cavern system within. Over the decades, and with great effort, it had been further hollowed out, with each exposure to the vacuum of space covered by double layers of cladding separated by gaps so that punctures were less likely to cause atmosphere to evacuate.

"Probably the only reason Patience is possible is that big field of blue and white asteroids back there," Kel said, pointing off in the distance. Rix lifted his eyes so he was no longer focused on Patience Station but was instead looking beyond. Just as promised, the asteroids behind were a shade of light blue and even looked like they had frothy white edges to them.

"Ice?" Rix ventured a guess.

"Got it in one," Kel said. "Water is the essence of life just about universally. Patience Station separates the water into hydrogen and oxygen; both are useful for about a million things."

"Not the least of which is breathing?" Rix asked.

"You're not wrong," Kel said. "But water alone is useful. Hydrogen is used by some of the smaller installations as backup power. Of course, the solid fuel is more energy dense, but with free hydrogen, there are plenty of applications for that. Space stations use a lot of power."

"I see the big pier up there, is that where we'll dock?"

"Yes, it's a pain, but I can't afford an interior berth," she said. "I don't suppose you'd want to take a look at that aft thruster I banged up, would you?"

"Let me get that communication mast taken care of. Then, maybe you could give me the nickel tour of the station. You're going to be here a minute, aren't you? Any thoughts on where I could stay? Do they have inexpensive rooms?"

"You can certainly stay on *Calypso* for a few days," she said. "I owe you at least that much. Besides, we're partners, right?"

"Su casa, mi casa?" Rix asked.

"Yeah, I guess, did you switch languages?"

"Spanish."

"Patience Station, this is *Calypso*, returning to home port, requesting permission to dock," Kel called over comms. "Technically, I could just run up there since this is our home base, but it's good practice to ask for permissions."

"Kel! Welcome home!" came a quick reply. "We saw your little maneuver getting around that Dravari patrol. Are you okay? We saw rock dust on G-12249-A."

The mention of G-12249-A brought a visual of the asteroid they'd briefly collided with onto the navigational display. Suddenly, *Calypso* appeared and was sliding around, when its aft grazed an outcropping, tearing off a fist-sized hunk of the asteroid and sending out a shower of dust.

"Hi, Hutari! Thank you. I brought a visitor home and we have a fresh load of fruit from Xandarj aboard," Kel said. "Also, yes, we got a little cozy with G-12249-A."

"That was an insane maneuver sneaking in front of them like that. Everybody's talking about it," Hutari said.

"Oh, what are they saying—*Kel is crazy?*"

Hutari laughed cheerfully. "Some are saying that. Garba is here. She wants to know if you got the package or not?"

"It's aboard," Kel said.

"Thank you, Kel," came a much older-sounding voice. "We're running pressure at seventy-two percent, and I was just about to step that down to seventy. Now the big problem is getting it installed. Geoff says he's not sure he can get it put in. Apparently, it's not a good match for our current equipment and he doesn't know where to get an adapter. He said he'll try, though."

"Dravari, Garba?" Kel asked.

"They're sending the smaller of the two in," Garba answered. "You have twenty minutes."

"Send out a cart. We'll get the condenser off *Calypso*. Also, I'm reporting a failure of communication equipment aboard *Calypso*. That's why we couldn't talk to you until we had line-of-sight."

"That's unfortunate," Garba said. "I'll file your report, right away. You're cleared for docking. Patience Station out."

"A condenser adds O2 to the existing station air? Do I have that right? It's the business end of a scrubbing unit, if I have that right," Rix said.

"How'd you know to look that up?" Kel asked.

"It's one of the ten major systems of a space station," Rix said. "According to Beverly, at least."

"And you've read about it? That's suspicious, Rix."

"I might have taken a look under the tarp in the hold, Kel," Rix said. "I figured that since I'm aboard, not being held captive and have entered a partnership, I was probably just as liable for what you took from that Dravari outpost as you are."

"Is Geoff right, it's hard to install?"

Rix shrugged his shoulders. "I don't know what kind of units Patience has now, I'd have to see what we're looking at. Just shooting from the hip, though, these things aren't crazy complex. They're moving a large volume of air, so the mating connections are huge, which probably means they're not overly complex."

"If I hadn't seen your work, I'd say you're nuts," she said. "Would you feel badly if I volunteered you to help with the installation?"

"I'm good with that," Rix said. "Let's hope Geoff doesn't have a big ego, though. Sometimes folks don't appreciate a johnny-come-lately."

"You do know that using Earth idioms makes it harder for the translator circuits to work, right? But Geoff is a decent sort of guy. Sure, he's old and cantankerous, but at the end of the day, he wants what's best for Patience."

"Those words are so contradictory, I don't even know where to start," Rix said.

"But you're okay working with the equipment? I know you have issues with it being stolen," Kel said.

"Well, here's the way I'm thinking about it," Rix said. "If Patience Station is running at 70% pressure due to limited ability to replenish oxygen and we have a condenser that will do the job, why wouldn't we use it? At a minimum, until it's decided it's to be removed. I don't figure I have much to say about any of that, really."

"I'm glad you worked your way around all that. Philo, you're in charge of creative destruction of the communications masts," Kel said. "But, remember, we're going to want to repair them, so don't go too crazy with it, okay."

"Philo smash, but not too smash," Philo said, grinning widely. "Rixy good at fixing. Philo not break more than Rixy fix."

"I have a bad feeling about this," Rix said.

"Same," Kel admitted, tapping an adjustment to course as *Calypso* slid effortlessly into place atop a long, wide metal platform left open to space. "We can sit here for as long as we want, Rix. There's no reason not to drop the cargo elevator, if it's broken, this is where we're going to fix it."

"I'll head back," Rix said. "Is there gravity on the pier? Or do I need to equip magnetic clamping boots?"

"They're running half-gravity on the platform," Kel answered. "You won't have trouble staying in place."

Having worn a spacesuit for the last portion of their trip due to the potential for combat with Dravari, Rix only needed to engage the transparent mask to deal with the vacuum that occupied the cargo hold. Traversing the airlock, he pulled the tool bag he'd left in a cabinet in *Calypso's* hold.

"What Rixy need?" Philo asked a moment later, having followed him through.

"Persuader," Rix said, removing a two-kilogram hammer from his bag. Brandishing the hammer with a smile, he braced himself next to the bent portion of the deck that would lower to the ground under better conditions.

"Philo strong. I bang," Philo said.

"I don't suppose you'll do any worse than I would. Beverly, have him give me straight-down blows right at the corner," Rix instructed, grabbing the controls that would extend the actuators. The sound of straining metal transmitted through Rix's boots as he applied maximal force to lower the platform. "Now, Philo. Give it all you've got."

With more force than Rix might have imagined, Philo brought the hammer down, time and time again, but to no avail. "It's not working, Rixy."

"Okay, hold up a minute, we're going to need to do something different," Rix said, moving to the side of the hold and grabbing a cutting torch.

"Cutting torch bad. Make hole in *Calypso*."

"You're not wrong, bud. Stand back, though," Rix said, first heating the bent metal. "Give that a few whacks while it's just hot. Let's see if we can avoid cutting."

"Good Rixy," Philo said when the platform jumped beneath Philo's hammer.

Rix moved back to the controls and powered the actuators again. This time, with Philo beating the corner with as much force as he could manage, the platform lurched down and then fell into place, slowly lowering under the control of the actuators, as if it had always worked that way.

"Beverly, let's grab some measurements and see where we're off. I think we deformed the plate when it got bent back and things have stretched. I imagine we need a good grinder and a cutoff line," Rix instructed.

"It is as you say, Rix," Beverly said. "The platform is extended five millimeters on one end and seven on the other. Do you really intend to grind that much metal?"

"Is there another option?" Rix asked.

"Well, maybe not on Patience Station," Beverly said. "Grinding could take as long as a couple of hours, though. It is work most would not do."

"I could cut it with a torch, but I'll end up getting too much and spending just as long repairing," Rix said. "The problem is, I don't have a quality grinder. We'll have to see if there's one I can buy or borrow. I haven't seen one in Kel's tools."

"She does not have a grinder like you are suggesting."

"That's too bad, I had a bunch of them back home. They can't be that expensive, can they?"

"It is not a matter of expense. It is a matter of availability."

"One step at a time," Rix said just as a small vehicle, not too dissimilar to the one used by the Xandarj kids to haul the crates had used, arrived.

"You must be Geoff," Rix said, crossing the deck with his hand extended.

"And you are this wunderkind who can fix anything?" Over Geoff's head on Rix's HUD, details appeared. Geoff was of the Vorruk species and stood to about Rix's shoulder, but with a broad chest. Beneath the spacesuit, Rix made out thick, gray leathery skin that was pockmarked and scarred from prior injuries.

"I'm human," Rix said. "According to Galactic Empire, I'm semi-sentient, so probably not what you're hoping for. I don't mind working though. Can I help get this condenser onto your cart?"

"I was told that you would figure how to install a square peg in a

photonic barrier powered. It sure made maintenance a whole lot easier since we could work in heated atmosphere. Now, it takes too long to cycle airlocks, so we leave the shop without atmo."

"Too much power draw?" Rix asked.

"Well, I said that wrong," Geoff said. "The photonic barrier projector broke. We can't afford the replacement parts. It's dumb. The piece I need isn't big, but I don't rightly know the specs and the photonic projection pattern is complicated."

"I'd love to take a look at that later on," Rix said. "I've never worked on a photonic barrier before."

"Well, you're welcome to see what you can do. It's not doing me much good right now," Geoff said. "Do you see the big pallet jack there? Jump out and switch the trailer out for that. I'll back the trailer in first."

"Yup, can do," Rix agreed.

Five minutes later, Rix had the big pallet jack switched out for the trailer and was back inside the truck next to Geoff. "Good," Geoff said.

Rix grinned. It hadn't taken much to get his first compliment from Geoff and while it wasn't much, it was a good start.

With a little help from Rix's block and tackle set up, the two men managed to slip the big pallet jack beneath the heavy condenser. With it loaded, Geoff started the process of slowly trundling the machine along the long pier. Once clear of the platform, Rix retracted the actuators, but as expected, was unable to fully close *Calypso's* hold.

"Kel, we're off," Rix said. "The hold platform won't fully retract, but it's mostly out of the way. I need to look at this condenser with Geoff, but after that, I'll come back and see what can be done for your elevator."

"Good copy, Rix. Thank you," Kel said. "You should probably move Geoff's truck, though. We don't need Dravari asking questions."

"Yeah, that's the plan. I'm supposed to follow Geoff with the truck once I'm done here."

"Good deal, we'll catch up after I deal with Dravari, how about?"

"Thanks Kel. Good luck."

"I don't really need it," Kel said. "They can't do much to me out here beyond searching *Calypso* and confiscating contraband, which there isn't any."

It took Rix a moment to figure out how Geoff had set the little, open-air truck to moving, but with Beverly's help, he finally started rolling. He'd only gone a few meters when the back end of the truck bounced and when he turned, he found Philo swinging through the truck bed and then into the cab next to him.

"Antennae smashed. Rix fix later," he said. "Where going?"

"I'm helping Geoff install that equipment you brought back," Rix said.

"Oh, Philo get off. Geoff mad mans. No like Philo."

"That's too bad. I'd love your help."

"Rix like Philo help?"

"Of course I do. Philo is good with tools and machines."

"Aww, Rixy good mans."

It didn't take long for Rix to catch up to Geoff, who was close to the entrance to Patience Station. Catching up, Rix followed him through the large rolling door where Geoff motioned for Rix to park and follow him.

"Any trouble?" Geoff asked, but before Rix could answer, he stepped aside. "I'll have you control the jack, just follow me. And, why's he here?" Geoff said, looking skeptically at Philo.

"He's my good helper," Rix said. "We've been working on *Calypso* for the last few weeks together."

"As long as he's your problem and doesn't get in my way. You read me?"

"Loud and clear, boss," Rix said. "Philo and I are good to go."

"Rix, you need to get clear," Kel called over comms, "Dravari just set down and are already banging on my hatch. I'm going to have to let them in. There's a pair headed to the station already."

"We're moving, Kel," Rix answered and then turned to Geoff. "I don't suppose this thing has a higher gear. Dravari are inbound."

"Don't sweat that. Garba has the station on lock down. She'll meet them at the entry and run interference. We just need to make it to the maintenance elevator, and we'll be just fine."

With anxiety, Rix guided the heavy pallet jack, loaded with the even heavier machine. Following Geoff, they barely fit into the maintenance elevator and as Rix looked down the hallway, he found that a pair of white clad soldiers had entered the long hallway. He ducked back into the elevator car, hoping he hadn't drawn their attention.

19

DIRT

"Through those doors," Geoff directed, pointing right, when the large freight elevator doors opened.

Rix grunted as he pushed on the heavy machinery to start it forward again. It took some effort to see around his load and keep it from hitting the railing which ran along an open atrium on his left. Level 3 Maintenance was painted in orange on a large placard which hung from the rock hewn wall to his right. The doors Geoff indicated were twenty meters down the long hallway and Rix found that he had to keep adjusting steerage as the machine didn't track particularly straight.

"Beverly, can you bring up a high-level overview of how an industrial oxygen condenser is installed? Also, I'm feeling dizzy, could I be getting sick this soon?"

"You're suffering from what is called altitude sickness on Earth," Beverly answered quickly. "The only relationship to altitude is that Patience Station has low atmospheric pressure due to limited oxygen availability. Exertion will be difficult for as long as a few days. Lift the helmet of your spacesuit, you have a portable oxygen condenser."

Rix did as she suggested. The relief was almost immediate and even though he earned a raised eyebrow from Geoff, he didn't lower his helmet.

"Is Rixy okay?" Philo asked, catching up with him and jumping atop the machinery so he could ride along.

"Get off there," Geoff snapped.

"He's fine. He's not hurting anything," Rix said defensively.

"Vorruk can cause a lot of trouble," Geoff growled. "If he breaks anything, that's going to be on you."

Rix didn't hear a question in the conversation and chose not to answer. Pushing the unit through the double doors, Rix felt a change of temperature and humidity from the cavernous walkway open to a soaring atrium to an enclosed hallway. Looking to the wall placard, he discovered they were now in Level 3 Environmental. After another ten meters, the hallway opened up to the left into a room about a third the size of a football field and two stories tall. Large translucent cylinders and pipes occupied much of one side of the room while wide, open tubes hung over a space where there was line of machinery sitting with panels off and equipment strewn about. The sounds of water dripping from multiple locations and the musty smell of mold met Rix when he lowered his helmet upon Geoff gesturing for him to stop. To his eye, the entirety of what he was looking at was in very poor repair.

"As you can see, this unit isn't the same size as those," Geoff said, pointing to a wall of metal cabinets.

"You said that before and I'm not disagreeing. I just wonder if there's something we can do to help match things up. I'll have to open things up if you're okay with that," Rix said.

"It's not like you're going to hurt anything. Neither of those two end units have worked in the last decade," Geoff said. "We were fine with one of them being down, but now with 1 and 2 down and Unit 5 throwing codes, we're in something of a pickle here."

"Are there tools I could use? Everything I had got left behind," Rix said.

"Tools are in cabinets on the north wall. Don't take anything with you," Geoff said. "I have other work to do. Keep your hands off Unit 5.

I've been working on it. Also leave units 3 and 4 alone. For the record, what you're doing is a giant waste of time and Kel risked her life for nothing grabbing that mismatched piece of crap. It's irresponsible bringing Dravari attention out this way."

"I'll stick with Units 1 and 2, then," Rix said, glancing around the space. In the war, he'd been moved from base to base, often after combat had ravaged the efficiency of the maintenance operations. Making do was just part and parcel of how he solved problems. Getting help from Geoff would have been ideal, but the grumpy old maintenance technician clearly didn't believe Rix could help.

"Beverly, do you read the model number of this condenser unit?" he asked, moving to Unit 1.

"I do, Phegile 200, manufactured sixty-two years ago according to the serial number," she said. "Could you locate an interface scope in the tool cabinet? With that, we could look at the last run diagnostics." As Beverly had been talking, she'd appeared in a recess in the first unit, wearing work overalls and a red polka dotted scarf.

"You should try different looks," Rix said. "You keep showing up as Rosie the Riveter. It's a fun look, but you could be more unique than that, couldn't you?"

"I didn't know this was a game," Beverly said. "I was just trying to look appropriate for the task."

"Why can't it be both?"

"Ooh, intriguing," Beverly said. "I like the way you think."

"Philo, let's go check out what tools are available," Rix said, walking over to the wall cabinets. Philo raced him over and had the first set of tall doors open before he arrived. Rix's heart fell. The original organization system of the cabinet was clear, each tool having an outlined place to hang and shelves with pictures of the supplies that should be stocked atop them. The reality of the situation was significantly different with a smattering of tools strewn across the shelves and open, disorganized boxes sitting in the bottom of the cabinet. "Oh, good lord." Rix shook his head. "Beverly, could you scan and organize this? This is insane."

"Yes, Rix," Beverly answered. "Open the other cabinet as well. I'll have Philo scan and then we'll get a complete list created."

"I'm going to want to organize things before I get going too much," Rix said. "This is mind-boggling."

"Are you open to a suggestion?"

"Probably."

"I see the diagnostics scope," Beverly said. "It is in the box at the base of the first cabinet on the right side. The end of it is sticking up from the box with the large oil stain on its side."

Rix crouched and pointed his finger at first one tool and then the next until he received a familiar green flashing light. "How do I know if it works?" Even as he asked the question, he found a button on the side of the device and tapped it, causing a small screen to illuminate and a prompt on his HUD, asking if he'd like to interface with the diagnostics scope, to which he answered yes. A blank screen showed, which made sense since he hadn't connected to a condenser yet.

"Open the video that shows how to pull the shrouds off and get these panels opened for maintenance," Rix said. "Philo, can you help me locate the correct wrenches?"

"I've got them, Rixy!" Philo exclaimed a few minutes later, setting a trio of long hand wrenches next to an expanding pile of tools behind him. "This, this!" Philo excitedly held a single tool to Rix. "Make toolbag with rest, okay, Rixy?"

"Thank you, Philo."

It wasn't lost on Rix that Geoff was still in the room, albeit on the opposite side where he acted as if he was tending to a translucent pipe that had a diameter of nearly a meter and held a greenish, brownish brackish water that had a thick yellow foam atop it. Noticing Rix's attention, Geoff turned away, but didn't leave, either.

With tool in hand, Rix started cranking on connectors, which he piled in a neat row as they were removed. In all, he removed five large panels and three additional shrouds which gave him walk-in access to the guts of the first condenser unit. Not unexpectedly, the parts were covered with old grime, in some cases so badly that he had to use the equivalent of a putty knife to uncover them in order to utilize his tools. The port for the diagnostic scope was equally filled with crud and worst yet, the cap which could have kept the material out was thoughtlessly embedded in a skiff of sludge only a few centimeters away.

"What is it, Rixy?" Philo asked, crawling up next to him.

"We're going to need solvent and a small brush to clean this out," Rix said. "I'm hoping we have a parts washing station somewhere in this mess. I can't believe they use a unit this dirty to collect air for people to breathe."

"Geoff says broken. No air for people."

"Solvent?" Rix asked, reminding Philo who stood close, looking at him.

"Yes yes," Philo said, bounding off.

As Philo was away, Rix set up a trio of light posts Philo had brought along. The lights, tiny in implementation, easily affixed to the interior of the machine, provided much needed illumination. Unable to help himself, Rix used his putty knife to clean surfaces, allowing the gunk to fall to the floor.

"Here here," Philo said, returning a few moments later.

"Good work, Philo," Rix said. He'd learned back on *Calypso* that encouragement for Philo took two forms: nice words and snacks. Having brought along a pocket full of sweet nuts from their haul from Xandarj, Rix gave over a handful as reward.

The solvent Philo had found was old and cloudy, clearly having never been strained between uses. Rix wondered if it was lack of effort or knowledge that had the systems in such poor repair. In the service, the level of disorder found would probably have resulted in court marshals, or at the very least, disciplinary actions. Scrubbing away with a fine brush, Rix cleared the diagnostic scope port and made connection. The list of diagnostics errors shown were as long as his arm.

"Beverly, can you prioritize these errors?" Rix asked. "What are the things that would make this machine shut down entirely?"

"Sorting," Beverly answered. "Look now. There are five critical issues. First and foremost is the failure within the charge couplings. Four of six of them are burned out."

"Highlight those for me, would you?" Rix asked.

"Behind the panel," Beverly answered, highlighting a panel a meter wide and half that tall.

Rix set to opening the panel and soon had it set on the floor outside of the machine in his neat row of unassembled parts. Back within the machine, he looked at the complex little pieces called charge couplings. The good news was the couplings that were burned out, were really burned out, visible because of their blackened state.

"Good stuff, Beverly," Rix said. "Can you look up the pattern for replacing these? Is that something we can create on the manufactory?"

"Those parts are quite expensive to reproduce," Beverly said. "Twenty-three thousand credits, each."

"No, for one of them?" Rix asked. "That's ridiculous. Is it really that complex?"

"That is the nature of intellectual property, Rix," Beverly said. "This part is unique and specific to condensers."

"Okay, that's problem number one. What about the other four?"

"Number two is a blockage in the primary intake for the ice manifold," Beverly said.

"Blockage? Show me," Rix said. Opening another panel, Rix was presented with a large chunk of icy rock that was completely frozen to the interior of the exposed chamber. "Philo, I'm going to need some sort of heating element, a pick and a big hammer."

Rix had spent significant time learning about how oxygen condensers and concentrators worked for large installations. Not only did the unit remove impurities from the manufactured atmosphere, it also pulled oxygen directly from water, often derived from large chunks of ice, which was the only water available to remote space stations. The requirement that the ice be pure and devoid of rocks was repeated constantly within the literature, but someone had missed that requirement on Patience Station at some point.

"How long has this unit been out?" Rix asked. "And what happens to those charge couplers if they run without water in the reservoir?"

"Your intuition is correct, the infiltration of rocky sediment would lead to a condition that eventually would overload and burn the charge couplers out," Beverly said.

Philo returned and handed a length of steel that had an electrical connector on one end. Without asking permission, he set the heater in place and plugged it in. A small trickle of water became evident after a several seconds.

"That's going to take a minute, next critical?" Rix asked.

And so it was that Rix moved through the entire list of critical diagnostics and then started on the next level down. After he'd worked through the first unit, he moved to the second and found it was in similar shape and suffered from a catastrophic issue where a whole part of the machine had been removed and never replaced. As was usual, he lost track of time and was just getting back to the ice blockage when he heard Kel's familiar voice.

"What's going on down here, Rix?" she called. "You've got to be getting hungry."

"Oh, hey, Kel," Rix said while he used a mop to herd the collected water over to a drain he'd already cleared several times in the afternoon.

"You're so dirty. Are you making any progress?"

"Well, I think I can get this Unit 1 going by harvesting parts from Unit 2," Rix said. "These units are neglected, though. Just getting them running isn't enough. They're filled with gunk that we can't afford to be blowing all over the station. People would get sick."

"What about the new one we brought in?" she asked.

"I haven't even looked at it, I've been so focused on these other two, I haven't had a chance."

His answer brought a frown to her face. "But, Rix, people are suffering. We need this unit up and running," she pushed, almost whining.

"How long has it been like this?" Rix asked.

"We've been running on three for a long time," Kel said. "But now, one of those is failing. Geoff says it's a matter of time before that one fails, too."

"Who's in charge of gathering the ice for these units?" Rix asked.

"What's that got to do with anything?"

"Look at this," Rix said, gesturing for Kel to climb into the unit with him.

"I'm not going in there."

"I need you to see this."

"What am I looking for?" Kel asked, stepping in next to him, still pouting slightly.

Rix reached into the compartment where fresh ice was thawed and interacted with the charge couplers. He pulled a handful of wet gravel and sand and dropped it into a bucket that was already half full of the material.

"That is supposed to be pure water," Rix said. "Whoever harvested that ice ruined this machine. Also, there isn't a single filter inside this machine that's clean. Hell, some of the big particle filters are missing."

"Are you saying you can fix this first unit?"

"Given a week, maybe," Rix said.

"A week?"

"And some budget. We need filters, fresh solvent, brushes and small pieces for the brackets that have been busted off. I'll need at least an hour of time on the manufactory for everything. Beverly and I have been building a list."

"Manufactory time is expensive."

"Is it?" Rix asked. "Or is it the patterns that are expensive? Who owns the manufactory?"

"Fine, patterns."

"You're not tracking. I need time, not patterns. Most of what I'm manufacturing are parts that have been ruined by poor maintenance and neglect. Those parts aren't available because they want you to buy the entire assembly."

"So you make money by creating your own parts. You're a smart one, Mr. Banner," Kel said.

"You make it sound tawdry," Rix said. "I'm just trying to get this air handling system running without poisoning everyone. Haven't you noticed how bad this air smells? It smells for a reason, Kel."

"Can you put this down for a while? Dravari are finally gone, and Garba wants to meet you. She's going to make dinner. It's an important invitation. You'll need to clean up, though, you're a mess."

"Are you getting hungry, Philo?" Rix asked, looking over to where Philo had sat back on a pile of crates and fallen asleep. While his eyes were still closed, Rix suspected the small alien was tired of working and wasn't fully asleep.

"Philo big hungry," Philo said. "Rixy making Philo work hard. Not enough treats."

"Oh, buddy, you're so dirty," Kel said with affection. "Let's get you cleaned up and we'll get a nice dinner."

"How do we even get out of here?" Rix asked. "I've been on station for most of the day, if not for Beverly, I wouldn't even have known where a bathroom was."

"I thought you were working with Geoff," Kel said.

"Not so much."

"Garba said he was working down here with you, and you were going to get the new condenser installed. I assured her that you could figure out how to match up the two systems," Kel said. "Garba is a big deal here. It'd be helpful if we impressed her."

"You're going to walk me through that, huh?" Rix stated dryly.

"Hey, don't be like that," Kel said. "You've been hanging in there tough so far. We're in the final stretch here. Get Garba on our side and we'll figure out all this debt stuff, right? That's basically what you said, isn't it?"

Rix laughed as Kel walked him over to a bank of elevators. "I don't recall the Garba thing being part of my pep talk," he said.

"Aside from helping me get out of debt, what is it you want, Rix?" Kel asked, stepping onto the elevator.

"Well, up until I met you a few weeks ago, I wanted to have a successful shop, make good money from the diner, find a girl I wanted to marry and settle down in a house," Rix said.

"Right, that was clearly a dumb dream," Kel said, tapping on the panel of the elevator car, sending it upward. "What about now?"

"Wow, that was a dumb dream," Rix said, clutching his chest. "Stab me in the heart, already."

"Tell me you aren't excited about the future, Rix," Kel said. "Until you met me, you didn't even know aliens existed. Now you're a spaceship mechanic, getting your hands dirty in the guts of a space station ready to meet the mayor of an asteroid colony. I'm asking, what it is you want now? You need to fix that in your mind so when you're talking to Garba, you're focused."

"I'm not that complex," Rix said. "I like working on things, fixing things. I'd like to have a shop where I could fix spaceships and maybe space stations now. I'd like to make enough money so I can live in a nice place and maybe meet a nice girl."

"Oh my gosh, you're repeating yourself. Let me guess, you want to settle down, buy a nice house, find a girl, get married and have little Rix Banners running around. Don't you want more than that?"

"I. Geez. I don't know. Mostly, I want to work on spaceships, now," Rix said. "But I want to make good money so I can build a shop where people want to bring their ships so I can fix them."

"Good, that's a start. Let's focus on that. The reason you want Garba on your side is because she has space on Patience Station. Space that could be turned into a shop like you're asking for. What is it you have that Garba might want, Rix?"

"Well, heck, that's easy. Her maintenance guy isn't doing the job. I don't know what he's doing, but maintaining the condensers and air handlers isn't it."

"And you can, right?"

"I can't do worse. And if that last condenser fails, it's not like anyone's living here much longer."

"See, there's your conversation. But you need to be gentle. Don't say bad things about Geoff. Focus on what you bring to the table, right?"

"Let me guess, Geoff and Garba are related somehow."

"Got it in one."

20

SERVICE CONTRACT

Stepping from the elevator onto the fortieth level, Rix took his first looks at Patience Station's public areas. The picture in his mind of spotless, tidy, well-maintained passageways looking out over vast expanses of space with exotically dressed aliens bustling about their business like what he'd seen on Dralli Station were crushed. Only slightly cleaner than the maintenance area, Patience Station showed years of neglect. Chipped paint on the walls gave way to shiny bare metal, smudge marks and dings one would expect from high traffic areas, only at that moment, only Kel, Philo and Rix were present.

"You look disappointed," Kel said.

"I didn't know what to expect," Rix said evenly.

"And this is less than what you'd thought, huh?"

"Dralli Station is my only other experience with space stations."

"Ah, Dralli Station, the Xandarj are so industrious, don't you think?" Rix's attention was drawn by the appearance of an older Fimil woman. Aside from a small, wrinkled elephant nose, she looked quite human.

"Garba Klex," Kel said, turning to face the woman. "Meet Rix Banner. He's the genius Earthling who rescued me from Dravari. I think he and Geoff were working on installing the condenser I brought back. Thank you for taking lead with the Dravari patrol."

"It was nothing, dear," Garba said. "Dravari need to know their place. We are a free people, and they have no claim, beyond might, on properties within Surnak Belt." As she spoke, she looked at Rix, clearly interested in teaching him about local geopolitics. "Welcome, Rix Banner. I understand there's a bit of a problem with the new machine. It is too big or something along those lines?"

"I haven't looked at it as hard as Geoff has," Rix said.

"Oh, I was under the impression you spent most of the day in the atmospheric engineering space. Compatibility seems a rather obvious concern, wouldn't you agree?" Garba said, giving a quick smile which disappeared just as fast as it had appeared. "But where are my manners. We've invited you to dine and I am always one to enjoy a meal before discussing business. Join us?"

"Of course," Rix answered, not overly interested in getting into a discussion about Geoff's opinions on anything.

The hallway Garba led them down was only ten meters long and as they walked, the overall repair of the space significantly improved until they arrived at a long window that started at waist level and soared overhead, disappearing into a deck above them. Rix couldn't help but stop and gaze out at the scene where in the far distance Narlux-4's star was poking out from behind a massive asteroid.

"That's Talos, one of the five Guardian asteroids, you're looking at," Kel said. "Talos is our watcher. If you look closely, you can see blinking red lights where our sensor buoys are located. Its rotation is perfect for the job of warning us about pending impacts. That reminds me, if you ever hear a warning about an impact, follow the instructions on your HUD. We don't always have a lot of time before impact."

"Impact?" Rix asked. "How often does that happen?"

"We haven't had a decompression event for over two years," Garba said with evident pride. "The iron composition of this beautiful rock along with our Guardians keeps us safe. Don't you, girl?" To emphasize, she patted the window frame affectionately.

"In Patience we trust," Kel added somberly.

"That's my girl," Garba said. "I understand you brought a load of fruit from Xandarj. That was very thoughtful, dear."

"We had room, so I funded what I could. Rix even added some of his own money to the haul," Kel said brightly.

"Oh, did he now? I thought you were a new citizen. Just emigrated from Earth. Word is, you're semi-sentient, but I'm sure not picking that up from you. Don't worry, though, you can take a test if you would like to remove that designation. It's mainly for your protection, though," Garba said, stopping in front of a double set of doors that were clad with a wood veneer. To Rix's eyes, the doors might have once been elegant looking, but time had taken a toll, and it looked like someone had simply glued wood pieces to a steel door and made no attempt to hide the transitions.

Rix hadn't heard a question, so he remained quiet as Garba opened the door to her suite and ushered them inside.

"You've a beautiful home, Ms. Klex," Rix said after taking in the interior. Different than the poorly maintained public spaces of the station, Garba's house was tidy, every surface clean and furniture all in good repair. Even more, the walls glowed with lights Rix was unable to locate, giving the space an open, airy feel.

"You are too kind, Mr. Banner," Garba answered.

It struck Rix that the atmosphere in the room was heavier than where he'd spent the day working. Glancing at his HUD, he saw that indeed the space had air pressure similar to sea level back home.

"Geoff is in the kitchen. Let's join him," she said. "Geoff, our new friend has arrived."

Standing at a cement counter, Geoff looked much different than when they'd met earlier in the day, having changed from dingy coveralls to clean one-piece space suit that was flattering for the older man.

"We've met," Geoff said guardedly. "Did you have any success with the first unit?" he asked.

"I can't be sure," Rix said. "I was hoping to go over what I've found with you, but I don't think the girls would be that interested, maybe in the morning if you're willing to let me take another crack at it."

"I thought the first two Phegile condensers were broken beyond repair," Garba said. "Why would you be spending any time on those?"

Rix looked at Geoff for help answering the question. If anything, Geoff seemed just as interested in an answer.

"Well, if we're going to replace either of those units, I figured I should find out why they broke in the first place. No sense making new trouble, don't you think, Geoff?"

"Not really," Geoff said. "Those Phegile condensers are nearly as old as this station. They're beyond their maintenance periods and need to be scrapped."

"So it doesn't hurt that I'm working on them, then?" Rix asked. "I can't break what's broken and if I can pull a rabbit out of the hat, then we're just that much further ahead. I guess that's how I look at it."

"And if you don't install the unit Kel brought back from the Dravari outpost, we're all going to suffocate," Garba said with obvious agitation.

"All I'm asking for is a few days and a small budget on your manufactory," Rix said.

Geoff snorted derisively. "To fix one of those Phegile units? Absolutely not. We're not throwing good money after bad."

"I say we table the discussion until after dinner," Garba said. "Rix, tell me about Earth. Had your civilization progressed to the point of living in cities? I understand this can be quite complex for sentients who are still developing."

"Running water, electricity, airplanes and even nuclear bombs," Rix said. "The town I lived in was about thirty-five hundred people. That's small compared to the larger cities which can be in the low millions."

"Very interesting," Garba said, gesturing to the places where they were all to sit. "And you were an engineer?"

"Not by Earth standards," Rix said. "I'm a mechanic. I fix things."

"Like spaceships," Kel said. "You should have seen it, Garba. With the most rudimentary tools, he fixed *Calypso's* engine, gravity repulsor and her inertial systems. His fixes are so basic that they border on genius."

"Is that so, Rix?" Garba asked.

"It sounds like he got lucky," Geoff said.

Rix placed his hand on a red drink on the table and had started to lift it when Garba and Geoff had pounced on him. "Oh, do drink that before you respond. I want to know what you think of it," Garba said.

Rix shrugged and took a sip of the drink. There was a small amount of alcohol in the fizzy, berry flavored drink. From Rix's perspective, that it was served at room temperature was a mistake, but the flavor was good.

"I like it," he said, setting the glass down. "And you're right, Geoff. I got lucky with those fixes. If they'd been broken in other ways than what I found, there's no way I could have fixed anything. Kind of like the Unit 2 condenser. It has ridiculously expensive parts that are completely ruined. There's no way we're bringing it back, but I was wondering if you'd be okay with me pulling some of the parts that aren't ruined over to Unit 1?"

"You need to let that fantasy go," Geoff said. "You're not getting either of those units going again. We're burning through charge couplings like they're made of lace."

"I was going to move over the working charge couplings to Unit 1," Rix admitted.

"And it'll run for maybe a week before it burns up, too."

"How do you get your ice supplied?" Rix asked.

"What's it to you?" Geoff asked.

"Geoff, be friendly. Rix is a guest at our table."

"Me and Collie Berg collect it from a local ice asteroid. It's hard work," Geoff said.

"I bet," Rix answered, taking interest in a plate put in front of him by Garba.

"Not all of that will be to your liking, Rix. You don't mind if I call you Rix, do you?" Garba asked.

"I'd prefer it," Rix answered. "Just dig in, or are there customs to observe?"

"Dig in. What a wonderful colloquialism," Garba said. "Please, by all means, *dig in.*"

"What's wrong with the ice, Banner?" Geoff growled, not bothering to pick up his fork.

"Well, I'm not sure," Rix said.

"Sounds like you are," Geoff answered. "Don't be makin' me look bad just because you don't know what you're doing."

"Hey, that's not fair," Kel said, interrupting.

"Now, now," Garba said. "Let's stay civil while we have our meal."

"No, he's starting something, he needs to be out with it," Geoff said.

"I imagine getting ice is hard work," Rix said. "I've been doing some reading which suggests that some asteroid ice contains too high a level of silica grit, which fouls the charge couplings and burns them out. So, I was thinking ..."

"That's bunk. Nobody has pure ice on a space station. The whole idea is to melt the ice because it's not in water form," Geoff said. "You're just a dumb, backwater, semi-sentient, ape. What is it that makes you think you can come here and tell me anything? I've been maintaining this station for twenty years. I don't need to take this crap from you, especially not in my house."

Geoff tossed his utensils onto his plate as he stood and then stormed off.

"Geoff, stop, please," Garba called after him. And when it became clear he wasn't listening, she turned back to the table. "He's full of passion, that one." That she seemed unperturbed was startling to Rix, but he kept the thought to himself.

"This corniq is really good, Garba," Kel said. "Did you make it yourself?"

"Thank you, dear," Garba said. "And no, I had Abistel make it for me. You were such a good friend delivering her load to Dralli. She's barely surviving with her meager income and with those kids to feed, I don't know how she does it all."

"Davile put her in a horrible spot, leaving like he did," Kel said and then seemed to understand that Rix had no idea what they were talking about. "Abistel is the clothing maker, we delivered those crates to Bopar for her. Her dad, Davile, was an asteroid miner, but he took a job a quarter arc around a few years back and hasn't been heard from. He left Abistel to take care of her three siblings. She's got a big heart for a girl of seventeen."

"And then some," Garba agreed. "Tell me, Rix Banner. Are you trying to make a job for yourself by acting like you can fix those condensers? Because, if that's your play, it's not going to end well for you. We don't need more people with their hands out around here."

"He's not like that," Kel said. "And if he is, he's my problem. I got him into this mess and we wouldn't have that new condenser if not for him, so maybe take it a little easy," Kel said, irritation gilding her voice.

"Hold on, let's just take it down a notch," Rix said. "I know everyone's excited here and for good reason. If that fifth unit breaks before we have a fix, people are going to suffer much worse than they are now. I'll be the least of your problems if that happens. If you must know, I have some credits already."

"A couple of credits isn't what you're going to need to survive out here. You need a job," Garba said.

"I don't disagree. Convince Geoff to let me keep working on Units 1 and 2. I need a week, and three thousand credits and priority runs on a manufactory."

"Three thousand credits won't buy you much where industrial repairs are concerned. The last time we manufactured charge couplers we spent nearly seventy-five thousand credits. I don't think Geoff wants you working on his systems. He's had more than his share of people looking for a job who make trouble and just walk off after the first payday."

"You have nothing to lose with me," Rix said.

"Three thousand credits."

"Okay, okay, hold on then, I have an idea," Rix said, tapping empty space and bringing up his HUD. With another day of sales of his manufactory part and the credits returned for the sale of his share of the fruit from Xandarj, he was sitting at sixteen hundred credits. "Give me a place to stay for two weeks, including basic food, water and atmosphere. I'll invest fifteen hundred of my own credits into the manufactory bill for the repairs. You come up with the other half. You convince Geoff to let me continue my work on Units 1 and 2 for six days. If after that time, I can't bring up Unit 1 by scavenging parts from Unit 2, then you kick me off the station and keep my credits."

"And if you succeed? What do you get?" Garba asked.

"I need a good deal on a space where I can open my own mechanic's shop. I need access to local space, minimum three hundred square meters with ten meters' clearance," Rix said.

"That's a lot of space," Garba scoffed.

"You're right, it is. You'll also give me the first year rent-free," Rix said.

Garba sat back and took a long drink of cherry fizz. "You're saying that, for fifteen hundred credits' investment and an apartment for two weeks, you'll fix Unit 1 with parts from Unit 2. I have to keep Geoff off your back and if you're successful, I give you, rent-free, a three-hundred-square-meter space for a year."

"That's right."

"You'll pay taxes just like everyone else."

"Only sounds fair," Rix agreed.

"What about the unit Kel brought back?"

"I'm not negotiating a second deal before we've completed the first," Rix said. "I have absolutely no leverage here aside from the hope that I know what I'm talking about. And, given that I'm from a backwater world, you're grasping for hope. Give me a chance and when I'm successful, we'll both be talking from stronger positions."

"I'm not giving you credits directly," Garba said. "I'm putting fifteen hundred credits on account to Patience Station, earmarked for Project Clean Air. I've sent you a draft of our agreement. Your signature, along with fifteen hundred credits of your own funds deposited to the Clean Air account, will signify your acceptance of this contract. Do we have a deal?"

"I need to read the contract," Rix said.

Beverly took this moment as her cue to appear and she did just that, appearing on the table, wearing a black pinstriped suit and a fedora with a white satin band around it. With a cigar clenched between her teeth, she looked up at Rix with a grin. "I read the contract, see?" she said, doing her best 1920's mobster impression. "It's a good contract, see? You should sign it or swim with the fishes, see?"

Rix grinned and shook his head at Beverly's antics. "Can you move the money for me?"

"I don't have that authority," Beverly said. "But acknowledge acceptance of the transfer that is showing now."

On his HUD, a button appeared, and Rix quickly tapped his acceptance. "How upset is Geoff going to be?" Rix asked, closing his HUD.

"I suspect the two of you won't be friends any time soon," Garba said. "Unfortunately, he's always been territorial about maintenance tasks on Patience Station."

"That's unfortunate," Rix said. "I don't need him as an enemy."

"I can help with that," Garba said. "Assuming you get that condenser fixed. If we're about to lose Unit 5, like you say, we'll be put off the station and none of this will matter. Geoff can see that, even if he won't admit it."

"Where are you putting him up?" Kel asked. "Is it nice?"

"I was thinking Belflower," Garba said. "I'll take it out of what they owe me already."

"You'll like Belflower, Rix," Kel said. "Long-term hotel is probably the best description. They have two- and three-room units. Some of them are super nice. Can he have one of the view rooms? I know they're more, but it'd help him get settled."

"Will you be preparing your own food?" Garba asked.

"Ideally, but I don't even know how to get groceries here yet. I've always cooked for myself."

"Okay, Jesif is saying he has a room that'll work," Garba said. "Rix, a lot is riding on you not lying right now. Patience Station is struggling for survival. That Dravari scout left, not because he thought we hadn't done what we were accused of, but because the air quality is so bad, he didn't want to spend time on our station. Our air is bad and that can be the death of a station if word gets out."

Rix started to speak but bit off his words.

"What was that?" Kel asked.

"Nothing. We have our deal," Rix said and then turned to Philo. "I don't suppose you'll be available to help, some, will you? I can't pay you anything beyond treats once in a while, but I really could use your help."

"Rixy fun to work with," Philo said. "Needs good treats. Philo help."

Rix reached across and tousled Philo's hair. "You're a good sort, Philo."

"Thank you for your hospitality, Garba. I apologize for making Geoff mad. We were trying to avoid that," Kel said.

"I'm not sure it was avoidable," Garba said. "Don't make me a fool, Kel. I trust Geoff and going against him is going to put a rift between us. I don't like that."

"I'm not looking to step on his back," Rix said. "I'll do my best to patch things up with him."

"Get Patience Station some air. Geoff is carrying a lot of guilt about not being able to keep these old systems running," she said, standing to signify she was done with dinner. "Help Patience Station and things will work out with Geoff."

"Okay, Garba," Rix said, standing and extending his hand to her. When she looked quizzically at him, he explained. "Humans shake hands to express agreement and general good wishes."

"Good wishes to you then," Garba said, shaking his hand.

"How about a station tour on our way to Belflower Suites?" Kel asked brightly. "I love this time of evening. Everyone is out, talking. They'll want to meet the new guy. Petju probably even has frozen comera tonight."

2 1

UNDER PROMISE

"Beverly, would you show me a layout of Patience Station decks?" Rix asked. While he'd been working, the lack of information related to the space station had been tugging at his curiosity. Standing outside Garba's apartment while Kel finished saying goodbye, seemed like a perfect time to get an idea of the layout.

"Of course, Rix," Beverly answered just about the same moment a three-dimensional drawing appeared in front of him with each floor shown as translucent wireframes. Upon first inspection, the shape of the cavern within Patience Station's asteroid was illuminated. Each floor or level had its own distinct shape with few straight lines on the edges. To Rix's eyes, if taken in its entirety, the shape resembled a large potato. And when he focused on any particular level, he received a summary of that level's primary purpose or usage. Garba Klex's suite was on one of the highest levels that had any sort of straight lines, which Rix quickly understood to be where the cavern of the asteroid was open to space and windows had been stretched across.

"This station is huge," Rix said, taking it all in. "How many people live here?"

"Six thousand one hundred forty-three if we include present company," Beverly answered. "Patience Station was originally designed for a comfortable operational population of twenty-four thousand, and a maximum of twenty-eight thousand."

"Not even thirty percent of maximum," Rix said.

"Who are you talking to?" Kel asked, catching up with him by grabbing his arm with her own.

"Getting a lay of the land," Rix said. "What did Garba have to say?"

Kel pulled Rix over to the elevator and didn't respond until they started moving downward with a destination of Level 17 Atrium had been chosen.

"She is concerned you aren't getting along with Geoff. What happened in the basement, really? Geoff was already pissed off when he got to dinner."

Rix gave Kel a surprised look. "After we delivered your condenser to Level 3 Environmental, I asked him about the other units that weren't working. He told me to look for myself and then left. I didn't see him the rest of the day."

"Garba says he feels guilty that everything is breaking under his watch."

"The equipment isn't well-maintained, Kel," Rix said.

"What do you mean?"

"You saw it. There's sludge inside the air-handling components. There's gravel sitting on the charge couplers. All of the drains are clogged so even if there was water flowing like it should, it'd be running inside. Every filter that's still inside is fouled to the point where they're only twenty-percent efficient. It's like he's never looked inside one of these machines, even though Unit 5 has been opened up and it looks like someone's working on it."

"Was he?" she asked.

"Working on 5? Not today, he wasn't."

"Can you fix it?"

"I have no idea. I'm not getting near anything he's working on. I have no idea how he might respond." Rix said. "With six thousand inhabitants, can't we afford better maintenance? I know the components are expensive, but there are plenty of people to share the costs. Isn't that the job of a local government?"

"Patience Station has paid huge for replacement parts. The last three times we had a shipment due to come in, Dravari impounded them because we're late on tax payments."

"Why not use the manufactories to create the parts?"

"Dravari have shut down our ability to use those patterns until we're paid up."

"Why aren't we paying our taxes?" he asked.

"Well, first, Dravari have no right to tax a space station in an unclaimed asteroid belt," Kel said, stepping from the elevator. "Second, they are assessing taxes as if we're running at maximum population. People here don't have much money. Our jobs have dried up because Dravari make it impossible to ship goods to or from Patience because they impound everything."

"What's that all about? If they're choking off commerce, that's no way to create a tax base," Rix said.

"Who knows? All I know is that they've created an impossible situation and people are suffering. The only reason Garba is going against Geoff is because you said you could fix Unit 1 without using original equipment manufactured parts. You're kind of screwed with Geoff, though. If you do fix Unit 1, he's not going to like it. If you don't, he'll be first in line to enforce the part of the contract that puts you off Patience."

"Great," Rix said.

"Put that out of your head. I have some really great people I want to introduce you to. Look at the time. It's 1930 local. That's when everyone gathers on the Atrium level. Some people just go for a walk. Sometimes people put out stands where they have things to trade. There's always music. It's not much, but it's something we all look forward to."

"Do Garba and Geoff go?"

"Not very often. On the other hand, Belflower Suites main entry is right off the main portion of Atrium, so it'll be super convenient for you."

"Where do you stay?" Rix asked.

"I move around," Kel said. "Sometimes I sleep on *Calypso* because the low atmospheric pressure bothers me, and I have allergies. There's something on Patience Station, maybe mold, that makes it a little harder for me to breathe. You can probably hear a little crackle in my chest. I have medicine, but it's getting expensive due to Dravari tariffs. I smuggled a bunch back from Xandarj, but the patrol that searched *Calypso* took them."

"I can't believe they took your medicine."

"It was either that, or I had to pay the tariff directly. It was too much for me to afford."

"That's terrible."

"Who's your friend, Kel?" a middle-aged man wearing a frayed embroidered golden robe asked.

"Skef, this is Rix Banner. He's a new spaceship mechanic from Earth," Kel said, smiling. "Rix, Skef is an environmentalist and is responsible for the beautiful plants in Atrium."

A look of pain crossed Skef's face as he opened his arms in greeting. "It is indeed nice to see a new face on Patience. I wish you could have visited when our atmospherics were working correctly. We've lost so much of the biodiversity we once had."

"Lost?" Rix asked.

"Oh yes and we're losing more. It's such a shame."

"Do you have a greenhouse so they're not lost forever?"

"I'm not following."

"Take cuttings from the plants that are in danger and build a self-contained room where you control the air pressure, temperature, all that. When things get better, you can take these plants and put them back," Rix said.

"Oh, you are an optimist," Skef said the smile on his face not reaching his eyes. "Things on Patience Station never improve. Dravari have seen to that."

"You're opposed to the idea, then?" Rix asked.

"No, it is a good idea. I'm afraid I don't have much energy for such a project. I don't even know how we could create such an environment, given how things on the station are."

"Let's you and I think on that," Rix said. "I just feel like there's something more we could do."

"Skef's got it right, you are ever the optimist," Kel said, tugging Rix along.

"Good to meet you, Rix Banner," Skef said.

"This used to all be filled with plants," Kel said, gesturing grandly to encompass the entire three-story tall space they'd entered. Most of the width and breadth of the station, the Atrium seemed massive, and to Skef's point, much of the greenery had a sickly look to it.

"Skef seemed depressed. It must be hard to watch his hard work die," Rix said.

"Your idea for a greenhouse is good, though," Kel said. "It'd at least give him something to do. What do you need to make that work?"

"I don't know how to build things here. Back home, we'd make a framework of glass so the natural sunlight could come in. There were vents to allow heat to leave, plumbing for watering, benches to hold potted plants, you know, basic growing stuff."

"Building panels aren't generally hard to come by. We'd have to get Garba's permission, though," she said. "And it'd be best if Skef was the one who proposed it."

"Sure."

"Oh, you absolutely need to meet Petju, she has her frozen comera. And Hutarj is setting up her music. You're really in for a treat. All the best of Patience Station is here tonight!" Kel said, pulling on Rix's arm so they bumped into each other. Rix hadn't seen as big a smile on Kel's face the entire time he'd known her, and the last vestiges of distrust melted away as he finally came to understand what she was so interested in protecting with her illegal activities. "What?" she asked, looking at him, her face glowing with happiness.

"These are your people. You're happy here," he said.

"You're my people, too, Rix," she said, releasing him and giggling as she embraced Petju and then accepted a pair of what looked to Rix to be waffle bowls with a frozen dessert in them.

"Ice cream?" he asked. "And it's very nice to meet you, Petju."

"Your words don't translate exactly right, but I think it is close," Petju said. "Try it. I hope you'll like it."

"Whoa, that is really sour," Rix said, puckering on first bite.

"You need to get some of the bowl with each bite," Petju said, grinning at Rix's facial expression. "The comera by itself can be quite tart for some. Could you taste anything but the sour?"

"It's a good taste, for sure, but oh man, I don't know if I can survive the tart. I'll try, though," he said, this time trying a bite with a good-sized hunk of the waffle bowl. And true to her word, the bowl's bland flavor somewhat reduced the frozen treat's punch.

"It might take a few times," Kel said. "Save it for Philo, he really likes comera."

The evening continued much in the same way as Rix met many of the people who had come out to walk the Atrium that evening. Finally, Rix found that Kel had escorted him to an arched stone entrance that stood out from the rest of the station's architecture. Etched into the white stone façade were the words Belflower Suites.

"Very elegant," Rix said as she escorted him to the front desk. "Jesif, this is Rix Banner."

"So I've heard," Jesif answered. Like Garba, Jesif was Fimil and had a small elephant trunk where his nose should be. Much larger than Garba's, Jesif's trunk hung past his chin and was distracting for Rix who fought to ignore it. Unlike the others Rix had met that evening, Jesif was distant, even annoyed. "You're in Eighteen-A. Don't get used to it. Eighteen-A is one of our nicest rooms and I only offered it because Garba called me directly."

"That's very nice of you, Jesif," Kel immediately said. "Do you want me to take him up?"

"Oh, I didn't know you were together," Jesif said cattily.

"We're not," Kel said. "I was trying to save you the effort."

"Whatever you would like," Jesif said. "You know where the security tags are kept. Go ahead, I'll get back to my evening."

"This way," Kel said, pulling Rix around the front desk where she grabbed a small gun looking device. Tapping on the display on the back of the device, she nodded approval and then pointed it at Rix. "This won't hurt."

Text floated across Rix's HUD: *Belflower Suites security access granted for suite Eighteen A. Duration fourteen days, six hours.*

"I got it," Rix responded.

"There are stairs if you don't mind the walk. The elevator is slow."

"Stairs are fine."

Rix almost regretted offering to take the stairs after they'd walked up four flights. Fortunately, that was the extent of it and Kel showed him where the entrance to his apartment was. "Just palm the security panel."

Rix did and they entered the suite, which by Earth hotel standards was elegant if small. "Is everything small in a space station?" Rix asked.

"That's right. Head is through there. You have a galley if you decided to prepare your own meals. Bed is over there, and the best part of this suite is the view. Check this out."

A narrow window—half a meter wide but floor to ceiling in height —sat embedded in the flat face of the wall which looked out over the Surnak Asteroid Belt. "Nice to have a sunward view," Rix said. "Does it ever get old?"

"Never," Kel agreed and then shifted gears. "What's your schedule for tomorrow?"

"I'm hoping to pick up tools from the manufactory. I had to make some since what Geoff had in the cabinets wasn't much," he said.

"Oh, I bet I can get you more tools. Let me know what you need by sending a comm and I'll put out a call. People will donate or lend tools," she said.

"I noticed you didn't tell anyone what I was working on."

"At this point, I don't want to build anyone's hope, especially since you'll probably have a better idea of how this is going to go over the next day or two," she said.

"So you recognized I was bluffing a little with Garba?"

"Garba knew you were bluffing as much as I did," Kel said. "What she didn't know is that you're harder on yourself than anyone else could be. If you think you can but aren't sure, that's like most people being certain."

"I don't know about that."

"What is it with humans and the whole 'aww shucks' routine?"

"I learned something when I was repairing airplanes in the war," Rix said.

"Oh yeah?"

"Nobody minds if you get something done early. Everybody hates someone who is late," Rix said. "One of the men who trained me when I was young told me that I should always under promise and over deliver, that this was the best way to establish trust."

"It's driving you nuts to be out on a limb with this repair, then, isn't it?"

"Like you can't imagine."

"I just swiped an atmospheric condenser from a government outpost," Kel said. "I know something about stress. I can imagine a lot."

"I stand corrected," Rix answered, checking out the bed that sat next to the narrow window.

"You're tired. Would you mind if I brought food tomorrow morning?"

"I plan to be to work early," Rix said.

"I'll call and figure out where you're at," Kel said. "I'll have a nice treat for you. I think I know what you like at this point."

"Sounds great, but don't spend a lot of money. I know food here is expensive."

"Don't worry about me."

Rix saw Kel out and then stripped off his clothing, jumping into the shower. Warm water helped settle his stomach, which was upset due to the swimming feeling he'd had since entering the space station. He took a short shower and was in bed within fifteen minutes, staring out the window at the unfamiliar scene of the asteroid belt. He'd just started to wonder how long it would take for the view to become familiar when he dozed off.

Morning came with little warning. He'd set an alarm for 0530 and sat up, working to remove sleep from his eyes. "We're going to need a coffee pot at some point," he acknowledged, pouring a glass of water instead. With nothing else to do, he exited his suite and retraced his steps to the elevator bank. There were only a few people around the Atrium when he walked through and likely due to the early hour, only friendly waves were exchanged.

Level 3 Environmental was the sign opposite the elevator when he finally arrived. Lights flicked on in response to his presence. Arriving at Unit 1, he sat cross-legged inside.

"Beverly, can you hear me?"

"Of course, Rix. I have a link with your HUD," she answered. "You are up at an early time. You have work you intend?"

"Today, we're going to work on cleaning things to my satisfaction. I'll need that power sprayer for the solvent. Also, do you have measurements for the ice basket I'm planning?" he asked.

"I don't know about a planned ice basket."

"My mistake, I thought we'd discussed it. Let's assume the ice Geoff is gathering will always be dirty. I'd like to build a table that will pre-melt the ice with a chute to the side that allows the gravel to tumble out. We'll need a screen on the bottom and then a way to shake the table to keep things rolling out."

"The material will need to be capable of withstanding the heat of the charge couplers," Beverly said.

"We're talking seventy degrees Celsius maximum, right? Boiling would be too much," Rix reasoned.

"You are correct. I believe an alloy of iron, chromium, and nickel would be appropriate."

"Stainless steel," Rix acknowledged. "Agreed."

"Let's get started on a design," Beverly said. "Tell me more."

Through conversation and the use of his HUD to project a design, they worked for a couple of hours, until Rix was satisfied. "Let's make one basket so we can test it before we make more. Also, could you add the cleaning tools I've identified? I'll need some sort of coveralls to wear when I'm cleaning. I'm going to get rather dirty."

"I've added all of these items to the manufactory queue. It is inexpensive to have them delivered and the benefit is you pay the courier directly, so it's good for the economy," Beverly said.

"I'm down to a hundred credits," Rix said.

"I believe that has been updated, you are at two hundred thirty," Beverly said.

"Sales are good. Yes, pay for courier."

"Very well. The items will be delivered in thirty minutes."

"Okay, we'll take out all of the charge couplers from Units 1 and 2," Rix said. "We'll clean those first. Can you pull up that part of the manual?"

"Of course."

About halfway into the job, Rix was interrupted by both Kel and the parts courier. The basket he'd designed was big and he wondered how exactly he would get it installed. Paying the courier, a younger kid named Boogs, Rix turned to Kel.

"You are disgusting," Kel said.

"Just part of the job," Rix said, wiping his hands down as best as possible. He had no idea what kind of gunk was on the inside of the condenser and hoped he wouldn't inadvertently poison himself with extended contact. "What do you have there?"

"Prota-egg and vat-sausage sandwich," Kel said. "And a big coffee."

"Not exactly coffee, but my taste buds are starting to buy it," Rix said. "Thank you for breakfast."

"Things look less put together than last time. Are you sure you'll have enough time?"

"We'll find out."

The two ate in companionable silence and soon enough Kel departed and Rix got back to the task. Working the afternoon and late into the evening, he removed all twelve charge couplers from both units and had them cleaned and set safely within the wall cabinets.

"Are you going to work all night?" Kel asked, catching him at 1900 that evening. Did you get anything more to eat?"

"No, and I'm starving."

"You need a shower. Does your room have a working textile cleaner?"

"I didn't try it," Rix said. "Hopefully."

"Well, I know Jesif has one for the bed sheets. You should hurry, there's good music tonight in the Atrium," she said. "I don't want to miss it."

"How do I go about getting dinner?"

"Paste for one credit, a good solid meal for fifteen. There are snack options in between."

"How about you let me buy you dinner for showing me around," Rix said. "I'll figure out the paste thing tomorrow."

"Did you make good progress today?"

"Everything takes longer than you expect," Rix said. "But I'm making progress."

"Good."

22

SABOTAGE

"Lift a little higher," Rix instructed. Seven days had passed, and Unit 1 was finally clean enough that he was willing to start the reassembly process with the addition of the new gravel filter he'd customized.

"Rixy, Philo need ladder," Philo said, pushing the stainless-steel gravel basket as high as he could manage.

"That's it, buddy," Rix said. "Now, over to me three fingers." While Philo struggled with normal measurements, Philo understood things like fingers width and arm length just fine.

"Stretch Philo," Philo complained but then, with a satisfying clunk, the gravel pre-pass filter dropped into place.

"Nice job!" Rix said. "Let's get this thing buttoned up!"

Just then, a clanking noise came from Unit 5, followed by a release of steam and then it grew quiet. In response, a muted yellow light started pulsing along a strip on the wall at waist level.

"Rix, are you there?" Kel called.

"Go ahead, Kel," Rix said, walking over to Unit 5. Crouching in front of the machine, he shined his flashlight into the interior and saw exactly what he'd expected—a layer of fist-sized rocks locked in by smaller gravel all sitting atop the charge couplers, blocking the flow of ice.

"Get away from there!" Geoff's voice boomed from the elevator. "What have you done!? I'll have you spaced for this!"

Rix stood and considered the older man as he stalked angrily toward Rix and Unit 5. "Calm down, Geoff," Rix said. "I didn't have anything to do with your condenser unit failing."

"Like Groden you didn't," Geoff said and then tapped on his shoulder. "Garba, send Quixly, we have a saboteur in Environmental."

"Rix, what's going on?" Kel asked.

"If I'm not wrong, I think I'm about to be put in the brig," Rix said. "Unit 5 just turned off for some reason."

"Did you have anything to do with it?"

"Do you really need to ask?"

"I'm coming down."

Rix stepped back from the failing condenser unit so that Geoff could approach unhindered. "What'd you do, Rix Banner?" Geoff asked. "I saw you messing with this condenser."

"Seems like you've already decided my part in this," Rix said. "I'll wait to talk to someone without a chip on their shoulder, if it's all the same to you."

"Why, you, frakking arrogant garrod-loving, septic-mouthed, half-wit," Geoff said, his small nose-trunk turning bright red as he approached, pulling a fist back.

"Hey, now," Rix said, redirecting the older alien's overly telegraphed punch by slapping it to the side. "I was just looking. There's no reason to get violent now."

"I'm going to pummel that moron mouth of yours into red paste." Geoff, having been redirected, turned back to Rix and bull-rushed him. Having a strong boxing background, Rix stepped aside and with open hands, once again pushed the older alien away.

"Hey, you, stop!" Quixly's voice called from the elevator. Rix had only once met Patience Station's constable and hadn't yet formed an opinion. "What's going on down here, Geoff?"

Rix, still back pedaling, stopped as Quixly's call had brought Geoff up short. "Arrest this human half-wit! He sabotaged Unit 5! I told

Garba it was dangerous to let him be down here by himself. Now he's done killed the station!"

"Nothing I could do would be worse than your sloppy maintenance, Geoff," Rix said angrily, immediately regretting his words. The problem was, he'd been up to his elbows in crap for the better part of a week and had feelings that apparently wanted to be heard.

"Are you going to listen to this idiot? Humans don't even have space travel. What's he know about fixing space stations?" Geoff asked.

"Let's all just slow this down a beat," Quixly said. "I was under the impression that Rix Banner was supposed to be down here working on the air handling. Do I have that wrong?"

"No. You. Do. Not!" Geoff said. "But he was supposed to be working on Units 1 and 2. When I got down here, he'd just shut down Unit 5. We don't have enough pressure to keep people alive, Quixly."

"Is that right?" Quixly asked.

"Unit 5 failed, I was looking at it when Geoff got here," Rix said.

"Turn around. Hands behind your back."

"What? Why? You don't want to stop me. I'm trying to get Unit 1 back online," Rix said.

"That's Unit 1?" Quixly asked, pointing at the mess of parts and panels that lay disgorged from both Units 1 and 2.

"Yes."

"Looks like sabotage to me," Quixly said.

"It's not!"

"Quiet. You'll have your chance to say whatever it is you want, later."

"Rix!" Kel said, running over from the elevators. "Quixly, what are you doing!? Rix is trying to fix the air. You can't lock him up now. You'll condemn us all to die."

"Look, Geoff oversees station maintenance. If he says this guy is a problem, I have to believe him."

Rix didn't fight the restraining cuffs Quixly placed on him and was led over to the elevators and taken to Level 15. "Look, Rix Banner, if you did this, you're hurting a lot of very good people and I'll see to it you pay hard. I'm not a man who appreciates violence, but you shouldn't take that as weakness. Are you looking for some sort of payout?"

"For Unit 5?"

"What's that supposed to mean? For anything? Are you a snake hiding in the ductwork?"

The idiom struck Rix so oddly, that he wasn't exactly sure what he was being asked. "I didn't sabotage anything."

"Save it for the judge," Quixly said, pushing Rix through the foyer of the constable's office and back behind a small desk which led to a hallway where there were four cells lined up along one row.

"I'm being charged with something?"

"No. You're being held as a possible threat to the station."

"I see," Rix said, almost stumbling as Quixly gave him a push into the first cell. Irritated, he walked over to a bench which likely served as both bed and seat. He could hear muffled voices and felt it likely one of them was Kel, but he wasn't sure. "Beverly, can you hear me?"

With no response, Rix imagined there was something in the cell that blocked communications. Sitting for several minutes, he struggled to calm. After an hour, he lay back and wondered what it would feel like to slowly die with too little oxygen to breathe, even as he lay there, he observed that his respirations had increased, likely to make up for the shortage of oxygen in the thinning atmosphere.

"On your feet," Quixly demanded some time later.

"What have you done, Rix Banner?" Garba Klex asked, walking into the hallway in front of the cells.

"Done? Nothing to Unit 5," Rix said. "I was working with Philo. Ask him. We were working on putting Unit 1 back together."

"That's bunk!" Geoff said from outside the hallway and then stormed in next to Garba. "I saw you messing with Unit 5 and then it broke!"

"Is that right, Rix Banner?" Garba asked.

"I can see how he got there," Rix said.

"Ah! Hah!" Geoff said. "What did you do!?"

"Do I get to talk?"

"No, you witless moron, where you're going, nobody talks," Geoff shouted.

"Geoff, we're trying to figure out what's happened," Garba said. "You have to let him talk."

"Why? He did it! He's trying to kill us all."

Rix's look of surprise was genuine and he saw a similar look cross Garba's face. "Quixly, would you help Geoff find a place where he can rest a minute? Perhaps get him a glass of water, please?"

"Yes, mayor."

"What? You can't do that," Geoff sputtered but didn't further resist as Quixly led him out.

"You can talk now," Garba said.

"It's not very complex. Philo and I were working on Unit 1 when we heard some noises from Unit 5. Not too long after that, Unit 5 stopped working. I figured I should have a look, so I went over and shined my flashlight in. I was reaching up to feel the heat on the charge couplers, but I hadn't even touched it when Geoff came in hotter than a branding iron," Rix said. "I think my HUD has all this recorded."

"Why would your HUD have this recorded?"

"When I'm working, I record so I can go back and look at things when I'm not actually doing the work. I get ideas so I want to check things out," Rix said.

Garba looked over to Quixly, who'd returned from helping Geoff.

"Quixly, why haven't you looked at his recordings?"

"Well, I didn't know he had them," Quixly said with a huff. "You should have said something."

"Funny."

"Why is that funny?" Quixly asked with a threatening tone in his voice.

"I was still recording, constable," Rix said. "What do you bet Ms. Klex here would see that you're not such a good listener if she replayed it."

"You runt."

"Men, stop," Garba said, scratching the back of her head in frustration. "It doesn't matter in this moment. Send me that video. If it went the way you said, we have a new problem."

Rix sent her the video. "What's the new problem?"

"The parts Geoff needs to fix Unit 5 are embargoed by Dravari."

"What's that got to do with me?"

"Look, you might be good, but you can't invent parts. We're almost at the end of your contract and you haven't produced anything, Rix Banner. I don't blame you for trying, but I have six thousand people who need air and I can't waste time with this."

"For the love of God, woman, just let me finish what I was doing, already," Rix said. "In the middle of a crisis that requires a working condenser, you've taken the only person on this damn station that can give you one and put him in jail because your boyfriend is jealous. I just need you to get out of my way instead of always making things harder."

"What do you mean, always?" she asked.

"Do you think it's a coincidence that my tools keep disappearing? How many people have access to Level 3 Environmental? If it wasn't for Kel finding me spare tools, I'd have been stopped a while ago."

"And you think Geoff took them?"

"I have no idea," Rix said. "Someone did. I'm just saying that for people who want a condenser working, you sure spend a lot of effort making sure it won't. Maybe you should think about that? It feels darn intentional. Maybe get Quixly to look at that for a minute."

Rix hadn't intended to say nearly so much but he'd reached a point of frustration. The missing tools had slowed him down, but he hadn't said anything because he had no reputation to accompany his claim. As he'd been talking, Garba had been swiping at the air, presumably moving video on her HUD.

"Quixly, let him out," she said after swiping away and closing the video.

"But, ma'am," Quixly objected.

"Review the video yourself. Rix Banner never came in contact with Unit 5. If you find any video that proves otherwise, let me know and we can review it together. For now, you need to post a person by the condensers and make sure this man isn't interrupted again. Do you understand me?"

"I don't take orders from you," Quixly said.

"Well, in this case, you do. As mayor, I can hear cases and that is legally binding. If you'd like me to bring this to the council, I can. You're up for reappointment in two months. How do you want that to go? Not like it will matter if we don't get a working condenser."

"Fine. I'll post someone."

"Rix Banner, is there anything I can get you that would help progress? Do you need people? Supplies? I can have lunch and dinner brought in. Would you consider keeping a cot in Environmental?" Garba asked. "This is truly do-or-die time."

"Let me out, please," Rix said. "Food would be helpful, especially for Philo. And no, I don't need more untrained people touching my work."

"In twelve hours, atmospheric pressure will drop to an unsustainable level," Garba said. "How much time do you need?"

"I don't know, I do know that talking isn't getting it done."

"Open the door, Quixly. Now!"

"You better be right, human," Quixly said threateningly as he opened the sliding door.

Rix looked the constable in the face and held his gaze for a moment. "Why does it seem that you're in the way here?"

"I never," Quixly said, quickly stepping out of Rix's way.

"I'm not sure that was a good idea, Rix," Kel said. "Quixly isn't someone you want to be on the wrong side of."

"Sure, but I figure I either get this condenser working and I'm a hero, untouchable by Quixly, or I don't. At which point I'm probably going out an airlock," Rix said. "High stakes mechanic's work at its best."

"Bet you never thought you'd say those words," Kel said.

"Oh, this? This is nothing. In the war, our enemy bombed the plant where I was working. Another time, I was at a forward airbase and that position got overrun. I hid in the oil pit for several hours until I could sneak out."

"Is that why you're so calm when everyone's yelling at you?"

"I guess. And for the record, I lost my cool back there with Garba and Quixly. I shouldn't have let them make me mad."

"You didn't sound that mad," Kel said. "Are you sure you don't need more help?"

"Just Philo for now," Rix said as they entered Environmental together. With a cursory glance, Rix discovered that his work area had been changed. Someone had moved his parts around and slashed the fabric of the large filters he had ready for installation. "You've got to be kidding me. Who would do this?"

"Someone was mad," Kel said. "I can think of someone that fits that bill."

"Be careful. We can't blame someone without knowing for sure," Rix said.

"How bad is it?"

"Beverly, can you scan the work area? I need to know what's missing," Rix said. Beverly appeared up in her miniature version, wearing a medium-blue lab coat with a pocket protector filled with pens and had a slide-rule sticking out the top. "IBM Corporation advertisement in *Popular Mechanics*, January 1951."

"You do have quite the good memory," Beverly said. "The parts appear to be all here with the exception of three of the manufactured filter brackets. I am able to trace the path of someone kicking their way through the work area. They were in a hurry or were possibly interrupted."

"Can you create an order to reproduce the brackets and replacement filters?"

"We are out of funds, Rix," Beverly said. "You need an additional five hundred credits."

Rix had checked his balance that morning and knew that he was back to eight hundred credits from the sales of his part on the manufactory store. "Take that from my account. We can settle up with Garba once this is running again."

"I'm going to report this to Garba right now," Kel said. "This is ridiculous."

"Sure, that's fine, but Kel, you might consider getting a weapon," Rix said.

"Why? There's no way Geoff is coming back."

"Right, and I know it looks like he was mad and stomped through here. What if that's not actually what happened? What if someone is trying to bring the demise of Patience Station?"

"Frak. You're right. I'll be back in twenty minutes," she said. "Keep your eye out until I get back."

Rix climbed into the condenser and got to work installing and reattaching old parts and new. Twenty minutes sailed past and Kel arrived with a long rifle slung over her back. "Any trouble?" Rix asked just about the time the new parts arrived.

"None, but people are scared Rix. What if Unit 3 or 4 die? There's no way to move six thousand people out of here with enough speed to save everyone," she said. "Those people who have ships are starting to leave. There's fighting in the Atrium."

"Give me another hour and we'll be ready for a test," Rix said.

"That soon? Can I tell people? It would do a lot to help people calm down."

"No, because if it takes longer, we'll have new problems."

Rix continued to work, and the pile of parts started diminishing rapidly as Philo continued handing them one by one to Rix until finally Rix climbed out from inside the condenser and closed a large panel behind him.

"Is it done?" Kel asked.

"I've run diagnostics on most of the subsystems," Rix said. "It's looking good. We might as well give it a try."

A laser bolt ricocheted off the deck between Kel and Rix. Philo, who was standing nearby cried out and then jumped onto the nearby station superstructure and climbed away.

"Take cover, Rix," Kel said, spinning down to one knee, searching for the gunman.

"Beverly, patch me through to the constable," Rix said, lunging for the control box that would allow him to power up the new condenser.

"This is Quixly. What do you want?" Quixly's voice was flat with irritation.

"Someone is in Environmental, shooting at us," Rix said.

"Shooting? Are you serious?" Quixly asked.

"Good Lord, do I have to argue everything with you? Yes, I'm serious," Rix said. At the last moment, he pulled his hand back from the control box just as a laser bolt buried itself in the circuit, slagging the small assembly. "You've got to be kidding me."

"I see him," Kel said returning fire. "He's getting away!"

"Because he did what he wanted," Rix said.

It took a few minutes for Quixly to arrive and when he did, he wore armor and had a helmet on over his normal clothing. "Excitement's over," Kel said when he approached.

"What happened?" Quixly asked.

"This happened," Rix said, showing the melted control box to Quixly.

"That looks important. Is it ruined?"

"Yes. Do you have security cameras down here so you can figure out who's after us?" Kel asked.

"No. This is crazy. Anyone on this station knows we need this equipment to work if we're to survive."

"Right," Rix said angrily. "Your perpetrator wants or needs this to fail. Do you have any guesses as to who benefits if Patience Station fails by catastrophic failure of air handling? Because, this isn't just poor maintenance at this point."

"Stop telling me my job," Quixly said, matching Rix's ire.

"Both of you stop," Garba growled, joining the conversation. "Rix Banner, I think I understand what's happened. Can it be fixed?"

"Yes. It might take twenty minutes, but there's another control box I can take from Unit 2 that's fully compatible," Rix said.

"How can we help?"

"Keep people from shooting at me while I do it?"

"That sounds fair."

"I need to find who's doing this. I don't have time to watch a human fumbling around with technology past his understanding," Quixly said.

"Bub, if you can fix it, I'll stand by with a gun and watch your back," Rix said.

"You really do bring out the best in people, Rix Banner," Garba said unfairly. "Quixly, get someone down here and ensure Rix Banner's safety. I will stay here until that is done."

"That's too dangerous, Mayor Klex," Quixly said. "I insist that you leave. Now!"

"Can I get started?" Rix asked.

"Yes, yes, go ahead," Garba said.

It was a simple matter for Rix to remove the existing, ruined control box and then to repeat the process with Unit 2's control box. Moving it over, the entire process was complete in thirty minutes.

"And that's it?" Garba asked. "This unit will work?"

"It'll be our first test run. I'll start diagnostics capture and we'll give our first try," Rix said. "And it's starting, now. Give it a couple of minutes, it'll be a slow start due to the diagnostic tracing."

"We need this immediately," Garba urged.

"Right, and if it's broken, we need to know why even sooner," Rix said. As the system control fired up the individual subsystems, Rix watched the free-scrolling events. Every so often an error would come up and he held his breath as he looked into each error. Fortunately, none of the errors were critical and the condenser continued its slow start. Finally, icy crystals dropped into Rix's new gravel trap and water began dripping onto the charge couplers. Industrial fans kicked on and Rix's ears popped as clean new air was introduced into Patience Station.

"It's working?" Garba asked with guarded anticipation.

"With some issues," Rix said. "But we can fix those in a couple of days, after we recharge the station."

"Is it supposed to be doing that?" Garba asked as gravel tumbled out the back of the machine, missing Rix's bucket. Rix repositioned the bucket after sliding the gravel out of the way.

"Sure is," Rix said sheepishly.

23
FRESH AIR

"Can you smell that?" Kel asked.

There hadn't been further gunfire in Environmental and with the constable posting a guard to watch the area, most of the excitement had diminished.

"Smell, what?" Rix asked, lounging back in one of the reclining chairs that sat beneath a large leafy tree.

"The air is a little sweeter."

"I don't know about sweet, but those filters have pulled quite a lot of the suspended particles out. I think this is closer to how air should smell," Rix said. "Head's up. Petju is coming over."

The middle-aged spacer woman approached cautiously and with a big smile on her face. "I hope I'm not interrupting anything."

"Not at all, Petju," Kel said, eyeing the pair of comera cups the woman was carrying. "What do you have there?"

"Word is, all this wonderful fresh atmo is because of your work, Mr. Banner," Petju said. "Is that right?"

"I certainly had help," Rix said. "But, sure, we were able to make repairs to Unit 1. It's nice to have enough air volume to get the pressure restored."

Petju handed the cups to both Kel and Rix. "I don't have much to offer, but I wanted to do something. You have no idea how depressing it has been to live with the fear of running out of air. I just don't understand how someone so unfamiliar with our systems could have possibly done something our own maintenance couldn't."

"He's just that talented," Kel said.

"I've heard a rumor that you're opening your own spaceship repair shop," Petju said.

"Word travels fast around here," Rix said. "And that's at least the idea. I don't have many tools, and truthfully, I don't even know what tools I'll need, but I'm not letting that get in the way of my dream."

"You're so full of hope. Please don't lose that!" she said. "Will you continue work on the station? I heard Garba hired you."

"It's hard to know what the future holds. As of this moment, I've completed the contract I had with Garba. I think it's likely this sort of work will transfer back to Geoff."

A flash of concern passed over Petju's face but was just as quickly replaced by a smile. "Well, regardless of all that, thank you, Mr. Banner. Today you've provided a fresh breath of air to all of us and that is something we'll all feel quite a lot of gratitude for."

Rix made a show of digging a scoop of frozen treat from the cup. "I feel your gratitude, Petju! Also, please just call me Rix."

Petju nodded and then walked off with a smile on her face. "You're becoming quite the hero, aren't you," Kel said.

"Not something I'm looking for," Rix said. "Is it weird that people aren't talking more about the shooter? Someone was shooting at the station's air supply. That feels like good reason for concern."

"Hold on a minute, I just got a message from Garba."

Rix shrugged and continued eating his comera. While his body had adjusted to the lower air pressure with which they'd been living, he was glad to be back at what amounted to sea level.

"What's up?" Rix asked after Kel finished reading her message.

"Garba wants to talk. Are you up for a stroll? She said she was working on a meal," Kel said.

"I wonder if Geoff will be there. He sure was salty last time," Rix said.

"No idea. Are you up for it?" Kel asked, standing in front of Rix's recliner.

"Sure," he said, holding out a hand so she'd help him up.

"You're stout, did you know that, Earthling?" Kel asked, grunting as she pulled him from the chair.

"Difference between spacers and natural gravity," Rix said. "Patience Station is sixty percent of Earth."

"Or maybe you're just getting fat on all this free comera and dinners with the mayor."

"Or that," Rix agreed, gaining his feet. "I imagine Garba wants to talk about maintenance going forward. Is that what you're thinking?"

"If we hadn't been fired at yet," Kel said.

"You don't seem overly shaken up by all that, though," Rix said as they stepped onto the elevator.

"They were shooting at you. I just needed to keep out of the way. I've been shot at plenty of times in *Calypso*. I suppose you just get used to it after a while," Kel said, leaning against the wall outside Garba's penthouse. "Are you ready for this?"

"Probably not," Rix said but pressed what amounted to a doorbell all the same.

"Kel, Rix, welcome!" Garba said. "Come in, I was just about to pull out the casserole."

"You work fast," Rix said. "We just saw you in Environmental a couple hours ago."

"I think better when my hands are busy," Garba said.

"I'm the same way," Rix said. "Is Geoff joining us?"

"I'm not sure," Garba said. "I let him know we were meeting, but he's been put off by having a second hand in the maintenance."

"Then let me step away," Rix said. "We've completed our contract. You have a working condenser, complete with a refit of its filtration system and a way to keep the gravel off the charge couplers. I know, that's a lot of technical jargon, but you're getting ahead."

"Except we're not," she said. "I've read the reports that detail the work you completed. How were those units so dirty and where were the filters that came out of them?"

"I don't know. I cleaned them and rebuilt the brackets to hold the filters. Someone will need to replace those filters every month and sure, you'll need to buy the filter media, but that's the cost of breathable air and totally worth it. I can't imagine that's not already in your budget."

"Our budget is tight, and maintenance is high on that list," Garba said.

"Look, I'm not here to second-guess anyone," Rix said. "I think we need to turn the conversation over to Geoff. He has the experience."

"Between us," Garba said ominously. "Are the current units well maintained? Was this preventable?"

"I can't answer the second as I have no idea the conditions of what Geoff was working on. The first is just as much trouble, though. I haven't looked at any of the three Units 3, 4 or 5. Units 1 and 2 were out of service, so being in poor shape is to be expected."

"Your answers are quite politic," she answered.

"I don't want anyone second-guessing me anymore than Geoff wants me second-guessing him," Rix said. "I can say that Unit 5 failed because the ice that was delivered was full of gravel which is extremely hard on the charge couplers."

"So we're just buying time by fixing Unit 1?"

"Not at all. I created a gravel pre-pass filter and now that extra gravel is dumped out the back. Someone will need to empty the gravel bucket from time to time, but it's better than trying to pull it out of the condenser after it's caused damage."

"I see. I'll talk to Geoff about that," Garba said typing on a tablet. "Putting that aside. We briefly talked about installing the unit brought back by *Calypso*. Geoff is insistent that it is an impossible fit, but you sound more optimistic. Your original optimism could have been written off to a crazy, semi-sentient, off-worlder. Now, that argument seems less pertinent."

"Are you asking if I think the new unit can be installed where Unit 2 is currently?"

"Yes."

"I do," Rix said.

"Can you do this work?"

"Yes, but we need a different type of deal," Rix said. "I took most of the risk on our first contract. When someone vandalized Unit 1, I had to pay for the replacement parts."

"That's not entirely fair. You didn't ask to be compensated," she said.

"True, but my reading of the contract said I only needed fifteen hundred credits from Patience Station," Rix said. "Would you not have enforced that?"

"It would have been a judgment call," Garba said. "Hold on, let me get the casserole out. Kel, be a darling and grab plates from the cabinet to the left of the sink."

"Feel free to transfer five hundred credits if Patience Station wants to make me whole," Rix said.

Garba stopped what she was doing and swiped at her HUD. Just then, Rix heard a chime in his ear and realized it was acknowledgement of the receipt of additional funds from Garba, bringing him back to thirteen hundred credits. It wasn't enough money to start a business, especially one that would take as much capital as working on spaceships, but it was progress in the right direction.

"Are you satisfied of my good faith?"

"That is generous, thank you," Rix said. "I think the contract I'd be interested in for installing the Dravari condenser is something along the lines of: Patience Station pays for manufactory costs, which is only fair, I'd be open to barter for equipment useful for my spaceship mechanics business."

"You don't want credits?"

"Bartering is beneficial for both of us. You've taken over, or bought out people who've left the station, right?" Rix asked.

"I'm surprised you've considered this," Garba said. "But you're right. There have been cases where I've purchased equipment and supplies from folks who are moving on. Although, in some cases, they've abandoned that equipment. Before you ask, I'm not handing it to you for free."

"I'm not asking for free, but there should be wiggle room. We all benefit from business success and let's be truthful, if I fail, you'll just get the equipment back."

"It sounds like you've thought about this. Do you have any idea what you're looking for?" she asked.

"I'd need to see what you have available. Mostly, I need general tools and tool cabinets," Rix said. "I imagine you've a warehouse where you've stockpiled equipment. Would you give me a chance to look through it?"

"I don't suppose that would hurt anyone," Garba said. "Something's been bothering me, though. You said there's too much gravel in our ice and it's ruining the condensers. Why wouldn't Units 3 and 4 suffer similar fates?"

"It takes time for the failure to occur," Rix said. "I believe they will eventually fail for the same reasons as Units 1 and 2."

"I thought you didn't want to comment on another man's work."

"Right. Regardless of how Geoff feels about me, I'll let him know what I've done to fix the gravel problem," Rix said. "I assume he'll want to be proactive and install my new gravel filters."

"Or he'll be stubborn and ignore it entirely."

"Your words, not mine," Rix said.

"When can you start on the replacement of Unit 2?"

"Would you be willing to take me to your warehouse?" Rix asked. "I know one thing I'd like right off the bat and that's the broken photonic generators by the maintenance entrance. In that they're broken, I'd say they're not worth a tremendous amount."

"And ridiculously expensive to replace," Garba said. "If you fix them, they're worth in excess of sixty thousand credits."

"Doesn't change that they're broken," Rix said. "Let's call that half my fee for hooking up Unit 2."

"I do not think I am going to enjoy working with you, Rix Banner. You ask for too much and yet if I turn you down, Patience Station will fail," Garba said.

"I see value in items that have no value to you at all, Garba," Rix said. "You look at the photonic generators and think of the value of them when they're working. How long have they sat there in that same state, unrepaired because it's too expensive? It's possible I won't be able to fix them or that I won't be able to afford the parts. Your risk on this is nothing beyond your perception of value."

"Semi-sentient. What kind of joke was that?" Garba snorted derisively. "You've got me. Fifty percent of the payment is the broken photonic barriers."

"I'll go easier on you with the tools," Rix said, starting on the casserole. "And this is delicious. You are quite a good cook, Garba."

"Thank you," she said. "Perhaps it is a good thing you are a strong negotiator, but I have to say, I do not enjoy it in this moment."

"I'll take that as a compliment."

"I'm not sure that is what I intended."

Rix smiled and quickly finished the casserole in front of him. Garba saw how quickly he'd devoured his food and offered him a second helping, which he gratefully accepted and quickly put away.

"Should we get going?" he asked.

"Yes, I think that is reasonable," Garba said. "If we run into Geoff, please allow me to do the speaking. He will not like that you have been given access to our warehouse."

"Well, think of it this way," Rix said. "Tools have no value if they're left on a shelf. The tools we agree are part of this contract will be utilized to repair the people of Patience Station's spaceships and small craft. I imagine they'll also be used to repair the very station itself. In both cases, the value of Patience Station is increased, just as it was when I repaired the first atmospheric unit and just as it will be when I install the second. This is a win-win, Garba. At least that's how I view it."

"I … you're very convincing. Let us go see what you might have interest in."

"Perfect," Rix said.

And without further discussion, the three of them set off for the warehouse, which was located on Level 8. Arriving, Rix found the expanse of equipment, including residential furnishing and rows and rows of neatly stacked crates.

"I believe there are tools over in this direction," Garba said, obviously referencing her HUD.

"Oh, here we go," Rix said with some satisfaction as he found a stash that included tool cabinets, varying sizes of gravity assisted lifts and myriad hand tools.

"Remember, everything you identify will be accounted for," Garba warned.

"If you give me two hours, I will set aside everything for which I have interest. After that, you can take a look and we can begin to haggle," Rix said. "I will try to be fair. Also, if you're okay with it, I'll keep track of items that I'm interested in but would be outside of the scope of our deal. That way for future contracts, we'll already have a baseline of items I find valuable."

"I don't suppose that would hurt. Kel, it is in your best interest to keep knowledge of this warehouse to yourself. Do we have an understanding?"

"Yes, Garba," Kel answered.

Rix waited a moment for Garba to leave and then proceeded. "What's with all the cloak and dagger?"

"Garba likes to pretend that we all don't know she's taken people's life-long possessions when they can't pay rent anymore. Technically, it's not illegal. She has a contract to back up what she does, but it's a sore spot."

"Does she have anything of yours in here?" Rix asked.

"Not yet. I'm behind on my rent, though, so it could happen soon enough," Kel said.

"You don't seem all that upset about it."

"I'm not, really," Kel said. "I can live aboard *Calypso* if it comes to that and I don't have a lot of possessions, otherwise."

"Didn't you get paid for delivering the Dravari condenser?"

"No. Geoff says it can't be installed. There's a damage waiver that says if I deliver an uninstallable unit, she only pays half," Kel said.

"Hold on. If I fix it, do you get paid?"

"I think she's going to try to wiggle out of the contract because she's having to pay to have it installed."

"That's cold. So, hold on, then. If she hasn't paid you fully, then she doesn't own the condenser and I'm not installing something that has a local claim on it. That's just bad practice."

"Rix, it's stolen. I hardly think you can make that claim with a straight face."

"Watch me," Rix said. "However, just in case we get that worked out, I should see what kind of tools she has stored down here. Beverly, could you help me identify tools most beneficial for work on spaceships? I already have a list started. I'll send it over."

"Hello, Rix!" Beverly said, appearing in front of him wearing spacer coveralls that matched what was commonly worn on *Calypso.* "Yes. Keep turning so I can record a good scan of the area. Oh, yes, that's good. What value are you shooting for in total?"

"Do you have access to some sort of book value for used tools vs new?"

"I will make reasonable adjustments."

"And then lower by forty percent."

"That is quite a discount. Why would you do that?"

"Just because. Let's shoot for five thousand credits."

"Oh, that is a small sum and much of this equipment is quite expensive."

"Target items that are repairable. I don't mind fixing things if it saves me money."

"Ah, good point. Also, congratulations on restoring atmospheric pressure to Patience Station, your efforts have increased the quality of life for thousands."

"That's generous," Rix said. "Thank you."

"I have your list. I took the liberty of showing options, depending on the style of work you're interested in to include repair for: *engine, hull, interior, gravity and repulsor, and electronics.* Select two of those five."

"That's easy. Engine, gravity and repulse technologies are my priority," Rix said.

Blue outlines overlay on Rix's HUD showing the items Beverly selected, and Rix started making piles. The first cut took twenty minutes and Rix started inspecting each of the items.

"What are you thinking?" Kel asked.

"Cabinets," Rix said. "I need organization in the shop, but I haven't even seen it."

"There are a few cabinets that would match the types found in your shop back in Cranberry Cove," Beverly said as new blue highlights showed in the distance.

"Good. So, give me your next choices, if we had a higher budget," Rix said.

"Okay."

And so went the process of Rix making several piles of tools and equipment of varying priorities.

"I didn't know there were so many sizes of boltguns," Rix said, turning a heavy boltgun over in his hand. "This thing looks like it could staple armor onto a battleship."

"You are not far off," Beverly said. "It is used for attaching skeletal members to a ship's superstructure. It is more valuable for hull repairs than what you'd specified, but it is not an expensive tool, so I made a judgment call."

"That's exactly the kind of judgment calls we need."

And for another hour, Rix, Beverly and Kel continued moving items between piles until finally, Rix sat back in a comfortable chair, tired from the exertion.

"Are you making progress?" Garba asked, showing up unexpectedly.

"I'm adding this chair to the list," Rix said.

"What is all this?" Garba asked, gesturing at the piles.

"Let's get to that in a minute," Rix said.

"Okay, what's on your mind?" Garba asked.

"Apparently, you haven't paid Kel for the condenser she brought back from the Dravari outpost," Rix said.

"You're not wrong. According to Geoff it's damaged and now I'm paying because of carelessness."

"Hey, wait a minute. That's not fair," Kel said. "We extracted that thing without a single scratch or dent."

"That doesn't change what we agreed to," Garba said.

"Right," Rix said, cutting off Kel's hot retort. "But, also, that means that condenser is Kel's and I don't have any right to install it for Patience Station. You guys need to work that out before I do anything with it."

"Is that how you see it, Kel?" Garba asked.

"I'm behind two months on rent," Kel said. "I was counting on that money to pay it off. I didn't choose that condenser, Geoff did. It was his responsibility to verify that it'd fit. I'm not a maintenance person."

"One month of your back rent," Garba said. "That's fair and you know it."

Kel shrugged. "I suppose."

"And, this is too much," Garba said, waving a hand over all the piles. "You have at least twenty thousand credits worth of equipment here."

"That you don't have a lot invested in," Rix said and before she could argue, he continued. "But, I agree. This is aggressive. How about these three piles." Rix gestured to three piles of the equipment he most wanted.

"That's still a lot," Garba said.

"And I bring a lot of value to Patience Station which means tax revenue and people having money in their pockets because they can be productive. It's a win-win."

"You keep using that phrase when what you really mean is you're getting a great deal," Garba said.

Rix pushed his hand out to Garba. "Shake my hand and seal the deal, Garba. You know as well as I do that we need to get that Dravari condenser installed."

"Were you this good a negotiator back on Earth?" she asked, shaking his hand.

"Honestly, it didn't come up that much," Rix said. "I've just sent you an itemized list. Please double-check. I'd hate for there to be any misunderstanding."

"Your list looks good. We have a deal."

24

UNDER FIRE

"Hey, you need to take this," Kel said, handing a small pistol to Rix. Evening had passed and they'd met for an early breakfast as Rix wanted to get started mapping out the installation.

"I'm glad you're taking my advice on being armed."

"The constable hasn't caught the shooter yet," Kel said. "There's no reason to think he or she won't be back."

"I agree," Rix said and changed subjects as he stowed the pistol. "Do you know who sells snacks that Philo likes? I need a stash because he said he'd come help me today."

"Petju has a dried fruit protein bar that he likes. It's better than the full glucose snacks he buys for himself when he has credits to spend."

"I'll send her a message. I noticed she doesn't open her shop until later," Rix said.

"Okay," Kel said. "And I know you're busy with all this, but Vigno contacted me yesterday. He's talking about taking *Calypso* back if I can't make some progress on what I owe him."

"How much does he want?" Rix asked.

"Two thousand by tomorrow," Kel said. "Another five thousand by the end of the month, which is only twenty more days."

"Do you have anything?"

"A little over a thousand, but that needs to keep me alive until I make another haul," she said.

Rix checked his bank balance and was pleased to see it had grown to twelve hundred. He'd listed the gravel pre-pass plans on the manufactory marketplace and had sold a unit for three hundred credits and made another hundred credits from other sales.

"Use that to make the payment," Rix said, flicking a funds transfer of a thousand credits. "I have money for groceries and an idea about how we might make a little more, let me think while I work on the install."

"How do you have this money?" Kel asked. "I've been there for all your deals with Garba. You're not getting credits from her."

"I've been selling IP on the manufactory marketplace," Rix said. "Apparently, nobody thinks about these problems the same way I do. I'm probably just lucky, but it's making an income stream."

"That's crazy. I'll go ahead and pay Vigno. You should know, the two thousand doesn't reduce our forty-seven thousand in debt, it's a penalty for late payment," she said.

Rix sighed and holstered the pistol on his belt. "I see why nobody gets ahead here. Everyone has their hand in everyone else's pocket."

"People are just trying to survive, Rix," Kel said defensively.

"Okay, enough philosophy for the morning, then," Rix said. "What are you up to today?" Kel didn't answer immediately and shifted her gaze elsewhere. "What's that about?"

"I don't really have anything to do. My skill is transport, but Dravari patrols won't let me do anything in system."

"What about the rest of Surnak Belt?" Rix asked. "Best I can tell, Dravari have nothing to say out here."

"It's dangerous, Rix," Kel said. "The belt is filled with pirates looking to jump unsuspecting freighters."

"But you're not unsuspecting and you're also fast," Rix said. "What's the closest settlement that has goods worth trading? What if we made some sort of speculation run? Are there things we could trade from Patience Station that others would like?"

"Well, clothing, I suppose. And, Petju has those travel snacks."

"That's fine, but you're not thinking big enough," Rix said. "Patience Station has extremely cheap fuel. Why is that? Is that the same with other colonies within a few days travel? What about Beaker's Black Rum?"

"That's just a hobby."

"Is it? What if you bought a case on speculation and just tested the waters on a trip. It only costs you fuel to find out," Rix said.

"I don't have money to front a load."

"Forget that for a minute. Do you have a destination that would work?"

"Sout Atal is three days, if you take Dravari space, six days if you take Inner Passage."

"Explain Inner Passage."

"Through the asteroids. There's a route that works. It can be hairy if you're solo, because you have to stay alert for long stretches. I haven't been to Sout Atal for years," she said.

"We're partners, right?" Rix asked.

"Sure. Why?"

"I'll front two thousand in six days," Rix said. "You take the next six days, work your contacts to find a buyer for a mix of goods you can get here on station that Sout Atal doesn't have, or at least not at our price. But promise that you'll get a case of Beaker's rum, even if you don't have a buyer."

"Do you really think you'll have two thousand credits in six days?"

"No, I think I'll have that in five days, but I'm playing it safe," Rix said.

"Well, heck, okay then," Kel said her eyes lighting up. "If you really think this will work, I'll try it. Beats sitting around the station waiting for something else to break."

"That a girl," Rix said. "Now, I got to get to work. Pick up those Philo snacks for me once Petju opens, okay?"

"Got you covered," Kel said.

Rix smiled and was surprised when Kel gave him a quick hug before they went their separate ways. His smile doused when he felt the unfamiliar weight of the pistol at his side, reminding him that someone had recently shot at him for the simple task of trying to fix Patience Station's air supply.

"Beverly, is there some way you could keep a look out for me today while I'm working? Paying attention to what's around me is hard when I'm focused on fixing things," Rix said.

"Yes, I will have Philo bring one of the security cameras from *Calypso* to set up near your workspace," Beverly said. "Do you mind sharing your plan for installing the Dravari condenser?"

"Today will be all about removing Unit 2," Rix said. "Instead of just pulling it out as a single unit, I'm going to take it apart. That way we have the parts handy for the other units if we need."

"I estimate you have added six hours of work to your schedule," Beverly said.

"Did you add cleaning?" Beverly chuckled. "You don't do that very often, Beverly."

"Laugh? It was involuntary. I find your fastidiousness to be quite adorable," she said.

"Most equipment works more efficiently if kept clean," Rix said. "Although, if I'm honest, I do prefer cleanliness."

"It is not a fault," Beverly said. "Just a funny consistency."

While Rix had been talking to Beverly, he'd entered the elevator on the way down to Level 3 Environmental. When he exited the elevator, he noticed a figure near the condenser units he'd just fixed.

"Hey, you! What are you doing over there?" he called when he heard the clanging sound of a hammer on metal. With a quick start to his step, he rushed forward, which between his shout and his movement, caught the eye of a second person near the units. Old instincts kicked in as he felt before he saw the rifle swing in his direction. "Oh, crap!" Rix threw himself to the deck and slid forward on his backside, until his shoulders rested against a pile of crates, which gunfire sailed over top of.

"Beverly, call the constable, I'm under fire down here!" he said pulling the pistol from its holster.

"Constable Quixly is not immediately answering. I will continue trying. As well, I will alert Garba Klex."

"I'm going to pop up, but I'll return. I need you to see where they're at," Rix said.

"Go," Beverly said.

Rix scooted to the side and popped up and then just as quickly sat back down. "Did you get anything?"

"Yes, there are two wearing masks. Only one has a weapon, look forward, I will project a picture of where the rifle wielder stands. I believe this person awaits your appearance," she said.

"How good is your geometry, Beverly?" Rix asked.

"Extraordinary by human standards," she said.

"I thought you might say that," Rix said. "I'm going to hold my pistol around the end of this crate. I want you to line me up so I either hit the shooter or I'm at least lined up close."

"Why would you not care if you hit?" Beverly asked.

"People's aim is significantly decreased when they are being fired at. Especially people who haven't shot at others often," Rix said. "I don't think our shooters are professionals."

"Why would you say that?"

"Because I ducked into cover and haven't fired a shot. The good money is in rushing my position before I can find a weapon or courage," Rix said. "Bold actions in combat are rewarded. At least that's what my lieutenant used to tell me."

"I wonder if your lieutenant simply had an ulterior motive to get you to do things against your best interest."

"Save the argument a minute, if you don't mind," Rix said, sliding over and poking his pistol out so it pointed in the general direction of the air-handling units. Instead of giving Rix verbal instructions, Beverly displayed something akin to the sweep hand atop a compass. When Rix adjusted the aim of his pistol, the sweep hand pointed toward a big arrow. Similarly, a second compass like display was shown, the elevation of the shot. For the elevation, Beverly displayed where on the person's body, Rix's shot would hit. "That's good stuff, Beverly."

Aiming below the person's waist, Rix fired two shots in rapid succession. His fire was met with a yelp of pain and a shot that was fired and ricocheted into the steel girders above. More surprised than even his attackers, Rix couldn't believe his good luck at hitting home.

"Okay, we're going!" Rix shouted, jumping up, his pistol trained to the location Beverly had displayed. He was late, though as the two figures were already running away, one of which was limping painfully. Rix fired two more shots, but purposefully missed, not wanting to kill anyone. His shots elicited both more yelps and speed alike.

Instead of chasing them down, Rix made his way quickly over to the condenser units. He shook his head as he came upon the carnage of what looked like at least thirty minutes of vandalism.

"Rix Banner, please provide your status." Rix recognized the voice as belonging to Hutari, the young communications officer for Patience Station.

"I'm attempting to secure the atmospheric generators on Level 3 Environmental," Rix said. "I apparently interrupted two who were vandalizing our atmospheric condensers. They shot at me, and I returned fire. I believe one of them was hit below the waist. I am uninjured."

"The constable is alerted," she said. "Please stay on the line as help is on the way."

"Copy that," Rix answered, glancing over to where the pair had disappeared into a stairwell.

"Rix, are you okay?" Kel called. "I leave you alone for one minute and this is what happens?"

"I'm fine, Kel," Rix said. "I'm not sure the same can be said for the condenser units, though. Unit 3 took quite a beating and they broke Unit 4's control unit, although it looks like it's still working. How'd you hear?"

"I happened to run into Garba. We were talking and the call came in. She's on her way down. And I'm going out to *Calypso* to grab my assault rifle. This is getting dumb. The constable was supposed to have someone posted down there."

Rix heard the elevator arrive and glanced over as both Garba and constable Quixly exited. They were in the midst of a heated argument which they exited the elevator car to continue. Rix holstered his pistol and approached.

"What is this all about?" Quixly asked angrily. "Why are you shooting up my station?"

"Your station?" Garba asked angrily.

"Yes, my station. Patience Station is my responsibility," Quixly said.

"I'm the mayor, it is more my responsibility than yours and I ordered you to keep this area secured. An order you failed to execute," she said.

"There was no one when you came down aside from the reported assailants?" Quixly asked.

"Right and they did a number on Units 3 and 4," Rix said. "You might want to get Geoff down here to see what needs doing, they're outside of my allowed scope of work."

"If you know how to fix them it seems in everyone's best interest," Garba said.

"You're looking at eight hundred credits in repairs," Rix said flatly.

"Fine," Garba said with obvious irritation in her voice. "Fix them and you, Quixly, you stay put until you figure out why your man ran off. I want a name for the people doing this. Do you understand me?"

"You can't order me around," Quixly said.

"How badly do you want to keep that badge, Quixly? Because it's not going to mean anything if these atmospheric generators stop working, regardless of how it happens. And so far, Mr. Banner is the only one who's shown any aptitude for doing so."

"He's just a dirty human."

"Keep that crap to yourself, Quixly," she said. "And if you give him any trouble after I'm gone, I'll hear about it and I will make it my mission to make your life miserable. Do you read me?"

"Loud and clear."

"Loud and clear who?"

"Mayor," Quixly said hesitantly.

"Now put it all together," she pushed.

"Loud and clear, Mayor." By the end, his tone had lost its petulant edge.

"Mayor, there's a part in your personal store that would be helpful. Are you willing to let me grab it?" Rix said, interrupting the awkward moment.

"That's fine."

"Kel, if I give you a picture, could you grab it for me?" Rix asked.

"Of course," Kel agreed.

Rix got to work on disassembling the damaged units and ignored the chatter behind him. Several minutes later, he realized he was alone with Quixly.

"What's with the daggers, already?" Rix asked.

"Daggers?" Quixly asked, irritation evident in his voice.

"You don't like me. That much is obvious," Rix said. "I don't get it. I keep to myself for the most part and I'm working to make Patience Station a better place to live. What's your malfunction?"

"I'm not here to be your friend. Get back to work," Quixly said, and it was at this moment when Philo showed up with the security device they'd talked about. "That's just perfect. Now I'm babysitting a whole batch of rodents."

"Quix always grumps," Philo said, handing the device over.

"Is that a security recording device?" Quixly asked.

Rix figured there'd be no reason to lie, so he set about installing the video sensors. "Yes. I'll provide access to the feed if the constable's office would like access."

"You can't setup a video recorder in a public space. Take that down."

"That's interesting that you consider this public space. To my understanding, this is municipal space and controlled by Patience Station."

"Don't argue with me. This is my station. Take it down. That's an order."

"Sure," Rix said, setting the sensor aside. "Feels like it'd be a useful tool to figuring out the guys causing all this damage."

"I don't need you telling me how to do my job."

Rix bit back the words he wanted to say and was surprised when Philo piped up. "Quix need help. Not do good job."

"Keep it to yourself midget ape."

"Philo, I'm sorry he's being a jerk," Rix said. "Would you grab the welder from *Calypso* and a small sheet of the wall panel steel?"

"Yup yup!" Philo said, bounding off.

Rix looked at Quixly, waiting to see if the obstinate constable had any more to say. After a few moments the quiet became uncomfortable, but Rix was unflinching. Finally, Quixly turned his head, spat on the deck and walked off grumbling.

With the excitement over, Rix concentrated on the task at hand, which was to repair the broken, but still operable units. Having sent out Kel and Philo to fetch items, he resumed with repairs. Without a break, Rix worked through the afternoon and finally stepped away from the units. He discovered that at some point in the day Kel and Philo had pulled chairs over and both were lightly dozing.

"Hey, do you guys want to grab some dinner?" Rix asked. "My treat. I sent the bill off to Garba and she's already paid up."

Kel blinked lazily and wiped sleep from her eyes. "Did you say something about eating? I'm starving."

"Yeah, my treat."

"Where did Quixly go?"

Rix pointed to an alcove thirty meters away. "It's not Quixly, but his deputies are taking shifts patrolling this level. They're mostly leaving us alone."

"Philo said there was some excitement about installing the video surveillance," Kel said. "What was that about?"

"No idea. Quixly wasn't a big fan, I'll tell you that much."

"We can't set it up? Why not call Garba? She seems to have his number."

"I was thinking that maybe Philo could climb up and install it in the station's superstructure, up there," Rix said, pointing above.

"Philo treat first," Philo said, stirring from his chair. Rix had anticipated Philo's request and tossed him two dried and candied pieces of fruit. "Good good!"

"Wait for us to leave. We'll walk out past Quixly's deputy and keep him from seeing you climb, okay, Philo?"

"Yup yup!"

Rix and Kel set off and were soon confronted by the constable's deputy. "Hello Berg," Kel said flatly when they approached.

"Why are you coming out this way?" Berg asked.

"Just showing Rix the station," Kel said. "What, are you hiding something?"

"No," Berg said petulantly. "But you don't need to be coming back here."

"You're not in charge, so stop acting like you are."

Berg tapped the pistol in its holster and raised his eyebrows. "Is that right?" he asked. "Because I'm telling you we're going to have a problem if you keep coming this way."

"Not worth it, Kel," Rix said, grabbing Kel's arm.

Kel frowned but allowed Rix to pull her away. When they were back near the atmosphere generators, Kel finally said something. "I don't need you telling me what to do, Rix," she said with irritation. "I can fight my own battles."

"There's something going on in this station. And Quixly is in the middle of it," Rix said. "We don't want to be fighting any battles right now. Let's see what those video sensors pull up."

"You lost an entire day on installing the Dravari condenser," Kel said. "What if that was the objective."

"To keep us from fixing the condensers? Who would want that? Living here would be impossible without atmosphere," Rix said. And then he smiled and nodded. "Yeah, I heard it. It's obvious that someone is trying to shut down Patience Station. And it seems like they don't care if a bunch of people die."

"Damn. You're not wrong," Kel said. "What do we do?"

"For whatever reason, we're right in the middle of this thing," Rix said. "I think we use those cameras to figure some things out and I keep fixing things. Eventually, whoever's behind this is going to overstep."

"I love your optimism."

"Let's eat and then I'll probably go back down and see if I can get started on removing Unit 2. Do you find it weird that we haven't seen Geoff at all today?"

"Yes, and do you ever relax?" Kel asked.

25

LOOSE LIPS SINK SHIPS

"I thought I might find you here," Garba said, startling Rix. Two full days had passed since he'd started working on Unit 2 and he had considerable progress to show for his efforts.

"Hey there, Garba," Rix said cheerfully. "I was just wrapping up the afternoon, thinking about some dinner."

"You're in a good mood," Garba reflected.

Rix wiped greasy hands on his coveralls and stepped away from the disassembled Dravari condenser unit. Garba's conversational attitude was new, and it piqued his curiosity.

"What's shakin?" he asked, trying to keep things light.

"That's a strange question, but assuming you're asking why I'm here, that's not so hard," she said. "I was interested in an update of your progress and wanted to know if we'd had more excitement."

"Whatever you said to Quixly sure put his men on their best behavior," Rix said. "It's been as quiet as a morgue around here. Perfect working conditions."

"Can you get it done?"

"It? Do you mean install the Dravari condenser?" Rix asked and when Garba answered, he pushed on. "For sure, Mayor. All we really needed was a mating hood to match the old plenum with the new unit's output port."

"And you found one?"

"No. I made one, though. I spec'd what I figured would mate the old with the new and sent it over to the manufactory. It's the dark purple piece over on the deck. I just got it installed. The next step is rebuilding the Dravari condenser on top of that piece and completing the connection with the station return air."

"You make it sound easy. I'm told it's not," she said.

"Most of the time, if you break down a project like this into small steps, you can focus on just one step at a time. For me, that's the easiest way, otherwise I'd get overwhelmed by the project size," he said. "I don't imagine that's what you came down here to learn, though. If I put my customer service hat on, I'd guess you're looking for a completion date. My best estimate is two days, three days maximum, assuming there's no more gunfire."

"I can't imagine how Patience Station will feel with four working atmospheric generators," she said. "Have you seen Geoff? I was thinking he was maybe down here maintaining the other units."

"Haven't seen him," Rix said warily.

"What's that look for?" Garba asked.

"It's not my place to say, Mayor," Rix said. "You asked me to fix a unit and install another. I figure it's best if I keep to the business at hand."

"This is a private conversation, Mr. Banner," Garba said. "If you have something to say about Geoff, I want to hear it."

"You two are close," Rix said. "I know better than to step between a couple."

"This is about the other condensers, isn't it? You'd like a shot at fixing them before they break like Unit 5 did," she said. "Am I right?"

"Honestly, I think with the current population of Patience Station, once I'm done, we'll have more than enough air," he said. "My standards were born of necessity in a time of war, and I understand that my exacting standards aren't for everyone. I don't need to be causing trouble."

"And you think that by telling me Geoff isn't doing a great job of maintaining the condensers, that'll cause trouble?" she asked.

"I certainly do."

Garba gave a wry grin. "I'll say you did a great job of telling me without speaking the words yourself. I have a responsibility as mayor and primary principal of Patience Station to put its well-being above the pride of anyone and that includes Geoff."

"Makes sense."

"Forgetting about Geoff for a moment, what would you suggest for the remaining units in terms of maintenance?" she asked.

"First, I'd want someone to do a survey on the ice fields where we source the ice to feed these condensers," he said. "For some reason, we're getting a higher-than-expected concentration of inert, silicate matter within the ice. Second, clean out the units and replace filters. Blowing good air over mold makes the entire station smell. It's unnecessary. Finally, I'd bite the bullet and repair Unit 5 by buying new charge couplers, but not until we install my pre-pass gravel screens, assuming we can't find a cleaner source of ice."

"The pre-pass gravel screens would be good prevention, though?"

Rix studied the woman's face for a moment. He'd had trouble getting her to open the checkbook for repairs and had resorted to bartering. "Certainly," he said cautiously.

"Would you be interested in the job? I know you've barely had a moment to explore the station or even step into your new space, given you've spent every waking moment working on fixing our air handlers."

Rix had anticipated the question, although Garba's new, open attitude was somewhat unexpected. "I took the liberty to create an invoice that shows the work required for each unit," Rix said. "I don't know if any of the charge couplers are salvageable, so that's where a lot of your expense comes in on Unit 5. My labor fees can be offset with picking your warehouse for tools. All in, assuming we can agree on the barter, you'd be looking at eighty thousand credits with a ten percent grace for overages due to unforeseen issues that are uncovered."

"Ninety thousand credits," Garba said, her voice having lost all of its conversational tone. "And you don't get paid aside from bartering for old tools."

"That's the best I could come up with," Rix said. "You could take seventy thousand credits out of that price if we don't fix Unit 5. I'm just not sure how you feel about that. I know money is tight everywhere."

"One of the reasons we lose citizens is because of the state of our repairs," she said. "You should know, I've spent over three hundred thousand credits on charge couplers alone over the last two years. Now, I learn it's because of dirty ice. Or so you say. The thing is, for no obvious reason, I trust you. Every time you say you'll do something, you do it and it's done better than you commit to. I like that."

"Thank you," Rix said.

"I'll review your invoice. In the meanwhile, I've given you access to my warehouse again. Go make your piles and let me know what it'll take to keep you on the job," she said.

"I'll head up there after dinner. And I have a question that might be a little tricky. Do you mind?" Rix asked, and when Garba nodded, he continued. "A few days back, I brought a security video recorder down and was going to install it so I could see who was messing with the station's equipment. Quixly stopped me, saying there were privacy issues and that it was his responsibility to install that sort of thing. Did he follow up on that with you? If someone's tampering with our equipment, it'd be good to see who it is, wouldn't you think?"

"I'll talk to him."

"Seems like an easy answer," Rix said. "Maybe there are things I'm just not aware of, though."

"Most likely."

"Talk later tomorrow?" Garba asked.

"I'm not available for at least two days," Rix said. "And truthfully, I'd like to take a couple of weeks off after this project since we'll have almost doubled the volume of atmosphere being generated since I arrived."

"Hmm, I suppose," she said. "I'd really like to see this work get done. I am putting up ninety thousand credits, after all."

"If that money was coming to me, I'd say you have a right to push," Rix said.

Unexpectedly, Garba laughed. "Well, I had to try, at least. Finish on the Dravari unit and we'll get you paid up. If you can visit the warehouse, I'll look over your invoice and we can at least come to a deal. Does that work with your vacation plans?"

"Sure," Rix said. "Are you going up? I think I'll call it quits for the day. I'll ride with you."

It was a short ride up to the Atrium where they parted company. Having quit a little earlier than expected for the day, Rix decided to finish some exploration he'd been doing over the last several days and headed down one of the back hallways in search of the Hidden Room, which aside from poor signage, wasn't otherwise overly hidden.

"Welcome, stranger," a man called from behind a two-meter-long bar. Like so many other bars, there were bottles of liquor on shelves behind the bar, but in this case, there weren't many bottles and none of those bottles had labels on them.

"Hello," Rix said, allowing his eyes to adjust to the dim light. As he did, he realized the bar had room for upwards of twenty people with several booths and a few tables and just as important, that he wasn't alone and was likely being listened to. Two groups of men turned his way, likely just curious at the new face. Rix decided to ignore the attention and approached the bar.

"Kel was telling me you served a concoction of yours that you call Beaker's Black Rum, that right?" Rix asked.

"Might be a bit much for an Earthling," the man said, glancing over to a table of men who were playing a game that involved both sticks and cards. His comment earned him a round of derisive laughs.

"Is that right?" Rix asked, turning to the loudest of the laughing men. "Don't suppose you have an extra seat available for your Pony game, do you?"

"What's an Earthling know about Pony? And aren't you a refugee? This is a man's game. We're playing for money," the man said.

"Oh, that's good," Rix said with evident relief. "I was afraid you all were too sophisticated, being all intelligent like, that you didn't play for cold, hard credits."

"You got credits, human?"

"Name's Rix," Rix said. "What's your name and what are the stakes?"

"Greasle," the man who'd been talking said. "Five credits minimum bet. Gotta stake for at least fifty."

Rix turned back to the man behind the counter. "Round of Beaker's for the table," he said, pulling an empty chit from his pocket and charging it with fifty credits. "And deal me into your next hand, if you're open."

Rix had learned that the game of Pony had a betting style like poker and a play style that went a few more rounds, with some gin rummy type elements included. Having played endless hours of cards while in the war, he hadn't found it hard to catch onto when Kel had taught it to him.

"Be careful, Rix," Beverly appeared on the table in front of him, wearing a cocktail server's dress and holding a tray full of drinks. "The rules of Pony vary. You should observe a few hands before you get in too deep."

Glasses were set on the table in front of the men, including at an open chair, which the bar tender gestured for Rix to sit in. "We'll take it easy on you, Rix," Greasle said. "Get you broke in all nice like."

"Appreciate it," Rix said, resting a hand on his drink. "Strong stuff, you say?"

His question caused a new round of laughter at the table. "Oh, no, it's sweet as golben milk."

"Golbens are an insect that store a milky substance similar to honey," Beverly said.

Rix winked at the Fimil man and tipped the Beaker's Black Rum onto his tongue, swallowing about a quarter of it in one go. The familiar burn of alcohol on his tongue gave him a warning that the drink failed to follow through with. Even so, Rix coughed like it had been an overly strong drink. "Phew, not bad," Rix said.

"Okay, Doble, deal 'em out," Greasle said, pushing a stack of sticks to Rix, which were used like poker chips.

"If that's too much for you, slide it over," Doble said as he flipped cards out to the table.

"I think I'm okay," Rix said, picking the glass up and taking another drink. This time, he didn't add the gasp.

"Just here for some cards and a drink, then?" Greasle asked.

"Not only. I was hoping to talk to Collie Berg," Rix said. "I heard he's the one who makes this rum."

"What's it to you?" Greasle asked, setting out a bet on the table.

"Well, that'd be business between me and Mr. Berg, I'd say," Rix said.

"I can get him," the man behind the bar said, obviously listening in on the conversation.

"Shut it, Yook," Greasle said. "We're just havin' conversation."

Rix matched Greasle's bet. "How about you help me find Mr. Berg after we make a game of this, eh, Yook?"

"What kind of hand you got there?" Greasle asked, scratching a stubbly beard and twisting the end of his elephant trunk nose.

Rix set down another five credits' bet. "Cost you five more to find out." He was fairly sure Greasle had the cards to beat him, but it was worth another five credits to learn more.

"I'm out," Yook said.

"Same," another said.

"Well, I guess I have five credits to find out just that," Greasle said, setting his cards on the table. To Rix's surprise, his cards were better, and he winced as he set them down, winning the hand.

"No way you won that," Greasle said. "Are you some sort of cheat?"

"Beginner's luck," Rix said, taking the sticks off the table.

They continued to play for another hour and Rix found that he had to work to lose against the men at the table. Either he was the luckiest guy in the world or these were some of the worst card players he'd played with. Finally, when he was down to about half his chips, he announced, "Boys, you've done worn me out. I'm going to take what's left of my pride and grab some dinner."

"Ah, you didn't do all that bad for yourself," Greasle said. "We'll take your money anytime you like. We've got a game going just about this time every week."

Rix tipped his third glass of rum up and drained it. The taste of the rum was pleasant enough, but the alcohol content was about a third of what he was used to and as a result, he wasn't feeling much of its effects. Purposefully, he shuffled his feet as he walked toward the exit and when he looked back, he saw satisfaction on Greasle's face.

"Hey, I called Collie, he's on his way down," the bartender said.

"Tell him to meet me out by the fountain," Rix said. "I'm already late, meeting a friend."

"I'll tell him."

And with that, Rix left and made his way back to the center of the Atrium, where he found Kel sitting on a bench next to a fountain. "You're late," she said. "Where'd you come from? I was watching the elevator bank for you."

"Hidden Room," Rix said. "Met Greasle, Yook, Marbary and Shixen. Upstanding group of men if ever I met some."

Kel's eyes raised. "Rix, you can't be doing that," she said. "Shixen is a bad man. Dangerous. He's Vigno's enforcer. Tell me you didn't take their money."

"I did not take their money. Trust me, reading a table is important if you play cards. Those boys didn't look like they'd go for a new player taking their money."

"Why'd you play?"

"Mr. Banner?" a man asked, approaching before Rix could answer.

"Collie?" Kel asked. "How do you know Rix?"

"I heard he was asking about me," Collie answered. "Is that right?"

"No?" Kel asked.

"Asking about his rum, Kel," Rix said.

"What about my rum?"

"I'm trying to convince Kel to take a speculation run over to Sout Atal with *Calypso*. I figured we'd pile up some fuel and a small load of your Beaker's. I was hoping if I bought bulk, you'd give me a discount so I've some wiggle room when negotiating."

"You want to make a run with my rum over to Sout Atal, huh? I don't think I can help that much. I only make what I run through Hidden Room. I don't have a lot of extra."

"How about a dozen liter bottles and I'll go market rate for this first run, seeing as how this is all about speculation," Rix said. "What's a good price for you?"

"Twenty credits a bottle is what I sell it for."

"Would you take two hundred credits for twelve? Might be best if they're in bottles that have some sort of branding on them, but that'd be on you, unless you want me to own every part of the deal," Rix said.

"Two hundred ten credits and you get the bottles I have," he said.

"How about I go two hundred fifty credits, and I make up my own name for the rum?" Rix said.

"But it's my rum."

"And I'm rebottling and renaming it for sale off station," Rix said. "Can't hardly cut into your business since I'll put it in a contract that I won't sell any here."

"You're kind of a fast talker, aren't you?"

"Just a businessman," Rix said. "Do we have a deal for twelve bottles? Doesn't have to be anything more than that. Two hundred fifty credits can't feel too bad, can it?"

"Well, I suppose I could start the next batch early."

"There's the spirit," Rix said, plugging numbers into a contract he'd already formulated and flicking it to Collie. "Read that over. I'll give you the two hundred fifty credits two days from now when you sign the contract and drop off the case of bottles at *Calypso*. Deal?"

"Well, I never said anything about delivery."

"But you don't mind, because it's good money, right?"

"Well, I suppose that's right."

Rix offered his hand and explained the significance. Collie seemed to appreciate the idea, and the two men shook.

"We don't even know if we're making that run, yet," Kel said. "As it is, the only thing we're bringing is a case of rum. Are you really going to make your own bottles?"

"Sales is all about marketing," Rix said. "Beverly, could you design a bottle that looks like that Kopke bottle I had back home? A liter is too big though. I need it closer to a fifth."

"Yes, and the volume you are considering is seven-hundred fifty milliliters," she said. "How many bottles do you want?"

"Ten cases of a dozen delivered to the shop?" Rix asked. "What's that going to set me back?"

"How soon?"

"Forty-eight hours?"

"Material?"

"Ooh, I'd like glass and cork for the top," Rix said. "I need a case that looks old and a label that says Collie's Select Black."

"This is not inexpensive. You will spend three hundred fifty credits for ten cases and bottles," she said.

"Perfect. Do you mind submitting? I'll get in and pay right away."

"Certainly."

"Rix, wait, what are you doing? Why are you spending money like this?" Kel asked. "How do you even have this money?"

"Maybe this isn't the best place for this discussion," Rix said. "You said fuel was cheap here but not so much in Sout Atal. If we brought a thousand in fuel on a spec load over to Sout Atal, what could we make?"

"A thousand credits? We don't have that kind of money," she said and then in a much quieter voice. "Do we?"

"We do, Kel," Rix said, flicking a transfer of a thousand credits to her account which brought him down to two hundred twenty.

"Did you borrow money, Rix?" she whispered. "You can't do that. It will catch up with you. Vigno is very dangerous."

"Ooh, yeah, no that's not my style," Rix said. "I've been making good money on the sale of IP on manufactory listings. Apparently, lots of people like how my little inventions help solve their problems."

"You're crazy."

"The real question is, are you crazy enough to take a load of fuel, rum, comera and natural clothing over to Sout Atal in a couple of days?" Rix asked.

Kel's eyes darted around, clearly concerned about who might be listening. "Rix, you can't just let people know what we're doing. Most of the people around here are good, but some of them are pirates, too. We don't need people to know what we're doing."

"Sorry. Loose lips sink ships. I should know better."

"I have no idea what you're saying."

"That makes sense to me."

26

SPECULATION

Rix closed the cabinet door and tapped a sequence of keys on the control panel. It was early afternoon, and he'd finished the install of the Dravari condenser earlier than he'd promised.

"Garba, come in, this is Rix Banner," he called over comms.

"Go ahead, Mr. Banner," Garba answered after a few moments.

"I'm about to start Unit 2," he said. "Do you want to inspect my work?"

"No, I've been receiving regular updates from a work monitor I left behind. Congratulations on another job well done. Patience Station thanks you for your efforts," she said. "Have you had a chance to think about what you need to service and repair the other units?"

"Yes, I've selected more tools from your warehouse as payment. The tools were more expensive, so there are not nearly so many to review. Would you look at them and let me know what you think? I tried not to get too exuberant."

"Do you not have enough tools for your business by now?" she asked. "Each of our contracts has you choosing tools over credits. I understand outfitting your shop, but how is it you are surviving without credits?"

"Right now, I live in a space you provide and the only thing I've done for the last couple of weeks is repair atmospheric generators," he said. "It's not a spendy lifestyle."

"I will keep my eye on you, Mr. Banner," she said. "I have accepted your proposal for maintenance and repair of Units 3, 4 and 5. The tools you have selected are in excess of the value of your services, but I find that I wait with anticipation to see how you will utilize these items that sit idle in my warehouse."

"You're welcome in my shop any time," Rix said. "Also, just so we're on the same page, part of the price for the Dravari condenser install was that broken pair of photonic barrier generators. I plan to transport those to my shop this afternoon, along with all the items in your warehouse that we previously agreed upon. Are we in agreement?"

"Yes. Enjoy your time off and please return quickly. There is work to do," she said.

Rix terminated the comms and closed the cabinet where the station's tools for the Environmental Level were stored. Unable to help himself, he'd cleaned and organized the cabinets, easily fitting all tools into a single location. Satisfied with a job done well, he tapped his communicator again. "Collie Berg."

"I was just packing up your bottles, Banner," Collie said, answering the comm. "Do you still want them at the address you provided? That's an empty old industrial part of the station that's been abandoned for years."

"I'm renting a unit from Mayor Klex, and I'll be there in forty-five minutes, give or take."

"Understood."

Closing the comm, Rix tapped Kel's contact. "What's shakin', Rixy?" Kel asked jovially.

"Have you been drinking?" Rix asked.

"That's cute. Did you call to check on me?" she asked.

"No. Sorry. I'm finally headed down to the shop and could use some help moving a few things. Any interest in helping out?" Rix asked.

"What's in it for me?" she asked coyly.

"You mean, aside from getting my shop up and going so I can make permanent repairs to *Calypso* for the ridiculous price of free?" Rix asked.

"Sold," Kel said, laughing. "I'm hanging out with Philo. I'll bring him along, too."

"Okay, meet me by the maintenance entrance on Level 5. I'm going to swing by and grab the crates and bottles from the manufactory and then meet you there," Rix said. "Give me a twenty-minute head start, please?"

"You've got it. Just enough time for another quick game," she said and then terminated comms.

Rix made his way to Level 7 and over to a long bank of lockers. He'd received notice that his bottles and crates were ready for pickup. Placing his palm on the security sensor, the proscribed locker opened, and he set to unloading the contents onto a grav-pallet he'd checked out for the purpose of moving the items. He smiled. The bottles had turned out even better than he'd hoped.

"Level 13," Rix announced when he got onto the industrial elevator, which was reserved for moving equipment. Stepping off on Level 13, Rix found himself in a poorly maintained and clearly abandoned section of the station. The lights flickered on as the station powered up the wide hallway he'd stepped into. Trash and random debris littered the hallway in both directions and the air smelled dank.

The sound of another elevator car opening caught Rix's attention as he was pushing his loaded cart into the dilapidated hallway. "Wow, you really know how to show a girl a good time," Kel said with Philo following close behind. "There are rumors that folks use these abandoned levels for nefarious purposes."

"Like what?" Rix asked, consulting his HUD to determine which direction his shop was from the elevator. Finding it, he directed Kel and Philo to follow him. "We're this way."

"I can't believe this is your first time checking out your space, Rix. What if it's a complete trash pit?" she asked.

"As long as it's the size we negotiated, I'll figure it out," Rix said. "What kind of nefarious purposes? I kind of got that same vibe from Collie."

"Some people don't like to have other people paying attention to the things they're doing," Kel said. "Use your imagination."

"I have a big imagination," Rix said, holding up as Philo moved a broken crate someone had left lying in the hallway.

After walking nearly a hundred meters to the end of the hallway, they arrived at an unassuming, man-sized door. Without his HUD, Rix wouldn't have been able to read the numerals over the door which provided the address, because the paint was faded and the illumination had been fully off for the last ten meters.

"Geez, this isn't a very nice place, Rix," Kel said somberly.

"That just means there's lots of opportunity for improvement!" Rix said, pressing his hand to the security panel. Nothing happened.

"That's not good," Kel said. "I think power is out down here. You should get Garba to turn it on before we go in."

"Maybe it's just the hallway," Rix said, opening the small bag of tools which he'd been carrying along.

"What are you doing?"

"Opening the door," Rix said, depressing a small latch on the side of the security panel housing. The action caused a small piece of metal to flip open, exposing two corroded copper terminals.

"Are you seriously hacking in?" Kel asked.

"Not at all," Rix said. "These security panels have an external power shunt for just this scenario." From his tool bag, he removed a magnetic powerpack and stuck it to the wall above the security panel. Pulling a pair of leads and attaching them to both power and the panel, Rix was rewarded with the screen lighting up. "It'll take a minute to update."

"How do you know this stuff, Rix?" Kel asked. "And don't say you were reading."

"I don't have to, you said it for me," Rix said. "I wanted to know if the security panels were private or municipal. Turns out they can work either way, but since I'm renting, I have to leave it tied into the municipal systems." As they were talking, the screen showed status messages as it made contact with the central system and updated its authorization list. Rix placed his hand on the screen and checked the unit's reserve power. "Looks like we have a month of energy. Hopefully, I can fix it before it needs a new charge. Carrying around portable power is annoying."

"You never cease to surprise me, Rix Banner," Kel said as Rix grabbed the manual door handle and struggled to operate it. "Here, let me help." Rix made room for Kel and between the two of them, they managed to open the door. "One more thing to fix?" she asked, grinning.

"You wouldn't believe how long my repair list is," Rix said pushing at the door. At first, the door resisted, but when Rix put his shoulder to it, he found he was able to make progress in moving the door and junk that had been piled up against it. Stepping inside, Rix shivered, his breath freezing as he exhaled. In the dim light, Rix got a good sense of the space, his HUD immediately projecting a green wireframe onto the scene ahead. The floor was littered with junk from the previous occupant, but he was still mostly concerned that it was spacious enough.

"You're renting a concert hall," Kel said, her voice echoing. "Or the universe's largest deep freezer. You need to get heat turned on in here, it's barely above freezing."

"I'll admit, I was hoping for a little better from Garba," Rix said, tapping a discarded but intact crate with his toe. "I wonder if there's anything of value in this junk."

"Looks like a lot of work to me," she said.

"It appears I have plenty of time. How about we go get those photonic barrier generators," Rix said. "This place would be a whole lot cooler with a good view."

"There's no way those generators work," Kel said.

"And yet, I see only possibilities," Rix said.

"I guess that's why I like you."

"You like me?" Rix asked, grinning. "Aww. I'm touched."

"I like Rixy," Philo said, poking through the trash on the floor.

"Same, Buddy," Rix answered.

"There's someone in the hallway," Kel said quietly. "I hear voices."

"I'm guessing Collie is making his delivery."

"There are two of them," Kel said.

"What's up, fellas?" Rix asked, when he stepped into the hallway and was faced with a trio of men he'd never met before, although one of them seemed vaguely familiar.

"What are you doing here?" The biggest of the three asked.

"Rix Banner," Rix said, extending his hand. "You must be the welcoming committee." The big man looked at Rix's hand and then back to Rix with a quizzical glance. "Sorry, Earth greeting. Maybe you boys aren't into pleasantries."

"No," the bigger man said. "You need to get out of here. You don't belong."

"Well, that's going to be a problem," Rix said. "Garba Klex is renting this space to me, so we're going to mark that down as we do belong."

"Why? Earth? You're that mechanic that's been messing with the atmospheric units people been talking about," the big man said.

"True."

"Don't come back," the big man said. "You've been warned."

And with that, the trio turned and left.

"I'm not sure we're going to get along with the neighbors all that well," Rix said.

"Did you see that tattoo over his eyebrow?"

"Wasn't sure. It could have been dirt."

"Don't make fun. Those guys are Graveborn. They're bad news, Rix," Kel said.

"I'll have to keep the security systems in good shape, then," Rix said.

"I don't like it," Kel said.

"What a dump." Rix recognized the voice but couldn't place it. He'd been expecting Collie, but quickly recognized Shixen, one of the men he'd played cards with a few days prior. Shixen was holding an open case of odd sizes of bottles, some of which had the word *rum* on them.

"Back home, we call these fixer-uppers," Rix said, accepting the crate from Shixen. "And thanks!"

"I saw those boys in the hallway. Are you sure you know what you're getting into down here?" Shixen asked.

"Is there something I should know?"

"Doesn't seem that complex," Shixen said.

"I'll take it under advisement," Rix said. "Tell Collie thanks for the delivery."

"Will do, and Kel Warp, Vigno says that you need to make good on your debt or we'll be looking at alternative payments. Are we communicating?"

"Yes, Shixen. Five thousand by the end of the month. That'll take care of the vig and pay down by a thousand," Kel said.

"Fifteen days. Don't be late." And with that, Shixen also left.

"Only twenty percent of that is going to pay down your principal?" Rix asked. "That's robbery. We just made an interest payment."

"I'm late, Rix. I knew the rules."

Rix shuffled through the room, tossing mostly empty crates to the side as he did. "Hey, looks like there's an airlock down here. Want to see what's on the other side?"

"I'm guessing space, Rix."

"No, what view," Rix said. "Of course it's space."

Rix tapped the security panel and discovered it was also unpowered.

"I wouldn't override that one, Rix. An airlock can operate without power, but there are too many things that could go wrong," she said.

"Fine," Rix said. "Let's go get my tools and the projectors. Did you purchase Petju's comera for our trip?"

"Yes, and the fuel is waiting for us at the terminal. We can load that as we leave. Do you want to take the rum and a single case with us up to Level 5? We could drop the alcohol off on *Calypso*."

"Good call, I also need to return the grav pallet to the manufactory," Rix said.

And for the next few hours, Rix, Philo and Kel spent their time moving items between *Calypso*, Rix's new shop, and Garba's warehouse. Their final task had them moving the heavy photonic generators.

"I know we're all exhausted," Rix said. "But is there any reason we shouldn't set sail for Sout Atal after we grab some dinner?"

"I'm broke, Rix," Kel said. "Some meal paste is about all I have."

"Dinner is on me," Rix said. "I couldn't have done this without your help. Also, could we double up on the fuel?"

"You have another thousand to spend on speculation fuel?" Kel asked in disbelief.

"I do," Rix said. "Let's make it another eight hundred. That way we can load up the galley for our trip. I'll make spaghetti while you get us on the road."

"Well, okay," Kel said. "It doesn't seem like I'm adding a lot to this partnership."

"Other than a ship, your skills as a pilot and having the right contacts," Rix said. "Because where I come from, that has quite a lot of value."

"Okay, but we're going to talk about this more," Kel said with reservation in her voice.

"Beverly, could you get us a load of foodstuff delivered out to *Calypso*? I have two hundred to spend. Plan on us restocking at Sout Atal for the trip back," Rix said.

"Certainly," Beverly said.

It was 2300 local when Kel, Philo and Rix finally rendezvoused at the fuel terminal having loaded everything else aboard. Loading the dry fuel, given Patience Station's original charter as a refueling station, was the easiest task they accomplished and twenty minutes after their arrival, *Calypso* had its entire load aboard.

"Patience Station, this is *Calypso*, we're requesting permission to disembark," Kel called over the local security channel.

"Happy sailing, Kel," came Hutari's cheerful voice after a few moments of delay. "Can I log when you expect to return?"

"Twelve days, give or take," Kel said.

"I've got you down. Be safe," Hutari answered.

As promised, Rix got right to the business of cooking the spaghetti he'd promised. One of the things he'd learned on the trip from Earth to Patience Station was that Kel had little interest in cooking. Even worse, *Calypso*'s galley was in poor shape for much more than boiling water or heating pans, which made simple recipes important. Just looking around the galley, Rix could only imagine what it would be like to strip the entire space down, burr out the rust, fair the surfaces and lay down new paint. After that, he imagined installing modern equipment that would make long trips much more enjoyable. Of course, if they couldn't get Vigno paid off, none of that would make any sense.

"How's it going up here, Cap?" Rix asked, handing a steaming plate over to Kel.

"Good," she said distractedly. "In two hours, I'm going to need you to take a six-hour shift through an open space, because after that, I'm going to need to have solid concentration for the next eight."

"Pirates?"

"Ish," Kel said. "Mostly, it's just a lot of maneuvering around space junk. I have some older maps, so there'll be new asteroids that haven't been updated."

"Yikes," Rix said.

"Sounds worse than it is," Kel said. "Now, if we're being chased, that could get dicey. But, I don't think anyone knows where we're going, so, unless someone's sitting in a ship waiting for us, we should be reasonably safe on the way out."

"What about on the way back?"

"Depends on what kind of trouble finds us."

"That's not exactly encouraging."

"Welcome to Surnac Belt, Rix. Everything out here is a risk," Kel said. "For the record, I like our chances."

"Okay. I'm going to grab two hours of shuteye. I'll set an alarm," Rix said.

"Good."

And so went the first four days of their journey to Sout Atal. It wasn't until the fifth day that they ran into their first hostiles.

"Rix, Philo, get strapped in, we have company," Kel called over ship's comms.

Rix was close to the bridge, working on a project to clean the main hallway's deck of built-up grime. It had been hard work, but he was down to bare metal over most of it and he'd started sanding and filling divots and other holes caused by years of neglect. With his proximity, he jumped into the bridge and strapped into the navigator's seat, his eyes searching first the open space ahead of *Calypso* and then the tactical display, where he saw a pair of twelve-ton, short range ships racing toward them.

"They look fast," Rix said.

"They are," Kel said. "You know, if you were in the needler turret, you could dissuade them more quickly than me getting all jiggy."

"Jiggy. You mean maneuvering at high speeds and making me feel sick," Rix said. "Give me ten seconds to get loaded."

Racing back to the needler turret access, Rix scrabbled into position. He'd barely strapped himself in when Kel maneuvered hard to starboard and then dove toward a dense cluster of asteroids. Rix struggled to locate the pursuit but found them on *Calypso's* tail. Instead of firing right away, he waited for a clean shot, which took almost ninety seconds, given Kel's violent moves.

A neat line of needles sprayed out behind *Calypso* and passed through the side of one of their pursuers. A cloud of gas sprayed from the small ship's fuselage and just like that both ships gave up pursuit.

"That doesn't hardly seem like they're trying," Rix said.

"They didn't think we had teeth," Kel said. "Good job. Why don't you stay up there for a while. There could be more."

But there were no more pursuers and after an hour of smooth sailing, Rix returned to his work, cleaning *Calypso's* main hall deck.

"Do you ever rest?" Kel asked early the next morning as he plopped into the chair next to her.

"Oh, I'm done," Rix said. "We need to stay off the floor for twenty minutes. I have a new coat of white deck paint down. Are we getting close?"

"Sout Atal is just around that big group of knight asteroids," Kel said, point off in the distance. With considerable magnification, Rix's HUD showed a grouping of larger than usual asteroids. "Think of them like our protectors."

"Patience Station has something similar, is that common for space stations out here?"

"Unless you're on the outside edge of the belt, yes," Kel said. "We're four hours out. Get some sleep, because I need our lead negotiator ready to go."

"Copy that."

27

SOUT ATAL

"Sout Atal, this is freighter *Calypso* requesting permission to dock, please respond," Rix called over comms just as he'd been prompted by Kel. Waiting for sixty seconds, he repeated the call.

"Local space time has us at 1400, I imagine we'll get an answer fairly quickly," Kel said. "If we were after 2200, it could take all night before a smaller station like Sout Atal responded."

"What do you do then?"

"Just what you'd expect, we heave-to. Sout Atal has moorings at five clicks that fall within their protection but don't require permission to tie up to," Kel said.

"I imagine that grabs someone's attention, though," Rix said.

"Depends on how much trouble they've had recently," Kel said. "I haven't been to Sout Atal for several years, so I don't know anything about their security status just now."

"According to what I could find, Sout Atal is deep enough in the asteroid belt that they're fairly isolated," Rix said. "Last census showed them having a population smaller than Patience Station."

"*Calypso*, this is Sout Atal. How many aboard and what's the nature of your visit today?" On the forward tactical screen a middle-aged humanoid, with rough skin that resembled walnut wood and long black hair that hung past his shoulders, appeared wearing a dark blue Mao-collared tunic.

"Samess, this is Kel Warp," Kel said, acknowledging and permitting video transmission per Samess's encoded request. "There are two, nope, strike that, three. You probably remember Philo and next to me is Rix Banner, he's not from around here, but he's catching on quickly enough."

"I was hoping you hadn't lost *Calypso* whilst gambling. I know how your love for cards does not match your skill at gambling," Samess said. "Or perhaps that is only when you've had too much of Jaknie's grog."

"Samess! Don't be giving away all my secrets to my new business partner. You'll run him off," Kel said.

"Business partner, is it, Rix Banner? Why, for the sake of the Lords of Gavenar, would you fall into business with that old pirate. Please tell me she's made you her se ..."

Kel interrupted the comms with a quick mute, but Rix found he was able to read Samess's lips all the same. "I wasn't aware that was an option," Rix said.

"It's not," Kel said. Rix couldn't help but notice that her cheeks had pinked even as her body had shifted from the narrow, hard form she showed to outsiders back to the curvier form that was her true self. "Samess behave yourself or we won't bring our hold full of trade goods aboard."

"Finally," Samess said. "You're cleared for slip A12. Remember, energy weapons over ten kilojoules need to be left aboard your ship."

"Thank you, Samess. Drinks after your shift?" Kel asked.

"Gog's Hob at 1900. I assume you remember where that's at," he said. "Rix Banner, if you're interested in cards, there's a game with a fifty-credit buy-in. You're most welcome to join in, although if you're sleeping with Kel, you should know, her credits don't typically last beyond the first hour and she's not always the best sport about things."

"I am too a good sport! Jelaki was cheating. I caught him dead to rights and you know it," Kel defended immediately.

"Always with the fire in your eyes," Samess said with fondness in his look. "See you tonight, precious." He then terminated comms.

"Now do you see why I didn't want to come?" Kel asked.

"It seems perfect, Kel. People know you. You have contacts, that's what we need to get trading going," Rix said.

"You do understand that a good portion of Sout Atal personnel belong to pirate gangs, right?" Kel asked. "Some of them might even have been in those ships that fired on us on the way in."

"That's not very friendly," Rix said. "Will they continue shooting at us on Sout Atal?"

"The general rule of thumb is to not poop where you put your head down for sleep," Kel said. "It's more of a guideline than a rule. We'll carry sidearms and this is a shoot-first-ask-for-forgiveness-later kind of situation here. Someone draws down on you, don't hesitate."

"Feels like we should have some sort of armor if that's how this works," Rix said.

"Armor is expensive, and I have maybe three hundred fifty credits to my name," she said.

"More than three hundred, then?"

"You're serious."

"Somewhat," Rix said. "A flexible piece of armor for our torsos that goes beneath our clothing wouldn't be a horrible idea."

"That might work for you, but it definitely won't for me," Kel said. "I have something of a reputation to keep up here."

As she was talking, her body shifted, but this time, not in the direction of the angular shape she used when interacting with Dravari. Instead, her height reduced by a few centimeters and the extra mass that became available shifted.

"Oh boy."

"I wondered if that'd be your reaction," Kel said with a grin on her face. "Like it?" she asked, spinning around.

"Why would you go onto a pirate space station looking like that? You'll attract a ton of attention. Holy cow," Rix said, struggling to keep his eyes schooled as he looked at the now voluptuous alien.

"The primary reason is that this is the persona I've always used on

Sout Atal," Kel said, her voice having raised half an octave and taking on a slightly breathy quality. "A girl needs to be consistent, don't you think? Wait until you see the clothes I brought along. I think you'll like them."

"Oh, boy," Rix said. "Am I okay wearing what I have?"

"The street clothes we manufactured," Kel said. "Go with the dark blue pants and the nicer cream-colored shirt. We'll need to get you some jewelry or maybe a tattoo."

"Philo ready," Philo announced appearing in the hallway just outside the bridge. Wearing a pair of black pants and a white sleeve-less t-shirt and black suspenders, he looked something like a 1920s gangster, especially with a small pistol tucked into his belt.

"Let me guess, you have a girl here," Rix said.

"Of course, Rixy," Philo said. "Tell Philo when to help unload. Philo has friends to see."

"Lock down the moorings and we'll see you tomorrow," Kel said.

"Hey, how are you doing for funds?" Rix asked.

"Twenty-three credits, Rixy. Tight times for us's," Philo said.

Rix tapped Philo's armband and transferred fifty credits. "Does that help?"

"Ooh, thank you Rixy!" Philo said and gave Rix a big hug. "I get moorings, Kels. Big funs tonight!"

An hour later, Rix looked up from the couch where he'd been hanging out waiting for Kel to finish getting ready. While it had taken him fifteen minutes to shower and change clothing, Kel had taken longer. When he looked up, however, he struggled to rectify the woman wearing a dress tight on her hips and loose on top but with a deep v and the woman he'd spent most of the last several weeks with.

"You're gawking, Rix," Kel said with a knowing smile.

"My gosh, I had no idea," Rix said.

"Your jaw has flapped open," Kel said, grinning. "You had no idea of what? That I could shift to alluring? You do know this is a façade, right? I've invented this personality specifically for places like Sout Atal."

"Help me understand *places like* …," Rix said, finally managing to take his eyes off her.

"Where charm and allure are a benefit to negotiations," she said. "Men often struggle to keep their wits about them when presented with a woman such as this."

"That's a weird way to say that. You're talking about you," Rix said.

"No more than the clothing you're wearing is you," she said. "I'll admit, I enjoy much of the attention such an outer shell garners. That attention can also be overbearing and down-right disgusting. I hope you do not mind me hanging onto your arm this evening. It will be more enjoyable for us both, I believe."

"I wondered why you hadn't been back to Sout Atal. It seemed like the right place for you to make trade runs, but this is the real reason you don't come back. Is there someone you're specifically avoiding?" Rix asked.

"Can you be okay with just being my partner in this?" Kel asked.

Rix saw a mixture of sadness and pleading in her face. He nodded agreement. "Sure, that I can do. You'll let me know if there's someone I need to shoot, though, right?" With the last, he raised a single eyebrow and hinted at a grin.

Kel barked a laugh. "I don't know how you always turn an awkward moment funny."

"Nothing awkward about wanting to keep a few of our own secrets," Rix said. "I remember back at the high school prom. I was dating this girl, Bethany. Boy howdy, I thought she was the one. I'd been smitten with her since junior high and when she asked me to prom, I thought I'd hit the jackpot. It turns out, her mother made her go with me and she really wanted to be with this other boy, Brad Anderson. Well, Brad and Bethany snuck away from the dance, and I ended up waiting for her for two hours outside in the parking lot so I could take her home. Which I did."

"That's horrible."

"Yeah, I even got yelled at by Bethany's dad for keeping her out late."

"And you didn't tell him the truth, did you?"

"Her parents forbade us from seeing each other. Which she was fine with."

"She should have said something," Kel said. "You're a nice guy."

"Naïve is the word you're looking for," Rix said. "I should have known better."

"You're telling me this because you think I might have something embarrassing I don't want to talk about," Kel said.

Rix shrugged. "Nah. I just figured it's easier to know that everyone's human."

Kel laughed again. "You know that particular statement doesn't work that well anymore, but I get what you're saying. Thank you, Rix."

"What's our first stop?" Rix asked, changing subjects. "Our biggest load is fuel. Are we selling to individuals or are you looking to make this a regular thing and sell to a distributor?"

"I hadn't thought about selling to individuals," Kel said. "We could probably make a better profit if we did."

"But you'll never sell to a distributor if you take their customers," Rix said. "I checked fuel prices when we came into range of their data networks. We bought this fuel at a quarter of the price they're selling it here at retail. I know you got a little discount on Patience, but I doubt that was fully wholesale, so we can probably get a better price in the future. I'd say we don't get greedy and see about selling at sixty-five percent of the price here, but to the distributors. That has us splitting the profit evenly with them."

"Which distributor should we talk to?"

"Pick one," Rix said. "The most likely case is they'll tell us to pound sand."

"Why? They can't be buying it for less than your offer," she said.

"And they probably have a deal with whoever is delivering what they're getting today," Rix said. "They won't want to jeopardize their contract with a one-off purchase like this."

"Then why did we even bring it out if you already knew that?"

"Trust the process," Rix said. "Who's first."

"Pjenga Tirsk has the fuel for the fuel depot on the pier. His prices are higher because of convenience," Kel said. "He's not a very nice Thugna."

"Let's go," Rix said.

Kel nodded and placed a hand on the security panel that opened to the concourse that had connected to *Calypso* after they'd docked. At the end of the ramp, she gestured to the right which coincided with posted signs for spaceport operations, security and business offices.

"This is it," Kel said when they'd arrived at an office that had a sign out front that read Tirsk Services. Opening a door that hadn't been cleaned for some time, the room they arrived in was unimpressive and had a pair of desks flanking the entrance to a longer hallway. At one desk a thick alien woman sat with a bored look on her face. Her species, Thugna, was unfamiliar to Rix aside from pictures he'd browsed. In person, he found her features curious. It was as if she had been molded from modeling clay by a less than proficient artist. With no hair atop her gray head, her features were muted with a thick forehead and protruding brow.

"Yes?" she asked in a flat monotone.

"We were hoping to meet with Mr. Tirsk," Rix said. "We don't have an appointment but perhaps have something of interest to him."

"He's not in," she answered, looking back at Rix, expressionless.

"I guess if the man isn't in, he isn't in, right, Kel?" Rix said.

"Sure," Kel said, not understanding where he was going with the conversation.

The Thugna woman remained expressionless, but her attention was still on Rix. "How about this. You probably know his interest in things. My partner and I have a load of fuel that we're willing to sell for seventy-five percent of your current retail. If Mr. Tirsk has interest in that, we'll be here for a couple of days, looking for a buyer."

"Is that it?" Kel asked.

"The man's not in," Rix said, grinning at Kel's unwitting straight-man setup for the line he wanted to deliver. He turned back to the woman. "On to the next stop. Thank you for your help." He then turned and was about to leave when he heard a voice at his back.

"Hold on a minute." The voice was a man's, although equally flat as had been the female Thugna's.

Rix and Kel turned around. "And you are?" Rix asked.

"Pjenga Tirsk. I own this place," the male Thugna said with obvious pride.

"Oh, certainly, what can I do for you, Mr. Tirsk?" Rix asked, causing a look of confusion on Tirsk's face to slowly form.

"It is you who asked for me," Tirsk said slowly.

"You've heard my deal," Rix said. "You stopped me from leaving because of your interest. How can I help you?"

"What volume have you transported?"

"Nine hundred kilograms," Rix said.

"That is not a large haul. I do not prefer to deal in such small quantities."

"But also, would it not be true that your supplier wouldn't be any the wiser if you were to procure a small load on the side? It's a nice way to make a little more profit and I'd bet anything you're running short," Rix said, recalling the warnings of fuel shortages on a station bulletin board. "Prices will naturally be going up. An extra nine hundred kilograms has real value, does it not?"

"Forty-five hundred credits for your entire load and you will not speak of this transaction," Tirsk said.

"Forty-five hundred is our public number. Our private number is five thousand two hundred," Rix said.

"Five thousand, not a credit more."

"A tough negotiator, you are," Rix said. "I feel I've made a poor deal. You barely blinked at my offer."

"Thugna don't have eyelids, Rix," Kel said quietly.

Tirsk didn't respond to the banter and continued to stare at Rix, awaiting a counter proposal. "How soon can you have the funds transferred?" Rix asked.

"Once the fuel is transferred, I'll give you a chit," Tirsk said. "Will you be on station next morning?"

Rix looked at Kel who nodded. Rix held out his hand and was once again met with a confused look. Kel, however, recognized the disconnect. "Your hands should touch. It is a human convention for signifying agreement," Kel said.

Tirsk's expression didn't change but he reached his left hand forward. Rix smiled and grasped it with his right and shook. "We have a deal, then. Tomorrow morning, you'll contact us when you're ready, then?"

"Yes."

"Join us for a drink later?" Rix said. "We should celebrate the first of many deals to come!"

"Tomorrow we will drink."

"Okay, then," Rix said, looking around uncomfortably. "I guess we're done here?"

"Yes." Tirsk said.

Rix had been addressing Kel and found the humorless Tirsk's terse conversation funny. He struggled to keep from laughing as he placed a hand on Kel's back as the two of them exited his office.

"That was easier than I expected," Kel said.

"Agree! The secretary really saved us time with her little routine," Rix said.

"Because she told us to leave?"

"Yes, we didn't have to threaten to leave, we put our deal out there and it placed the onus on him to move forward," Rix said. "That's a good profit margin if we can keep it going. I'm not sure how much fuel you want to haul, but it's good to know we won't lose our shirts on it."

"Five thousand credits for eighteen hundred invested? That's a good deal no matter who you are," Kel said.

"I'd like to know why he was so quick to accept. His margins can't be that poor, can they?"

"If he's getting fuel from Dravari, he's probably marking up ten percent or less," Kel said. "No doubt they set the price."

"Dravari? Are they really involved out here?"

"Yes. Not on Patience because we have our own refining and the right composition of asteroids," Kel said.

"Man, they're everywhere."

"What's next?" Kel asked.

"Your turn," Rix said. "We should try to sell the comera and the clothing. Maybe comera first since I'd really like to grab something to eat that's not from Patience Station."

"Be careful about what you ask for," she said. "Station food can be hit and miss. Although, there is this one place. I hope it's still there. We'll try to sell the comera and worst case, we'll get a good meal."

They were in good spirits when then entered Sout Atal Station. Like Patience Station, Rix was struck by how dirty everything was. Similarly, the smell of the atmosphere belied poor maintenance practices, which he imagined he would always notice. They spent a long afternoon walking between small shops and visiting hole-in-the-wall diners. With only four hundred invested between comera from Petju and clothing from Abistel, Kel managed to raise six hundred credits.

It was in good spirits, if not exhausted, that they finally found themselves entering the pub Hob's Gob, which sported the green-skinned head of what looked like a pig but had an earring in its left ear mounted above the door.

"Should I ask?" Rix asked, glancing upward.

"No, for sure not," Kel said. "I'll tell you more when we're back on *Calypso*."

"Sounds ominous."

"You're looking to sell your rum here but you should tread carefully. Jacknie is not someone to be trifled with. Just go easy, okay?"

"Jacknie is dangerous is what you're saying."

"That's exactly what I'm saying," Kel said. "This bar is his office but it's not how he makes his money."

"Pirate?" Rix asked quietly.

"Pirate, information broker, trader, oh there are so many hats a person can wear."

Rix stiffened as a man's voice drifted over a divider near the front door. From behind the panel, a man Rix could have mistaken for human, stepped. With a slim, elegant build, the man walked with grace which befit the expensive, albeit all black, clothing he wore.

With an open neckline, tattoos ran from beneath the fabric and twisted up his neck, stopping short of his chin.

"My apologies. It was a question and I've spoken out of turn. I mean no offense," Rix said.

"Oh, such manners," the man said with a dramatic flair. "And Kel Warp, gorgeous as ever. I will never get over how you broke my heart. Please tell me you've returned to take me back."

"Jacknie, I've missed you," Kel said embracing the man.

"Ah, you do feel so good, my dear. I do thank you for wearing the Kel I know and remember so well," Jacknie said, sparing a glance at Rix so that Rix understood Kel's nature wasn't a secret to him. "Tell me you are not with this plain-spoken man of substance. Have you changed so much?"

"Jacknie Dark, meet Rix Banner. Rix, Jacknie was my partner several years ago. And yes, Jacknie, Rix is my partner now," Kel said. "Don't let him fool you. Our parting was of mutual agreement."

"Was it, though?" Jacknie asked.

2 8

INKING DEALS

"What brings you to Hob's Gob, Rix Banner? I have heard rumors that you have been making trade deals all throughout Sout Atal. Have you some offer that you wish to discuss with your new girlfriend's lover?" Jacknie asked, gesturing for Rix and Kel to sit at his private table.

"Rix, if this is too much, we don't need to stay here," Kel said. "Jacknie is showing his true nature today and wishes to make you feel jealous."

"Is that what I'm doing?" Jacknie asked. "That doesn't seem very sporting of me."

Kel started but Rix raised a hand, giving him a moment to speak. "We haven't spoken of Kel's prior romantic relationships at all, to my knowledge. And as amusing as it is to watch whatever this is, you're right, that's not why we came into your elegant establishment. A question, how long have you been on Sout Atal?"

"Is that your question?" Jacknie asked.

"Not specifically, I don't know you very well and I'm trying to build rapport so I can figure out if there's business we can do together," Rix said.

"Aw, well, in that case, I've been on Sout Atal for twenty-three years. Prior to that I spent a great deal of time moving from one colony to the next. It was all something of a blur. My family is from Grevlox, my father a lowly plant supervisor, my mother, well, let's just say she kept busy. And you?"

"Earth, currently quarantined, but for some reason, I've been pulled along because Dravari decided to blow up my life," Rix said.

"Ah, the common thread you were searching for: we both despise Dravari," Jacknie said with mild contempt in his voice. Rix wasn't sure if the contempt was aimed at him or Dravari, or more likely both.

"Talk to me about your grog," Rix said.

"My grog? This is social, then?" Jacknie asked. "I make a simple, yet tasty beverage that is a hit here on Sout Atal. Here, I'll bring out a round. I imagine people from Earth also imbibe in spirits?"

"We do. In the meanwhile, I thought to get your opinion on something." Rix pulled a small bottle from his pocket and set it on the table. Unlabeled, he'd half-filled the bottle with Beaker's Black Rum prior to disembarking. "Since you're an aficionado, I was interested in your take on this."

"What is it?"

"A new product from Patience Station. It's a specially bottled version of Beaker's Black Rum called Collie's Reserve. As you probably know, Collie Berg is the proprietor who distills this for folks on Patience Station much like what you have done here with your grog."

A tray of three short glasses was set on the table by a scantily clad young waitress which brought a smile to Jacknie's face. "Thank you, love," Jacknie said, resting an overly familiar hand on the small of her waist.

"Anything else, Jacknie?" she asked.

"Three empty glasses, if you'd be so kind."

The waitress smiled demurely and nodded as she walked away.

"I see you haven't suffered greatly since I left," Kel said with more than a little jealousy in her voice.

"Don't fret, gorgeous, she's nothing more than a pastime," Jacknie said, picking up a glass of grog and nodding for Rix to do the same, which he did. "It's maybe a little strong for an Earther but do give it a go."

Rix watched as Jacknie swallowed the equivalent of two shots from the short glass in a single swig. Following suit, he brought the licorice-tasting black liquid into his mouth and rolled it around on his tongue, testing its taste. Weak for a spirit, he estimated the alcohol content to be half of a good whiskey from home. The taste wasn't bad, although he thought it could be improved if chilled.

"That's delightful, Jacknie," Rix said, smiling. "Back home, that taste is associated most with anise."

Jacknie turned his head quizzically. "Well, I appreciate the compliment. It wasn't too strong for you?"

"I have a good poker face," Rix said. "It burned all the way down. I thought I was about to lose a lung."

"Not a simpleton," Jacknie said, mostly to himself. Just then three empty glasses were set on the table. "You've been a good sport and tried mine. Let's try your Collie's Reserve. A black rum, you say."

"Patience Station's finest," Rix said, pouring out doubles into each glass, even though Kel hadn't touched her grog. Gesturing to her glass he continued, "Do you mind, Kel? I'd like to take another swing at Jacknie's brew."

"Grog. Sure," she said absently and then under her breath whispered. "Be careful, Rix."

"Oh, yes, be careful," Jacknie said. "The big bad Jacknie will fleece you out of your underthings, otherwise."

"I didn't mean it that way," Kel said, although Rix imagined that was exactly what she meant.

Under Jacknie's curious gaze, Rix quickly drank the extra grog and then picked up his own glass of Collie's Reserve. "To new friendships," Rix said, raising his glass.

"I like him, Kel," Jacknie said with a predatory grin. Following Rix's lead, he swallowed the entire glass of black rum and coughed slightly as it went down. "Oh, my, that is strong. What a treat."

"One more?" Rix asked, holding the bottle out to pour.

"Oh, no, I have a business to run. Is that your plan? Get Jacknie drunk and take advantage of him?"

"Not me," Rix said. "I'm a straight-up businessman. I'm looking to make a trade."

"Keep talking.

"I have nine liters of Collie's Reserve packaged in elegant 750ml bottles," Rix said. "Originally, I was looking to get forty-two credits per bottle, or five hundred credits."

"Hmm, a fair retail price, but I don't pay retail," Jacknie negotiated.

"Agreed," Rix said. "I'd like to arbitrage and instead, trade twelve bottles of Collie's Reserve for twenty-seven liters of Jacknie's Grog."

"Thrice?"

"Yes," Rix said. "The value in Collie's Reserve on Sout Atal is novelty. Sell it only to your most exclusive customers. People want to feel special as much as they want variety. On Sout Atal your grog is an expected commodity. I'll take it back to Patience Station and sell it to Collie Berg as a novelty. Everyone wins in this. I'm positive your cost to produce thirty liters of grog is significantly less than what you can ask for even six bottles of Collie's Reserve."

"You keep doing that."

"Doing what?"

"You say twenty-seven and then in the next sentence you upgrade that to thirty."

"I suppose I do. Thirty is just easier to say than twenty-seven," Rix said.

"Twenty liters and you can't sell to anyone else on Sout Atal."

"Twenty liters, you can't sell spirits to anyone on Patience Station, I can't sell spirits to anyone else on Sout Atal, and you have to exchange at least fifty liters of Collie's Reserve each year for a hundred liters of Jacknie's Grog, or this deal is voided," Rix said.

"You do drive a hard bargain. When can I get my spirits?" Jacknie asked.

"Can you have someone bring out the twenty liters of grog tomorrow morning? I have the bottles just waiting for you," Rix said, extending his hand. After an explanation, the two shook on the deal and then created a digital contract.

"Look who's thirsty!" Jacknie said, scooping Rix's unlabeled bottle of rum from the table and secreting it into his pocket.

Following Jacknie's gaze, Rix found that Samess, Sout Atal's second in security had arrived with a small group of friends.

"I am ready for some grog, Jacknie. There is no doubting that. And, I was promised a card game. Tell me you're well and goodly liquored up so that I have a chance of keeping my paycheck this week," Samess said with good nature.

"Maybe we could get something to eat while we play?" Rix asked. "And you might need to show me how to play, unless it's Pony, in which case I've played a couple of times."

"Pony it is," Jacknie said. "And we have some of the best tub-raised fried fish you've ever had. It comes with fried red roots. Ten credits gets you quite a load."

"Tub-raised fish? I don't think we have that on Patience," Rix said.

"We don't," Kel answered.

"That's interesting," Rix said. "I wonder if we could get a hundred kilograms of frozen fillets to bring back."

"Well, Terg is probably playing tonight," Samess said. "She's the fish farmer."

"Who's the fish farmer?" a swarthy female fimilint asked, with a big smile as she approached the table.

"Speak of the dark lord herself," Jacknie said with some irritation in his voice.

"Don't be like that, Jacknie. I won't always take your money. And who is this delicious youngster who's joined us?" Terg asked, looking at Rix.

"A new customer," Jacknie said. "He's looking to transport a hundred kilos of your fillets. Do you have that much available?"

"Hmm, that'd be a thousand credits," Terg said, sitting at the table. "Do you have that kind of bank?"

"Can you deliver in a frozen case to *Calypso* in the morning?" Rix asked.

"I'd need a deposit on the frozen case," she said. "Make it eleven hundred and I'll give you fifty credits back when you return the case."

"Sounds like a deal," Rix said. "Kel, do we need red root?"

"No, that's not hard to grow on Patience."

"Just looking to figure how to make a buck," Rix said. "Not every idea can be a winner."

A few more locals joined the table and the card playing started in earnest. With a fifty credit buy in, Rix started with plenty of chips and his stack grew and shrank on the whims of the table, while Jacknie's stack mostly grew as players were forced out of the game.

"So you're setting up spec runs," Jacknie said. "Dangerous work sailing the inner passage. Pirates love picking off fat loads of goodies. Especially if they're chasing broken-down little freighters."

"I'm curious about how you'd know that," Terg asked, causing the entire table to laugh.

"*Calypso* is hardly a broken-down little freighter," Kel said defensively, tossing her cards angrily onto the table. "Why, Rix is a master mechanic, capable of fixing just about anything."

"Oh, is he now?" Jacknie asked with a cocky grin. "I'm not sure how an Earther knows a thing about our tech, much less can figure out how to fix it."

"Well, I'll tell you this much," Kel said. "He fixed three atmo generators on Patience. You can ask Garba, if you doubt my word."

"That's enough, Kel," Rix said. "He's just trying to rile you, so you go on tilt."

"Don't you go patronizing me while I'm defending you," Kel said angrily.

"You're right, my bad," Rix said. "And we shouldn't underestimate how a talented pilot makes a tough run look easy. Isn't that right, Kel?"

"That's right."

"You know, for a bit of change, less than you'd expect, we could probably find a clear corridor for *Calypso*," Jacknie said, dealing a fresh hand.

"Here we go, Rix," Kel said. "Don't listen to him."

"Hold on," Rix said. "It can't hurt to listen."

"Smart man," Jacknie said. "Ten percent of your load and I could guarantee that you won't be hassled one bit between here and Patience."

"That's robbery, Jacknie," Kel said.

"Or a tax," Jacknie said.

"Ten percent on profit, not cost of goods," Rix said.

"Gross profit, not net," Jacknie negotiated.

"This trip is gratis," Rix said, extending his hand.

"Kel, you could learn a lot from this man," Jacknie said.

"This is forgie crap!" Kel said, throwing down her cards and pushing away from the table. "You didn't even consult me, Rix. Sleep in your own bunk tonight!"

Until that moment, Rix thought he was likely in bad shape with Kel. That he slept alone in his own bunk all the time was something Jacknie didn't know.

"Don't wait up," Rix said. "And I'm in for another ten credits."

"You better chase that one," Terg said. "She's got a temper. You might find your bunk's been set on fire if you don't make things square."

"You're probably not wrong," Rix said. "But cards is cards."

"Cards is cards," Jacknie echoed. "And unless you picked up three smokers, I've got you beat this time, my boy."

"I have not," Rix said, showing his hand and acting properly rueful.

"That's all I have tonight," Terg said as Jacknie scooped the sticks from the table. "I'll be over first thing with those frozen fillets. Make good with Kel. I don't like drama in the morning."

"Nobody likes drama in the morning," Samess said, grinning.

"Do you boys mind if I ask a question?" Rix asked. "It's about Patience Station."

"Not exactly our home base, Rix Banner," Samess said.

"No, but you fellas deal with trouble on the regular, you might have some ideas."

"Tell us what's on your mind, Rix," Jacknie said.

"Someone's been sabotaging the atmospheric handlers on Patience Station. I can't figure why, though," Rix said. "Geoff is Garba's guy, both at home and for station maintenance, but it's like he looks the other way."

"You might be getting in over your head, Rix Banner," Jacknie said. "There's a group called Sable that runs out of Patience. I know a brother who's friendly. What's it worth to you to find out?"

"Find out, or find out with proof?" Rix asked.

"Either."

"I have no idea how much these things are worth, Jacknie," Rix said. "I've a little money saved up. What could I get for five hundred credits?"

"A name," Jacknie said. "Two thousand would get you proof, assuming Sable isn't behind the trouble."

"What if they are?"

"If Sable is making a run at Patience? I just don't see that as their thing. I'll tell you, though, whoever's behind this is paying Sable to look the other way," Jacknie said. "They might even be doing some of the grunt work, but it's just a job."

"Here's fifteen hundred," Rix said, flicking a credit transaction at Jacknie. "Whatever you don't use, we can apply to transport tax going forward."

"You give too much in faith," Jacknie said. "I've taken a liking to you, though, so, I'll do what I can. You probably won't like the answer, though."

"The truth is what it is," Rix said. "I'd rather know and not do something about it than not know at all."

"Betting everything, then?" Jacknie asked, pushing in a stack of chips the same height as what Rix had remaining.

"Gah, why not, it's getting late," Rix said.

"I hope your luck in business is better than it is at cards," Jacknie said, turning over his cards.

"Me too," Rix said, tossing his hand onto the table in disgust. "At least we don't need to worry about cashing me out. And I'm done for tonight, boys. Grog delivery in the morning?"

"I'll send my girl over around 0930."

"I'll set an alarm."

"Drink lots of water, Earther. The grog will catch up with you," Jacknie said, chuckling as Rix feigned stumbling away from the table.

Making it back to *Calypso,* Rix tried to be quiet as he entered the ship so as not to wake Kel. Not unexpectedly, she intercepted him.

"You are patronizing, you do know that, right?" she asked.

"I didn't think it was all that," Rix said.

"Making deals without even giving me a chance to have my say isn't being a good partner, Rix."

Rix took a long breath and gave himself a moment to think. While the grog wasn't overly strong, he'd had enough that he knew better than to say the first thing that came to mind. "You're right," Rix said. "I wasn't being thoughtful. I can do better at that."

"I want to be able to trust my partner, Rix. I know you're this crazy smart person and everything, but I have good ideas too," she said.

"Okay, what do we need to fix?"

"Thank you for saying *we.* Also, that's what I'm finding frustrating. You played Jacknie well. He's going to stab you in the back at some point, but right now, he's intrigued and you're getting the full charm offensive," she said. "He's nothing but a snake though. You can't trust him."

"You're not super angry?"

"No. I owe you a lot and I don't want to sound ungrateful, but I also don't need a partner who won't listen to me, either," she said.

"Message received," Rix said.

"Do you have five hundred credits left over?"

"I will tomorrow morning," Rix said. "What do you have?"

"Flour. I can get five hundred kilograms at a credit per kilo," she said. "They have a serious overstock."

"Any chance it has weevils?" Rix asked.

"What is that?"

"Bugs that infest flour. At least back home they do."

"That's a good idea, we'll run a bio scan and we're on the hook for picking it up," Kel said. "That's why we got it so cheap."

"Good, that's a good deal, Kel," Rix said. "We'll have a nice load to bring back to Patience."

"I hope so, because if I don't have five thousand to give to Vigno the day after I get back, he'll take *Calypso*."

"It'll work out," Rix said. "Trust me."

Kel stilled for a moment and Rix couldn't help but look at her again. She'd changed out of her evening gown and had put on loose pajamas but hadn't switched back from her voluptuous form. "I do trust you, Rix," she said quietly. "And that's what scares me."

Rix leaned in and stopped two centimeters from his face making contact with hers. He felt the warmth of her skin and saw the decision in her face as she made it and leaned in the final distance. Their lips touched and they lightly kissed.

"That was nice," Rix said when they separated.

"Yeah, it was. Good night, Rix," Kel said and then she turned and padded off to her bunkroom.

"Cold shower it is," Rix said, turning down the hallway.

Morning came more quickly than he'd hoped as Kel knocked on his bunkroom door at 0700. "Rise and shine, space boy," Kel called cheerily. "You and Philo need to run and grab a big load of flour. I've put the scanner out on the table and there's breakfast in the galley. I'll be out for a couple of hours, working some new deals I have a line on."

"Hold on, do you need more credits?" Rix asked, leaning against the doorframe as he opened his bunkroom.

"You look rough, Rix," she said. "And your breath stinks."

"Hazards of wining and dining new suppliers," Rix said.

"I could use two hundred fifty credits. I have a line on some goods I think we can make thirty percent on," she said. "It's not great, but we might as well fill the hold."

"That sounds about right," Rix said. "If we get loaded today, are we shoving off?"

"If you're okay with that," she said. "How does 1300 work for you?"

"You're the boss," Rix said.

"Best for you to keep that in mind."

"Are we going to talk about … you know?" Rix said.

"I know?"

"The kiss last night?"

"Probably not."

And with that, Kel walked off whistling a happy tune.

29

BILLS TO PAY

"How does it feel?" Rix asked as they pushed away from Sout Atal and turned to the asteroid belt.

"I don't love Sout Atal," she said. "But it was nice to catch up with some friends last night. What did you do? And how does what feel?"

"*Calypso* has its second, mostly full load and is headed home," Rix said. "And I spent my time reading what I could about local events in Sout Atal. They have an interesting archive of local news. It's mostly invitations to social gatherings, but there's talk about Dravari and pirate activity sprinkled in, too."

"That sounds boring," Kel said. "Also, I wish you'd talked to me about paying Jacknie that extortion money. I can get around his pirates just fine."

"I don't like it any better than you do, but he would have known when we were taking off and would have alerted his crew to be waiting for us," Rix said. "I didn't see much of a choice."

"That's what I'm saying. You need to trust me and trust *Calypso*," she said.

"Okay," Rix said. "I won't enter another agreement like that without talking with you first. For now, we'll pay him. A time will come when he decides to up the fee. We'll tell him to pound sand when he does."

"Do you promise?"

"Yes."

"Are we going to have enough to pay Vigno when we get back?" Kel asked.

"Five thousand credits, right?" Rix asked.

"Yes. That's mostly interest, but I think it pays down a thousand of my debt, too," she said.

"The fuel got us five thousand credits alone. We used some of that to buy the fish, flour and the other items you picked up. I traded for twenty liters of Jacknie's Grog. I guess what I'm saying is that overall, we're going positive at some level."

"Are you going to pay protection for your new mechanic's shop? I'm telling you that once you get into the business of paying protection, it won't be long before everyone wants a piece of you," she said.

"That sounds like experience talking," Rix said.

"I just know it's a bad idea."

"It might be the best in a list of bad ideas, though."

"I can't fully disagree with that, Rix, but you need to know, once they have their hooks in you, they're not letting go," Kel said. "They'll bleed you dry."

"I understand the danger."

"What are you reading about now?" Kel asked, noticing that she wasn't getting Rix's full attention.

"Photonic generators, or more accurately Glatius Corporation's photonic barrier generator, Model 14A," Rix said. "I'm trying to get some perspective on how they're put together."

"I'd ask if you think you can fix that pair you got from Garba, but I already know the answer," she said. "What's something like that cost, anyway? It can't be cheap if it's made to keep a space station's atmosphere from leaking out."

"New, they're about sixty thousand," Rix said. "I doubt people pay that much for a refurbished pair, though. I'd like to put them in my new shop so it's easier for folks to pull their ships in for service."

"That'll get attention," Kel said. "You don't see a lot of photonic barriers out this far."

"I'm trying to figure out if Garba will want them back once I get them running and if she does, what a fair price looks like," Rix said.

"Garba Klex has deep pockets and short arms," Kel said. "If she wants photonic barrier generators, she should go buy them."

"Sounds like you have big feelings about all this," Rix said.

"Don't get me started. Garba has taken advantage of so many families who were just trying to hang on," she said. "Garba could have loaned them money or given them a break on rent, but no, she's always a stickler."

"Talk to me about your loan with Vigno. If you're only paying off a thousand credits per five thousand credits paid, that means your interest is four thousand credits a month," Rix said.

"That's the deal," Kel said.

Rix did some quick mental math and shook his head. "You do understand that every year you pay down a quarter of the debt but you've paid the full amount of the debt in interest. He's getting four times pay back on his loan over four years."

"I've accumulated interest when I couldn't pay," she said. "It started out as a three thousand credit payment."

"Do you have papers on this loan? Can you pay it off early?"

"I don't think so," she said, shaking her head. "Sometimes people buy someone else's debt. I don't really know. I told you I was a bad bet, Rix. You shouldn't have thrown in with me."

"Well, I don't see it that way," Rix said. "You're not defined by the old decisions you've made. We make changes, we figure things out. Heck, I just paid Jacknie to keep pirates off our six and lookie there, pirates are headed right this way."

"Aww, crap," Kel said, looking at the tactical display. "That's three of them and those are Model 72s. We might be able to outrun them, but with three, that's not a good bet."

"Okay, no problem, let's see what they want," Rix said. "Just keep sailing along like we haven't seen them."

"We're getting hailed. I'm answering," Kel said. "This is *Calypso*, go ahead *Black Sparrow*."

"*Calypso*, this is just a friendly checkup, please state your destination."

"*Black Sparrow*, we're sailing the Inner Passage, en route to Patience Station," Kel said. "We've had clear sailing. Over."

"Safe travels, courtesy of Draven Knights. We'll ask that you report any ship traffic you pass while underway to the attached address. *Black Sparrow* over and out."

"And so it starts," Kel said. "No doubt Jacknie told them to make their presence known so we'd feel the investment was worth it."

"That sounds about right," Rix said. "You do understand that if Jacknie sent them to let us feel his presence, he could have sent them to board and take our cargo, right?"

"Or worse," Kel said.

"If you put aside the pirates and extortion, it's an interesting trip, don't you think? We're making some money and even more importantly, we're making contacts," Rix said. "Talk to me about your dreams for *Calypso*."

"I'd like to have that short-haul freighter pilot's license so we could make runs within the system," Kel said. "It's one thing to trade alcohol and snacks within the belt, it's another thing to contract actual loads with legitimate shippers."

"Do they really pay that well?"

"Yes and no, but that's not the appeal," Kel said. "With a freighter pilot's license, we get some protection from Dravari. They can't just willy-nilly board us and search. Galactic Empire Trade Federation hands out fines to localities that harass licensed pilots. Now, if they catch us hauling something illegal, that's another issue, entirely."

"But you'd start hauling legitimate cargo, right?"

"That depends. Dravari have a chokehold on the settlements in Surnak asteroid belt. If I see a way to even the score a little, I'll do it," she said.

"Like taking their atmospheric condenser," Rix said.

"That's right."

"But don't you risk losing that license you don't even have yet?"

"It's a matter of principle, Rix," Kel said.

"A principled thief," Rix said. "Sounds like the title of an obituary."

"I don't get you, Rix," Kel said. "You pay off thugs and let Dravari stomp all over good people and you don't seem to upset about it all. That's not me. I'm not putting up with that crap."

"Your problem with me is that I don't fight against organizations that can crush me?" Rix said.

"That's right, Rix, you have to make a stand once in a while, let people know you can't be shoved around, otherwise, that's all they're going to do," Kel said.

Rix nodded but didn't answer. Kel wasn't wrong and he knew it, but he also didn't think they stood a chance against pirate gangs and immoral governments. It was a tough position to be in and her logic was starting to make more sense.

"Do you really think you could outrun those Model 72s?" Rix asked.

"I think the question is, would Jacknie have sent them after us for half a ton of flour and fish? There was a minimum of nine pirates aboard those ships. What kind of payout would that have been? Sure, maybe they make initial contact and chase us when we rabbit," Kel said. "How hard do they push things once we really get into the rocks. We're running for our lives, but they're burning fuel and endangering their crews for basically nothing interesting."

"Damn, I hate it when you make sense," Rix said. "So what do I do when Sable approaches me and wants protection money to leave me alone in my shop?"

"Tell them you'll give them a friends and family discount for repairing their ships," Kel said. "Trust me when I tell you there's nobody out here who repairs ships like you do. Their actual risk is that you deny them service because they're leaning on you."

"And then they start breaking legs and everybody goes home unhappy."

"I just know we're better off if we don't let these guys have a piece of us," Kel said.

"Your deal with Vigno is a good example."

"Right. Now we're talking. And getting your legs broken is something that Patience Station's medical bay can fix easily."

Rix laughed ironically. "I don't think that's the point. I think breaking legs hurts a lot."

Kel grinned. "I'm glad you're starting to see things my way on this."

The trip quieted down and the two took shifts sitting in the pilot's chair as they worked through the asteroid belt. Five days later, they finally arrived at Patience Station, both ready for a change of scenery.

"Meet me at Hidden Room this evening?" Rix asked.

"I never go in there," Kel said. "The men in there are all part of Sable. We talked about this, Rix."

"Shixen plays cards there," Rix said. "I figured we'd grab a drink and get Vigno's money delivered for this month."

"I'm not sure we'll have all the fish and flour moved by then," Kel said. "I'm tight on credits."

"Well, I can pay you your part of the load right now, or I can take your share out of what I pay Shixen for *Calypso's* mortgage," Rix said.

"My share is only fifteen hundred credits," Kel said. "I'm not even breaking even if I hand it all over to Shixen."

"Do you have money to live on?" Rix said. "I'll make the payment to Shixen and cover the difference."

"And now I owe you more?"

"My terms are better than Vigno's, Kel," Rix said. "You're fighting for survival and Vigno's interest rates are ridiculous. Nobody can survive that. Besides, you're a good investment. We couldn't do any of this without *Calypso*."

"I can't help but think we're barely breaking even," she said. "And if you look at it, I'm not."

"You haven't tried to sell the trade goods you bought," Rix said.

"I'm going to need a place to put those, by the way," Kel said. "Would you mind if I set up a shelf in your shop for just a little while? I need a place where I can show things off and my apartment is too small. I could show them out the back of *Calypso* but that feels sketchy."

"I don't see a problem with setting up a few shelves with your import goods," Rix said. "Eventually, you'll need your own shop when your inventory grows enough. Also, who should I try to sell this flour to? I was thinking Petju."

"Let me sell it from the shop," Kel said. "Same with the fish. All I need to do is put word out that we have fresh food and people will come out of the vents to buy it."

Rix tipped his head to the side, not understanding the vents comment, but then realized it was an idiom like "coming out of the woodwork." "Perfect. I plan to go work in Environmental today, do you think you could get Philo to help move the fish, flour and barrel of Jacknie's grog?"

"Sure, we'll rent a grav pallet."

"No need, I have one in Garba's warehouse. We just need to pick it up."

Philo picked that moment to stick his head into the bridge. "Land soon? Philo sleepy. Want to take nap."

Kel and Rix laughed together as Philo had spent the majority of the time they'd sailed between Sout Atal and Patience Station fast asleep in his bunk.

"Hey, Buddy," Rix said. "Are you up for making some credits today?"

"Hard work, Rixy?" Philo asked.

"Moving equipment and supplies, Philo," Rix said. "I'd give you seventy-five credits to help unload *Calypso* and also grab the tools I earned from Garba for fixing the atmosphere condensers."

"Seventy-five credits! Yes yes, Rixy! Rixy good friend," Philo said excitedly.

"Hidden Room later this afternoon, then?" Rix asked as *Calypso* settled into her berth.

"Sure, just send a comm when you're on your way."

Rix waited impatiently for the telescoping concourse to connect to *Calypso's* side and then jogged through once complete. Mostly, he was worried about vandalism while he'd been away. And just as he'd worried, he arrived to discover that someone had indeed torn into

Units 3 and 4, causing significant damage, leaving both on the edge of catastrophic failure.

"Garba are you available?" he asked, tapping his comms. "We've had a new incident."

"Rix Banner, are you on station? I hadn't heard you were back yet."

"I just got in and came down to Environmental," Rix said. "Units 3 and 4 are in trouble. I'm going to have to take them offline if we're going to save them."

"What now?"

"It looks like the same sort of vandalism using something like a big hammer. They really went to town on it," Rix said.

"That's an odd phrase. Have you contacted constable Quixly?" she asked.

"No, you're the first call. We're in an emergency here. I need to shut those units down. Do I have your permission?" Rix asked.

"Yes, do it. How far back are we set?" she asked.

Rix moved around to the power controller and shut the units down one at a time before responding. "Maybe two days?" Rix said. "I'll go time and materials on this. We don't have time to negotiate something else."

"I'm coming down there and I'm bringing Quixly with me," she said.

"Copy that," Rix said, glancing into the rafters where Philo had placed the recording device that might show who'd damaged the units. He didn't locate it and sent a message to Kel, asking for access to the unit's video stream.

Grabbing tools and getting to work, he had the enclosure removed by the time Garba and Quixly arrived.

"You again?" Quixly asked.

"That's a strange question," Rix said. "I basically live down here, fixing these things because they keep getting damaged. Who else would you expect to see down here after I call and report damage?"

"How long have the units been this way?" Garba asked.

"Five days," Rix said. "I have the log pulled up and that's about the time we started taking all these errors."

"Where were you then?" Quixly asked.

"Sout Atal, we had dinner and drinks with a local trading partner," Rix said. "Why, do you need their name to validate I wasn't on station?"

"Every time there is damage, you are here," he said.

"Did you install a camera so we could see who's doing this?"

"No. It is against our policies."

"That's absurd," Garba said. "I'm hemorrhaging credits trying to keep air in this place. I order you to install monitoring devices immediately. Do you understand how critical this is, constable? Without air, this station is uninhabitable. Someone is trying to run us out of here. Is that what you want?"

"I will install a device using an emergency declaration," Quixly said.

"You do that," Garba said. "How long before you can get one of these units back online?"

"Tomorrow afternoon if I work through the night," Rix said. "I'm going to charge double time if that's what you need, though."

"I'll pay it."

Rix nodded and got back to work, later receiving a message from Kel that the video device they'd placed in the rafters had been mysteriously removed with no video evidence of who had taken it.

"Kel, how is that possible that we don't have a record?" Rix asked.

"Someone used a jamming device before they took it down. That's not a common thing to have, but we are dealing with pirates, so that's likely."

"I'll be honest, I feel like Geoff is somehow involved, but I can't prove it," Rix said. "We should ask around to see if anyone's seen him."

"I can do a little digging," Kel said.

"Thanks," Rix said and hung up.

He got back to work on the unit and at 1800 he sent an invite to Kel to meet him at Hidden Room, asking her to bring ten of the twenty liters of Jacknie's Grog with her. They ended up meeting next to the elevators as they arrived at the same time.

"How'd the unload of *Calypso* go? Did you have any trouble with my shop's neighbors?" he asked.

"Someone came by looking for you. I didn't catch his name," she said.

"Did you tell him I'm tied up for a bit?"

"I did," she said. "On the positive, I sold twenty kilos of your fish for two hundred credits and I think Petju wants to buy half of your flour. Will a thousand work? That's twice what you paid and it's a good deal for Petju."

"That's perfect," Rix said. "Any hits on your trade goods?"

"Interest, no sales."

"It's early."

Smoke vapor wafted from the bar when Rix pushed open the door and wheeled in the grog with Kel right behind him. Scanning, he was gratified to find everyone he wanted to talk to present. He first went up to the bar where Collie Berg was cleaning glasses.

"Well, look at what the space monkeys have sent us," Collie said in a not unfriendly tone.

"Collie," Rix said by way of greeting.

"What's in the canister?"

"Well, first, you'll be interested to know that the good folks of Sout Atal quite enjoyed Collie's Reserve rum," Rix said. "So much so, that I traded the entire stock you sold me for a batch of Jacknie's Grog. I have to wonder if you've ever tried it."

"Don't know that I have."

"It's a sweeter taste than your rum," Rix said. "It might appeal to a different crowd."

"I suppose it might," Collie said guardedly. "I'd need to taste it to know."

Rix let the cart rest and smiled. "I have business to discuss with Shixen, why don't you give it a try and let me know if you're interested."

"Sounds fair, but Shixen is playing cards, he might not like sharing business with the boys. Let me call him over, you fellas take a private booth," Collie said, pointing at a booth away from all other customers.

"Solid plan," Rix said.

It took a few minutes for Collie to grab Shixen's attention and then a few more minutes for him to extract from the card game and join them.

"Kel, Rix, want to tell me what's important enough to interrupt my card game?" Shixen asked.

Rix handed Shixen a chit with five thousand credits. "I believe that's mortgage for *Calypso*. Looks like we're back to forty-six thousand owed. Is that right?"

Shixen looked at Kel with mild surprise. "Finally shacked up with a sucker, eh? Well played."

"Hey, he's a business partner, nothing more."

"Forty-six thousand eight hundred, Banner," Shixen said. "Next payment in thirty days. Five thousand."

"Would Vigno be open to selling Kel's debt?" Rix asked.

"For the right price, anything is for sale."

"Next time you talk, could you ask what that looks like?"

Shixen nodded. "Do you have that kind of money?"

"No, but I like to know what we're shooting for," Rix said.

"Fair enough," Shixen said. "I'll get you a number. If that's it, I'm gonna move on."

"Thank you for your time, Shixen," Rix said.

"Yup, sure."

"That all okay with you?" Rix asked Kel after Shixen had left.

"You're really something, Rix," Kel said. "That's such a load off my mind."

"Well, stick with me kid, we're going places," Rix said and got up from the booth to join Collie at the bar. "What'd you think?"

"What do you want for what you've brought in here?" he asked.

"Twenty liters of your black rum," Rix said.

"That's a lot," Collie said. "I'm not sure I have enough material to make that."

"It's a fair price," Rix said.

"People like my rum."

"They sure do and we're building a market for it in other places,"

Rix said. "Do the math, Collie. Sell Jacknie's grog at a premium because it's new and different. You'll make twice what the bill is for the ingredients for another batch of rum."

"Who else are you selling this grog to?"

"You're my first customer on Patience Station," Rix said.

"How much more do you have?"

"Another ten liters."

"I'll give you thirty-five liters of my rum for twenty liters of Jacknie's grog. I don't want you selling to anyone on Patience."

"You're asking for a discount and exclusivity at the same time," Rix said. "How is that a good deal?"

"Where else will you get my rum?"

"It cuts both ways," Rix said. "I can think of three other people on Patience who have the means to buy twenty liters of this grog for full retail. I'm working with you because you have something I want. I can just buy the grog instead of trading it for rum. The value for both of us is keeping this a bartered deal. I'll let you think about it. My price is two for one. Let me know."

"I'll have forty liters ready for you in a week, but you have to leave the grog you brought," Collie said.

"Deal," Rix agreed.

30

SUSPENSE

"You've done a whole lot more work than just set up shelving," Rix said, looking around his new shop. Kel and Philo had moved all the bartered tools from Garba's warehouse and instead of just dropping them haphazardly, they'd neatly arranged the toolboxes and filled them with the loose tools. Further, they'd made an effort to move the piled junk and debris off to one end of the shop. There was more to do, but it was a considerable improvement.

"I'm calling these shelves our boutique," Kel said, pointing to the shelves where she had set out the various smaller trade goods she'd picked up on Sout Atal. Next to the shelving were stacks of bagged flour, the empty Collie's Reserve bottles Rix had manufactured and the remaining ten liters of Jacknie's Grog. "I have appointments already setup tomorrow to let a few folks in to look around. I think the flour is going to all move tomorrow, I've been getting comms all afternoon asking about it. It might take a minute to get word out about the fish. At ten credits a kilo, it's a good deal, but people don't have a lot of money."

"If you have to, discount it to seven and a half credits per kilo," Rix said. "I'd rather move it quickly than hang onto something perishable. Besides, it's a benefit for people to know that we're in business."

"Okay. Talk to me about what happened in Environmental this morning. More vandalism?" she asked. "Is that why we're running low on atmospheric pressure again?"

"That's right. I have to run down there after this and get to work," Rix said. "They really did a number on those units again."

"But you can fix them."

"I was already going to work on them. I'll get Unit 3 back to limping along and then clean up Units 4 and 5. I can't understand why Quixly isn't more interested in finding out who's doing all this. The whole floor should be locked down."

"Do you think he's behind it?"

"I was hoping we'd get something from that security video Philo installed." As they were speaking a comm arrived in his inbox. "That's weird, I just got an anonymous comm. I didn't think that was possible."

"What is it?"

"A video clip," Rix said. "Beverly, would you mind projecting the clip onto the wall so we can all see it?"

"I thought you'd forgotten about me," Beverly said, appearing on one of the shelves, wearing an usher's uniform as was common in movie theaters.

"No, we've just been running hard," Rix said.

When the video started, it was clear that the camera was being worn by someone, possibly on their belt or in a button on their front. The angle wasn't perfect, but as the person moved, Geoff came into view and he was seen speaking with a uniformed Dravari officer.

"That Dravari was the guy who chased us in when we first arrived on Patience Station," Kel said.

"Are you certain?"

"Oh, yeah, he searched *Calypso* and was a complete jerk about it."

"*You need to take care of this,*" the Dravari officer could be heard saying.

"*We have this under control. You showing up like this isn't helping anything,*" Geoff said with irritation evident in his voice. "*This is taking too long.*"

"*They can't install your condenser, I've seen to that,*" Geoff said. "*That newcomer might be trouble. I'll need to hire local muscle to help.*"

"*Get it done, or we'll find someone who can,*" the Dravari officer said, holding out a credit chit. "*This is your last until this place is closed. The Prefect is impatient.*"

The video was cut off.

"When was that video taken?" Rix asked.

"Hold on, who would send that to you?" Kel asked.

"I paid Jacknie some money to look into the vandalism," Rix said.

"We talked about getting involved with him, Rix. It's a bad idea. Jacknie is dangerous," Kel said.

"This was before we talked," Rix said. "And paying unsavory types for information is different than paying them for security."

"Not really," Kel said.

"That video was time encoded to the day when you arrived at Patience Station," Beverly said.

"We need to show this to Garba," Kel said.

"Not yet," Rix said. "We need to get things back online first."

"Why?"

"Because we need to show this to Quixly, Geoff and Garba at the same time and see who blinks," Rix said. "Quixly could be behind this, too. His security is terrible."

"At least now we know why station maintenance is so bad," Kel said. "People are going to revolt once this video gets out. Garba's going to have trouble keeping peace. We can't sit on this very long."

"Let me get Unit 3 working and then we'll confront Geoff. I'm working on an idea. Trust me for a couple of days on this?"

"Okay," Kel said skeptically.

"Look, Kel, people need air. Once we start confronting people, things could change and we might not be able to get Unit 3 back online. It's too dangerous to get in the way of that," Rix said.

"Okay, but I'm going to watch your back while you're working. This just got more dangerous," Kel said.

"I wouldn't mind the company," Rix said. "Meet me down in Environmental when you're ready. I need to get back to work."

It was in the wee hours of the morning when Rix knocked off work for the night. Instead of sleeping in their apartments, the three of them decided to sleep on sleeping rolls and keep watch over the equipment with Beverly monitoring while they slept.

"Man, I'm sore," Kel complained as she rolled over. Her eyes defocused for a moment as she checked comms. "Hah! Petju has fresh sweet rolls this morning. She totally used that flour we sold her, I knew it!"

"Grab some and bring them back?" Rix asked wearily. "Also, strongest type of coffee you have, okay?"

"You'll be okay?"

"Or I won't," Rix said. "We can't live on top of each other forever."

"I know."

Rix got to work as Kel and Philo left to gather breakfast. He'd been at it for twenty minutes when he heard a noise and turned. He'd long ago lost his startle reflex but was surprised when he saw Geoff standing not two meters from him, with a heavy wrench in hand.

"Geoff, it's been a while," Rix said, setting down the cleaning wand he'd just finished up with. "Can I help you with anything?"

"What are you doing here, Banner?" Geoff asked.

"You know what I'm doing here, Geoff," Rix said. "I'm fixing these condensers. Apparently, it's turning into a full-time job because someone's been trying to ruin them."

"That's not what I mean, and you know it. Why'd you come to Patience Station and I'm not buying the poor, dumb semi-sentient Earthling story. What are you and what do you want on Patience?" Geoff asked.

"At this point, I'm just trying to keep a few thousand station residents alive," Rix said. "The longer part of that story is that I needed a new place to live and this was the most convenient place to land."

"You're going to get hurt, Banner," Geoff said. "People don't like you. You're putting your nose into people's business that don't appreciate it."

"Are you threatening me?"

"I'm telling you how it is."

"Are you planning to use that wrench?"

"As a matter of fact, I am," Geoff said.

"On me?"

"No. I have a black water problem that needs addressing," he said. "I don't appreciate you telling people my ice crystals are dirty and I don't want those prepass filters on my equipment. Up to me, you'd be fired and I'm sure Garba is one-step from doing just that."

"The units are working flawlessly. Or they would be, if people with big, heavy tools would stop hitting them," Rix said angrily.

"Be careful, Banner," Geoff said. "Don't be making accusations if you can't back them up. That could get a person hurt around here."

"Hey! What's going on over there!?" Kel called from a distance.

"And that goes for your girlfriend, too."

"Business partner," Rix corrected.

"Sure, whatever you want," Geoff said and then stalked off in the opposite direction.

"What in the heck was that all about?" Kel asked, handing Rix a small box that was warm to the touch.

"Geoff being Geoff," Rix said, opening the box. Inside sat a frosted pastry with orange colored fruit. "Man, this smells fantastic."

"Philo's had three of them," Kel said, grinning. "Oh, got a coffee here for you, too. Seriously, though what was that about?"

"Geoff just showed up and was acting weird."

"Do you think he knows we're onto him? I wouldn't put it past Jacknie to be playing both sides of this," Kel said.

"I hadn't thought of that."

"Oh, he's a snake, alright," Kel said. "How close are you getting?"

"Two more hours and I'll have Unit 3 fired up," Rix said. "Then I'm taking a break. I'm spending so much time fixing these things that nothing I want to do is getting done."

"Well, we do all appreciate breathing. So, I'd say it's worthwhile."

"Until Geoff and his thugs beat the life out of it again."

"True."

After eating the pastries, Rix got back to work while Kel guarded his back. True to his word, two hours later, he pushed closed the cabinet and directed the unit to start up. Which it did.

"How much did that cost?" Kel asked. "I saw the manufactory delivery down here at least three times."

"Manufactory bill was thirteen thousand. I'm billing twelve hundred in emergency repairs," Rix said, filling out the invoice and sending it along to Garba. His comms immediately lit up after sending the bill. "This is Rix, go ahead."

"Rix, Garba Klex, I see you got us going again, great work," she said. "The invoice you sent is only for Unit 3, what about the other two?"

"I'm short on sleep and have a few of my own issues to deal with," Rix said. "I'll get started again tomorrow. Any reason to stay in emergency mode? I figured with Unit 3 we could stick to our original contract."

"Okay, whatever you think is best," Garba said.

"Any chance we could get Quixly to post a guard down here. I'd hate to see this get ruined again," Rix said.

"I've talked to him," she said. "He has a plan and I trust him."

Rix knit his eyebrows at the statement. So far Quixly had been anything but trustworthy on keeping the critical equipment secured. "So, hey, I have something I need to show you. It might be interesting to Quixly and maybe even Geoff, too. Is there any chance you all could meet me in my new shop sometime tomorrow?"

"Won't you be working?"

"I'm going to take a day, but I'll get started the day after," Rix said.

"Would mid-afternoon work for you?"

"Yes. I'll just be cleaning the shop, that should work fine."

"I'll bring them both," Garba said. "Thank you for your hard work, Rix. Patience Station would be in a serious bind if not for your help."

"Glad I could be of service," Rix said, closing comms.

"She sounded like she was in a good mood," Kel said.

"Well, she won't after she gets the next bill. That'll be nearly eighty thousand considering the parts we have to manufacture," Rix said.

"She's really putting a lot of money into the station," Kel said.

"It's not her money, Kel," Rix said. "The repairs come from tax revenue. I did some checking. Want to guess who owns the manufactory?"

"Garba?"

"Got it in one."

"Wait, do you think all these repairs are about running tax money through the manufactory?" Kel asked.

"Ever since I've been here, those manufactories have been running a backlog and she's the primary benefactor," Rix said, "Maybe it's a coincidence. Does anyone audit Patience Station's books?"

"I have no idea. That's a good scam. Geoff oversees maintenance and knows which parts generate the most profit on Garba's manufactory. Garba signs off on the repairs. There's no one to catch them. That doesn't explain that video clip, though," Kel said.

"Agreed, but I think we'll get to the bottom of that tomorrow. I have a plan," Rix said.

"What?"

"Not yet," Rix said. "I need your help getting the shop ready for our meeting tomorrow. Can you do that?"

"I hate suspense, Rix," Kel said. "I'm not going to wait long."

"If I'm right, you won't have to," Rix said.

The trio returned to the shop. Getting right to work, Rix set the pair of photonic barrier generators he'd spent so much time researching on a bench and opened them up. Tracing circuits and testing power pathways, he was deep in thought when a loud rap at the door invaded the moment.

"That's probably Petju looking for more flour," Kel said. "She told me if the pastries were a hit, she'd take the rest of it."

"Good job," Rix said distractedly, not taking his eyes off the project. He'd identified a couple of small parts that looked burned out and was pleased to find that for a thousand credits he could manufacture a run of four of them, two more than he needed. He'd just submitted the order when he recognized the conversation at the door didn't sound like a baker looking to pick up flour. "Who is it, Kel?" he asked.

"Uh, Rix, it's Greasle. He wants to talk to you," Kel said.

Rix flicked his HUD so that the magnification of the photonic assembly no longer occupied his entire field of view. Just inside the doorway stood a pair of men doing their best to look intimidating, in front of those men, Greasle stood, looking over Kel to Rix.

"Greasle, welcome," Rix said. "Sorry I haven't had a chance for a game lately. Things have been busy down in Environmental lately. We haven't got things too well set up, but you're welcome to look around. Kel has some new items just back from Sout Atal."

"It's not that kind of visit, Banner," Greasle said, pushing Kel out of the way and walking over to him.

"You look irritated," Rix said. "What's going on?"

"Bossman says you can't work here without paying rent," Greasle said.

"That's fully reasonable," Rix said. "But I am paying rent ... to Garba. According to her, she owns this space. Am I missing something?"

"Level 13 is Sable territory," Greasle said. "If you want to set up business here, you have to pay."

"I'm new around here, you know that," Rix said. "Work with me a minute so I can understand. Sable wants me to pay to rent a place that I've already paid for?"

"Seems like you understand," Greasle said.

"How much?"

"It depends. What are you doing here?"

"Spaceship repairs. The whole space station fixing thing is a side gig," Rix said.

"Where'd you get all these tools?"

"Not sure it's your business, but I bartered my repair skills with Garba to fix the atmospheric generators. I took tools instead of credits," Rix said.

"Five hundred a week," Greasle said.

"No."

"If we don't leave here with five hundred, my boys are going to make you wish we had," Greasle said. "It's not personal. Just business."

"You're not going to do that," Rix said.

"Why not?"

"Because I'm going to give Sable preferential service when I fix your spaceships," Rix said.

"You'll do that anyway," Greasle said. "You don't have a choice. This is our territory."

"You keep saying that, and I believe you. But you need to ask the question. Do you want a happy mechanic who fixes things really well, or a pissed off mechanic and you don't know if your spaceships are going to break when you're in the middle of something important," Rix said.

"If you don't do a good job, we'll end you," Greasle said.

"There are lots of people making threats," Rix said. "You've come into my place and now you're telling me you're going to hurt me if I don't give you my money. That doesn't work for me."

The sound of blaster capacitors charging warned Rix of pending danger and Greasle extended a telescoping wand. "Everybody needs to feel the stick. I don't like doing it, but it's for your own good," Greasle said.

Rix tapped a button on the bench in front of him. At first nothing happened, but then Greasle's baton sagged toward the deck dropping from his hand. Similarly, the pistols held by his crew were torn from their grips and landed on the deck noisily, just as did several tools.

"No," Rix said. "Talk to your boss. Tell him I'm a reasonable guy and if he brings his business to me, I'll get you the friends and family discount for repairs. I'm not going to be threatened and if you all need to take me out, that's just how it goes. I imagine, you'd rather have a competent mechanic available. I've seen the ships around here and I can see they all need work."

"You can't win like this," Greasle said. "You're just going to get hurt."

"And without me, this station fails, and you guys are looking for a new place to live," Rix said. "I bet your boss can find five hundred credits a week of value in keeping me alive and happy. Go talk to him. I'll be here."

Greasle leaned over to grab his baton but found he couldn't pick it from the floor. "Let it go," he growled, stepping toward Rix threateningly.

"Buddy, you need to understand something. Just because I'm looking for a peaceful solution, doesn't mean I can't do this the other way," Rix said. "Make your move if that's what you're about, but know this, it won't go like you think."

Greasle stared Rix in the face and leaned close in, his muscles bunching as he worked through the conversation. "This isn't over, Banner."

"You can collect your weapons in the hallway later this afternoon," Rix said.

Greasle and his crew exited the shop with nothing further than angrily grumbled words. "Was that you not provoking them?" Kel asked.

"You said I couldn't make extortion payments," Rix said. "That's me not making payments."

"You're too much."

"Maybe. Bring me those blasters. There are some changes I'd like to make," Rix said.

"How did you do that with the guns?"

"This whole bay has a magnetic lock down," Rix said.

"But it didn't affect me," Kel said.

"That was my doing," Beverly said. "I cordoned off the fields to just where the Sable men were standing."

"We're probably not done with those guys," Kel said.

"Nope," Rix agreed, getting back to work. "We're not even done with the worst part of the day. Oh, and I have a favor to ask. I need you to do something for me while I meet with Garba, Geoff and Quixly tomorrow."

"You don't want me to back you up? Quixly has a temper," she said.

A new rap at the door broke their attention. "Beverly, who is it?" Rix asked.

"Manufactory delivery," Beverly said.

"Perfect timing." Rix walked over to the door and accepted the new parts. "I can't wait to get this thing set up."

"You fixed the barrier?"

"I'm hoping," Rix said, gently inserting the new parts into place. "That's a good fit. I'm glad someone made that pattern. Give me a couple of minutes, we'll give it a test run."

"Geoff is going to be mad when he sees this. That's an expensive piece of equipment," Kel said.

Rix nodded as he got back to work. Thirty minutes turned into an hour and then two. Finally, he started reassembling. "Got it," Rix said triumphantly as he carried one of the two devices over to the external hatch. Connecting to station power, he returned to the bench and brought the matching device and installed it too.

"What now?" Kel asked.

Rix leaned down and tapped a button on each device's housing. At first nothing happened but then, suddenly, a translucent blue photonic field appeared, fully covering the hatch.

"Hmm, probably be safest if we tied ourselves down before we test," Rix said. "We can at least crack the hatch, though. It won't open if it senses a pressure differential. Beverly, can you help?"

"Opening a crack," Beverly said, standing on the workbench wearing a white lab coat and goggles. In her hand, she held a rectangular box with two buttons one red the other green. She tapped the green button and as she did, they heard a loud pop on the hatch side of the barrier. Everyone jumped, but then nothing more happened.

"More," Rix encouraged. Beverly depressed the green button and as she did, the hatch continued to slide open until they were looking out into the asteroid field. "Well, heck, that's really satisfying."

A pair of small runabouts sailed past and then turned around, and sailed closely to the station, passing in front of the newly opened hatch. When he waved, his wave was returned by the pair of curious pilots.

"That was Belta and Fienna," Kel said. "I hope you weren't looking to keep this a secret because everyone will know you have a photonic barrier now."

"Why's that?"

"Those two are terrible gossips, just like everyone else on this station," Kel said.

"Perfect," Rix said.

31

SPACED

"That should do it," Rix said to himself, pushing off the deck as he finished bolting down the last of the tool cabinets in place. Brushing off his knees, he set the boltgun on his worktable, satisfied that it was the only tool out of place.

A loud rap on the station side hatch sent a jolt of adrenaline through his system. He'd been anticipating the meeting he'd called for with Garba and was uncharacteristically nervous. Instead of opening the hatch right away, he placed a peephole device on the door and shook his head as he took in the ensemble outside. Instead of just Garba and Quixly, as he'd hoped for, Geoff and Greasle had also come along.

"Beverly, do you see this?" Rix called over comms. He'd sent Philo and Kel away, not wanting them involved in the meeting.

"Rix, you should not open that door," Beverly said. "There can be no good that comes from this."

Rix blew out a hot breath and steeled himself. "You're not wrong," Rix said. "But I'm moving forward, anyway. Record this, will you?"

"I am," she said. "I wish you would reconsider."

Rix closed comms and opened the hatch. "I guess we're getting to the bottom of all this today, then?" Rix asked, his eyes locking on Greasle.

"It is your meeting, Rix," Geoff said but his words were cut off by Greasle's response.

"I told you we'd be back," Greasle said.

"I'll admit, I didn't see that coming," Rix said, turning to Geoff. "I wondered if you were connected to Sable. I figured you were just running your own play."

"What? Rix, you called me. I brought the constable and Geoff like we talked. Greasle is here at Geoff's request," Garba said.

"Is this where you tell Quixly or do you want me to show what I have?" Rix asked.

"All you needed to do is go along, Banner," Geoff said. "You had a good gig fixing the atmo generators. You get paid for fixing things and give a little gravy on the side to the boys. Was that so hard? I thought we had an understanding."

"Show me what?" Quixly interrupted, his face flush with anger.

"You know that if you're not part of this, you're in danger," Rix said.

"What are you talking about?" Quixly asked.

"Why don't you show us this video that's got Garba here all worked up. Then you can tell us what you think you know," Geoff said.

"And don't get any fancy ideas about your magnet again," Greasle said, showing a pistol made of polymers.

"Put that away," Quixly said angrily. "Garba, you vouched for this man and now he has a pistol out."

"Put it down, Greasle," Garba said. "Play the video already, Banner."

Rix had set up a small projector and tapped a virtual button on his HUD launching the video. As before, it showed the Dravari officer exchanging a credit chit with Geoff as the officer expressed Dravari dissatisfaction with the station not shutting down.

"You're working with Dravari?" Quixly asked, his eyebrows high with surprise.

"You can't be that simple," Geoff said. "Dravari paid us to ruin Patience Station. We're just milking the last few credits we can out of the manufactory."

"Hold on, so the damage to the air units was all you?" Quixly asked. "You were the one taking out all of my security systems."

"You used station power," Geoff said. "All I had to do was cut their power. You're not too bright for a constable, but of course, that's why we hired you."

"You're an asshole, Geoff," Quixly said. "You're going to murder good people if you kill the atmo generators. We can't possibly unload the station fast enough."

"That's what Dravari wanted," Geoff said. "We needed a body count so nobody else would try to settle Patience. But then, this guy came along and started fixing things. It just prolonged the inevitable, which made the story all that much more believable."

"You're the mastermind, Garba?" Rix asked. "I know it isn't Geoff. He doesn't have the brains for it."

"Here's the problem," Garba said. "You're smart and you think quickly on your feet. I could use a man like you."

"I don't see a problem," Rix said.

"The problem is that you want to be a hero. This isn't that moment. This is the moment where you go along to get along. Only, I'm certain you don't know how to do that. I can't figure why you let us in the shop today. You had to know Geoff was bad from the video. Greasle doesn't make any bones about his allegiances. You had to know I was involved. So why meet?"

"I wanted to know if Quixly was involved," Rix said. "He runs the security. If we're to survive this whole mess, we need someone who isn't trying to tear it down."

"A bit too late for that. Push them out the airlock, Greasle," Garba said. "We'll tell people that the barrier failed, and they got sucked out."

"But I want to shoot them."

"Not this time."

"Let's go, Quixly," Rix said extending his hand.

"What are you doing?" Quixly asked. "We need to fight."

"I'd rather get spaced than get shot and then spaced," Rix said.

"Greasle, now," Garba said angrily.

Rix was already halfway to the barrier when Greasle angrily grabbed Quixly and started shoving him toward the exterior hatch. The laser blaster went off and Quixly fell to a knee.

"Hey, man, I've got this," Rix said rushing back to help Quixly up. "Trust me," he whispered hoarsely to Quixly.

Greasle pushed Quixly's back and raised his pistol again. "Keep moving."

"How are you so calm?" Quixly asked through clenched teeth.

"Hold your breath," Rix said wrapping his arms around the constable. "Beverly, now."

A clanging sounded from the shop's interior station hatch when it popped open. "What in the heck?" Geoff asked. His question was cutoff when suddenly the photonic barrier generators blinked out. Suddenly, Rix and Quixly were expelled from Patience station only to be followed by the others a moment later.

Calypso slid into view, her cargo hold open as Kel perfectly aligned on the tumbling figures of Rix and Quixly. The solution was inelegant and Rix felt a bone snap in his arm as he slammed into the forward bulkhead of *Calypso's* hold. Snapping shut with emergency protocol, *Calypso's* hold door sealed, and atmosphere was pumped in.

"What did you do?" Quixly asked. "Where are we?"

"Thank your lucky stars that Kel is such a good pilot," Rix said.

"Wait, you knew that was going to happen?" Quixly asked.

"Not exactly that," Rix said. "But they were for sure going to space us, or at least me. I didn't know how much you were involved. It could have just been me."

"I can't believe Geoff was behind all this."

"Geoff was part of Sable," Rix said. "I guess the real question is are you part of Sable, too? Because if you are, I've made a big mistake here."

"I know of Sable," Quixly said. "I'm not one of them, though. Mostly, they stay out of my way and I stay out of theirs."

"And if you need to look the other way once in a while?"

"Look, out here, it doesn't pay to get too curious," Quixly said. "I don't have enough budget to run Sable off Patience Station. So we coexist."

"She put me on Level 13 on purpose, then?" Rix asked.

It was then that the atmosphere finally equalized, and Kel came running through the hatch, pulling Rix into a big hug.

"Ow, ow, ow!" Rix complained as his broken arm got pulled around.

"Oh, I'm sorry, Rix," Kel said. "I'm just so glad you're alive."

"I must admit, I appreciate how it worked out. We need to get a wound dressing for Quixly. Adrenaline has him forgetting he got shot on the way out," Rix said as Quixly slumped to a nearby bench.

"If we land in your shop, it's faster to medical," Kel said.

"Tell Beverly to turn the photonic barrier back on in that case," Rix said.

"Oh, she did that right after those other three came tumbling out," Kel said. "I tried to grab them, but I couldn't get all five of you. That was fast thinking, grabbing Quixly like you did."

"Well, I suppose," Rix said. "Will someone go get them?"

"There's an emergency team responding," Kel said. "They have a chance. It's not great, though."

Landing *Calypso* in Rix's shop, they rode the cargo elevator down and with Philo's help, they made their way to Medical on Level 14.

"What will you do with them, Quixly?" Rix asked as a medical bot worked on his broken arm.

Quixly sat on a bed next to Rix's and considered the man. "Funny, until a few minutes ago, I would have sworn you were involved in the vandalism," Quixly said. "And we have a jail to hold them in. There's a travelling justice that comes by every month or two. If they're convicted, we can pay to transport them to a Galactic Empire facility or hold them ourselves. We'll likely release Greasle to Sable with an agreement he won't step foot on Patience again."

"You really thought that was me?" Rix asked.

"Look at who was getting paid to do the work."

"Fair point."

"How will Patience Station move forward?"

"It's not that complicated. We'll have an emergency election for Mayor. You'd have a chance if you were interested."

"Or you," Rix said. "I have no interest other than to get my shop opened up and get back to fixing spaceships."

"I understand you're under contract to refurbish Units 4 and 5."

"Will that contract be honored?" Rix asked.

"Depends on if the contract was registered or not," Quixly said. "I can check when I get out of here. I'm probably acting mayor, so it's my responsibility. I'll make sure it's still intact if you're still willing to follow through."

"Sure, it's a worthwhile project," Rix said. "And, since we're being honest. I thought you were behind the vandalism. I just couldn't figure out how you kept missing the guys doing it. Will you do anything about Sable? Did you know Greasle was trying to make me pay for Sable's protection?"

"I had an idea that Greasle was doing Sable's business. Now it's clear that Geoff was either paying Sable to vandalize or he was part of Sable," Quixly said. "Last election, I tried to get money to hire more security. Garba was opposed and enough people followed her to defeat it."

"Small town politics are messy back home. I guess things just aren't that different in outer space."

"I don't suppose."

EPILOGUE

Rix set the last crate of frozen fish fillets onto a shelf in the freezer of a previously abandoned restaurant soon to be named Petju's Pub. A week had passed since learning of Geoff and Garba's plan to ruin Patience Station. By some twist of fate, the trio; Geoff, Greasle and Garba had been rescued by a quick-thinking runabout captain and escorted to station's small jail per Quixly's order.

"I'll need more variety of food if I'm to keep this pub running," Petju shared with Rix. "Is there any chance you have a trip to Dralli Station in your future?"

"I'll talk to Kel about that," Rix said. "I'm not sure what we have to trade with Dralli, though, and a deadhead run isn't ideal for profits."

"I understand you were able to trade fuel with Sout Atal," Petju said. "Perhaps you could do that on Dralli as well."

"I'm not sure how you heard about that, but that deal needs to stay on the down-low," Rix said. "Dralli Station's fuel contracts are certainly locked down."

"We need to find an export that's something other than black rum," Petju said. "Collie's producing about as quickly as he can already."

"Or he needs help in going to the next level," Rix said. "Petju, you successfully ran a small stand business making just comera and you more than survived, you thrived. Now, with a menu limited by flour, fish, and produce from Xandarj, you're opening a pub. Show Collie how to increase his production and then add his black rum to your menu."

"I asked about that, but he wants to remain exclusive," Petju said.

"So don't sell it directly. Use it as ingredient," Rix said. "Rum cake, rum glaze, and tiramisu are all things from my home that use rum as a base ingredient. You're creative. Get him to see that there's an advantage to both of you if you cooperate. He needs to see that you're not competition, you're a customer. Not to mention—he gets free advertising."

"I'll invite Collie for a nice lunch made with his rum," Petju said.

"That's good thinking," Rix said. "While you're at it, create a list of items we can look for when we're at foreign ports and what a good price point is. Also, considering shorter runs, if you had access to Grevlox, what would your list look like?"

"Grevlox has just about anything we could want," Petju said. "They're one of only a few major trading hubs in this system. Getting a licensed pilot out this way is next to impossible."

"We're working that," Rix said. "With all that fish, have you considered fish and chips?"

"An Earth delicacy?"

"I first had it in London, after the war," Rix said. "Nothing more than breading fish and deep fat frying. The chips part of it are deep fat fried potato rounds or wedges. There are a couple of sauces we could make to go with it."

"Write it down," Petju said. "I'm game."

"I'll do just that," Rix said. "Thanks for buying out our fish and flour. It sure makes it a lot easier to fill *Calypso*'s hold when we've got money to spend."

"No thanks needed, they were good choices," Petju said.

"Let's hope we can keep that going," Rix said. "We'll let you know when we plan our next trip."

When Rix arrived back in his shop, he found Quixly and Shixen waiting for him just outside. "What's up, fellas?" he asked.

"Can we step inside and talk?" Quixly asked.

"As long as everyone is behaving," Rix said. "Last time didn't work out so well."

"It's not that kind of meeting," Shixen said.

Rix nodded and palmed open the hatch. He was expecting Kel to be back soon and was interested in getting through whatever it was the constable and the local Sable pirate gang leader had to say. "I feel like Kel's loan is up to date," he said preemptively. "Am I wrong?"

"You are not," Shixen said. "We have another matter."

"No time like the present," Rix said.

"Bottom line is I'm turning over security of Levels 10 through 13 to Sable," Quixly said.

"Here we go," Rix said shaking his head.

"No, hear me out," Quixly said. "As acting mayor, I've seized all of the properties that Garba Klex titled in her own name as citizens were pushed out. It's possible the district judge will find this an illegal seizure, we'll find out in a month or so. In the meanwhile, if you want to move your shop to a slightly smaller bay we have on Level 8, you can do that and be outside of Sable territory. Otherwise, you need to negotiate with Sable to stay here. There is one advantage on Level 8 that you don't have now, which is there is a pier directly adjacent that you would have full access to."

"How big of a pier?" Rix asked.

"You can go look," Quixly said.

"I had a year contract here with Garba for fixing the station. I feel like Patience Station should honor that," Rix said.

"Changing times," Quixly said. "I'm willing to honor the duration of the contract, but this location won't be under Patience Station control."

"Is that a forever kind of thing?" Rix asked.

"Two years, but I can see it being extended significantly if Sable remains peaceful in our quadrant," Quixly said.

"You're under a false impression of Sable, Rix Banner," Shixen said. "We're just like everyone else. We want a clean, safe place to raise our families. We just don't want someone else telling us what to do."

"I imagine you have a proposal then, Shixen," Rix said.

"I wouldn't be much of a businessman if I didn't," Shixen said. "Two thousand credits a month for rent. For that, you'll get Sable's legendary security presence and full, unhindered access to the elevator for you and your customers. As we were not included in your contract with Garba, that rent would start next month."

"How long of a term would you give me at that two thousand credit rate?" Rix asked. "And what about limits on future adjustments to that rate?"

"You've negotiated for real estate before, I see," Shixen said. "Five percent annual adjustment applied automatically. If you sign a three-year contract now and renew for another three years, I'll guarantee your rate for six years."

"That's a fair price, other than the fact that I'm losing an entire year of use, which I worked hard for," Rix said.

"Can't be avoided," Shixen said. "I have bosses, and we don't give away property. I have another matter to discuss with you that might have some bearing."

"Shoot," Rix said.

"I'm not sure that's a phrase I'd use with folks like me," Shixen said, allowing a small smile. "It's about your partner's debt on *Calypso*."

"Oh?" Rix asked.

"Walk away from this shop, leave your tools, the lifts and the photonic barriers. Sable forgives *Calypso's* debt."

"Aw, man, you've got to be kidding," Rix said, looking around at his neatly organized shop. He'd yet to have his first customer, but he hadn't started advertising and was certain he wouldn't have trouble finding them, given the state of the small ships he'd seen sailing around Patience and even Sout Atal.

"It is a good deal for you," Shixen said. "What does a mechanics bay need with a photonic barrier, anyway. Simply void the atmosphere when a new vessel arrives. It is a minor inconvenience, likely experienced less than daily."

"Let me keep a cabinet of my choice with the tools already in it," Rix said, fretting at the loss. Due to the problems on the station, he hadn't been given a chance to work on *Calypso* and complete her repairs. Finally, with time and tools available, he had plans to do just that.

"You keep an empty cabinet, and you can fill two crates with whatever tools you wish to keep, but no more than a hundred kilograms," Shixen countered.

"Oh, also, the shelves with Kel's trade goods," Rix said. "Sorry, I forgot about those."

Shixen waved off the comment. "Certainly. Do we have a deal?"

"It's never a full win around here, is it?" Rix said mostly to himself. "Yes. How much time do I have to get my items out of here?"

"Take the week," Shixen said. "And just as a show of good will, you may take one of the grav pallets."

"I guess I'll be taking that space down on Level 8 then, constable," Rix said, shaking Shixen's hand. "I assume you'll send some sort of final payment notification to Kel freeing her of her debt."

"She'll receive that within moments," Shixen said. "I'll let you get to the business of clearing out."

"Thank you, Mr. Shixen," Rix said. "Can you show me the new space today, constable?"

"I'm sending you the address. Security will be programmed by the time you make it down there," Quixly said as Shixen exited the space. "I appreciate you being flexible today, Banner."

"I didn't see a lot of choices," Rix said.

"You made the best choice of those available. Doubling down with Sable by signing a lease would have drawn you closer to them. I'm sorry about the loss of your business."

"It wasn't my business yet," Rix said, shrugging. "It was just tools."

"Good luck, Rix Banner." And with that Quixly also left.

Standing alone in his now defunct garage, Rix could already feel the alienness of the place. Only moments ago it was his place and felt like home. That was gone. He was still considering this when Kel and Philo arrived, carrying food.

"I ran by Shixen and Quixly in the hallway," Kel said. "Is everything okay?"

"Check your comms," Rix said, accepting a bag that contained a leafy wrap with spiced protein loaf.

"What? Why? How, Rix?" Kel asked.

"Which question?"

"I just got a message from Vigno. My debt is paid off for *Calypso*," she said. "What did you do?"

"That's good news, right?" Rix asked, smiling.

"Rixy! *Caly* is ours!?" Philo asked, biting down on a wrap of his own.

"That's right, little man," Rix said. "The bad news is, I had to sell the shop."

"You did what?" Kel asked. "You can't do that, Rix. You've worked so hard to get this far. You're right on the brink of making it work. Tell him deal's off."

Rix pulled out a pair of empty crates and loaded them on a grav pallet so the tops sat at roughly waist height. "Look, being tied to a mobster with nearly one hundred percent interest rate is no way to live," Rix said. "Quixly is giving me a spot on Level 8 where I can set up a new shop. I have to leave most of the tools, but I get one cabinet and a hundred kilograms of tools. We also keep your boutique."

"Nobody is going to come down to Level 8 to look at my boutique," Kel sad.

"Well, Quixly gave Level 10 through 13 to Sable," Rix said. "I doubt your prospects were going to improve here."

"Wait, what? He gave away a part of the station to Sable?"

"Long-term lease," Rix said. "Although I'm fuzzy on the payments."

"Are you sure you want to do this, Rix?" she asked.

"Look, it frees up five thousand credits a month and it's not like I had a customer base already," Rix said. "What if we rented a storefront on Level 17? You could sell our stuff out of there."

"How could we afford that?"

"Most of those storefronts are going for one to two thousand a month," Rix said. "Get a small one if you're feeling squeamish, but it's a lot less than the five thousand you were paying for *Calypso*."

"I had a hard time making those payments and sailing through pirate territory all the time is going to wear on us," she said. "It's not like Sout Atal had a wealth of things we wanted to trade. Wait, what about your photonic barrier generators? Are you at least taking them?"

"No, they're staying. I think that was most of the deal. Without, this shop is just a neat pile of tools."

"Oh, Rix, you must be very upset. You were so excited to get those generators fixed up and running," Kel said. "I'm so sorry."

"I'm not. From when we left Earth, we're one hundred percent better off than we were," Rix said. "We'll load *Calypso* with the agreed upon items and get out of here. It can't take much more than an hour to get loaded."

"Philo will help," Philo said.

"Good. Help me by placing the most used tools and stacking them on this table. I'll pick out what I want and put them in the crates."

"Okay, Rixy."

Ninety minutes later, they were all loaded into *Calypso*. Rix felt a lump in his throat as the lights turned out in the shop and Kel slowly backed out. Once free from the station, Beverly closed the exterior hatch and turned off the heat.

"Nothing ever quite works out like you expect, does it?" Rix asked, sitting back in the pilot's seat.

"Not really," Kel said. "But owning our own ship is a big step for our little company."

"I agree, and also, I think you should get your short-haul license," Rix said.

"Bub, we've had a spendy day," Kel said. "And I don't have twenty-five hundred credits."

"The good news is, I do," Rix said. "And I can't think of anyone better to get the license than you. Patience Station needs import goods from reliable sources."

"Really? You'd front the money for that?" Kel asked. "How do I pay you back?"

"You only owe me half," Rix said. "Our company will benefit from your license, so it's a company expense."

"When?"

"Now," Rix said, transferring twenty-five hundred credits.

"Dang, just like that," Kel said. "How do you have this money all the time?"

"My little inventions on the manufactory marketplace are a nice trickle of funds each day," Rix said. "I'm spending just about every-thing I make, but most of those expenditures are investments I'm certain will pay off sooner or later."

"That's impressive," Kel said, her eyes glassy as she navigated prompts on her HUD. "And now I'm officially Captain Kel, queen of the short-haul."

"Just like that?"

"Yes, I've done all the required coursework and logged the hours under sail. I just never had enough credits to pay for the license. I'm not sure what to think. We're legit, so what now?"

"Well, I have some ideas," Rix said.

But, of course, that's another story entirely.

JUMP DRIVES AND COFFEE STAINS

What follows is a preview of the second novel in the *Spaceship Mechanic* series titled *Jump Drives and Coffee Stains*. The full novel will be available in the first quarter of 2026.

Chapter 1 - Alas, Pirates

"Rix, you gotta get that thing off me, already!" Kel called over comms, raucously tipping *Calypso* to port and dashing behind a fast moving, semi-truck sized asteroid.

"Frak, Kel, you're jumping around like a Texas frog on a hot sidewalk," Rix answered. With significant effort, he tried to line up on the Model 72 Falistad light attack craft with *Calypso's* needler weapon's targeting reticle.

"Deal with it!" Kel answered.

Rix tapped a thumb stud on the yoke, which caused his turret to jerk around so that it once again aimed straight at the pirate's ship. With one eye on the acceleration vectors virtually tailing off behind their attacker and a quick mental calculation, Rix pushed the targeting reticle some three hundred meters ahead of their attacker and sprayed a ten second volley of needler darts.

"If you're going to make a move," Rix said. "Now's the time. I just ventilated their cockpit. It's going to take them a minute to adjust."

Just then, the attacking pirate ship swung hard to starboard and its aft engine clipped a refrigerator-sized asteroid, which sent it into a high-speed tumble.

"Uh, oh." It was all Kel could manage to say before the Falistad craft wrapped itself around another asteroid moving in the opposite direction. For a moment, it almost looked like the pirate spaceship would become forever engaged with the asteroid but then it exploded.

"Recording debris field for Inner Passage map," Beverly said, appearing virtually as a ten-centimeter-tall woman wearing a scholarly robe and sketching on an unrolled map with a quill pen.

"Copernicus robes?" Rix asked. He and the four hundred nanometer long alien symbiote who had hitched a ride on the third of *Calypso's* crew, Philo, played a game where it was Rix's responsibility to guess what sort of costume Beverly was wearing when she showed up.

"Ding, ding, ding, we have a winner!" Beverly answered.

"That was close," Kel said, relief evident in her voice. "Is everyone okay?"

"Philo okay," Philo, the short, bearded alien added. "Need suit. Fell to sleepy." It wasn't uncommon for Philo to sleep in his small bunk. That he didn't have easy access to a vacsuit was something Rix noted to talk to him about. The combination of asteroids, space combat and lightly armored *Calypso* meant the odds of loss of pressure were significant, especially considering that Philo was trapped in his bunk because the main part of the ship was venting atmosphere, currently.

"Stay put, Philo," Kel said. "We'll get to you shortly."

"I guess Jacknie wasn't too happy with our decision to stop paying for security," Rix said. "How is this approach better. Feels like taking down a pair of his short-range fighters is going to escalate bad feelings between us."

"Agreed. Sout Atal is going to be tricky for us for a while," Kel said.

"Tricky? I imagine we won't be going back," Rix said.

"At least we have a hold full of flour and fish again."

"I have a dozen subsystem failures reporting right now," Rix said. "We're going to lose money on this trip."

"It cost Jacknie more than it did us," Kel said. "Two Model 72s, even old ones like that are worth at least a hundred fifty thousand."

"You're not making it better," Rix said. "Where do you think Jacknie's going to want to find payback for those?"

"Look, Rix, that's not my problem. Someone shoots at me and mine, we gotta do what keeps us alive," Kel said. "That's just the law of the deep dark."

"I'll be below deck to see if I can get us patched up so we can limp home," Rix said. "We're leaking coolant from the main."

"Turn off the reservoir," Kel said.

"Right, we're in an asteroid belt if you didn't notice," Rix said tightly. "Cutting power to the main seems like a bad idea."

"Well, shoot, you're not wrong. Can we make it another forty minutes? Cactus Flats isn't that far away," Kel said. Cactus Flats was a wide-open area where the asteroid belt thinned, allowing pilots to make up lost time when sailing the Inner Passage.

"I'll know in a couple of minutes," Rix said, pulling the deck tile up so he could swing beneath to the 'tween deck. A cloud of steam greeted him as his feet hit the hull. Clouding his vac suit, Rix steadied himself as his suit struggled to clear vapor from his transparent face shield. "Beverly, could you give me a wireframe? I can't see anything."

"Of course I can," Beverly answered.

An overlay of green lines projected onto his view and even through the steam, Rix had enough detail to orient his feet and move aft to where Calypso was reporting both a hull breach as well as a critical subsystem loss of the cooling system.

"What are you seeing?" Kel asked.

"Trouble," Rix answered. "That last hit we took scarfed out a chunk of the main coolant tank across all four of the baffles."

"I don't know what you're telling me aside from – we took damage and it's bad," Kel said.

"No coolant will cause the main engine to overheat in a few minutes," Rix said. "If they'd known, they could have just avoided us for a few more minutes and we'd have been sitting ducks."

"We can't exactly sit around here," Kel said. "Or the asteroids will finish off what Jacknie's crew started."

"I need to shut down power for at least a couple of minutes, tell me when you have a window," Rix said.

"Now. You have ninety seconds, max," Kel said.

"Okay, good," Rix said, turning off the coolant supply.

"What Rixy do?" Philo asked, catching up with him. Rix gave him a double take, wondering how the little alien had escaped his bunk with the low atmospheric pressure they were currently maintaining.

"Looks like we're patching." Rix grabbed a roll of duct tape, grateful for its fantastic ability to adhere to anything. "Hold these rods in place for me, would you?"

"How's it going down there?" Kel called over comms.

"Don't pressure me," Rix said, stretching tape around the temporary spine Philo was holding in place. Five strips of tape high, Rix filled in the missing coolant walls with duct tape.

"Buddy, I need main in twelve seconds," Kel said.

"Frak," Rix growled. Instead of the shape he'd intended, he pushed the duct tape wall over so it grabbed onto the opposite side and then placed one more piece atop it.

"Go now, Kel," Rix said.

Steam immediately poured from large gaps in the reservoir tank and Rix worked feverishly to apply duct tape patches. It wasn't anywhere near his best work, and in the end, he had a big silver-gray ball that no longer leaked.

"Are we okay?" Kel called after a few minutes.

"Kind of," Rix said. "I don't know how long my patch is going to last and best I can tell, we lost way too much coolant."

"We're still a couple of days out, Rix," Kel said.

"I know, I know," Rix said. "It's holding for the moment. Let me look at the other less critical issues first and I'll come back to this. We need to coast through Cactus Flats to give me time to deal with this."

"If you can get us there, I have a path that'll give you thirty hours of free sailing," Kel said.

"Sold. Philo, do you want to start with the hull patch? I'm going to work on subsystems," Rix said.

Rix moved from one problem to the next, his estimate of the costs of the trip escalating with each issue. "Man, maybe those guys did exactly what Jacknie wanted," Rix said after spending thirty minutes reviewing the critical issues. "Talk to me when we're clear for shutting off the main engine."

"You're good to go, Rix," Kel said. "Engines at full stop for thirty-one hours, twenty-two minutes. Going slow will chew into our timeline, though. Ordinarily, we'd burn hard through this spot."

"I wouldn't recommend it," Rix said, tapping a small sheet of steel into place with his boltgun. As expected, fixes applied while sailing were often temporary. While he was able to get all but the coolant problem dealt with after two hours, the fact that they had burned off all of their coolant in both the primary and reserve tanks was a problem he wasn't sure how to fix.

"Talk to me, Rix," Kel said as he joined her for a meal of cold cereal. "You're looking uncharacteristically glum."

"Any idea where we can get some coolant? Do we have contact with Patience? Maybe we could get Freda to bring some out?" Rix said.

"We have a reserve tank. Did you find that?"

"The reserve took a bigger hit than the primary," Rix said. "Of course, the primary was hot enough that when it got hit, we lost all but a couple of liters. It's not enough."

"How much do we need?"

"Five liters if we limp in," Rix said.

"We can't make it with two?"

"You'd burn up the main in four hours, give or take."

"How could you possibly know that?"

"The specs are publicly available," Rix said.

"And you just happened to have read them?"

"What can I say, I'm curious and I like to read."

"But manuals. You like to read manuals."

"Not only," he said. "Let me take five hours for sleep. I'm irritated that I don't have a better solution than calling Freda."

"Freda is six days out and if she agrees to it, we're probably talking twenty-five hundred credits just to get her to come," Kel said. "And that's assuming I can bounce a radio signal through all this crap and get it to her."

"I'm taking a nap," Rix said, pushing back from the table and standing. "Let me know if something breaks."

"Are you mad?"

"A little."

"At me?"

"At the situation," Rix said. "I'm pissed that Jacknie sent those fighters after us and even more that six crew are dead because they did what he told them. It was senseless."

"If you hadn't shot them, we'd be the dead ones."

"I know. I'll be in a better mood with a little sleep."

"Okay," Kel said. "Want me to tuck you in?"

Rix looked back at her. The comment was unexpected given they'd shared exactly a one, one-sided kiss in the past. She wore an impish grin which caused Rix to shake his head. "You're too much," he said.

"Probably," she agreed. "But seriously, how can I make it better? I know, how about I make your favorite breakfast when you get up. You barely ate any of that cereal. We have enough in the refer for that egg wrap you like, and I'll make you some hot coffee, since that's the way you like it. I'll even clean out the warmer mug, so it doesn't get cold on you."

"That'd be nice, Kel," Rix said, grabbing a bar at the top of his bunk cabinet and swinging his legs in. Instead of the full-sized cabins found in larger spaceships, *Calypso* had rectangular bunks that were a meter and a half square on end and two and a half meters long. A person couldn't stand within the bunk but had plenty of room to spread out as they slept and even had a few drawers to hold possessions.

Rix closed the hatch next to the main hallway and tested pressurization. With individual atmospheric controls, he discovered that his bunk had two through holes and was one of the offenders of why *Calypso* wasn't holding cabin pressure.

"Philo, can I grab that hull patcher?" Rix called over comms. "My bunk is venting."

"Coming, Rixy," Philo said.

A moment later, he heard rapping against the hatch and he opened up, accepting the small tool that would force a plug into the hole and inject a foam sealant that expanded. Rix pulled back the blanket on his bed, only to discover it also had a through hole. "That's just great," he groused, tossing the blanket aside and filling two more holes.

"Sorry 'bout blanket," Philo said as Rix handed the tool back to his little alien friend.

"Thanks, Philo," Rix said. "It's not you. I'm just frustrated. Pirates ruin things. It's just such a waste."

Pushing his pillows into place, Rix stretched out, his foot immediately finding the hole in his blanket. It was not without effort that he tamped down his frustration. They were out of coolant. It wasn't even difficult or expensive material to come by back on the station. He allowed his mind to wander as he struggled for sleep. It was nice that Kel would let him use the warming mug for what passed for coffee. The lode bean, while easily adapted for growing on space stations and laced with a cousin of caffeine was much better as a cold drink as it cooled more quickly than it should. A warming mug was about the only way to enjoy it hot. These were the thoughts on his mind as he drifted to sleep.

Five hours later, he heard rapping on the hatch and grinned. "I've got it, Kel!" he said, opening the hatch and then repeated excitedly, "I've got it!"

"You've got what?"

"Lode bean coffee. Its thermal transfer rate is fantastic," Rix said.

"I don't know what you're saying," Kel said, her eyes going glassy as she reviewed a definition on her HUD. "It gets cold faster than it should. Yes, I know."

"Beverly, if we keep under forty percent power, can you run the numbers? Will it work?" Rix asked.

"Will what work?" Kel asked.

Beverly appeared between the two of them, her hair was white and wildly frizzy and she wore a white mustache. "Rix is considering using lode bean coffee as a coolant. It is poorly suited to the task, but my calculations show that forty percent power is achievable."

"Get to brewing!" Rix said, grabbing Kel and dancing with her. "We're going home, baby!"

"Now who's crazy?" she asked, grinning at his enthusiasm.

"Me. You're talking about me," Rix said with a big smile.

"I like this Rix a lot more than grumpy Rix," Kel said.

"That's fair," Rix said. "Me too."

"Burrito and coffee are waiting," Kel said.

After a long nap and breakfast, Rix was once again ready to take on the coolant leak which had once felt insurmountable and was now just a matter of brewing enough coffee. He chuckled to himself as he splashed some of the coffee on himself as he filled the makeshift reservoir.

"What are you laughing about?" Kel asked having accompanied him below decks.

"Coffee and duct tape," Rix said. "Who'd have thought the most sophisticated machines in the galaxy could be repaired with these things? It's like the universe is laughing at us."

"Someone has a sense of humor, that's for certain. How long before we know if this'll work?" Kel asked.

"It'll work right away, the question is probably more how long will it last," Rix said. "I'm hoping the answer to that is long enough to get limp back to Patience Station."

"Have you checked the hold yet?" Kel asked.

"Not yet," Rix answered. "I know there are some through holes in there because I tried to pressurize it and it didn't work."

"Philo says he's about done applying patches to the hold," Kel said. "We should be able to pressurize fully in twenty minutes."

"How about we check the hold before you fire up the engines," Rix said.

"You're done here?"

"For the moment, at least," Rix said. "I have a couple of parts we're going to need to manufacture. I'll put them in the communications queue, so they're done by the time we get back."

"Good plan. I'm afraid to ask. How expensive are we talking?" Kel asked.

"Twenty-one hundred credits," Rix said.

"Frak, that wipes out anything that looks like profit," Kel said.

Rix nodded and led Kel up through the main hallway and back to the hold. Pushing through the hatch, he initially wasn't sure what he was looking at. A cloud of dust hung in the air and there were large puddles of something milky on the deck.

"That's not good," Rix said, rushing over to where a cask of Jacknie's Grog had once been stored. In its place was the remains of the aluminum cask, its contents having been expelled due to enemy rounds piercing the hull. "Yeah, that's what I figured. They shot up the flour. I imagine there's a few good bags left, but this is a mess. Looks like the fish survived, though."

"How depressing," Kel said.

"Yes and no," Rix said. "We survived a two-on-one assault by superior craft due to your excellent flying in close quarters. We've had no casualties aside from some low rent grog and a few bags of flour. Damage to the ship is pennies to the dollar what we inflicted on our enemies. You, kiddo, are the hero in this."

"I got us shot up to all cognie," she said.

"Again, look at the other guys," Rix said. "When people come swinging for you, there's going to be pain. Your point isn't wrong, though. If we keep we want that."

"I think you're saying we need to drop the spec loads, and I need to use my shiny new short haul freighter license and start making some predictable, if not boring, income," she said.

"I'm not saying anything other than we need to figure out how to dial down the danger," Rix said. "We're not indestructible and we've been lucky."

Kel's face fell as she considered the conversation. "I know," she said and changed subjects. "No more than forty percent burn?"

"I'd keep it to thirty-five if you can," Rix said. "I know it's annoying, but who knows how much stress my fixes will take."

"Rix, if we've lost most of our load, I'm not going to have anything to stake our next run. I'm going to have to take a job if I'm going to hold up my end of the partnership," she said. "And before you offer to stake the entire thing, no. I know better. You're putting your mechanic's bay on hold. Have you even looked at the space?"

"We dropped off tools and a cabinet," Rix said. "Nothing beyond that."

"Okay, then. Can you deal with me taking *Calypso* out by myself? It's not like I don't know how."

"To do what?"

"There's a premium load on Gestalt Station that's six days through Dravari space. They'll pay for a deadhead to their station and twice standard to get the load safely to Majis on Grelvox," she said.

"Majis ... oh, there it is. It's a city of a million. Doesn't seem like a big thing. Why are they paying so much?" Rix asked, gesturing to his HUD's map.

"Dravari are choking off loads from anywhere in Surnak Belt," Kel said. "You know this."

"I do," Rix agreed. "How is it you plan to get around Dravari?"

"Oh, you're so cute," Kel said. "I've spent a lifetime avoiding Dravari. Now that I have a legit license, even if they catch me, there's not much they can do other than impound my cargo. And, if they do that, my client has insurance that covers the load if they hold it for more than thirty days. None of that works without my license, but now that I have it, I need to take advantage of the perks."

"You're assuming they won't lock you up for past crimes, Kel," Rix said.

"Assuming is such a strong word," Kel said. "My first choice will be to avoid them. After that, we'll see."

"And you want me to stay home," Rix said. "What if things break down."

"We'll come up with something, but Rix, I need you to do your thing," Kel said. "I've taken over your life enough, already. Tell me you wouldn't love to have the better part of a month to focus on your work. And maybe without me around, you might pay some attention to Namari. She has a daily exercise class in the Atrium gardens at 0700."

"Hutari's mom?" Rix asked. "Why would I do that?"

"Oh, Lords of Gavenar but you're as dense as a black hole."

ACKNOWLEDGMENTS

To Rachel Aukes for excellence in editing and word-smithery.

To my beta readers: Carol Greenwood, Kelli Whyte, and Lyle Clingman for wonderful and thoughtful suggestions. It is a joy to work with this intelligent and considerate group of people.

Finally, to Elias Stern, cover artist extraordinaire.

ABOUT THE AUTHOR

Jamie McFarlane is the father of three and lives in Lincoln, Nebraska. An avid runner, scuba diver and hiker, Jamie enjoys the active life writing fulltime affords him.

Word-of-mouth is crucial for any author to succeed. If you enjoyed this book, please consider leaving a review, even if it's only a line or two; it would make all the difference and would be very much appreciated.

FREE DOWNLOAD

If you'd like to receive automatic email when Jamie's next book is available, please visit http://fickledragon.com. Your email address will never be shared and you can unsubscribe at any time.

For more information
www.fickledragon.com
jamie@fickledragon.com

ALSO BY JAMIE MCFARLANE

Spaceship Mechanic

1. Boltguns and Duct Tape
2. Jump Drives and Coffee Stains (First Quarter 2026)

Junkyard Pirate Series

1. Junkyard Pirate
2. Old Dogs, Older Tricks
3. Junkyard Spaceship
4. Junkyard Veterans
5. Junkyard Raiders
6. Junkyard Ghost Ship
7. Junkyard Commandos
8. Junkyard Mercenary
9. Junkyard Saboteur

Oldest Starfighter Series

1. The Oldest Starfighter
2. Rogue Commander

Privateer Tales Series

1. Rookie Privateer
2. Fool Me Once
3. Parley
4. Big Pete
5. Smuggler's Dilemma
6. Cutpurse
7. Out of the Tank
8. Buccaneers
9. A Matter of Honor
10. Give No Quarter

11. Blockade Runner
12. Corsair Menace
13. Pursuit of the Bold
14. Fury of the Bold
15. Judgment of the Bold
16. Privateers in Exile
17. Incursion at Elea Station
18. Freebooter's Hold
19. Black Cutlass
20. Privateer's Supremacy

Space Troopers Series

1. Rebel's Call
2. Rebel's Run
3. Rebel's Strike

Privateer Tales Universe

1. Pete, Popeye and Olive
2. Life of a Miner
3. Uncommon Bravery
4. On a Pale Ship

Henry Biggston Thrillers

1. When Justice Calls
2. Deputy in the Crosshairs
3. Manhunt at Sage Creek

Witchy World

1. Wizard in a Witchy World
2. Wicked Folk: An Urban Wizard's Tale
3. Wizard Unleashed

Guardians of Gaeland

1. Lesser Prince

www.ingramcontent.com/pod-product-compliance
Lightning Source LLC
Chambersburg PA
CBHW072341020726
47506CB00004B/954